Lloyd F. Ritchey

STORMDRAGON

Wildgrave
www.wildgravepublishing.com

This is a work of fiction. The characters, names, incidences and plot are products of the author's imagination and are used fictictiously. Any resemblance to actual persons, companies, or events is purely coincindental.

STORMDRAGON

Print ISBN 978-0-9985785-2-1

www.wildgravepublishing.com
www.lloydritchey.com

Published in the United States of America

Printed in the United States of America.

Acknowledgements

To those who suffered early versions of this novel and offered valuable comments ... Thank You! Those helpful souls include my brother-in-law, Phillip Hamilton; my sister-in-law, Catherine Bearce, who is a wonderfully creative graphic artist; my brother, Stephen; the talented musician and artist Cy Brinson; and my wife Christine (an award-winning author), whose infinite patience, intelligence, and love helped sustain my effort in bringing Stormdragon to successful completion.

I also wish to thank the Dallas rock band, Hard Night's Day, for performing Helter Skelter (and other Beatles music) with such power and energy, thereby inspiring the incorporation of the so-very-appropriate song in the story.

Introduction

Before the reader dismisses the outrageous science in this novel as nothing more than the concoctions of a fevered brain, please consider the following:

There really was a genius named Nikola Tesla. He really did build a laboratory in Colorado Springs in 1899 from which he hurled man-made lightning bolts and conducted seminal experiments in wireless transmission of electrical energy. Legend has it that Tesla succeeded in transmitting enough power to light 100 Edison bulbs (about 10,000 watts) a distance of 16 miles. Modern technology has not replicated this feat.

There really is an auroral research station in Alaska. It is called HAARP (High Frequency Active Auroral Research Project), and it is currently designed to transmit a billion or so watts of radio frequency energy into the ionosphere. Its alleged purpose: communications. Its possible use: a weapon.

And speaking of history; it often deceives. Marconi is credited with the invention of the radio, but it was Tesla who demonstrated and patented an elegant wireless system years before Marconi began toying with his first crude designs. The U.S. Supreme court invalidated the Marconi patents in 1935, and again in 1943, granting Tesla credit for the invention of radio.

Additionally, Tesla invented all of the AC and polyphase systems of electrical power generation and transmission used today. Without them, Edison's electric light would be…well…a dim bulb.

When Tesla died in 1943 at the age of 87, the U.S. government seized his research papers and theories. Seems Tesla was working on some sort of energy-beam weapon, among other things. As of this writing, those papers are still classified.

And speaking of deception: your own government and big, well-known, respected corporate entities wouldn't lie to you, would they?

But, back to reality. Sleep tight. The government, multinational corporations, and the military-industrial complex have your welfare at heart. All is well.

Everything is under control.

Magnifying Transmitter

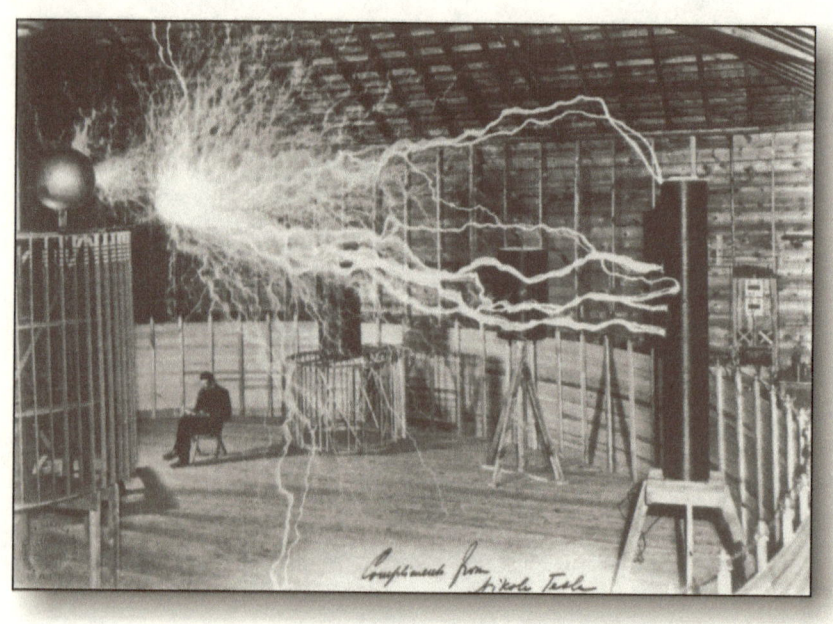

Nikola Tesla's Lab, Colorado Springs, 1899
—*Courtesy Nikola Tesla Museum, Belgrade, Serbia*

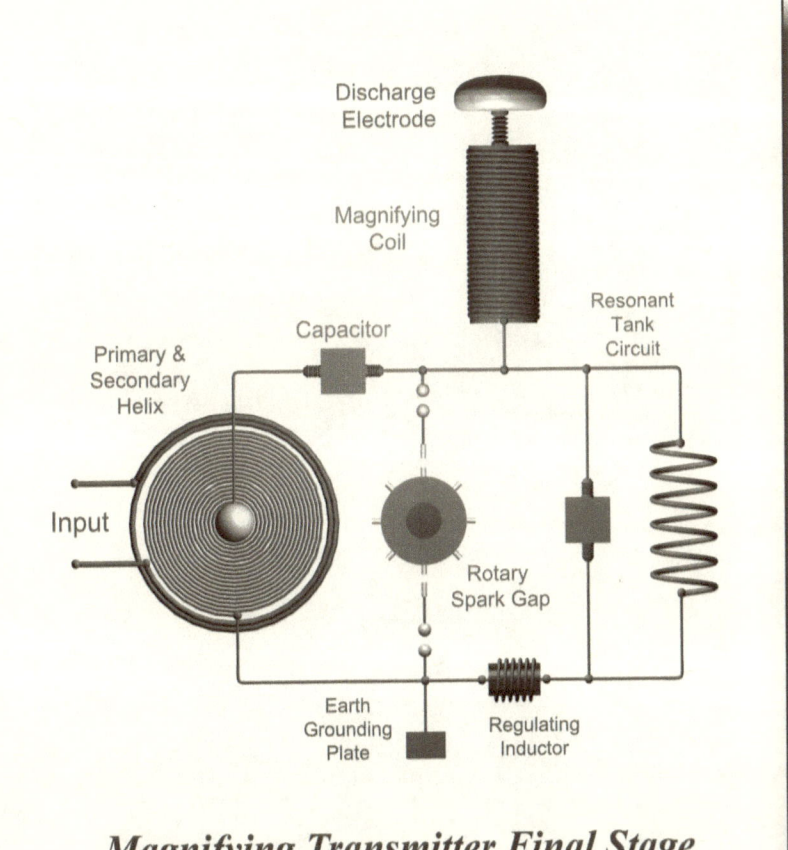

Discharge
Electrode

Magnifying
Coil

Capacitor

Resonant
Tank
Circuit

Primary &
Secondary
Helix

Input

Rotary
Spark Gap

Earth
Grounding
Plate

Regulating
Inductor

Magnifying Transmitter Final Stage

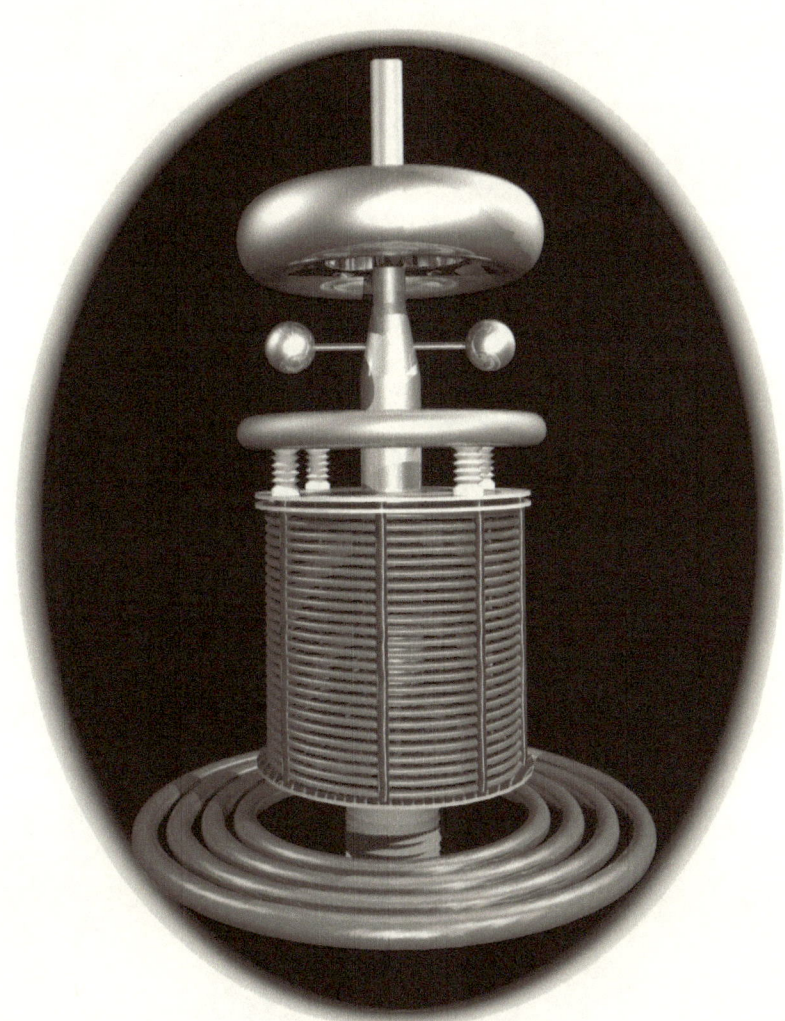

PART ONE

DISCOVERY

Prologue

Lightning split the sky above Pikes Peak, sending peals of thunder booming down the valley and grumbling across the plains. The concussions shook the square, barn-like structure crouching in a windswept field a mile east of Colorado Springs. The building's roof sloped upward to an open section, from which there rose a slender mast capped with a polished aluminum sphere. A sign beside the barred gate read, KEEP OUT! EXTREME DANGER!

A flash of atmospheric fire illuminated Nikola Tesla, who observed the storm through the broad west window. He smiled, his deep-set eyes scanning the approaching thunderhead. He turned his attention to a cluster of instruments on the slanted panel before him. The glowing dials were alive, needles jerking in response to the earth's electrical forces.

Mikhail, Tesla's assistant, watched the inventor closely. Tesla's concentration was unusually intense this night; the Master of Electricity had a final experiment to perform—something that involved the oncoming storm.

Lightning-fired shadows leaped across the laboratory's cavernous interior, followed by a thunderclap that rattled the windows and drummed the pine-planked walls. Tesla turned from the instruments and strode to a wooden platform overlooking the huge machine at the building's center. He climbed rapidly, his long legs taking two steps at a time. He spoke over his shoulder. "We haven't much time. See that the mast is secure."

Outside, Mikhail climbed a hillock where he could see the free-standing steel rod that rose one hundred and forty-five feet above the roof. Silver against the dark sky, the three-foot sphere atop the rod seemed to hover without support. The sun had fallen behind the horizon, and in the purple twilight, twinkling early stars framed the glowing thunderhead. Below the storm, the yellow lights of Colorado Springs winked in warm defiance.

Mikhail entered the building and latched the door. Tesla was on the platform, bending over the control console. From his elevated position, the inventor monitored the great instrument before him—the Magnifying Transmitter—a giant coil of copper interconnected with a wizard's tangle of electrical machinery.

"The mast is holding, sir," Mikhail reported. "There is very little wind."

"Good," Tesla said without looking up. "Raise the voltage. We will be operating at full power."

Mikhail snapped shut a bank of massive switches near the main transformer and walked to a long, insulated handle connected to the transmitting circuit. The handle would allow him to make adjustments while staying a safe distance from the lethal current that would soon surge through the apparatus. Following Tesla's instructions, he reached up and rotated a knob, placing the numeral 8 at the center of a large dial suspended overhead.

The drumbeat of thunder became louder and more frequent. Tesla placed his hands on the console and leaned forward, lifting his gaze slightly. He resembled, Mikhail thought, a ship's captain peering ahead toward uncharted waters.

Lightning glared through the observation window. Tesla turned to him. "Are you ready?"

Mikhail tightened his grip on the control handle. "Yes sir."

"Then we are starting—*now!*"

As Tesla spoke, an electric motor whined to life, followed by the whistling whir of the rotary spark gap. Tesla grasped the handle of the transmit switch and slammed it down.

The laboratory erupted in a fury of sound and light, as if the heart of the storm had suddenly burst inside the building. The rotary gap flared blue-white, blaring like a buzz saw ripping through an oak log.

Crackling, purple fire danced from the Magnifying Transmitter's central helix, clawing menacingly into the open air. Mikhail twisted the control handle and brought the overhead dial's needle back to center. Tesla had never operated the machine at such power, and Mikhail tensed, preparing to run if the voltage climbed too high. *Run?* He smiled grimly. There would be no opportunity to run.

He imagined the scenario: electrical streamers would arc around the control handle and penetrate his arm, locking him in a bone-breaking spasm of pain. In less than a second, searing tendrils of electricity would erupt from his body, splitting his skin, exploding his head, and blasting a froth of steaming blood from a thousand rent openings. His wife would die in horror from the sight!

Tesla thrust the power lever to the right, increasing the deafening roar of man-made lightning. The coil's crown of electricity now resembled a thousand serpents wriggling on their tails, their heads snapping and hissing as if seeking any prey foolish enough to come within striking range. Blue-white light flashed and bellowed beyond the open hatch, accompanied by a fusillade of shuddering booms. Tesla signaled that he was increasing the power to maximum.

Sound waves pounded the air. Mikhail thought his head would burst. A wind reeking of ozone and burnt insulation swept through the laboratory and rushed upward through the truncated roof. Mikhail glanced behind him; the rotary spark gap had become a mass of roaring, yellow-orange fire. Melting down from an overload of current, the whirling disk showered metallic sparks across the building like an overcharged Catherine wheel.

Mikhail jerked his hand from the control handle; the tingling in his arm was growing, presaging instant electrocution. *When will Tesla shut this inferno off?* He stared at the roof opening; long, zigzag streaks of electricity roared from the aluminum sphere high above the building and sizzled into the lightning-torn sky.

Tesla seized the power switch and yanked it open. Searing sparks blasted from the contacts, forcing him to cover his eyes and step back. As if imbued with a will of its own, the Magnifying Transmitter refused to stop—the noise and voltage were *increasing*.

"Mikhail!" Tesla shouted as he leaped down the steps. Mikhail anticipated Tesla's move and dashed to join him.

Violent, twisting channels of electricity erupted from the coil and lashed against the floor, the deafening barrage carving branching rivers of white fire across the wooden timbers. The frenetic discharges glared with stroboscopic light, throwing the running men into stuttering silhouettes of frozen motion.

They hurled themselves against the emergency disconnect, and the bar exploded free. An electrical spark three feet long buzzed from the top connector, trying to reestablish its path, then died. The men paused in the sudden silence, ears ringing, then released the lever, letting it swing, creaking, back into position.

Flames curled from sections of the transmitter and rose from blackened pockmarks where electricity had arced to the floor. Snatching soda-filled buckets, Mikhail and Tesla moved rapidly and snuffed the small fires before they could become a conflagration.

"It's ruined," Mikhail said, wiping the grime from his brow. "It'll take months to repair."

The inventor laughed. "Magnificent, wasn't it?"

The look of obsessive concentration was gone from Tesla's face, replaced by, what—elation? After a grueling year of development and testing, his greatest invention was destroyed, and yet he laughed. Perhaps, as some had said, he was a madman after all.

Tesla smiled, his eyes glittering. "The experiment was successful, Mikhail. This is a time for celebration." He clapped Mikhail's shoulder and guided him toward the door. "Come to the hotel after dinner. I'll buy us a bottle of the best wine they have in stock. I would ask your beautiful wife to join us, but tonight I will be telling you a great secret about this machine and the experiments. It would be better if you were the only one to hear."

Mikhail nodded. Secret or not, all he presently wanted was to return home to his wife and young daughter. Yet, he had been extended a great honor. Tesla was not in the habit of confiding secrets.

After a quick meal and bath, Mikhail donned his best suit and walked to the hotel. Tesla was seated at a table in the lounge, gazing through the front window.

As Mikhail approached, Tesla smiled and said, "Just in time. I was about to taste this bottle without you." He poured for both of them and raised his glass. "A toast—to successful experiments and the future of mankind." He paused, his smile widening. "And to the future of Mikhail Karsov and his family."

Mikhail followed Tesla's example and drained his glass. "Dr. Tesla, I greatly appreciate your kind sentiment, but I am completely baffled. I…"

Tesla interrupted. "You will have your explanation, Mikhail." He signaled for the waiter, then chuckled. "I think this will require *two* bottles of wine."

The inventor spoke for more than an hour. Afterwards, Mikhail was stunned, his hand visibly shaking as he reached for his wineglass. Tesla had thrown him a proposition that would affect his family for generations and have an enormous impact upon the entire world. If Tesla had truly discovered what he claimed, the future would be one of paradise—or of Hell.

Mikhail left the hotel, dodging puddles as he walked down the cobbled street toward home. Sleep would be impossible; he and his wife would soon have to make the most important decision of their lives. He stopped and looked back, sighting Tesla's room. The light would glow until early morning, for the inventor applied himself relentlessly to his work. Mikhail turned and resumed his walk, pulling his jacket tighter against the now cool, starry night.

* * *

Far to the south, the thunderstorm that had revealed such powerful secrets rumbled on, undiminished. It passed over the town of Pueblo and continued southward, dropping rain and hailstones on Raton Pass, then sweeping onto the plains of New Mexico, where it could be seen for a hundred miles.

2007

Captain Jack McCullough rocked forward and stared at the purplish light flickering on the horizon. "Pete—what the hell *is* that?"

Static crashed through the headphones, obliterating the copilot's reply. "…thing's huge. No transponder…"

Jack banked the 767 left and watched the object creep from his field of vision. An endless strata of cumulous clouds crested a thousand feet below, ragged tops a firestorm of red in the dying sun.

The static faltered, then stopped. Jack brought the plane back to wings level, his eyes searching the sky.

"It's gone," Pete said. "Bang. Just like that." He glanced back at the radar. "The trace was soft. Maybe it was some kind of atmospheric—"

The light ignited again, closer, exactly in their path. But it was no solid mass, rather a violet flame hundreds of feet across, with a guttering nucleus that crawled with patches of orange like molten steel in a crucible. Jack threw the plane into a hard left and shoved the throttles forward. As the airframe shuddered through a wall of turbulence, the light emitted a series of bright pulses and flamed out.

"That wasn't random," Pete said after an interval of silence. His voice had climbed a full octave. "And it sure as hell was no atmospheric."

* * *

Senator Jeff Travis felt the rising G-forces shove him downward as the plane arced into another turn. He reached beneath the laptop balanced across his son's legs and tugged the seat belt tighter. "Not to worry, tiger. They're probably just avoiding some weather."

Scott jabbed the keyboard; the battling karate figures had frozen in mid-kick. "Oh, it locked up. Just when I was gonna smash you…"

"We'll reboot and see what happens." Travis punched the start button and watched the screen. Instead of the usual chirps and beeps, the tiny speakers emitted a warbling electronic howl. There was a soft *pop*, and a wisp of smoke curled from the vents.

"Whoa!"

"Shh. Don't get everyone riled up." Travis lifted the machine onto his own lap and clicked it off. *Let an eight-year-old play with a thousand-dollar computer...* He nudged Scott, trying to divert his attention from the aborted karate duel. "Think you'd like to be a senator someday? I think you'd make a good one."

"Only if I get to play games."

Travis winked. "Oh, you play games, all right." His eyes shifted to the petite Oriental stewardess hustling along the aisle, shouting for everyone to buckle up. She looked worried—no, scared. He snapped the computer's lid shut and stuffed it back into its case. The aircraft pitched sharply to the right. A murmur rose from the passengers.

Travis felt the breath punched out of him as the plane slammed upward. It rollercoasted weightless, slashed sideways, cracked his ribs against the armrest. Metal screeched and banged; overhead bins burst and disgorged their contents into the aisle. Thunder rocked the cabin. He threw a protective embrace around his son. *Someone's detonated a bomb...*

* * *

Jack shoved the 767 into a dive as the violet-orange glare swallowed them. He felt the yoke seize up. "I'm losing assist!" Warning lights raged across the console. Alarms blared. "Engine fire! *Pete!*"

Jack glanced at the copilot. He had pitched back in his seat, eyes glazed and staring. A filament of blood trailed from his nostrils and branched across his jaw. Jack punched his shoulder. "Pete!" The man's head arched backward as taut cords of muscle stretched his mouth into a rictus. "Jesus Christ!" Jack shot his hand out and twisted the fire control handle. The entire sky blazed orange.

* * *

Pressure exploded inside Travis's skull. He bent forward and gasped, his insides climbing his throat. He turned and managed to focus on Scott. The boy's eyes had rolled back, eyelids fluttering over glistening slices of white. "Oh, my dear God!" *We've been poisoned, or—*

With a *crack,* sparks shot from the lighting panels above the aisle. Oxygen masks tumbled from their concealed pockets and swayed in unison as the plane lurched. The lights flickered and died, throwing the cabin into semidarkness. In the starbursts from the shorting wires, Travis could see passengers reeling in their seats. Hands clawed at faces, bodies jerked, screams bubbled from constricted throats.

Beyond the miasma, in the dark alcove behind the cockpit, a glowing orb materialized like the unlidding of a phantom eye. It was the size a beach ball, violet in hue, its core a pulsating yellow. Travis could hear it rasp and whir above the bedlam. It burst from its invisible socket and soared, spinning and twisting, down the aisle toward them. Tentacles of blue-white electricity uncoiled from its surface as it traveled and raked the cabin walls, punching out fountains of sparks where the neon shafts pierced metal, cloth, flesh…

Screams tore from Travis's throat as the fulminating horror loomed up beside him. Whether the torrent of pain came from the fireball or from another source, he couldn't tell.

*   *   *

A white-hot poker probed behind Jack's eyes. The instrument panel danced through a kaleidoscope of shattered colors. If he could force his hands to maintain an even grip on the yoke, he could pull them through.

Maintain! He stared into the seething, yellow-orange sky…

Jack and Mark are pumping their mountain bikes up the Lost Canyon Trail. Legs burning, lungs bursting, they coast to a stop on the Overlook. Jack plucks his water bottle from the bike's frame and holds it out. "Comin' at ya," he says to his son, as always after they reach the top.

Mark holds his own bottle aloft. "Comin' at ya."

Looking down, Jack realizes he is sliding toward the edge of the cliff. He must grasp the handlebars tightly, or the bicycle will tilt into the abyss. The bike is falling even now. He has to maintain—

There was only a searing incandescence, as if he had been suddenly thrust into Hell's furnace.

A digital editing system stretched across the darkened office, glare from its twin monitors mingling with sunlight spilling past the curtained windows. Kate McCullough scrolled to the video segment's beginning and hit the play button: A frowning woman stood before the elevated blade of a bulldozer. "Developers can't take it *all*," the woman said, gesturing toward the woods behind her.

Another scene flicked on: a man shouted into the microphone, his body framed by a chanting, sign-waving crowd. "Colorado Springs has had enough growth. We have to preserve quality of life, and unbridled development does not…"

Someone swept the door aside and strode heavily across the room. Kate paused the system. She knew it was Randall Mason without looking up. The nasal wheeze and nervous jangle of pocket change announced his presence. She swiveled around. "Almost finished, Randall."

"Ah…" Mason began, his pear-shaped body taking those mincing, half-step forward, half-step back movements she hated. "Angela has the story on that pileup in the Eisenhower Tunnel. We're running her in the prime spot. Your story about the, what do you call it? The…"

"Colorado Springs Overdevelopment."

He stopped prancing and leaned forward. "Don't make another crusade out of this. You're skating on thin ice with this… editorializing. We have sponsors to consider, not to mention policy." He stared at her, his hand molesting the junk in his pocket. "Play it down, or I'll pull the report."

Her protest died when she caught the hardened look in his eyes. "Right."

"Atta girl." He gave a final snort and stalked from the room, jangling like a trolley.

Kate sighed. Channel 12's editorial policy had taken a serious detour after TriConn's hostile takeover. They had appointed Mason, and under his iron rule the station now shoveled corporate-filtered propaganda and insipid crap into the heads of seventy-five thousand viewers. Worse, Mason had swapped her co-anchor for Angela Amesworth, an uninspired prima donna whose primary assets were a fountain of long, blond hair and an artificially amplified chest. Rumors hinted Kate was next to be tossed into the unemployment line. Kate wasn't a team player.

She jerked her fingers through her own short, black hair and stared blankly at the monitor. The show-biz clichés were probably true. She'd come to work some morning to find her name excised from the parking lot and her desk in the storage closet. She yanked the offending video segments, transferred the report to cassette, and steamed down the hallway toward the control room.

She nodded at Weatherman Fred, with his aw-shucks grin and nerdy bow tie, as he hustled into the forecasting center cradling an armload of printouts. Angela stood outside the newsroom, platinum locks swirling as she vamped a fawning group of male employees. "Hi, Kate," came the saccharine voice.

Kate gnashed a smile and ducked into the control room. The cramped space reeked of stale coffee and hot electronics. Against the opposite wall, the afternoon movie unspooled on the monitors, the audio muted. She walked to the soundproof window and watched the gaffer tweak borderlights for the new *Action-12* newsroom set. The warm wood-tones of the old set had been replaced by a monstrous, swoopy steel and glass concept she thought was more appropriate for a cheap sci-fi flick.

Gil Henderson, his cherubic face topped by an unruly burst of red curls, looked up from the console on her right. In the five years they had worked for Channel 12, Kate had become known for hard-hitting investigative reporting, and Gil had always been there, rolling tape, getting the hard shots. She slapped the bowdlerized cassette into his outstretched hand. "That arrogant putz...."

"Mason walk on your story?"

"Castrated."

"Ouch." He shoved the cassette into a slot and cued it up. "And speaking of cojones, Mason doesn't have any."

She flopped into the swivel chair. "I quit."

"Here we go again." Gil shook his head. "Professional suicide."

"This time I mean it." She paused. "It's obvious Mason wants me out anyway."

"TriConn owns every freakin' station in the southwest. Where you gonna' find work, Kate?"

"I have a plan."

Gil tilted his head and studied her. His voice softened. "You know...if you actually go through with this...*plan*, I'll back you up. Just like old times."

"Thanks, Gil." She stood, smiled and nodded, and walked out.

In her office, she picked up her notes for the evening's newscast, leaned back in her chair, stared at the ceiling. Even if they didn't fire her, humiliation would drive her out. She fidgeted with the notes for a moment, then tossed them aside.

Her gaze drifted to the plaques and awards dotting the wall. One touted her as "Colorado's most important news personality," another, "The best investigative reporter in the southwest." She could kowtow to Mason, and perhaps save her job. Or she could try to rekindle what the past two years of hell had extinguished and go independent. A desperate move, but it might open doors to a network position or a spot with an indie. But it would require a power story, a real jolt—a genuine, high voltage jump-start.

She turned to the computer and scrolled through her wish-list of potential subjects: Politics, Disasters, Weird Stuff. She clicked Weird

Stuff: Aliens, Witchcraft, ESP, ARC…

ARC. During a ceremony at the Air Force Academy a few years ago, she had overheard a small group of pilots talking about it, their voices hushed and wary. They said ARC was a sinister black project that harbored secrets greater than Area 51.

She opened the file.

Auroral Research Center: U.S. military investigates auroras and related phenomena by beaming radio waves into the ionosphere. Some believe ARC is a cover for a plot to monitor and control communications worldwide.

She remembered Senator Sam Hurwitz had championed ARC, saying it was essential to national defense. Others opposed the project because of its expense and secrecy. *Nope. Too big. I need something I can get my arms around.*

She printed the ideas and looked them over, her plan finally asserting itself, one that could salvage her career. Or destroy it. *Now or never.* She rose and strode briskly down the carpeted hallway to the station manager's office. The secretary confirmed she could enter. She smoothed her skirt, took a deep breath, and walked into Randall Mason's lair.

Her boss looked up from his gleaming chrome desk and raised an eyebrow. He motioned for her to sit, and she settled into a narrow steel and leather armchair. Kate remembered when the station had been under Tom Southgard's energetic management, when the office had been open and vibrant, the room bright and filled with framed cells of cartoon characters and photos of famous talent. Kate's own photo had occupied a prominent spot. Now the room was sterile, a few conservatively posed pictures of the station's current personnel spaced evenly along the wall. Kate's portrait was the smallest, squeezed ignominiously between two filing cabinets.

"Randall," she began, her voice not quite as forceful as planned, "I'm requesting some time to pursue what I do best, to regain—"

Mason made a dismissive gesture. "Time *off*? Angela is taxed enough as it is. You can't throw the entire program her way."

She held her composure, letting the insult wash over her. "You know my strengths lie in investigative reporting. My exclusives served this station well in the past and, frankly, I think it would improve ratings if we reinstated that format."

Mason's pink jowls darkened. "It seems we've had this conversation before." He gave her a condescending frown. "TriConn insists upon a tasteful, reserved approach, Kate. You know that. They're moving away from, well, sensationalism. Besides, Angela would need another co-anchor, and TriConn wouldn't fund it."

Kate steadied her voice with another deep breath. *Here goes.* "I'm willing to work as an independent contractor. I keep my office for the duration, but you only pay as I deliver. Of course, the station participates if a story goes into syndication. You can't lose." She paused to let that sink in, then added: "I'm just requesting that you harness my talents."

Mason tilted back in his chair and steepled his fingers, nodding as if in serious contemplation. Kate could tell by his suppressed smile that he favored the idea of her darting off as an independent producer. He expected her to fail. Dumping her would become much easier. But the response surprised her when it finally came.

"I like it," he said. "Not a bad idea, actually. I suppose I could intercede on your behalf with the owners. We could hammer out an agreement. So, yes, take some time. Investigate. Find us something with real punch." He sat forward, his comb-over glistening like lacquered plastic, and gave her a sly smile. "But remember, Kate, it's essential you demonstrate that gut instinct, that reportorial verve." He clenched a fist for emphasis.

Kate smiled, said thank you, she'd get right on it. She got up and walked rapidly back to her office. *Reportorial verve, my ass, you smirking S.O.B.* She hesitated just inside the door, a rubbery weakness stealing into her legs.

Now I've done it.

The screams woke her Saturday morning at seven.

Right on schedule.

Kate swung out of bed and walked into Mark's room. He was sitting up, covers askew, stripping off a sweat-soaked T-shirt. He glanced up, ice-blue eyes flashing beneath the black mop of hair curling low over his forehead. Guilt and anger colored his voice. "Sorry,"

"Same old nightmare?"

"Yeah. Same old, same old."

She sat beside him and squinted as sunlight glancing from the Navajo fetish in the window brushed her eyes. There was a low chuff as Buddy looked up from his mat, his gentle face filled with concern. She reached down and stroked the golden retriever's fur. "Hey, Buddy."

Mark pulled the covers across his chest. "'Comin' at ya.' That's what Dad always says."

"Comin' at ya?"

"From that dumb Aussie beer commercial. We always ride our bikes to the Lookout. He smiles at me and says, 'Comin' at ya.' Then…"

Kate knew what the recurring dream would bring next: his father would turn away and the world would explode in a brilliant flash of light—exactly what had happened to their lives two years ago, when Mark turned twelve, and Jack's plane vanished over the North Pacific.

Happy birthday.

She was trying to think of something comforting to say, something besides the usual inane platitudes, when the telephone jarred the silence. She rushed back to her room and lifted the receiver.

"Hello, Darlin'. Sorry to disturb you on your day off."

"Daddy? It's early—"

"How about you and Mark drivin' up here today, say, around eleven?"

"I'd love to, but—"

"It's time to let you in on a secret."

"What do you mean?"

"Something you have to see. Might be a big story for you."

She paused. "What on earth are you talking about?"

"Just come on up. 'Bye now."

She stared at the receiver. This was totally unlike her father. He was never coy, never played games. The idea of his having something worthy of primetime news was ludicrous. She shrugged. They were overdue for a visit. "Mark," she called out. "Get dressed. We're going to Grampa's."

* * *

They loaded Buddy into the old Wagoneer's back seat, drove to I-25, and headed north toward Garden of the Gods road. A few miles to the southwest, Pikes Peak glowed orange against a turquoise sky. The cog railway would soon haul its first load of tourists up the grinding, nine-mile track to the summit. In the silent distance, a training plane slowly descended, a glint of silver floating north toward the Air Force Academy.

Mark turned to her. "Gramps couldn't have any big-deal secret. There's nothing out there."

"You know Grampa. This will probably amount to nothing."

"Maybe he's giving the museum more money."

"Don't even joke about that."

Kate felt her hands tighten around the steering wheel. For some inexplicable reason, her father had spent a fortune on the new Colorado Springs Museum of Science, and she had been furious to see her parent's retirement squandered. Since Jack's death, money had been tight. They couldn't afford any more charitable obsessions.

From the side of a roaring, southbound eighteen-wheeler, a Crocodile Dundee clone grinned at them, his beefy arm unleashing a kangaroo-festooned bottle of Australia's Finest Lager, Comin' at Ya' stenciled in giant, arched strokes across the trailer's length. Kate stole a glance at Mark and noticed he had forced his gaze downward, away from the truck.

They passed the Garden of the Gods, its sandstone spires jutting skyward like pink fangs, and angled onto a narrow blacktop road that snaked westward into the hills. Twenty minutes later, Kate turned north at a sagging wooden gate, and the Jeep shuddered over a cattle guard and onto an entrance road of crushed granite. They crunched along the winding drive for a mile and crested an aspen-shaded hill.

Below them stretched the ranch.

The great barn, awash in morning sunlight, stood on their left. River stone formed the massive lower story. The upper two stories were of wood, painted maroon. A broad, white-trimmed cupola straddled the roof. Running in a deep channel, a creek plunged down from a hidden lake cradled in the hills and churned past the barn.

A large diameter pipe, made of wooden slats reinforced with iron bands, traveled on concrete supports just above the channel, then climbed through a concrete section in the building's western end. Kate thought it was strange to use such a large pipe for watering the livestock, but her father had always shrugged the question off, saying, "That's the way your great, great, grandfather built it."

In the back seat, Buddy pounced from one window to the other, his tail dusting the air in excitement. A wistful tone crept into Mark's voice. "Buddy thinks…all of us…are gonna' go riding up the trail together."

As the Jeep rumbled over the wooden bridge spanning the creek, Kate looked past the barn to the faint beginnings of the Lost Canyon Trail. She and Jack and Mark used to climb the path, her husband and son straining on their mountain bikes, Kate astride her black mare, Winnie. Buddy always led the way, pausing now and then to explore the trailside or herd the others along with an impatient bark. The trail rose into the folded landscape, arching over ravines with a series of narrow bridges, winding through the pines and around enormous sandstone boulders. It faded into the hills, a pathway to another time.

The rambling, three-story house nudged the woods five hundred feet to their right. A flagstone walk stretched from the front porch to the barn, carving a rust-colored path through a wide expanse of lawn. Kate noticed a late-model sedan in the graveled parking area. The message on its bumper leaped out at her: WHERE LEARNING IS FUN—COLORADO SPRINGS MUSEUM OF SCIENCE.

She swerved up beside the car and stopped, then sat quietly, searching for some innocuous reason why the museum car should be in her father's driveway. But there was only one possible answer: he was going to donate more money—money he didn't have. If not money, then what? The ranch?

As she clutched the steering wheel and made an effort to tame her nerves, Mark climbed out and opened the rear door. Higgins, her father's black and white Border collie, shot across the field and intercepted Buddy as he flew from the Jeep's back seat, and the two dogs bounced playfully around each other like a couple of furry basketballs.

Attitude stabilized, Kate stepped from the Jeep and inhaled a deep breath of crisp mountain air. From the creek came the whisper of rushing water.

Mark looked toward the house. "There's Gramps."

Her father came down the steps, his white walrus mustache aglow against weather-darkened skin, a warm smile pinching the corners of his eyes. As usual, he was wearing faded jeans and a blue denim shirt. He hugged Kate and gave Mark's shoulder an affectionate squeeze. "I've told you all about Professor O'Hanlon," he said as a smiling, portly man with a neatly-trimmed red beard and round, ruddy face walked up beside him. O'Hanlon wore a gray tweed jacket with a vest and tie. For his size, his movements were quick and energetic.

Kate tried to maintain a cordial composure. "Dr. O'Hanlon," she said, extending a hand. "This is a surprise." She was astonished to see the director of the Colorado Springs Museum of Science standing before her. Professor Patrick O'Hanlon had held a lofty position with the Smithsonian Institute before joining the Colorado Springs museum, the money to lure him away having been provided by her father's lavish sacrifice.

O'Hanlon gestured toward her father. "Well, of course I couldn't turn Jared down. He's one of our principal beneficiaries, and now he's promised something spectacular for the museum." His eyes glittered with enthusiasm. "And I must admit, my curiosity is about to kill me."

Kate shot her father a worried glance, but he seemed not to notice. "Well, come on, folks," he said. "You've got a lot to see." He hooked Kate's arm, gave her a curious wink, and stepped onto the flagstone pathway.

He turned toward the barn.

*   *   *

The barn was much larger than it seemed at first glance. The doors and windows were oversized, the proportions of the building combining to trick the eye. A sliding door rumbled back, and Mark followed the others inside and across a freshly swept concrete floor.

They entered the tack room, where the smell of leather joined the odors of hay and horse. Mark glanced at the left wall. His blue mountain bike still hung from the pegs where he'd left it two years ago, after the last ride with his father. It glimmered from the shadows like a talisman, and he fought a sudden urge to grab it and ride furiously up the Lost Canyon Trail to the Lookout, as if the effort could somehow turn back time, and his father would be waiting for him on the rock ledge.

With a sweep of his hand, his grandfather indicated a row of saws, augers, and farm implements dangling from a ceiling beam. "These tools date back to the eighteen hundreds, when the house and barn were built." He lifted an ancient bellows and compressed it, puffing out a cloud of dust. "This very room housed the forge." He turned and gazed at the faded panoramic photograph of the ranch stretching across the room's back wall. "This old barn is kind of a museum piece all its own."

O'Hanlon cleared his throat. "That's certainly true."

Mark saw the professor steal a quick glance at his watch. *Gramps, come on. This is just a bunch of ranch junk.* Now O'Hanlon was rocking back and forth on his heels, hands thrust into the pockets of his jacket, his expression polite but grim.

Mark had been in and out of the barn a thousand times. He had helped the farrier with the shoeing, sat on the corral fence while the horse trainers worked their magic, and watched a mare give birth. There were no secrets.

Jared walked up to the photograph and grasped a knobbed iron rod angling through a narrow slot below its frame. He shot a penetrating look at Mark, pale blue eyes twinkling, and tugged the rod down. A metallic clank came from somewhere beyond, and the wall silently moved back and to the left, admitting a soft rush of air. An enormous, dimly lit space yawned before them.

With a faint hum, the cavernous room filled with light.

"My God!" O'Hanlon whispered, his voice throwing back a faint echo. "Oh, my God."

A massive coil of copper, wound in perfect curves around supports of glass and porcelain, rose from the room's center and thrust into the dark roof cavity high overhead. An aluminum ring some twenty feet in diameter hovered above the coil, its broad perimeter carving into shadow. The effect was that of a great sculpture; beautiful; terrifying in its scale; imbued with an aura of sudden and ferocious power.

Mark finally worked his voice free: "What is it? How did it get here?" There was no way this monster could have been hidden from him. *No way.*

His grandfather started down a wooden ramp toward the floor below and looked back, grinning. "Come on. I'll give you the grand tour."

They descended and approached the towering machine, old pine planks squeaking beneath their feet. Tall steel boxes bristling with wicked-looking electrical insulators and interconnected with heavy cables sat in ordered rows. Complex instruments studded with meters, dials, and switches hugged the walls. Barn smells jousted with the odors of machine oil and metal.

Resting low on thick ceramic supports, two huge turns of copper encircled the tall central coil, forming a broad, flat helix. Mark bent down and ran his fingers over one of the turns. It was as thick as his leg. He rapped the burnished metal with his knuckles, producing a dull ringing sound.

"That's the primary coil," Jared said. "It's about fifty feet in diameter. That big aluminum ring at the top is called a torus. Whole thing's forty feet tall."

Mark noticed the machine actually had three main coils: the outside helix, a short, wide coil, and the tall coil that had first caught his eye. The successively taller coils were centered, one inside another, like the tiers of a skyscraper

"What in God's name is this?" his mother demanded.

Jared's gaze lingered on the machine for a moment, then shifted to his three guests. "It's called a Magnifying Transmitter, and it was built in 1903 by Nikola Tesla."

O'Hanlon seemed to have frozen in place. He cocked his head. "*Tesla?*" His voice became low and tremulous. "You do know, of course, this is one of the greatest scientific finds in recent history."

Anger spilled into Mark's voice. "You never told me—"

His mother's hand shot out, cutting him off. "Who was this…who was Nikola Tesla?"

But Jared wordlessly turned, leading them deeper into the vast room. Shaking his head in frustration, Mark followed. They passed a cluster of industrial-size electric motors and gearworks crouching within protective wire cages. Ahead loomed a sinister looking apparatus comprised of two large, vertically-mounted glass disks rimmed with metal spikes. Heavy cables fanned out from the device in ordered, parallel rows. "That's called a rotary spark gap," Jared said. "I have no idea what it does." He paused before a steel door set into the wall and turned the latch. The door groaned open, and they stepped over a raised threshold into a concrete chamber that smelled faintly of rust and mildew.

An iron mass as big as a Volkswagen Bus hulked up from the floor. "This is the generator." Thick cables erupted from the machine and snaked into a flat panel crowded with electric meters and switches with long black handles. "That pipe brings water down from the lake," he said, pointing to an enormous steel tube that curved into the lower half of the machine. He patted a wheel jutting from the generator's flared base. "To produce electricity, you open the floodgate at the dam, then you turn this valve to let water into the turbine. The generator does the rest."

Mark noticed his mother's shrewd smile. Maybe this Magnifying Transmitter, or whatever it was called, might be the story she desperately wanted.

O'Hanlon peered through an opening in the machine's iron casing. "How much power can it deliver?"

"About ten megawatts. It's one of Tesla's bladeless designs. About a third the size of a conventional turbine, so I understand."

"I read about these turbines. They use disks instead of blades. Tremendously efficient, but apparently Tesla was the only one who could make them work on a large scale."

"We won't need the generator. The lake can only supply water for a few minutes, and I doubt the old pipe could take the pressure anyway. I had the power company install underground lines years ago."

"Have you actually been operating this...this machine?"

"I just maintain it. Making it run is where you come into the picture."

O'Hanlon blinked. "*Me?*"

Again, the question was left unanswered. They were led back into the main room, toward stairs rising to a broad landing high overhead. As they walked, Mark began to realize how the huge space—nearly half the barn's volume—had been so cleverly hidden. A large portion of the building was supposed to have been used for grain storage, and shallow rooms, always choked with crates and bulky implements, had their true depth disguised.

They climbed to the landing and stopped beside a wide console that projected toward center of the room like the prow of a ship. Switches and enormous round dials studded the console's inclined surface. "This is the main control panel," Jared said. "You can operate everything from here."

The bulky, antiquated instruments, with their brass bezels and ornate lettering, reminded Mark of the submarine *Nautilus* from Disney's *20,000 Leagues Under The Sea*. "What does that do?" he asked, pointing to a brass globe suspended in gimbals just beyond the console. He could see the faint outlines of continents traced in tiny glittering dots across its surface.

"I don't know what this stuff does. I just know what some of it's called."

O'Hanlon was shaking his head. "It's astounding...that a device of this size and complexity could have been built so long ago, and then hidden for more than a century." He leaned over the rail and looked down. "This machine will be of tremendous interest to the scientific community, and it should even cause a stir among the general population." He paused, his gaze lingering on the huge central coil rising into the shadows above. "One thing does puzzle me, though. I don't understand why Tesla used such heavy windings, even for ten-million watts of power."

"Tesla was known for doing weird things." A metallic clanging drifted through the walls. "I hope you brought hearty appetites. That's the call for lunch."

*   *   *

Built of stone and logs, the sprawling ranch house echoed the architecture of the barn. The vaulted ceilings and exposed log construction imparted a rustic, comfortable feel. Indian rugs cushioned the floors and hung from the walls. The interior smelled of furniture polish, cedar, and, for the moment, Mexican food.

Mark's grandmother met them at the entrance. Like his grandfather, Jenny was slender, her face weathered and tanned. Her hair was pulled back into a loose ponytail that fell across her shoulders in a silver fan. She smiled. "Come in and make yourselves at home. María is setting the table for you."

As everyone drifted toward the dining room, she pulled Mark aside. Her eyes held him for a moment. "Figured any of this out yet?"

He shook his head.

"You'll see." She gave him a concerned smile. "Just hold onto your hat."

*   *   *

After lunch, they gathered in the great hall that served as living room and den. Over the decades, smoke escaping from the arched fireplace had painted a ghostly shadow across the mantle and two ancient Teutonic flags crossed against the massive stone chimney.

O'Hanlon settled into an easy chair. Mark shared a leather couch with his mother. His grandfather stood before the fireplace, gazing into the distance. Finally, he looked down at O'Hanlon. "Professor, you're very knowledgeable about Nikola Tesla—one of the reasons why I supported you for the position of curator. Anyway, please forgive me if I review some history you're already familiar with."

He cleared his throat and began. "Tesla was one of the most prolific, and eccentric, inventors in history. He designed electric generators for Thomas Edison, then moved to New York City, where he made a lot of major scientific discoveries. He invented the alternating current system we still use today and did some ground-breaking work with high-frequency electricity. In 1899, he came to Colorado Springs and built a big laboratory out on the plains. There, he performed experiments with a machine similar to the one you just saw. He said the Magnifying Transmitter was his greatest invention. An interesting statement, considering he gave us so many revolutionary ideas.

"In 1900, he returned to New York and started building a bigger transmitter at Wardenclyffe, on Long Island. With that machine, Tesla claimed that he would be the first to broadcast a radio signal across the Atlantic."

The tone of his voice dropped. "But I think he had another, secret purpose in mind. J.P. Morgan was funding the project, but for some reason he backed out. Maybe he found out what Tesla actually planned to accomplish. Anyway, when Morgan quit, Tesla abandoned the effort. History books say Tesla was bankrupt. Truth is, he was far from broke. He built the transmitter you saw today as the backup to Wardenclyffe."

"That's a considerable departure from the accepted history." O'Hanlon said. "Logic suggests he would have used the money to finish the New York project."

"He apparently intended Wardenclyffe as a test, to see if mankind was ready for his discovery. Thomas Edison lied about the dangers of Tesla's new AC current in order to protect his own, inferior DC system. People made a fortune using Tesla's patents. They stole his ideas. Scientists ridiculed his theories. Before revealing the Magnifying Transmitter and its secrets, Tesla decided to wait until the world caught up with him. He thought it would take a hundred years." He smiled faintly. "I wonder if he allowed enough time."

O'Hanlon leaned forward. "I don't understand. Marconi transmitted the first radio signal across the Atlantic in 1901. What did Tesla have that was worth holding back?"

"Yeah," Mark added. "That thing in the barn is just an old broadcasting station, right?"

"Ah." His grandfather said, a curious look crossing his face. "That's the heart of this whole story. We don't know what the Magnifying Transmitter is really for. It was apparently built to do more than just send signals." He folded his arms, silent for a moment. "Tesla discovered something significant in 1899. Something so profound he didn't want it revealed until now."

"Tesla died in 1943," O'Hanlon said thoughtfully. "He had more than forty years to change his mind."

"After the Wardenclyffe failure, Tesla made a pact with his assistant, Mikhail Karsov, who was also something of an electrical wizard. He helped build the transmitter in the barn. Tesla's deal required that Karsov and his heirs maintain the transmitter and then reveal it to the world after a hundred years, give or take ten. In exchange, they got money and this ranch. If they ever broke the pact, they would get nothing." He paused and directed his blue eyes straight at Mark, an odd twitch of a smile pulling at the corners of his mouth. "Mikhail Karsov and his heirs have owned and guarded the transmitter since 1903."

"That means…" O'Hanlon began.

"Mikhail Karsov was my great grandfather, and Mark's great, great, great grandfather."

Mark bolted upright. He was a direct descendent of Nikola Tesla's genius assistant.

"You will inherit all this," his grandfather said. "But you have to help get the transmitter in working order and do a proper job showing it off."

Mark scowled. Before today, he obviously hadn't been considered trustworthy enough to have shared in the secret.

His mother spoke for both of them, her voice flaring with indignation. "Why was all of this hidden from us? Why didn't you tell us—?"

"There was a secrecy agreement between Tesla and Karsov," Jared said, lifting a faded leather binder from the coffee table. "If the agreement is broken, Tesla's deal is off. We lose the ranch, the transmitter, and a generous trust fund."

He withdrew a folder and held it out. "Dr. O'Hanlon, on behalf of the estate, I'm inviting you to oversee the restoration, testing, and public release of Tesla's invention."

"Absolutely!" O'Hanlon sputtered. "I can make arrangements with the museum…take a leave of absence."

"There's a salary and a secrecy agreement. You can have an attorney look it over if you like." He faced Mark. "Would you consider working as a paid helper?"

The prospect of earning money thrilled him. "Yeah, sure."

"There's no need for an attorney," O'Hanlon said, lifting a pen from his breast pocket. "This is very straightforward."

"We can get started as soon as you're ready."

"Make it tomorrow morning. Sam Goodwin can take over for me at the museum."

Kate stood. "And I'll have a video crew here in twenty-four hours."

"Take pictures, notes, anything you like. But you can't go public until the machine is tested. It's in the agreement."

"How long will that take?"

"Depends. Several months, at least."

Her face fell.

"I'm sorry, Kate. This is the only way."

She was silent for a moment, frowning. "I'll shoot the restoration myself and write up the history. Gil can help edit, and I can trust him to keep quiet. We'll have a documentary finished by the time you're ready."

Jared nodded his approval, then said with an apologetic smile, "Now I have to get on with business. I've got a ranch to run."

As they left the house, Mark looked up at his grandfather. "I wasn't really mad at you."

"I wouldn't have blamed you." He ruffled Mark's hair and laughed. "Hey, you're gonna get paid, what do you want?"

They said their good-byes, and as Kate drove toward the bridge, Mark looked through the side window at the barn, its shadow growing long across the lawn.

He was heir to a monstrous machine of unknown purpose, a creation of one of the greatest—and strangest—inventors of all time. It had slept in its secret room for more than a hundred years.

What would happen, he wondered, when it awoke?

Traffic choked I-25 during the drive back home, and it was nearly five o'clock when Kate swung the Wagoneer into the driveway. As she entered the house, she heard Mark open the creaky backyard gate and begin warming up Buddy for their daily ritual. She watched through the den window.

Mark stood beneath the old sycamore, unleashed a Frisbee, and shouted the singular command that galvanized the dog into impossible bursts of speed: "*Faster than lightning!*"

In one fluid motion, Buddy streaked across the lawn, snatched the spinning disk from its arc, and dropped smoothly back to earth. Without breaking stride, he pivoted and sped back to Mark, fur rippling like spun gold.

Kate remembered the summer before Jack's death, when Mark had entered Buddy in the Summit Park Frisbee contest. Everyone thought golden retrievers were too heavy and clumsy for serious competition, but in the end it came down to Buddy and a terrier owned by a man who had come all they way from Denver. A large crowd had gathered to watch. It was an "instant death" playoff—an unfortunate choice of words, in Kate's mind, because she thought if Buddy strained much harder he'd have a heart attack.

Mark's opponent fired a smooth toss. The terrier rocketed across the field and jumped, but misjudged the height. Animal and plastic tumbled to earth in a sad heap.

Buddy was next. Mark cocked his arm and spun the Frisbee into a long, high arc—too high Kate thought—but Mark belted out "Faster than lightning!" and Buddy launched like a bolt from a crossbow. He leapt, ears and tail streaming straight back in a blur of yellow-gold. He met the Frisbee at its peak, clamping down on it like a ravenous hawk.

As the crowd cheered, Buddy trotted jubilantly back and dropped the disk at Mark's feet, mouth open wide in an excited grin. Mark hugged him and heaped on enough praise to last a year.

"Maybe he's part Border collie," said one of the judges as Mark walked onto the platform to receive his trophy. "Never seen a golden run so fast."

"Nope," Mark had replied. "He's purebred golden retriever. My dad bought him for me."

The reward for their effort was a year's supply of Uncle Ed's Pizza and a picture of Buddy on the delivery box.

The memory fading, Kate turned from the window and walked to the small downstairs bedroom she had commandeered for an office. A documentary about the Magnifying Transmitter would eventually go national. She was certain about that. But the story had to remain under wraps for an indefinite period, and she was hemorrhaging time and money. Besides, the overriding imperative was to prove she still possessed, as Randall Mason had so smugly demanded, "gut instinct." Sighing, she switched on the computer and opened the research file. The leads were taking her nowhere, and the clock was ticking.

* * *

Mark tugged the black case from beneath his bed, snapped the lid open, and lifted his most prized possession from its maroon velvet nest: a 1964 left-handed Hofner bass guitar exactly like the one Paul McCartney used. It had an intoxicating smell of polish and exotic wood. Even at rest its perfect shape evoked a sense of energy and purpose. Everything had its own vibration.

He strapped the flawless instrument on and plucked the strings. If anything compensated for being a southpaw, it was that he shared that distinction with Paul.

Buddy chuffed at the window, and Mark looked out to see the headlights of a rusted Chevy Malibu wash across the curb. The car stopped with a squeal of brakes, and a slight figure with severely spiked hair emerged. Shoulders hunched, hands thrust into the pockets of a tattered windbreaker, he trudged across the front lawn toward the house. Mark settled the guitar into its case, pounded downstairs, and opened the door.

Alex Graham looked up from the front steps and tilted an earringed head. "Me and about fifty primo hackers groveled this totally excellent program." He held up a CD and rotated it enticingly between his fingers. "We're talking split-key encryption, decryption. Only problem is, my DSL is down."

"You shouldn't be here. Mom's gonna have a cow..."

Alex continued in a low voice. "I scored a copy of the Panther... back doors to the FBI, CIA, secret government projects..."

Mark had heard rumors about the forbidden program, said to allow entry into the most inaccessible systems. Secret government projects had their attraction. He glanced back at the door. "You better make sure my computer's clean when you're done."

Alex grinned hungrily. "No problemo."

Mark ushered him quietly upstairs to his room. Alex pulled up a chair, loaded the Panther, and copied a program onto the hard drive. The modem squealed as he went on line. "We'll route through the museum computer and a couple of switching stations. They'll never trace us that way." His fingers blurred across the keyboard. "Done," he said after a minute. "Now, my man, where do you want to go today?"

Mark remembered something about a weird military project his mother had mentioned. "ARC," he said.

Alex scanned a list from the CD. "Got it." A moment later the screen darkened and a curt message appeared: "Password." He hesitated, then typed in the code. A long list of folders marched on, most of them a meaningless jumble of letters and numbers. "We're in."

Mark sighed. "Boring."

"Hey. Here's one called *Cerberus*."

"What's that?"

"To spy on the Internet, Dilbert. Don't you ever read the news?

It's that Gestapo program those government creeps are pushing. Like a V-chip for the Web. No privacy. No encryption. No *nothing*." He downloaded a file. "This one's coded. Ciphergraphics." He loaded the decryption program and clicked the mouse. "Now," he said exultantly, "we shred this baby."

The word CONSTELLATION slowly crystallized over a battle shield formed of stars. "*Yes!*"

Then text:

—The Greatest Threat Comes From Within—
Secret Research Project Attacks Freedom

The screen morphed into a photograph of a huge geodesic dome framed by jagged, white-capped mountains. More text blinked on:

This information is disseminated by Constellation, a watchdog group of U.S. citizens.

Project ARC is the ultimate weapon against your freedom. Operating as the Auroral Research Center, this Alaska-based system is designed to intercept and control communications worldwide.

Powerful ARC receivers and transmitters can spy on and disrupt the Internet and all broadcast communications, regardless of power or modulation.

Primary ARC supporters include Moral Alliance leader Frederick Crotty; president pro tem of the Senate, Sam Hurwitz; and General Thad Greggson, Chairman, Joint Chiefs of Staff.

Government propaganda claims ARC is an innocuous research project. However, the following communications blackouts coincided with ARC transmissions.

A long list followed, linking ARC to blackouts that had occurred over the past several years.

Mark shrugged. He lifted his battered acoustic guitar from its stand and quietly strummed the chords to *Lady Madonna*.

"Freaky," Alex said. "This data's a year old. But it looks like ARC snatched Constellation's site right off the web and then shut it down. That probably means Cerberus has been secretly active." He gingerly patted the top of his spiked hair with an open hand. "And they could listen and knock out, like, the Internet, cell phones, satellite—anything that uses radio waves." He stared at the screen for a minute in silence. "Whoa, check *this* out."

He read aloud: "Constellation has documented the suspicious deaths of prominent individuals who opposed ARC: Senator William Daniels, Professor Wesley Coolidge, Senator Jeff Travis—"

Mark's chest tightened. He silenced the guitar and stared at Alex, his mouth open in a silent exclamation.

"Senator Travis," Alex said. That's…"

"Read the whole thing."

Alex leaned toward the monitor. "Senator Jeff Travis: Plane crash over North Pacific. Undetermined cause. Crash coincided with powerful RF signal burst bearing similar characteristics to ARC transmissions. Senator Travis had fought Senator Hurwitz over funding and secrecy."

"That plane crash," Alex said softly. "That's the same flight your dad was on, wasn't it?"

Mark nodded. "Yeah."

"Sorry, man."

"This isn't somebody's idea of a joke, is it?"

Alex swiveled around to face him. "Cerberus didn't think so."

"Look!" Mark jabbed a finger at the screen. A message screamed: *Warning. You have entered a restricted site—*

The image froze as Alex yanked the cable from its jack. He stared at the monitor, shaking his head.

"What?"

"I don't believe it. I think they traced us."

"You said they couldn't."

"Maybe they only got as far as a switcher. Don't worry about it. They probably won't do anything." He paused. "Anyway, I saved the data."

"I want my mom to see it."

"Yeah, your mom," he said. "She could dig up the full shit on this."

She was downstairs at her desk, pale light from the monitor blanching her tanned face. Mark leaned in the door.

She glanced up. "Hi, honey."

"Alex is upstairs. He found something you've gotta see."

"Send him home. He's nothing but trouble."

"You said you were looking for a story…this might have something to do with Dad."

She stared at him for a moment. "What about your father?"

"About that secret government thing called the ARC Project. Alex found this site—"

Before he could finish, she pushed her chair back, rose, and rushed past him through the open door.

* * *

Kate watched as Alex scrolled through the Constellation text, her vision momentarily blurring as she read about the plane crash. Alex copied the encrypted file and handed her the disc. "Use the second disc to decrypt it."

She sat on the bed, turning the discs over in her hand. "What makes you think this is for real?"

"ARC censored it. That makes it important." He pointed to the CDs. "Don't let anyone see those. They're not exactly legal."

She gave Alex a stern look. "No more hacking, or you could spend the rest of your youth peering between prison bars." Privately, she wished he would continue. She wanted more information, and she wanted it fast. "So," she said mostly to herself, "what's next?"

Alex shrugged. "Obviously, try to find Constellation."

"Talk to somebody who knows a lot about electronics," Mark suggested.

Alex nodded. "Yeah."

There was a brief silence. "David Hightower," the two boys said in unison.

"He's a science fanatic," said Alex. "And he belongs to a bunch of ham radio clubs and stuff."

Kate was dubious. "A ham radio operator?"

"He'll be my math teacher this year," Mark said. "Alex had him for physics. He's totally cool."

She thought for a moment. People always suspected a bomb or sabotage when a disaster involved someone of prominence. Two years ago, although devastated by Jack's death, she had mustered enough energy to start her own investigation. But she had discovered nothing, and the government agencies had been worthless.

They never found the plane's black box. No bodies were recovered. But ARC's possible involvement was a totally new twist. Her heart raced. The inference that enemies of the ARC project were being murdered held a desperate hint of plausibility.

"I'll talk to Hightower," she said. "What can it hurt? And I'll research these Constellation people." She felt a twinge of guilt; Alex needed very little encouragement to start hacking again.

"Mom?" Mark said. She could tell by his tone that she wasn't going to like what was coming. "Let Alex work with O'Hanlon and me." He glanced at Alex, who frowned back in confusion. "Things will go a lot faster if he helps, and he knows a ton about electronics. I'll share my paycheck with him."

She felt a firm "No!" forming on her lips until her son cunningly added: "He could bring his laptop. Gramps has a DSL line too."

She was silent for a moment. Now she felt totally evil as she said, "I'll ask Daddy if it's okay."

Alex held a hand palm-up. "*What* project?"

"An electronic project you wouldn't believe."

"I could bring my computer?"

"And you'd get paid."

"Awesome."

Mark accompanied Alex to his car and returned to his room. His mother was still seated, staring ahead, lost in thought. He settled beside her, then finally said, "You're really gonna investigate this aren't you?"

She turned to him and, with a determination in her voice he hadn't heard since his father's plane went down, replied, "You're damn right I am."

*   *   *

That night, as Buddy slept curled up beside Mark's bed, his paws twitched as he dreamed:

Dark clouds tumbled and roared. The Frisbee sailed ahead, rising into an angry sky. He ran, forging through the wild wind rushing past. Mark cried out in the hidden distance.

As if answering, the sky cracked with a bright flash and a heavy boom. The call came again, weaker and farther away. A fearsome urgency goaded Buddy on. He sped, paws blurring above the ground.

Mark's voice, laced with a struggling terror, wailed with a desperate plea—*Faster than Lightning*—

5

Senator Sam Hurwitz tilted back in the oversized leather chair and huffed a stream of cigar smoke at the jaguar mounted on his office wall. The chair popped and creaked as his mass stressed its wooden frame. He leveled his cigar at the big cat. *Pow*.

Hunting trophies stared from mounting stands and wall plaques: Ibex, zebra, antelope, tiger. The elephant tusks he'd had to remove, having caught too much flak from the environmental nut bags. A lion's penis, stretched to full erection, poked forlornly from a wooden base beside his desk. He loved to watch the reaction of female visitors when he explained what it was.

He scanned the wall to his left. Campaign signs and bumper stickers shouted *Senator Sam—That's Who I Am*! Political cartoons, enlarged, framed, and punctuated with track lighting, hung in honored spaces. One depicted Hurwitz as a squat, cigar-chomping, wild-west marshal, guns blazing, clearing the Internet Saloon of nefarious looking characters labeled "Smut" and "Pornography." In another, a helmeted caricature of Senator Sam stiff-armed the legislative opposition, his short but Herculean form charging through their defending ranks while cradling a football emblazoned with the florid logo of the Moral Alliance.

He worried the cigar with his tongue, attempting to disguise the sneer forming at his lips. This morning, Dr. Joseph Krohner, president of EleKtrum Corporation, was coming to his office all the way from Alaska. Because the senator wanted it that way. Thanks to Hurwitz, Krohner headed the most important project in the nation's history—ARC. And ARC, in turn, would soon make Hurwitz the most powerful man on the planet.

Then his eyes fell upon the grim-faced visitor at his right. General Thad Greggson sat ramrod straight, silent, still as a wooden Indian, his broad chest supporting an impressive array of medals and ribbons. Greggson was proving to be difficult. In a twist of irony, the general constantly objected to the extreme measures necessary to implement their plan, yet he wholeheartedly supported ARC, which was itself as extreme as the mind could imagine.

The intercom buzzed and the secretary announced Krohner's arrival. Hurwitz plucked a fresh Montecristo from the carved wooden humidor, flicked the lighter, and sucked the flame against the cigar's blunt end. After a full minute, he informed his secretary that Krohner could enter.

Now it was time to chew some butt.

Krohner pushed the door open, paused at the entrance, then crossed the room and folded his long limbs onto one of the stiff, low chairs near the desk. He nodded at Greggson, who acknowledged his presence with the merest rise of an eyebrow.

Hurwitz studied Krohner's gaunt figure through the growing haze of smoke. He extracted the cigar from his mouth, rotating it between thumb and forefinger. "I told you I wanted to keep a low profile until everything was ready. Now, thanks to that fuck-up you pulled two years ago, we've got problems."

"What do you mean?" Krohner asked quietly, the Slavic accent evident even with so few words spoken.

Hurwitz tilted his head. "I mean Senator Reese Myerson. You *have* heard of Senator Myerson?"

"I have heard—"

Hurwitz cut him off. "Well, that sonuvabitch is gonna reopen the investigation. Constellation hacked your firewall and downloaded *everything* about the plane crash. They sent it to Myerson."

Krohner shrugged. "By the time they determine anything of significance, it will be too late for them."

"Myerson got hold of the lab report."

Krohner pursed his lips slightly. "They still do not have much, even with autopsies."

"Like hell."

Krohner withdrew a folder from his briefcase and held it out. "We are now ahead of schedule."

"Sez you. You missed too many deadlines already." Hurwitz snatched the folder, dropped it onto his desk, and jammed a finger into it as if poking Krohner's chest. "I don't get enough reports, I don't hear what's going on. You make too many independent decisions." He paused, staring into the other man's steel-gray eyes. "I can yank funding so fast you won't know what happened 'til the doorknob hits your ass."

Krohner remained silent, his helmet of black hair, with its girly little pig tail, shining greasily in the overhead light.

Hurwitz analyzed his cigar for a moment; then he lowered his voice. "I want you to take care of Myerson."

"I think it would be unwise until we are fully operational."

"You didn't think so when you nailed Travis, did ya?"

Krohner's mouth twitched into a hint of a smile. "No."

"Then handle it. Myerson meets in committee in three days. He'll leak the whole shitload before he leaves the building."

Krohner stared at Hurwitz, his countenance neutral.

Greggson's deep voice boomed out. "I think it's time we moved to other topics. He turned to Hurwitz. "People are getting nervous. Congressional oversight wants appropriations on hold until the NSC is satisfied."

Hurwitz grunted. "I throw a lot of weight with the oversight committees. I can delay a decision for six months. And DARPA is still on board, so forget about it. Our primary concerns lie with the president and the FBI."

"Which brings us again to Constellation." Greggson's eyes shifted to Krohner. "I thought your hot-crap computer freaks could locate them."

Krohner cocked his head, his features brushed with disdain. "The full system will be on line within a month. After that, it will be impossible for them to hide—or to survive."

Greggson's eyes flicked back to Hurwitz. "I want this done surgically. Since you lost the nomination, the collateral damage will be a lot higher. I don't want this escalating into a major confrontation with our own armed forces."

Hurwitz winced inwardly. His party had deserted him, leaving him fourth in a field of five candidates for the presidential nomination. President Williamson was a coward and a fool. Instead of embracing the immaculate ARC system, he had begun to probe for information—sensitive information. The situation would be so much simpler if Hurwitz were to take the presidency. The ARC technology could be implemented without a total bloodbath.

He turned to Greggson, mellowing his voice to a cajoling purr. "General, we all want to minimize casualties. But I know you're the man to make the tough decisions. Sacrifice is necessary in order to save this country. You knew that when you joined us." Hurwitz rocked forward and rested his elbows on the desk. Clamped between his interlocked fingers, the cigar swiveled back and forth like the barrel of a cannon. "In less than two months, we will be in full control. Worldwide. We will have *unprecedented* power."

He smiled serenely. "And Constellation, the president, and the FBI will be totally irrelevant."

Carrying a bulging leather briefcase, Senator Reese Myerson left his office in the Russell Senate Building and strode down the marbled hallway to the elevators. As the doors slid open, he nodded at the exiting security guard and rode down to the parking garage. A half hour later, the black Cadillac limousine deposited him in front of a spacious, two-story colonial perched on a gentle slope two-hundred feet from the boulevard. The maid had left the porch light and several interior lights on for him. Marion would be working late for the law firm. He'd take her to dinner.

He unlocked the front door and walked to the study, which faced the front lawn and side yard. He often worked in his home office, occasionally glancing up to watch the squirrels scamper across the great oak outside his window. He preferred this peaceful environment, always feeling he accomplished more here than in the frenetic surroundings of the Capitol.

He dropped the briefcase beside the antique mahogany desk and switched on a small television in the corner. As the evening news droned in the background, he opened a file cabinet and removed a thick folder labeled *Constellation*.

Evening's orange twilight faded to black, and the landscape floods switched on, highlighting the oak's graceful branches and providing subtle lighting along a winding garden pathway.

Myerson opened the folder and began reading, making notes on a legal pad. He picked up the television remote and increased the volume as anchorman Bob Massey launched into his report. Edward's own image smiled back at him from the screen.

Citing new evidence indicating that foul play may have been involved in the crash of a jetliner that killed Senator Jeff Travis two years ago, Senator Reese Myerson is pushing to reopen an investigation of the incident...

The sound dissolved into an inferno of noise as jagged diagonal teeth raced across the screen. Myerson punched the controls, but the grinding static continued. Muttering, he got up and switched the set off manually, then turned to the built-in bar and poured two fingers of scotch. He checked his watch. If his wife didn't return soon, he'd have Chinese delivered from Yee's.

He lifted the reading glasses from his nose and rubbed his temples; a sharp headache had begun pulsing behind his eyes, and he still had hours of work to complete. He fumbled the glasses back into place and sat down heavily. The desk swam in and out of focus. "Christ," he mumbled. "I wonder if I'm headed for a stroke." He shoved the chair back and came to his feet. ...he'd get some aspirin or Tylenol... He snatched his glasses off and dropped them onto the desk. Was it his imagination, or were the stems hot to the touch?

Something moving caught his attention: wisps of smoke curling lazily from the television. Myerson yanked the cord from the wall. *What's happening?* He walked haltingly from the room, carried by legs suddenly robbed of coordination. The floor began to tilt.

Fumes from the burning TV, that's what it was. He needed fresh air. He staggered into the living room and paused, a cold sweat shivering against his skin. A skittering sound came from above. Steadying himself against a chair, he looked up.

Holes the diameter of basketballs pocked the ceiling, their rounded edges funneling into darkness. Jointed limbs clawed through the openings, tugging forth bulbous, black and yellow abdomens. Lowering on lifelines of glittering threads, the creatures dropped to the floor and regarded him with multiple obsidian eyes—a legion of gigantic spiders. Needle-mandibles clacking, they scurried after him, their pointed legs ticking against the hardwood with a sound like autumn leaves before the wind.

Myerson lurched backward as the chitinous monsters wriggled up his legs, blanketed his chest, his head, and arced their curved fangs into his flesh. He reeled, screaming, his hands frantically clawing at the grasping, spiny horrors.

A torrent of pain shot through his body. His limbs jerked in a flurry of spasms and clenched. He pitched forward and fell. As he lay still, with his head twisted to one side, his unblinking eyes stared as blood crept across the polished oak flooring in a viscous thread.

The last thing he sensed was the terrible buzz saw whining inside his brain.

K ate felt like a fool. *Desperate times require desperate phone calls.* She closed her office door and punched David Hightower's number into the phone. He answered after three rings, recognized her name, confirmed that Mark would be one of his math students this year. The soft, clipped voice said yes, she could come right over.

Kate stuffed a digital camera into its aluminum case, grabbed a microcassette tape recorder, and marched from the Forest Creek building to the parking lot and the Wagoneer. She found Hightower's street in ten minutes, in an older neighborhood not far from her own home. She parked and walked across the neatly trimmed lawn to the front door. An electric motor whirred, and she looked up to see a wide antenna slowly turning, its long, horizontal elements slightly swaying. Evidently, the man was playing with his ham radio set.

She rapped with the brass knocker and Hightower appeared a moment later. Kate had expected a balding, fifty-something man with a paunch and tired, baggy eyes peering through outdated bifocals. The man in the faded jeans and black T-shirt standing before her was tall and muscular, with a narrow waist and broad shoulders. He had thick, dark brown hair worn close-cropped. Square face, outdoors-rugged, maybe mid thirties—no glasses.

He smiled, gave her a firm handshake, then swung the door wide, ushering her inside. The living room was decorated simply, with a handful of functional furniture and a few rugs. Spartan, but comfortable. He motioned for her to follow. "I'll show you the station."

Inside his den, David seated her beside a long desk occupied by a computer and clusters of electronic gear. Lights winked from some of the instruments and voices murmured fuzzily from a small speaker. Track lighting illuminated a broad world map spread across the wall. She accepted an offer of coffee, and he walked from the room. She watched him go. His voice and demeanor suggested a military background. She should know, having been married to a pilot for fifteen years.

David returned with the coffee and sat beside her. "You said you're doing some research on radio jamming?"

She nodded, hesitating. She always had to force the words when she discussed the tragedy. "My husband died two years ago, along with sixty-three others, when his plane disappeared over the North Pacific. They never found the cause. No wreckage was recovered, and the investigation stopped."

"I heard about it. I'm very sorry."

Kate sipped her coffee and set it aside. "Mark and his friend learned that some radio jamming occurred at exactly the same time my husband's plane crashed."

Hightower gave her a curious look. "Where did they get their information?"

"A web site. It claimed a radio project in Alaska sent the jamming signals."

"What was the date and time?"

She told him, and he jotted the information down. "Some amateur radio operators monitor RFI—radio frequency interference—as a hobby. They log the time the RFI occurred and its direction. Sometimes they record the signal." He turned to the computer and logged onto the Internet. "RFI sources have different fingerprints.

Some interference is accidental. For example, some guy might have a malfunctioning transmitter. Or it could be malicious. Intentional jamming."

A web site flashed onto the screen. David scrolled down. "Here it is," he said, leaning closer. "Lots of guys reported something on that date, mostly from the West Coast. They detected a microwave signal occurring intermittently over a three-minute period—hmm!"

"What?"

"Very strong signal. Started around ten megahertz and broadened to a complex transmission in the gigahertz range. Funny, though, it was as strong in Hawaii as in Seattle. No reports from Oregon, a bunch from California, and a couple from Washington. Japan has a few hits on that too." He read for a moment. "They think it probably originated in the northwestern U.S., maybe Alaska. But they can't explain the high signal strength in Hawaii, unless it was beamed and took a skip off the ionosphere. I know they've been experimenting with that."

"Who's been experimenting?"

"The military, independent groups, defense contractors, developing over-the-horizon radar and submarine communications. The Russian Woodpecker was like that."

"Woodpecker?"

"A beamed signal that sounded like a woodpecker, pulsed at around six to eleven hertz. We never knew what it was for, but the theory was they were experimenting with radar." Images of electronic apparatus filled the monitor. "This guy has some serious RDF equipment, including Doppler and geo-location. He recorded the Alaska signal, which I am downloading now."

"Radio amateurs have this kind of equipment?"

David nodded. "Some of them are really into it. They monitor everything. Only way you could find out more would be through the NSA, the National Security Agency."

"What do they do when they find—what did you call it—RFI?"

"It depends. If it's strong or malicious, they report it to the Federal Communications Commission. They can make arrests, even send people to jail." He glanced at the screen. "Download's complete. Let's see what it sounds like." A hissing noise began and abruptly changed to a pulsating squeal similar to a fax signal.

Kate folded her arms and shuddered. "Makes my skin crawl."

David cocked his head. "Strange signal." A jumble of sharply curving green lines jittered across the screen. "Here's the graph. The carrier was pulsed. Weird pattern." He started burning a copy.

"Could a signal like that cause an airplane crash?" Kate asked.

David regarded her with blue-green eyes, a muscular arm resting on the desk. "If the signal was powerful enough to disrupt the radionics—instruments, radio, and so forth—the plane could still fly, but the pilot would have only visual flight reference. At night or during heavy overcast, he could be in real trouble."

"It's too coincidental this jamming, or whatever it was, occurred at exactly the same time my husband's plane disappeared."

He retrieved the copied disc and handed it to her. "I'll contact the RDF people, see what I can find out."

She was silent for a moment. "Be very careful."

He looked puzzled. Kate took a deep breath. She had decided to trust him, tell him everything. "Mark's friend hacked a government web site, called Cerberus, and copied some files. That's where I got the jamming information."

David gave her a skeptical glance. "He must be exceptionally talented."

She dug into her purse and removed the discs Alex had made. "The files are on these."

Following Kate's instructions, David loaded them into the computer and applied the decryption program. He read the Constellation files in silence. Finally, he looked up. "Normally, I'd view this as a hoax. But if Cerberus actually confiscated this, it means they were afraid of the content. Also, Constellation was dead accurate about the RFI." He leaned toward Kate, his forearms across his knees. "Until we know more, I think Mark and his pal should stay as far away from this as possible."

She stood. "Thank you, David. You've been a great help."

"What's your next move, if you don't mind my asking?"

"I'll talk to my husband's best friend. He's an instructor at the Air Force Academy. He did a little of his own investigating after the crash. Then, I'll find out about Constellation. Oh, and I'll look up Senator Reese Myerson. He's reopening the investigation—"

"Myerson is in a coma. It was just on the news."

Cold ghosted through her midsection. "What happened?" she asked, almost in a whisper.

"They didn't give any details." He paused, frowning. "I guess *you* should be careful."

David accompanied her to the Wagoneer. "I think maybe you're on to something. I'll try to help." He looked off into the distance, then back at her. His voice grew softer. He seemed a bit sheepish. "I wonder if you'd like to meet me for lunch. That is…"

Kate smiled. "Yes. How about the day after tomorrow?"

"Perfect."

She had replied too quickly. *Oh God*, she thought as she drove away. *What am I getting into?*

This is *impossible*." Alex stared down at the Magnifying Transmitter from the landing, shaking his head in disbelief. "I can't believe this thing is sitting out here in the middle of nowhere in your freakin' *barn*."

Mark smiled at this. He thought that Alex, with his tinted hair, piercings, and scrawny body, would be laughed off the ranch. But his grandfather had given him a handshake and a pat on the back just like he'd hired some tough new hand.

He led Alex downstairs to the barn's eastern wall, and they stepped back as a tractor pulling a wagon laden with farm equipment rattled out through the sliding doors. José was sweeping the concrete floor near the entrance, stirring up clouds of dust that hung and glittered in the late morning sunlight. Looking back inside the barn, Mark saw another hidden door now open, revealing the Magnifying Transmitter's huge coils curving away into shadow.

His grandfather came striding up, with O'Hanlon in tow. "Let's begin a little project." He picked up a spade leaning against the wall and began digging into the compacted earth near the entrance. After a minute, he had exposed a creosote-covered board buried several inches deep. "There's another board about two feet over here," he said, pointing. "Start digging and prying them up. We'll bring in the backhoe for the rest of the job."

As Jared and O'Hanlon disappeared into the barn, Mark tugged on his work gloves and lifted the shovel. "Man, this is not what I had in mind." He made a half-hearted stab at the ground.

Alex grabbed a pickaxe. "Didn't you know? This is what electrical engineers actually do."

"Why doesn't he just tell us why we're digging these up?"

Alex's pickaxe bit the earth. "Because, dude, that wouldn't be any fun."

*   *   *

O'Hanlon followed Jared onto the second landing. They walked past the transmitter's sloping control panel and stopped before a door. Jared threw it open, revealing a spacious room with white paneling and a ceiling of stamped metal. An ancient oak desk and a plush leather chair sat against the opposite wall. The modern telephone resting on the desktop seemed glaringly out of place in the archaic setting. Behind the desk, a wide window overlooked the ranch house and woods beyond.

"This was Tesla's office," Jared said as they stepped inside

Wooden filing cabinets sheathed the wall on O'Hanlon's right. On the left was a row of glass-fronted cases crammed with thick volumes bound in leather. They entered an attached storage room, where antique electrical instruments nested on rows of heavy shelving. O'Hanlon raised his eyebrows. "My God, Jared. This is a veritable museum." He lifted a wooden box festooned with toggle switches and meters. Here was a priceless collection of electrical apparatus, some of which must have been designed by Tesla himself. O'Hanlon could easily spend weeks examining them. He replaced the box, resolving not to become distracted.

Back inside the office, Jared unlocked a tall case filled with rolled paper documents. "These are the blueprints for the Magnifying Transmitter." He walked to the desk and withdrew two leather-bound manuals from the top drawer. "First, you'll want to look these over.

They describe maintenance and operating procedures."

O'Hanlon opened one of the volumes and began thumbing through yellowed, handwritten pages filled with intricate drawings and schematics. "I can't wait to read these."

Jared tapped the manual with a forefinger and waited for O'Hanlon's full attention before speaking. "Patrick, there are some serious warnings here. The Transmitter is dangerous, and I don't mean dangerous for the obvious reasons. It's *major-league* dangerous. You'll see what I mean. I look forward to your opinion."

O'Hanlon nodded, acknowledging with a thoughtful silence. He lowered himself into the chair and ran his hands reverently along the desktop. "That the transmitter exists at all is beyond my wildest dreams. Now, with the discovery of this secret body of Tesla's original, and possibly most important work, I'm…quite overwhelmed." He started to get up. "I'll need my laptop."

Jared placed a hand on his shoulder. "I'll send Mark to get it. Let the youngsters do the leg work." He turned to leave. "I'll have María bring you up some coffee, or whatever you like. Lunch is at noon."

O'Hanlon called after him. "If today's lunch is as bountiful as the last, I won't be able to waddle up the stairs!" He opened the first manual and yanked the pull chain on the old brass desk lamp. Peering beneath its glass shade, he saw that the illumination came from a modern bulb. He laughed at himself. How could he possibly be disappointed that the lamp didn't contain an original Edison?

* * *

Mark stared at the greased steel shining dully in the excavated trench. After an hour of digging, he and Alex had uncovered twenty feet of narrow gauge railroad track and the base of a switching mechanism. The rails were an extension of a pair that came through the sliding doors of the barn and sank beneath the soil outside.

"Don't tell me," Alex groaned, pressing a balled fist against his lower back. "This is the railway for the Lost Tesla Mine."

Mark pulled up his shirttail and wiped the sweat from his brow. "I'm taking a break. I'm hungry." He tugged at his gloves. "And I'm getting blisters." He didn't bother speculating about the track's purpose; everything in his life now seemed to be an endless series of mysteries and incomplete answers.

*   *   *

O'Hanlon thought his nerves would calm as soon as he began studying the Tesla manuals. The thought fled as he read the first paragraphs.

> The Magnifying Transmitter has several fundamental capabilities, one of which is the wireless transmission of electrical energy, without loss.
>
> Should the specified operating parameters be altered, great danger will befall not only those within the immediate vicinity of the Transmitter, but also those at distant locations.
>
> The Third Manual sets forth the procedures for initiating and controlling the Transmitter's Ultimate Capability. Contents of the Third Manual will be revealed only after the tests specified in the first two Manuals have been carried out.
>
> Failure to follow the methods and procedures described will result in the gravest danger.

As he read, O'Hanlon muttered, "What sort of machine *is* this?" The first notes in his personal journal read:

- Wireless Transmission of Electrical Energy
- Third Manual
- *Ultimate Capability?*

Kate turned into the Air Force Academy's north entrance and drove past the Cadet Chapel, its sweeping multiple spires piercing the morning sky. To the south, a prop-driven trainer lifted off from the Academy runway, climbing north to join others circling Colorado Springs like lazy hawks

She spotted Major Sean Neill standing outside the Visitor's Center, arms folded across his blue flight suit. She hadn't seen him in months. For almost a year after Jack's death, he had dropped by often, sharing the rare bits of information he had discovered about the plane crash. But the visits had become less frequent.

Sean shared Jack's lean, wiry build and ready smile. He and her husband had been best friends, almost like brothers. She parked and stepped from the Wagoneer. Sean hugged her, and she gave him a peck on the cheek.

He guided her toward the Visitor's Center. "How's Mark?"

"Still has the nightmares. Wants to drop out of school and play in his rock band. He's sullen and angry. Other than that…he's just fine."

"Sounds like a typical teenager. You want me to talk to him?"

"The shrink says he needs time…" She ended it there. The truth, she knew, was that no one could help, and that months of counseling had provided only "give Mark time." How much more time, she wondered, until he shook the nightmares and began to deal with reality?

Seated at a table in the Visitor's Center, she told Sean about ARC and the strange radio signal David Hightower had transferred to CD. She handed him the disc.

"I've got an hour before I take a cadet up. I know exactly who needs to see this."

They drove to a two-story brick building south of the airfield, passed through security, and entered a room crammed with row upon row of rack-mounted electronic equipment and computers. Cooling fans hummed and hissed, the sound punctuated by an occasional outburst of electronic noise. Sean paused before a desk equipped with two monitors and a shelf of complex-looking instruments. "This is the Electronic Warfare Simulator."

A young cadet immediately rose to his feet. He wore glasses, seemed a little gawky for pilot training, Kate thought. But his eyes were intelligent and respectful. Mark would probably label him a nerd.

"Airman Stinton," Sean said.

"Yes, sir."

"This is Mrs. Kate McCullough."

"Ma'am," the airman nodded.

Sean held out the disc. "This contains an audio file. Can you check it out, see if it has a jamming signature?"

"Probably, sir."

Sean wheeled two additional chairs beside the desk while Stinton loaded the disc and started playback. Kate clenched her teeth as the eerie, fax-like screech warbled from the speaker.

"What do you make of it?" Sean asked.

"Sir, it doesn't match any threat signal I've ever heard. Sounds like a combination of white noise and rapid FSK, or frequency shift keying."

"Let's see the other file."

Stinton magnified and stretched the signal's waveform as its phosphorescent trace crawled across the screen. "It's a series of pulsed signals in the gigahertz range. There's some audio modulation and phase shifting." He pointed to the tallest lines. "The power in these pulses is maybe a thousand times above the signal's average." He studied the waveform a moment longer and asked, "What was the source, sir?"

"That's what we want to find out."

"Well, the signal-to-noise ratio is extremely high, meaning it was very strong. It's not a radar or fax signal. It's really an odd ball."

"Could it be used for jamming?"

"I suppose so, sir, although this wouldn't be the best waveform. But almost any signal can jam if it's strong enough."

"Corporal, as a personal favor, I'd appreciate it if you could find out what generated this signature and who might be using it."

"Yes sir, I'll try."

Sean drove Kate back to the Visitor's Center. He parked and turned to her. "That was pretty good sleuthing. It was smart to check with the amateur radio people."

"Actually, it was Mark and his friend's idea."

"Somebody wants this covered up, Kate. Tell Mark and his buddies to keep away from this business."

"I already have."

Sean worked his jaw. "Maybe you should consider dropping it too."

She frowned, surprised. "You know me better than that, Sean. You know how important this is."

"All right. Since you've started down this path again, there's something you should know." He paused, staring through the windshield. "They said they never found any wreckage. But I heard a rumor. I went to San Francisco. They had some pieces of the plane in a warehouse. Security caught me snooping around and threatened to have me arrested." He glanced at Kate. "Word came down for me to stop investigating or face serious consequences."

Kate's stared at him in disbelief. "What...?"

"About six months ago," he continued, "I heard that two bodies had been picked up by a fishing boat."

The word hit like a sucker punch. "*Bodies*?" She felt the sting of tears. "Jack was your best friend..."

"You were becoming obsessed with this, Kate. I thought you should stop, get on with your life. I couldn't confirm anything anyway. And I was afraid, for my own sake, to pry any further."

He lifted a notebook from his pocket and jotted something down. "This is the boat. It was probably operating out of Oahu. Maybe you could track down the skipper."

Still reeling, Kate read the boat's name—*Tombo Ahi*. She looked up. "I didn't mean to get upset. It's just that...we've always worked together."

His expression softened. "I should have realized... Look, if I find out anything else, I'll contact you. I promise."

Kate returned to Channel 12. She called the state administrative offices in Honolulu and was transferred to the Department of Land and Natural Resources. The *Tombo Ahi* was still registered as a commercial fishing boat. As a matter of policy, no other information could be given out.

She logged onto the Internet, found the Marine Directory of Commercial Fishing for Hawaii, and scrolled down the long listing: no Tombo Ahi. She began calling directory numbers at random. On the fifth try, someone recognized the boat's name and suggested she contact a Captain Josh Garrett. His number appeared in the Oahu online directory. She glanced at the clock: almost noon. It was three hours earlier in Hawaii. To ensure privacy, she decided to wait and make the call from her home office.

She found Gil in the control room, and they walked to a small deli in Forest Creek Center. Over sandwiches, she told him about the investigation.

He listened, wide-eyed. "Kate, this could get way dangerous."

"I know how to cover my tail."

"Yeah, but this is major spook stuff. No offense, but all we've ever worked on is local scandals."

"Just be there when I need you, Gil."

He studied her for a moment, smiled. "We'll edit one awesome tape. If the station won't handle it, we'll shop it to CNN and the networks."

"I knew I could count on you."

She listened to the news broadcast as she drove home: Senator Reese Myerson was still in a coma. Had he discovered a connection between the plane crash and ARC? Perhaps she should contact Senator Hurwitz. Why did he support ARC? Why was the project shrouded in secrecy? Maybe Constellation would know, assuming she could find them.

She had spent over a year investigating the crash, hammering away, getting nowhere. Now she had suddenly dislodged an avalanche of new leads.

The trick was to avoid being buried alive.

10

A flurry of welcoming barks came from the backyard as Kate walked into the kitchen. She called Buddy, exhorting him to use his personal mutt-entrance at the bottom of the kitchen door, but he recalcitrant animal just stood outside and barked louder. She bent down, pushed her hand through the top-hinged hatch, and called again. He graced her fingers with an enthusiastic snuffle. He stayed outside.

Relenting, she opened the big door and he rushed in, wagging and prancing, his paws thumping softly on the linoleum floor. She petted him. "Buddy, the doggie door isn't going to bite you. Why are you so afraid?" Two and a half years ago, Buddy had watched in stolid silence as Mark and Jack installed the pet door. He had sniffed it, pawed it, and barked at it, but despite the cajoling and pleading (including bribes of his favorite dog biscuits), he refused to go through it.

In her downstairs office, Kate dialed Honolulu and left a message on Josh Garrett's answering machine: she had some important questions. He could reverse the charges.

She logged onto the Internet, entered Auroral Research Center, and promptly got a multitude of sites brimming with newspaper reports and magazine articles: Senator Hurwitz touting the value of ionospheric research; protecting the Internet with ARC technology; and the quest for more efficient radio communications. He also alluded vaguely to ARC's military value because of its ability to monitor communications.

Senator Reese Myerson had argued that the project was too covert, too expensive, and that accountability was virtually non-existent. No member of Congress had been shown the entire installation, and if a U.S. senator couldn't gain full access, it was too dangerous to continue funding. Kate printed Myerson's speeches and logged off. A car door slammed: Mark returning from band practice. This initiated another round of round of anxious barks from Buddy.

She mumbled as she walked into the kitchen. "Buddy, Buddy, Buddy. If you'd just use the doggie door." She opened the people door and the dog flew out. Back in her office, she could hear Mark goading him with, "Run, Buddy, run. *Faster than lightning!*" She grimaced. Someday the dog was going to kill himself making one of those prodigious leaps.

The phone rang, jangling her nerves.

"This is Josh Garrett," said the gravelly voice.

Kate cleared her throat. "Is this the owner of the *Tombo Ahi?*"

"Owner and captain. How can I help you?"

"Captain Garrett, I'm a reporter for Channel Twelve Television in Colorado Springs. I'm investigating an airplane crash that killed Senator Jeff Travis two years ago." She paused, half expecting him to slam the receiver down.

"Yes?"

"I heard a rumor, that bodies had been found."

There was a brief silence. "Go on."

She drew a deep breath. "I have a personal interest in this, Captain Garrett. My husband was killed in that crash. He was the pilot."

"I'm sorry." More silence. "The government boys told me not to talk about this. They can be pretty persuasive."

"I'll be honest with you. I'm doing this on my own. The station doesn't even know about it. But I'm going to get my story, and when I do, it'll go to every network in the country."

Kate heard Garrett sigh. She continued. "Did you ever hear about the ARC Project?"

"No, what's that?"

He's losing interest. "They use powerful radio waves for research," she said quickly. "They were beaming a signal at exactly the same time my husband's plane went down—"

Garrett interrupted. "Radio signal, huh? Funny you should mention that." He took a long pause. Kate thought she had struck a note. "Look," Garrett continued, "I'm gonna tell you some things I never told the Feds. Hell, maybe you *are* CIA or FBI or something, but I don't think so."

"Please, if there's anything you can tell me…"

"You say you work for a TV station. If you promise to do a show about it, I'll talk to you."

"That's why I called, Captain. I promise."

"Okay, Ms. McCullough, here's the full story." Kate could hear a long intake of breath. He began. "We were about two hundred miles north of Hawaii, watchin' for albacore. It was evening, and the ocean was real calm. Ed, my first mate, said the radio was actin' funny. I listened to it, and it let out a loud, you know, screeching sound. Then it just popped and went dead. Later on, we found out the radar, Loran, and *all* our electronics was dead.

"Then Ed yells at me and says, 'Look at that!' I looked up and saw a jet way off to the northeast. And right in front of it was this big, bright ball of fire. The plane went through that fireball, and when it came out the other side, it was coming down steep. I told Ed to throttle up, and we headed toward it.

"It leveled off a little and crashed, throwin' up a huge spray. Just about that time, there was this big blast, like a sonic boom, and our starboard windshield blew in on us. But we kept going.

"It got late and we finally smelled kerosene. Jet fuel. We used our big searchlight and saw some floating stuff comin' at us in the dark. We launched the Zodiac and cruised around. Then one of the men spotted a man floatin' face down. We grabbed him and pulled him inside. Turned him over and shone the flashlight on his face. I don't know what in God's name happened to him. But with all due respect, Ma'am, the men scrambled out of the way like we'd hauled a monster on board.

"After they calmed down, we searched and found another body. He was just as bad as the first. My crew was worried about bringin' them on board, you know. But we did. Packed them in ice."

Kate fought back an image of Jack floating there among the bodies.

Garrett continued. "It was three days before we got back to the Islands. And I can tell you, something's not right. We brought those bodies back and the government boys took them without even a 'thank you very much.' They told me and my crew not to discuss it with anyone."

"What government people?"

Garrett snorted. "Said they were FBI, but who knows?" He paused. "One more thing. And this is secret."

"What?" Kate whispered.

"I thought it might be sacrilegious to do this, you know, but I took pictures of those bodies. No one but my crew and I know about it. I'll send them if you want."

She paused for a moment, stunned. "Yes. Send them, please. I'll pay for it. I'll keep your name out of this."

"Ma'am, don't worry. I've been keeping this under wraps long enough. I don't trust the government, but I won't be intimidated. Something strange is going on here. I think there's a cover-up. I'd bet my life on it." Another long intake of air. "And one last thing, ma'am."

"What is that, Captain Garrett?"

"I apologize for the pictures, because your husband was on that plane. I suggest you have someone with you when you look at them."

11

Kate pushed away from the desk and ruffled her hair in frustration. This morning's Internet search had yielded nothing new about ARC. And Constellation—*the* Constellation— seemed to have disappeared off the planet. Her cell phone chirped: David Hightower.

"Lunch?" he asked.

Her mood lifted. "I'm starved."

"There's a place called Back Street."

"I've heard of it. When can you meet?"

"I'll take you. I'm outside your building."

"Give me a minute."

Kate paused before the full-length mirror and gave her reflection a critical stare. "Too many years in the Colorado sun," she mumbled. The tiny wrinkles around the corners of her eyes seemed to deepen even as she spoke. *Here's our news anchor—Leatherface.*

David stood in the lobby, arms folded across his chest. He was wearing faded jeans and a black shirt. *Has a thing for black.*

He smiled. "You look great."

"Thank you. Secrets of TV makeup."

His black SUV waited in the parking lot. "It's a seventy-four Bronco," he said as he opened her door. The interior, of course, was black. Like his house, the Bronco was immaculately spare, with crank windows and a simple AM-FM radio. "It has all the important stuff: four-speed transmission, four-wheel drive, plus granny gears." The exhaust rumbled when he turned the key. Kate pictured a large engine beneath the hood—probably black. Mark would love it. She complimented his effort in restoring the machine.

He backed out. "The suspension is for off-road work. Makes the ride a little stiff." He shifted smoothly through the gears and they headed down Uintah to I-25 and accelerated south.

"I see a lot of these older Broncos around," Kate said. "What makes them so popular?"

"They have a narrow frame. You can go places the newer SUVs can't. The turning radius is tighter. I like the way they look. Functional."

The old brick building off Bijou displayed a red neon sign reading "Backstreet Bar & Grill." Inside, posters and memorabilia from the fifties and sixties dotted the pine-paneled walls. An ancient jukebox crooned a scratchy Fats Domino record. Kate and David settled into a purple, vinyl-clad booth near the back.

"Don't let this dump fool you," he said. "The food's great."

A smiling young waitress with a punk hairstyle and tattoos took their orders. David opened a notebook and handed Kate a diskette and a printout with columns of dates and numbers. "I queried some RDF groups about your mystery signal. Some of them have heard it sporadically for a couple of years. The signal strength varied a lot, but the origin points to Alaska."

Kate looked at the printout. "What are these?"

"Signal hits." He pointed to a column. "That was recorded last night. Stroke of luck. It was from the same guy whose web site we visited. He has very sophisticated equipment. He can tell, for example, whether a signal is moving toward you or away from you. The signal last night had both components. It either had some kind of repeater firing an identical signal back, or they found a way to bounce it back. In this case, the signal had an impossibly strong return, almost one-hundred percent."

"I'm not sure I understand. You mean the signal was moving?"

"Not likely."

David drew a circle representing the earth, then two small squares at the edge of the circle. He tapped one of the squares. "If a transmitter in, say, Alaska, wanted to beam a jamming signal to a point near Hawaii"—He tapped the second square—"it couldn't do it because of the curvature of the earth." He drew a straight line leaving Alaska, showing that the line couldn't reach Hawaii without penetrating the earth. He drew a circle around the earth. "This is the ionosphere. If they found a way to efficiently bounce the signal off the ionosphere, they could hit their target like a guy shooting billiards."

He drew a line from Alaska to the ionosphere, to Hawaii. "The signal last night, going out and then coming back almost as strong, suggests that maybe they beamed the signal into the ionosphere and reflected it back close to home."

"But how can we hear those shortwave broadcasts from all over the world?"

"They're reflected off the ionosphere, too. But there's a huge signal loss. If you wanted to jam someone a long distance away, you'd need a stupendously powerful transmitter, a highly efficient means of reflecting the signal, and an impossibly accurate beaming system."

"What is the ionosphere, anyway?"

"It's a region of charged particles circling the earth, ranging from around sixty to a thousand miles altitude. Solar activity, such as ultraviolet light and X-rays, knock electrons off air molecules. The result is a conducting plasma that can reflect radio waves of various frequencies."

Kate dug through her notes, then read: "A U.S. Government

project called ARC is bouncing signals off the ionosphere to investigate auroras. Some believe it's a cover for a project to monitor and control communications."

"Where did you find that?"

"An Internet site, months ago. But I was stupid—didn't save it and can't find it again. When I run a search for ARC now, I just get the PR version, with Senator Hurwitz's fat face in all the endorsements."

Their lunch arrived, a vegetarian meal for Kate, and trout for David. He grinned when she eyed the fish, and cut her a generous portion.

She told him about her conversations with Captain Josh Garrett and Sean Neill, and about the photographs. After a long silence, David said, "What do you think about paying ARC a personal visit?"

Kate sighed. There was only one option left. "I've already decided on going."

"Don't rush into this, Kate. You don't know what you're up against. Give me time to find out more."

She gazed up at him. "I trust your judgement, David, and I couldn't have made this much progress without your help. But I am going. Soon."

Across the table she clasped his hand.

12

The steel rails curved westward and climbed a gentle hill, where they disappeared behind a natural wall of granite boulders and tombstoned rocks. They reappeared in the pasture, flashing between islands of sawgrass and sage, and vanished again as they passed through the woods beyond the house. They finally emerged near the bridge and angled back toward the barn, completing the loop.

Mark watched as Carlos manipulated the backhoe, peeling up protective boards from the last hundred feet of track.

"Amazing," Alex said, tracing the loop with an outstretched hand. "It must be over a mile long."

"So what's next, we push an ore cart around it?"

Alex shot him a disdainful look. "Come on, man. This has got to be something…"

Jared's shout summoned them, and they walked through the sliding door into the barn, following the recessed rails as they curved left into a storage room. The track disappeared beneath a long wooden crate bearing a time-faded John Deere logo.

Jared held out hammers and crowbars. "Let's pry it apart."

Squeaking and groaning, the box ripped open to reveal an elongated mass wrapped in a heavy tarp. They peeled the covering away and stood back, staring at the black beast beneath.

Alex chortled. "Oh, *yeah*, baby."

Mark found his voice a moment later. "Wicked!"

An enormous round headlight gleamed from a recess in the blunt nose. Rows of narrow fins, like the cooling vanes of a motorcycle engine, streaked front to rear along the torpedo-shaped fuselage. The windshield, comprised of two round glass panels encased in a rakish metal frame, swept seamlessly up from the machine's body and angled back toward the cockpit. Exotic power and speed were etched into every curve and line. Mark grinned. He was looking at a crazy, Buck Rogers version of a locomotive.

They folded back the remaining canvas, revealing two sleek passenger cars coupled behind the engine. With help from four of the ranch hands, they pushed the heavy vehicle slowly over the rails, out of the barn into sunlight.

Jared walked alongside the train. "I haven't seen this old fellow in a long time. It's still in pretty good shape."

Mark opened the cockpit door and climbed in, the pleated red leather squeaking as he sat down. He ran his hands over the brass trim and touched the control knobs studding the metal dashboard. His grandfather leaned into the cab and pointed. "These meters show power and speed. And there's the throttle, brake, and transmission levers."

Alex unlatched a cowling forward of the windshield and swung it open, then stepped back and let out a surprised whistle. Mark left the cockpit and stood beside him. A scrambled, miniature version of the Magnifying Transmitter occupied the exposed compartment, with ribbed insulators, metal spheres, and strange electrical devices connected to spiraling coils of wire.

Alex pointed to the thick cables snaking into a massive iron cylinder. "Obviously, it's driven by an electric motor—a *big* electric motor." He stood and shrugged. "There's no room for batteries."

"I thought you'd have figured it out by now," Jared said. He was pivoting a tall metal rod into position on the engine's left side. "It doesn't need batteries."

Alex stared at the rod for a moment. "Don't tell me it gets power from radio waves."

"Yep."

"No way. You'd need a mega-power microwave transmitter and a reflector big as a barn."

"Tesla figured out a way to do it without all that."

Mark felt a shiver of anticipation. "When can we start it up?"

Jared led them to another corner of the barn and lifted a canvas cover from a hardwood cabinet the size of a kitchen stove. A sloping panel of burnished aluminum held a control knob resembling a steering wheel. Two meters stared from opposite sides of the knob, giving the apparatus the appearance of a startled robot. "This sends power to the train."

They pushed the cabinet on its swiveling wheels to the barn's entrance and settled it just inside the doors. Jared plugged a cable into the box, raised a metal rod identical to the one on the locomotive, and snapped a switch on the console's front panel. A red light glowed and a steady hum drifted through the vents. He clapped the dust from his hands. "It's time to get the Professor."

*   *   *

O'Hanlon massaged the frown creasing his brow. Revelations about the Magnifying Transmitter were astounding—even troubling. There were obvious dangers involved in operating such a powerful machine: electrocution, fire, explosion, RF burns. The manuals were clear about that. But they also hinted of a far greater danger, one that was not explained. The third manual, he supposed, would expound on this. Yet, for some inexplicable reason, that manual wouldn't be available until the machine was fully restored and tested.

Well, this was Tesla's baby. He had his reasons. It would be a miracle if the system worked at all. Understanding the machine's theory and deciphering the circuits could take months, if not years. But he didn't have to understand it in order to restore broken parts and test it. As long as they followed the instructions, it should be safe. Shouldn't it?

He looked up as Jared rapped on the open door. "You seem thoughtful, Patrick."

O'Hanlon sat upright, clasping his hands on the desktop. "I'm quite concerned about safety. I need more information about power levels and thresholds. I wonder if you could give me a hint about what the third manual contains."

"I haven't read it. Can't open it. The key is available only after it's tested."

"*Locked*?" This was extraordinarily odd. Surprises in the pursuit of scientific discovery were common enough. Surprises during the testing of an ancient megawatt electrical machine could be lethal. O'Hanlon stroked his beard. "I suppose we'll just have to move ahead. But, I must say that Tesla made claims about this machine that sound impossible. His manuals read like science fiction."

"If you want to glimpse some of this 'science fiction' in action, follow me."

*   *   *

O'Hanlon stared at the locomotive wide-eyed, taking in its quaintly streamlined, art deco contour. "Where in the devil's name did you find that?"

Jared opened the door to the first passenger car. "Climb in, Patrick."

Wearing impish grins, Mark and Alex looked back at him from the engine cockpit. Several ranch hands stood leaning against their shovels, watching with bemused expressions. O'Hanlon felt foolish participating in this *amusement park ride*, but at the same time was elated at discovering yet another cache of Tesla technology. He settled into the leather seat, privately wondering whether the machine could pull his weight. Buddy, who had been busily anointing a cast-iron wheel, leaped into the car and sat beside him, nose forward, eyes eager.

*   *   *

Mark jumped as a crackling sound sizzled from the train's antenna. A low hum rose from the engine compartment.

"Put her in gear and throw the direction switch," Jared shouted from the console.

The transmission lever engaged with a light clunk.

"Now give it some juice."

The brass throttle felt cold in Mark's hand as he ticked it forward. The humming sound became louder and—*yeah*—with a lurch and a clank, the train began to move. He glanced back at O'Hanlon. The professor's eyes had grown large, and he had braced his arms against the seat as if he expected the train to launch itself over the creek.

Alex tapped the dashboard. "Give it more."

Mark edged the throttle up, and the train pulled into the left curve and climbed, rolling between boulders and tufts of sage. A broad grin broke across his face as they crested the hill; the train was moving at a good clip, and the wheels were making a steely, metal-on-metal train sound.

The locomotive carved around the bend and accelerated to twenty miles per hour on the downhill run. Buddy lifted his head, sniffing the wind. Three horses playfully kicked up their heels and thundered past, nodding and snorting.

As they leveled onto the flat stretch, Mark pushed the throttle up again. The drone from the engine compartment rose in pitch, and the speedometer jumped to thirty. The machine rocked hypnotically as they shot along the field, the voice of the rails rising into the cockpit, vibrating through the controls and the padded leather seat.

Alex touched a control knob. "The limiter is set at one half. If you opened the throttle and Jared fed it more power, I bet this thing could do sixty—easy."

The rails twisted through the woods and the train followed, the antenna knifing through the low branches, dropping a light shower of pine needles on O'Hanlon and Buddy. They curved into the final bend south of the house, and the engine pointed its nose toward the barn.

"If you extended the track, you'd have a *really* cool ride," Alex said.

"Yeah, it could go for miles." Andrea would get a kick out of this, Mark thought. He pictured his girlfriend seated beside him as they cruised through the woods, her auburn hair flowing in the breeze, her adoring smile directed at him as he manipulated the controls. He clicked the throttle back to zero, pulled the brake lever into its locked position, and the train coasted smoothly across the intersection, squealing to a gentle stop.

His grandfather appeared at the cockpit. "Great job, boys."

O'Hanlon stepped from the car. "After I examine this machine," he said with a smile, "I insist on another ride—only *I* get to drive." He bent down and looked beneath the engine. "I see no insulators and no brushes, so it's not receiving power through the rails. Therefore, it must be battery powered."

Jared nodded toward the tall metal rod.

O'Hanlon stared for a moment. "Come, now. Don't tell me that's an antenna."

Alex had pried the cowling open again. "See, just a motor and receiving system."

"That's totally impossible! The inverse square law applies to omnidirectional antennas. The power falls off in proportion to the square of the distance. You couldn't begin to supply enough power—"

"Maybe the answers are in that third manual," Jared said. The clang of the lunch bell drifted across the lawn as he connected the main track with the section entering the barn. They pushed the train through the doors into its hiding place and started along the flagstone path toward the house.

* * *

O'Hanlon fell in step behind the others, then paused and looked back, frowning. What he had just experienced—beaming large amounts of power from a single vertical antenna—was theoretically impossible. And how much power had been transmitted? It had to have been at least fifteen or twenty kilowatts, directly to the moving train. That was impossible physics.

And impossible physics disturbed him very much.

13

Kate's heart tripped. The FedEx envelope on the Channel 12 front desk had a Hawaii sender's address: Captain Josh Garrett's photographs. She snatched them up, rushed to her office, and stared indecisively at the package. *I suggest you have someone with you...* She'd take the envelope home and open it there. *No.* She and David would examine the photos together. She dropped the envelope into an aluminum attaché case, snapped the lid shut, and walked to the control room.

Gil stood when she entered. "Back in the saddle?"

"I leave in a couple of days." Kate pulled a Nikon digital SLR and zoom lens from the shelf and loaded them into the case.

"Wish I was going with you."

"No need to put your career on the line, too."

Gil snorted. "And what career might that be?" He became serious. "Good luck, Kate. Be careful." She hugged him.

No one at Channel 12 other than Gil knew where she was going or what her investigation was about, and she wanted to keep it that way. She left the building and drove toward David's, the photos locked inside the case beside her. Bodies are just bodies, she told herself. But in the back of her mind, she feared that when she opened the envelope and slid the photos out, Jack's mutilated face would be there, staring back at her.

*   *   *

"This is it," she said, sitting on the couch in David's den. "The station's letting me have three weeks. They haven't come right out and said it, but it's either a story or my career."

He sat beside her. "I think they're a bunch of fools."

She handed the envelope to him.

Reaching inside, he withdrew a handwritten letter:

> *Dear Ms. McCullough,*
> *Please forgive me for what you're about to see. I can only hope these photos will help expose the truth.*
> *Sincerely,*
> *Josh Garrett, Captain of the Tombo Ahi.*

David pulled a thin sheaf of glossy photos halfway from the envelope, then pushed them back inside. "I don't think you should—"

Her voice was a quick whisper. "Let me see..."

He slowly handed the photos to her, his lips pressed tightly together. She lifted the first one and stared.

A man's face. Blood-engorged eyes bulged from the sockets, pupils a film of translucent white. Distended purple veins erupted from the skin like an invading alien life-form; the swollen black tongue lolled lugubriously between bared teeth, curling past lips stretched back in a rictal scream. It was as if a giant hand had seized the head and neck and squeezed—

The remaining photos were equally horrifying. As a reporter, Kate had witnessed the results of catastrophic accidents; drownings, burns, fights, maulings. But nothing even came close to these abominations. Her first thought was that the bodies weren't real, that they had been fabricated as a cruel joke. Her physical reaction, though, was immediate.

She rushed to the bathroom, forcing back the gorge crawling

up her throat. She cupped her hands beneath the tap and drenched her face. *Get a grip.* She dried off, stared into the mirror for a full minute, then walked to the den. David had placed the envelope out of sight. He helped her to an armchair. "Here," he said, offering a glass of water. "Or do you want something stronger?"

"Yes," she managed. "Whatever you have. Make it a double."

She was still in a daze when he returned with stiff drinks for both of them.

"I'm sorry," he said.

Kate's voice sounded harsh in her ears. "No crash could do that to a person. No fire, no poison..." She looked up at David. "Something monstrous happened on that plane."

14

The tiny Italian restaurant occupied a mining-era boarding-house in Manitou Springs. David guided her to a candlelit booth that overlooked the plunging, rocky channel of Fountain Creek. The horror of Garrett's photographs began to fade after the second glass of wine, and Kate raised her eyes to the quiet man seated across from her.

David met her gaze and smiled. "Welcome back."

"Sorry. Guess I overreacted…"

"I think shock would be normal." A spark of anger flickered behind the blue-green eyes. "I think the people aboard your husband's plane were murdered. Whether it was an act of terrorism, or something else, I can't say. But I have some ideas about how it might have been done."

"And."

"I don't want to dwell on that now. But if it's what I think it is, the concept is unprecedented. I also believe there are some nefarious types in high places pulling strings."

"You don't have to get more deeply involved…"

David's hand found her own. "Don't attempt this alone."

"No…"

"Someone with technical knowledge would be helpful."

His touch was warm.

"Please come," she said in a sudden low voice.

"I love adventures."

She sat back and chuckled. "It has occurred to me that I have just offered to spend several days with a man about whom I know practically nothing."

His smile deepened. "Give me your email address. I'll have the school district forward my résumé."

"You haven't mentioned kids, a wife, a girlfriend…"

He grew solemn, the playfulness extinguished. "My wife died a few months before you lost your husband. Cancer. It cheated us of children, then it took her life."

"I'm sorry."

"Before I moved to Colorado Springs, I spent fifteen years in the Navy. I was a communications officer, with a few…um… side specialties thrown in. Served aboard everything from the *Enterprise* to nuclear subs." He paused, a sad little half smile on his lips. "I always wanted kids. Maybe that's why I chose teaching." He glanced away, his cheeks reddening. "One more thing. I haven't dated, seriously anyway, since Carol died." His eyes found hers again. "But two years is long enough…"

He drove her home after dinner, and she turned to him as he pulled into the driveway. "Come inside for awhile. Mark is staying with his grandparents, and it's…"

"Of course."

The house was too quiet and empty. David stacked logs in the fireplace while Kate poured wine. As the flames rose in a steady glow, she sat on the woven rug with David behind her. He massaged her shoulders, her neck, his strong hands finding every painful knot. Kate closed her eyes, letting the warmth from the fire caress her body. She sighed, finally relaxed. David bent forward and gently kissed her.

"I should go," he said. He swept her up and settled her on the couch near the fire, then drew a wool coverlet across her legs and brushed her cheek with the back of his fingers. He turned and left.

*   *   *

She awoke with a start; someone was hammering at the back door. The fire had burned low, the hissing embers casting a feeble light into the dark room. She sat up groggily and listened. Her watch was barely visible in the gloom: past ten o'clock.

The knocking came again. A little frightened, she got up and walked to the window. She pulled aside the curtain and peered toward the back porch. Alex stood there, agitated, looking back over his shoulder. He jumped when she opened the door.

"Alex, what on earth…?"

"They're after me, Mrs. McCullough," he said breathlessly, "I really need to warn you guys—"

"Warn us?"

"Yeah. Could I…please…come inside?"

Kate guided him into the den. From the look of the boy, she thought he could use a drink, but brought him a Coke instead— caffeine free.

She sat on the couch and motioned Alex beside her. "Tell me what's going on."

He avoided her eyes. "I didn't tell you this yet, but that night we first hacked into ARC, they tagged us."

"Tagged?"

His features held a mix of worry and guilt. "They may have traced the connection to the museum's computer, or even here."

Kate nodded grimly. Moral Alliance-backed candidates were trying to pass legislation censoring the Internet through the proposed Cerberus program. The legal concept was broad: Cerberus would save everyone from immoral, dishonest, or "unseemly" material. Encryption codes, of course, would be strictly forbidden. The Internet was already aggressively policed, and hacking in any form was severely punished—a taste of what was to come if the legislature finally approved Cerberus.

Alex wrung his hands. "Now the FBI is after me. They went to the museum. Then they went to my house, came around in a van. I took off, but the van kept showing up wherever I went." He paused and gulped his drink. The rims of his eyes glistened. "I tried sneaking back home, but my mom, she threw me out…"

Wouldn't be the first time would it, Alex? Here was a teenage whiz kid with worlds of potential, anchored down by an alcoholic mother and a father who specialized in disappearing acts.

He looked at Kate with anguish. "Constellation says they're killing people."

"Who's killing people?"

"The people who run ARC. It's like I suspected. ARC and Cerberus are actually the same, and much more powerful than we thought. Constellation has new evidence against them, and now I've gotten all of you in danger. I'm really, really sorry. Mark will never forgive me."

Kate rested her hand on his shoulder. "You don't need to apologize, Alex. You don't realize it, but you've helped me a great deal."

He drew his fingers across his nose and sniffled. He looked away. The boy was exhausted. She got up and rekindled the fire. Alex was usually a cocky troublemaker, but now he seemed like a pathetic little kid. She sat across from him. "Tell me the rest of the story."

He drained his Coke and continued. "I got online and found Constellation again. They have to switch sites all the time because ARC tags them almost immediately and confiscates the data. If ARC thinks someone's dangerous enough, they'll kill them. I know it sounds unreal, but I'm afraid they'll try to kill me." He glanced up at Kate. "I hope you believe me about all this."

"I believe you." She thought for a moment. "Did you actually see these FBI agents?"

"No. I work part time on the museum's network, and they came there this morning—two of them—and they checked all the computers, got the names of everyone working there. And they were real interested in finding me. When I went home, my mom said they'd been there, searched my room, took my computer. So my mom got mad and threw me out. I could sneak back, but I'm afraid they'd find me."

She thought about calling David, but what if phone conversations were being monitored? Wait a minute, she thought. Even the U.S. government didn't have the resources to search for every teenage hacker, did they? She decided to wait until morning. "Stay here, Alex. Use the spare bed in Mark's room. We're all in this together now."

His body sagged with relief. "Thanks, Mrs. McCullough. I'll make this up to you."

"Don't worry about that. Come on. I'll make you something to eat."

She kept Alex company as he gobbled his sandwich, asking more questions about Constellation. At eleven o'clock, he dragged off to bed. Kate rummaged in the closet and found the Smith and Wesson revolver, the one Jack had bought her years ago, and tucked it under her pillow. She settled beneath the covers and tried to disengage her mind from the events of the last few days.

Within an astonishingly brief time, her investigation had jumped from "sinister" to "damned scary."

15

The low thrum of an idling engine clawed her awake. She tottered from bed, pulling her nightgown tight against the chill creeping through the half-lidded window. In the pale, pre-dawn light, Kate could see a gray panel van nudged against the curb, silver wisps from its exhaust curling up and dissipating into the still morning air.

Now she was fully alert, her pulse pounding. Her hand groped for the telephone on the bedside table, David Hightower's number flashing into her mind. But as she backed from the window, the van's engine revved, and it pulled away from the curb and faded slowly down the quiet street.

She dressed and rushed to Mark's bedroom, where Alex, illuminated by a wedge of light bleeding from the hallway, was still bundled beneath the covers. She shook him. "Alex."

He awoke with a jerk. "What…?"

"Shh. Get dressed. We have to go. Don't turn on the lights."

He emerged a few minutes later, fully dressed. "What's going on?"

"Just stay with me and keep quiet."

Inside the garage, she started the Wagoneer and punched the door opener. "Keep low," she said, motioning Alex down.

She eased into the driveway and scanned the still-dim street: no mysterious van. She backed out and drove southward, opposite the direction the van had taken. They parked two houses from David's. With Alex in tow, she trotted to his door and knocked.

Alex turned. "Someone's coming."

Moving with the easy stride of a long distance runner, a dark figure jogged through the gray light toward them. He slowed and came up the front walk, chest heaving. Perspiration darkened the front of his sweatshirt. It was David. "Kate?"

"We're being followed—"

He looked back toward the street, gave Alex a quick glance, and opened the door. "Come in."

She quickly told him about the FBI agents and the gray van.

"Give me your keys. I'll hide your Jeep in the garage." He paused by the door and smiled. "You guys had breakfast?"

Half an hour later, they devoured the southwestern-style omelette Kate had prepared. David added salsa to his second helping. "We should do this on a regular basis."

"What, you jog and I cook?"

"We both jog. Then you cook."

She chuckled. "Spoken like a true man." She lifted the coffee to her lips and cast him a furtive glance. Like Jack, he exuded a quiet confidence that made her feel safe, at ease in his presence.

She turned to Alex. "Until we get this sorted out, I want you to stay with Mark." He nodded, poking the omelette with his fork. She checked her watch: seven o'clock. She was tired of running, of reacting.

"Time to go on the offensive," she said to no one in particular.

*   *   *

A rising sun glinted from the science museum's gold-tinted windows, casting fiery rectangles across the vast green lawn. David parked in the east lot and scanned the area for unwanted company. Kate glanced into the Bronco's back seat and hissed at Alex, who had risen into a sitting position. "Keep down!"

She stepped from the truck and walked to the building's main entrance, where the uniformed security guard unlocked a door and ushered her inside. The museum would open to the public in an hour.

Assistant Director Madeline Atwell and another woman were upstairs in the big conference room, stuffing fliers into envelopes. Atwell looked up, peering through bifocals bound by a silver chain. She was around fifty, her gray hair short and curled. The executive granny.

Kate extended her hand. "Madeline, I'm Kate McCullough, Jared Thompson's daughter."

Atwell stood. "Oh, yes, I know you from Channel Twelve News. Your father has been such a great help to us."

Kate asked for a private conversation, and Atwell led her down the hallway to the assistant director's office.

"Alex Graham told me the FBI paid a visit yesterday..." Kate began.

Atwell frowned. "This isn't for TV, is it?"

"Not necessarily. I'm just a concerned mother. Alex Graham is a friend of my son, Mark."

"I don't want this getting out—that the museum was involved in some sort of crime."

Kate nodded. "I understand."

"Well, they claimed someone at the museum did some illegal hacking." Her voice took on a disapproving tone. "It was quite obvious Alex was the prime suspect."

"Tell me about the agents."

"There were two of them," she said, nodding as she spoke. "They brought a laptop and checked all our computers with it. Then they started asking about Alex, what he did here, that sort of thing. We could lose our Internet privileges, you know."

"Madeline, I think it's important for you to call the FBI and verify this. Right away."

"Why? You don't suspect…" Her voice trailed off. She looked thoughtful. "You know, now that you mention it, they didn't seem quite right for FBI men. They seemed a little, well, rough around the edges." She fished two business cards from a box on her desk and held them out. "Their credentials looked proper. They had badges, too."

"But," Kate warned, "if they're really not who they said they were, and they got access to all of your financial data, personnel files, business records, donors…"

Atwell's eyes widened. She sat down. "Oh, my."

"Please call them. I'm concerned for Alex, and for the museum's security. I'll help you out. I've got connections…"

Atwell slowly lifted the handset from its cradle.

Kate was already thumbing through the telephone book. "Here's the number for the FBI resident office. At least we know it's correct."

"Yes." She dialed.

Twenty minutes later, Kate rushed back to the Bronco and climbed in. "It's like I suspected," she told David. "The field office in Denver checked all the way to the National Computer Crime Squad, and they knew nothing about Alex, or hacking, or a visit to the museum. The men were imposters. FBI's sending a special agent to investigate."

David was silent for a moment, eyes focused on a distant horizon. Then he looked at Kate. "I think there's a dark entity, perhaps even beyond the so-called shadow government—the CIA, NSA, and so forth—protecting ARC. They want Alex and your son—and probably *you*."

16

K ate tensed as David flicked the Bronco into a narrow gap between two cars speeding in the right lane. Alex rode in the seat behind her, his eyes glinting from beneath the low brim of an oversized baseball cap. Seated opposite, Mark acted as sentinel, his wary focus on the glittering river of headlights winding behind them.

That morning, Kate had nearly come to blows with her father, who had made a searing plea for her to cancel her Alaska trip, to not get involved. "But we're already involved," she had replied. "And I can't trust the authorities." She had then looked straight into his eyes. "This is the most important work of my life. We have to find the truth. If they killed Jack and all those others, where will it stop? The only real safety lies in exposing them."

He had finally relented, but turned slitted eyes on David, saying: "I charge you with protecting my little girl. If anything happens to her, I will personally find the culprit, drag him across the cactus patch, and hang him from the tallest tree on this ranch." Kate thought there was as much truth as jest in her father's words.

She had decided to wait until dark before gathering trip essentials. The decision to allow Mark and Alex on the potentially dangerous return trek into Colorado Springs had been her own. It was selfish, she realized, but she would soon be taking her own maximally dangerous foray to Alaska, and she wanted the warm aura of family around her for as long as possible.

David turned off I-25 and wheeled into the dimly-lit parking lot of a burger joint. Alex walked to a pay phone and dialed. After a brief conversation he climbed back into the Bronco, his head down. "She's okay." Kate knew what that meant: Alex's mom was at least sober enough to answer the phone.

The next stop was Kate's own house. Inside the garage, they waited for the overhead door to whir shut before climbing out. "Keep the lights off," David said. His flashlight probed ahead, and they moved quietly through the dark hallway toward her downstairs office.

Kate gasped as she entered the room; a mass of papers torn from her file cabinet buried the desk and lay in a tattered avalanche across the floor. A green panel light indicated her computer was on. She tapped the keyboard and stood back, staring at the screen. "Damn. It's been wiped. Everything."

With David leading, they climbed the stairs to Mark's room. The flashlight beam glanced off piles of clothing, mattresses, books—everything her son owned—ripped, strewn, and broken. Mark cried out: his precious Hofner lay in a splintered pile where it had been hurled against the wall. "Oh, no," he moaned, kneeling beside the shattered instrument. "Why?"

"Look," Alex whispered. He stood beside the computer, the monitor's russet glow pulling his face from the dark like a Halloween mask. A blood-red message filled the screen: YOU ARE DEAD.

David jerked his hand toward the door. "Come on, we're out of here."

As they turned to leave, ragged patterns tore the monitor. The speakers pumped out a nerve-jangling screech.

Kate recognized the fax-like noise. "It's that *sound*!"

David grabbed her arm. "Move!"

They flew down the stairs and through the hallway toward the kitchen. In Kate's dark office behind them, the computer shrieked, its ghost-light flickering crazily through the open door. Alex stopped, looking back.

"Get in the truck." David yelled, throwing open the door to the garage.

As she crossed the threshold, Kate could feel the awful, rasping sound worming through her mind. She pressed her hands to her temples and let out an agonized moan. Strangely compelled, she turned, faced the dark doorway to the kitchen, and stared.

Something clawed along the floor and paused at the threshold. It was the wreckage of Mark's guitar, drawn together to form a skeletal, serpent-like thing. Tentacled strings coiling and whistling through the air, it wriggled through the door, down the steps, and into the garage toward her.

She stumbled, screamed as something wrapped around her waist—David's strong arm, lifting, thrusting her into the Bronco. Mark and Alex fell into the seat behind her.

As the door slammed shut, the guitar-thing rose up like a hooded cobra and crashed against the window by Kate's shoulder, the steel tentacles scratching and thrashing at the glass. If it broke through, she knew it would wrap itself around her neck like a garrote, tightening and jerking until it sawed her head from her spine.

David struggled into the front seat, the engine roared, and the Bronco exploded through the overhead door in a shower of metal framing and splintered wood. He braked hard in the driveway, jammed the transmission into forward, and they spun and fishtailed across the yard toward the street.

As they flew over the curb, Kate glimpsed a gray apparition—a van—that flashed by on the right. Her head began to clear as they roared away, but she was shaking as if she had been stuffed naked into a snowdrift.

David's voice was calm. "Everyone okay?"

Kate held a hand to her chest, gasping. "I'm alright." She suddenly felt fine, almost euphoric, despite the dull pain throbbing between her temples. But she was scared. Oh, yeah.

Alex nodded. "Me too."

"What happened?" Mark said. "Did you see that?"

David shifted gears. "Hallucinations. I think everyone saw something."

They drove steadily now, speeding up the I-25 entrance ramp.

David merged into the heavy northbound traffic and swerved into the outside lane. "Uh, oh."

"'Uh, oh,'" Kate echoed. "Uh, oh *what*?"

"Behind us," Alex yelled.

She jerked around.

A pair of headlights broke from the trailing cars, pacing them as David abruptly switched lanes. "Can you see what it is?"

"Just the headlights." Then, "No, wait!" as light from a street lamp painted the other vehicle. The wide, imposing body and flat windshield made identification immediate. "It's a Humvee!"

"Buckle down," David ordered. He dodged right, cutting in front of a delivery van, and rocketed down the Uintah exit. He flew through a stoplight, made a hard right, and accelerated eastward. The Humvee followed in their wake. The Bronco sped over a bridge spanning a wide creek and made a screeching left onto a street lined with big homes and oversized yards. They were halfway down the block when Kate saw the Humvee turn in behind them. "They're still coming."

Flashing lights and construction equipment jumped into view: ROAD CLOSED.

"Barricades!" Alex shouted.

Kate's body slammed against the seatbelt as the Bronco made a shuddering stop, big tires bellowing across the blacktop. David snapped the shift lever and they accelerated in reverse toward the approaching Humvee.

"What are you *doing*?" Kate cried.

The Bronco spun in a screaming, counterclockwise arc and faced the other vehicle head-on. The Humvee's wheels locked in a smoking sideways skid, its black mass blocking the street. The long barrel of a weapon slithered through its passenger-side window. David gunned the Bronco and they roared up the driveway of a large two-story house; dodged a silver Range Rover inside the carport; mowed down a hedge; careened into the back yard.

"Oh, shit!" David yelled.

Brightly-lit pavilions materialized in their path. Banners, pennants, and decorative lighting swung from overhead cables. Dozens of people in formal evening attire strolled across the lawn. Shattering a forest of potted plants, the Bronco skidded toward them. The crowd parted like a school of startled fish.

David arced left, as if to circle the house, then spun a severe right toward the creek—and the biggest pavilion. Punchbowls and food geysered up and rained across the Bronco as it exploded through rows of fully-laden tables.

Kate looked back. They had hooked a cable, and it whipped along behind them, dragging a joggling wake of decorations and chairs like an oversized "just married" tail on a newlywed's car. The black Humvee turned in pursuit, stalking as smoothly as a panther through the screaming partygoers.

The Bronco crashed over another hedge and plummeted twenty feet down the creek's steep embankment, thrashing over roots and boulders. David punched the gear case into four-wheel drive and they roared up the shallow creek bed, slinging mud, swerving giddily from bank to bank.

The Humvee lumbered down the slope behind them. "They're coming," Mark shouted.

A bridge loomed above. Beyond the overpass, the creek widened into a pool of black water that looked frighteningly deep. David cranked right and stabbed the accelerator. Rocks jackhammered the undercarriage as the Bronco slogged and skidded through reeds and clinging muck. He jerked the wheel maniacally back and forth, compensating as the truck's nose swung right and left.

A wall of glistening concrete raced toward them—the bridge buttress rising to the street high above—and the front wheels slammed against the sheer incline. Smoking and screaming, the knobbed tires found traction, and they began to climb. Kate felt her back pressing against the seat, her feet rising from the floor. It looked as if they were going straight up.

The Bronco bounced and shuddered as if undecided whether to keep climbing or yield in its battle with gravity and tumble backward. They crested the top, wheels bellowing, belching smoke, then sailed weightless into empty space.

The vehicle slammed the street with a teeth-chattering crash and bounced sideways. David recovered, made a rubber-burning U-turn, and gunned toward I-25. The exhaust roared a fountain of orange sparks as metal sawed pavement. They had lost the muffler.

Behind them, the Humvee dropped onto the street and turned toward the intersection.

"He's still after us!" Kate cried.

David yanked the shifter. "Time to play our ace."

The amputated tailpipe thundered as they shot beneath the overpass. David accelerated up the two-lane blacktop and spun into an alley bisecting rows of decrepit buildings. The headlights chattered across the ghost-gray walls as the Bronco leaped over mounds of dirt and construction debris. Like a heat-seeking missile, the Humvee followed.

David glanced into the side mirror. "Come on, you sons of bitches."

The rears of stores and back porches of old houses flashed past. If they went any faster, Kate thought, they'd end up in somebody's living room. A dark gap appeared ahead, where rows of dilapidated buildings encroached on both sides of the tight space. A tilted sign blurred past: "Narrow Alley."

"We can't make it," Kate screamed.

They launched into the slice of vertical blackness, the side mirrors snapping off with a ping as the Bronco pitched and banged between the rotting wooden walls. They finally burst into an opening, slamming aside trashcans and piles of cardboard boxes.

Kate turned around. Behind them, the Humvee's headlights blinked out. David braked, poked his head through the window, and looked back. The angry snarl of a revving engine and the burr of spinning tires echoed toward them.

"Aha!" David shouted.

The boys high-fived: "All *right*! Way to go!"

David gunned the Bronco and they sped on. Kate stared at him. "What happened?"

He chuckled. "The Humvee's too wide. The alley trapped them like a cow in a squeeze chute."

As they raced from the alley into the street, melding with the traffic drifting toward the highway, David held his hand palm-up. Mark slapped it. "Right on!"

"*Right on?*" Alex said. "Where'd you get that?"

Mark sniffed. "It's from before your time."

"You think this is *fun?*" Kate said, staring at each of them as if they had gone mad. "We almost got killed and you're *happy?*"

David turned to her with a gritty smile. "Score one for the good guys."

They headed north on I-25 and drove for several minutes without speaking. No headlights dogged them. The dangling muffler had finally clattered free, and David feathered the throttle, keeping the exhaust noise to a minimum. Kate could feel her nerves beginning to calm.

"Man," Alex said with a tinge of desperation. "I really have to pee."

Mark laughed. "Yeah, so do I."

The Garden of the Gods exit took them west into the hills, to the unmarked gate. They turned and sped along the gravel road toward the Thompson ranch.

17

The Bronco's headlamps swept across the great boulders and ranks of pine that enfolded the road like a cragged tunnel. Mark thought the wild terrain, scenic during daylight, now harbored sinister hiding places for Humvees and hallucinogenic monsters.

They crested the last hill. Below, cheerful beacons of light poured from the ranch house windows and stretched across the lawn toward the bridge. David parked, and as they climbed from the truck, Buddy darted out the front door and danced an anxious greeting at their feet. Jared strode up and played the beam of his flashlight along the battered Bronco. "You folks okay?"

Kate hugged him. "We're fine, Daddy."

"I could hear you coming a mile away."

David looked at the truck's ruined skin. "This old girl earned her stripes tonight." He turned to Jared. "Can we hide this?"

"We can put it in the tractor shed." He paused. "Then I want to know what the heck's going on."

* * *

The night was still and cold, arched by an infinite dome of black sky and glittering stars. Carlos kindled a fire in the big stone fireplace, and the warmth stretched across the room, sending fears scurrying back into the dark. María brewed coffee and hot chocolate.

On any other night, Mark thought, the setting would be perfect for a pleasant family gathering.

He settled into a big leather armchair near the fire and swung his feet onto the footstool. Buddy curled up at his side, but instead of dozing, remained alert, his eyes darting from one individual to another. Alex crammed himself into the overstuffed sofa and pulled a cushion onto his lap. Kate and David shared a couch.

Jared dropped into a chair. "I've got two men posted at the front gate, two more riding the fences." He patted the radio clipped to his belt. "They'll check in every ten minutes." He looked around the group. "All right. Tell me what happened."

The words tumbled out. Stories overlapped. They told of the ransacked house, the terrifying hallucinations, the panicked chase. After they finished, Jared finally said, "Folks, one thing is abundantly clear. You're in way over your heads. Call the sheriff, the police, the FBI. Get some help."

"They monitor communications," David said. "If we contact the authorities, they'll find us in a heartbeat."

Jared sighed. "Before you go running off on some wild goose chase, think about what you've said. If these people can listen-in on telephone, Internet, whatever, and they can somehow cause you to *hallucinate*..." He held his hands out in a pleading gesture. "How the heck are you going to deal with that? Stay here. We can defend ourselves. If we wait it out, maybe it'll blow over."

"Daddy," Kate said. "Don't you see? There's more at stake here than our immediate safety. Someone has to find the truth. If these people aren't stopped..." She paused, looked down, back up. "We've already discussed this. My mind is made up. David and I are making the Alaska trip."

Jared got up and paced the room. He took the poker off its rack and jabbed the burning logs, sending a small storm of sparks swirling up the chimney. The soft glow from the embers touched Mark's face and eyelids like a warm feather. Despite the disturbing reality that his mother would be heading off into uncertain danger, his thoughts began to drift.

The walkie-talkie squawked, pulling him from his trance. The sentries were checking in. Jared listened. "Everything's quiet." He was silent for a few moments, then spoke, his voice somber and resigned. "I'll see if James Kilbrew can spare a few men from his ranch. They can stay in the bunkhouse. That would make twenty guys on security, ten 'round the clock. Alex can stay with Mark here in the main house."

"Thank you, Daddy."

"How soon you figure on leaving?"

"In two days. That gives me time to shop. I'm afraid to go home for anything."

David said, "It also gives us time to work out secure communications." He nodded at Alex. "Maybe our chief hacker can help with a plan."

Jared cracked a smile. "We'll put Alex to work breakin' broncos and mucking out stalls."

Mark laughed as a momentary panic seized Alex's face.

"This house has enough bedrooms for everyone," Jared continued. "So when you're ready, Kate will show you a room. As for me, I'm taking my tired old carcass to bed." As he left, he glanced back over his shoulder and with a wicked grin said, "Breakfast is at a quarter to six."

* * *

The next morning, Kate sat at her father's computer and logged onto her email account. Sean's message sent a jolt of apprehension through her system.

> *Extreme danger. Must talk. Meet at usual place*
> *at 0900. Don't use telephone unless emergency. —S.*

David drove her to the Air Force Academy in the Ford pickup, and they parked close to the Visitor's Center. There was no sign of Sean. She walked into the building, but saw only a small knot of tourists clustered around the information desk. Back outside, she punched his number into the cell phone and waited. A busy signal beeped back at her.

"Something's wrong," she told David as she climbed into the truck. "He's never late."

"Try again."

She waited a few minutes and redialed. The busy signal returned.

David started the engine. "Where does he live?"

Fifteen minutes later, they pulled up in front of a small condominium in the rolling hills northwest of the Academy. She remembered the day Sean had bought the Spanish-style condo. He had invited her family over for a cookout and a swim in the pool. He had pointed out with pride that you could sit on the tiny balcony and watch planes take off from the Academy airfield.

She looked around. Only a few cars were parked along the quiet cul-de-sac. Sean's car was probably in the garage. She tried the cell phone again and received the same aggravating busy signal.

At his front door, she punched the buzzer and knocked. No one came. Retracing her steps, she searched the small patch of landscaping and at last found it—the silly fake rock holding Sean's emergency key. David unlocked the door, swung it slowly open, and they stepped inside and paused in the silent entryway. "Sean?" Kate called out, her voice sounding shrill in her ears. Then she noticed the faint odor. Her stomach tightened. "Smoke."

"Fried electronics," David said, stepping ahead of her. He flipped the light switch, but the room remained dark. They walked silently through the den and entered the kitchen. The phone still rested in its cradle on the wall.

"That leaves the office and the bedroom," Kate whispered.

The peculiar smell sharpened as they approached Sean's office. As they stepped inside the room, the fear prickling Kate's spine turned to alarm. Stripped of their contents, disc storage boxes lay in a disheveled pile beside the computer.

She began backing out the door. "Let's go, get out of here—"

David placed a hand on her shoulder. "One more stop."

The bedroom door was partly open, exposing an ominous slit of darkness. David motioned for Kate to stand to one side as he cautiously pushed the door wide. He glanced inside and froze, his breath escaping in a long sigh. She nudged up beside him and peered into the gloom. Pale light filtering past the curtains revealed a man's body sprawled beside the bed. She stifled a scream. "Oh God."

"Careful," David said as they approached the crumpled figure. The man was clad only in jeans and lay on his stomach, with his head turned to one side, a stare of horror locked into his face. They knelt beside him.

"It's Sean," Kate moaned.

David placed two fingers across the man's carotid artery. After a moment, he shook his head. "I'm sorry."

Kate sobbed. "This is my fault."

"You're not responsible for this."

She looked again at the body. Sean's outstretched hand clutched his Colt .45 automatic, the one he and Jack had used when teaching her how to shoot. Sean had attempted to defend himself. Against what? Another man—a hallucination? Through a haze of tears, she glimpsed something hidden beneath his curled left hand: the small leather notebook he carried for names and appointments.

David took her gently by the arm. "We'd better go. We'll call an anonymous nine-one-one."

On impulse, she reached down and snatched the notebook as she stood. They turned and rushed from the condo. Kate maintained control until they reached the turnoff to Garden of the Gods. Then her body shook with sobs.

"I'll take you home," David said.

She dabbed at her eyes. "I just need someplace quiet. Just for a minute." She paused. "That little restaurant you took me…"

* * *

The Backstreet Bar and Grill was quiet and cool. Kate ordered a Bloody Mary, David coffee. She nursed her drink for several minutes and cradled the glass in her hands, rubbing the cold surface with her thumb. She shoved the drink aside. Red was the wrong color. "We called him Uncle Sean," she finally said. "He loved Mark…loved all of us. He never had a family of his own. He and Jack were best friends."

"Kate, maybe you should rethink this investigation. Take your family and disappear—"

"No!"

She looked at David. His blue-green eyes were full of sympathy and concern, an expression that seemed unnatural for that square-jawed face. Her tears were gone now, and instead of shock and sadness and pity, another emotion raged to the surface. "No matter what it takes," she said, fighting to keep her voice even, "I'm going to find them. I'm going to find them and bring them down. All of them."

18

The landing gear thumped, shaking Kate from the clutches of a dark dream. She stretched, glanced at David in the seat beside her, and looked out through the window. A curve of rough land rose against blue-black ocean. Islands dotted the shoreline. Bays probed toward glistening-white mountains framed in greens and grays.

"Ice fields," David said. "We're over the Kenai Peninsula. The Cook Inlet is on our left."

He squeezed her hand, and she entwined her fingers with his. Anticipation sparred with apprehension. The pilot's voice crackled from the overhead speakers: they would be landing shortly. The temperature in Anchorage was sixty-three degrees. Scattered clouds.

* * *

They drove the rented Ford Explorer eastward along the International Airport Road. On their left, brightly-colored floatplanes rose in an endless line from Lake Hood, ferrying passengers and cargo into the wilderness. The long curve of the Chugach Mountain Range stretched out behind them, gray in the hazy distance. To the right, Kate could see a cragged mass of snow and shadow shouldering above the horizon: Mount McKinley, highest mountain in North America. The Athabascan Indians named it Denali, *The Great One*.

The Minnesota Bypass took them to City Center, the heart of Anchorage, where a sprawl of generic office buildings lay, mantled gold in the constant sunlight. Their hotel, a rustic-modern on West

Fifth Avenue, had a large common area with a walk-in fireplace. Kate thought the building would pass muster in Aspen or Vail. Their single room on the second floor overlooked a broad green lawn and a meandering hiking trail. Some two hundred yards beyond, the glittering waters of the Knik Arm lapped the rocky shoreline.

David placed the laptop on a table near the window and plugged it into the telephone jack. Kate watched as he logged onto the bulletin board Alex had specified. David left a message: *Arrived safely. Having a great time*, and signed his Internet alias, *Arthur*. He logged off, locked the laptop to the bed frame, and slid it beneath the mattress.

Kate drew out Sean's leather notebook. Earlier, she had found "Constellation—ARC sig. matches deaths," and an underlined name: Professor Bernard Winstead, Anchorage University. She looked up the university's number and dialed it. Her call was transferred, and she reached a secretary; if they hurried, they could catch Winstead in the geophysics building.

They drove five miles southeast to the sprawling A.U. campus and parked near the three-story Geophysical Sciences building, a brown shoebox shoved into the side of a bald, dome-shaped hill. Winstead's office was on the second floor, where a hand-lettered note on his door directed them to the laboratory at the end of the hall. The core analysis lab was open, and inside they saw a robust, bearded man in overalls wrestling a rough-textured cylinder of gray rock from a cart. He cradled the cylinder in his arms and laid it carefully beside a row of similar specimens neatly arranged on a massive wooden table. His full beard and heavy, black eyebrows reminded Kate of photos she'd seen of early Alaskan gold prospectors. He smiled when he saw them.

"Professor Winstead?" David asked.

The man dusted off his hands. "That's me. What can I do for you?"

David introduced Kate and himself, giving assumed names: "Donna and Arthur Reston." Winstead offered a firm handshake.

Kate said, "We're doing some research. Can you spare a moment?"

"Depends, what do you want to know?"

"We're trying to find the source of an odd radio signal." She paused for a moment. "We thought it might have come from the

ARC project."

The professor's smile vanished. He scrutinized them for a moment, as if sizing them up for a difficult job. His eyes narrowed. "Who are you working for?"

Kate watched his face closely. "This is personal."

Winstead shut the door, then motioned them to lab stools beside the table. The rock cylinders gave off an earthy, slightly oily smell that mingled with a background odor of chemicals. Winstead ran his fingers along one of the core samples, tracing lines in the fractured surface. "Tell me."

"Professor Winstead, have you heard of an organization called Constellation?" Kate asked.

The black thicket of eyebrows rose. "Yes. I know about them."

"Their web site made some disturbing claims about radio transmissions originating from ARC. I want to verify that claim."

"Why is this important to you?"

Kate took a deep breath. Her instincts about people were usually accurate, and Winstead seemed innocuous enough. "Two years ago, my husband was aboard a plane carrying Senator Jeff Travis. Constellation said ARC might have caused the plane to crash. Everyone was killed."

"I'm very sorry." Winstead's mouth twisted into a wry smile. "So, naturally, you want to prove ARC was responsible and bring them to justice."

"That's what I intend to do."

"That's been tried. You realize the media in this country is owned by only a handful of people, and they all kneel before the omnipotent Moral Alliance. And the Alliance supports ARC."

"I can get the news out."

Winstead sighed. "What do you already know?"

"We know the ARC transmitter can cause strong radio interference, maybe destroy electronic equipment."

David said, "We assume there's far more to the system than the government is telling us."

"You assume correctly," the professor replied. "Have you seen the installation?"

"No."

"You should fly out to the mountain. You wouldn't believe the scale of the thing."

"Mountain?"

"I'm surprised you didn't know. ARC is built into a small mountain near Denali. The installation is huge, unbelievable. The antenna system occupies about a hundred square miles."

"We want to photograph it," Kate said.

"The air boundary is fifteen miles out. If you fly any closer, they'll shoot you down."

Kate grimaced. Getting a decent photograph from fifteen miles away would be nearly impossible.

David pulled a map from his jacket and spread it across the table. Winstead bent over it and tapped his pencil on an area south of Denali. "It's here." He traced a blue line threading its way through a cluster of mountains. "This river runs between two small mountains. They bored a tunnel through one of them and built a bridge over the river. The antennas wrap around this mountain just to the north. The transmitter is buried inside."

David marked the spot and folded the map. "What's your connection to all of this, Professor?"

Winstead sat down and hoisted one leg over the other. "First, I'd like to know how you found out about me."

"Through a friend," Kate said. She stifled a sharp emotion as she thought of Sean. "He was helping me analyze the radio signal. I don't know how he got your name. We maintain everyone's anonymity."

Winstead nodded. "Eight years ago, I worked in the ionospheric research department for A.U. Fairbanks. That's when the military started building ARC as part of the High Frequency Auroral Research Program. The university was supplying some engineers, and I was invited to support the ground-penetrating tomography effort. But once I found out what they were doing, I opted out."

Kate took out a pen and notebook from her purse. She missed her microphone and Gil Henderson's comforting presence as cameraman.

"Do you mind if I take notes?"

"No. Just don't connect my name with any of this."

"What was it that disturbed you about ARC?" she asked.

"Secrecy and the power levels they proposed using. I thought it was environmentally unsound, beaming intense microwave radiation into the ionosphere. Plus, Senator Samuel Hurwitz and his buddies were pushing for it. Those fine fellows who want to destroy free speech.

"They brought in that guy, Joseph Krohner, and his company, EleKtrum. He had the super high-power microwave technology. They took over the mountain and thousands of acres and dug in."

"Do you believe they've injured people with that technology?" Kate asked.

Winstead puffed out his cheeks. "Like you, I've heard stories."

David dug into his jacket and brought out a miniature tape recorder. "Does this sound familiar?" He jabbed the play button and a warbling screech filled the room. It was the sound he had recorded off the Internet, the same noise Kate heard the night of the hallucinations. She had begun calling it the "death fax."

Winstead frowned. "Sounds something like the ARC signal. Sometimes even TV sets would pick it up as far away as Fairbanks."

"Know why they would modulate a carrier like that?"

"That's a mystery." He paused. "Maybe it would be helpful if I gave you more background." He thought for a moment and began. "The technical theories originated around the turn of the century with an inventor named Nikola Tesla."

Kate almost dropped her pen. "Tesla?" She exchanged glances with David.

"Heard of him?"

"Yes. I've…heard about him."

"Well, he had some ideas about injecting radio waves into the earth-ionosphere waveguide and tapping the energy at a distance. He knew about the ionosphere decades before it was actually proven to exist, and theorized about beaming energy around the planet using it as a reflective surface.

"Around 1981, an inventor named Eastlund took out a bunch of patents based on Tesla's ideas. He sold the patents to Atlantic Richfield. They had huge gas reserves near Gakona and thought they could use the beaming technology to transmit the energy.

"But they sold the patents to E-Systems, a company that developed secret technology for the military. They built the first phase of the test installation. Then along comes Raytheon and buys E-Systems. Raytheon is a multi-billion dollar company that does all sorts of classified stuff.

"Apparently, they proved some of Tesla's theories, because somebody got really excited. Senator Hurwitz buddied up with EleKtrum, the Moral Alliance, and some general with the Joint Chiefs. They got a giant chunk of the taxpayer's money and started building ARC."

"What's so special about EleKtrum?"

"Like I said, they have technology that can generate and beam super-powerful microwave energy." Winstead lowered his voice. "The ARC installation is dangerous as hell, and the scariest part is the people who are running it."

"What happened to Raytheon? Are they out of the picture?"

"Apparently. Once things disappeared into the dark zone, you couldn't find out anything. Like Area Fifty One. All we hear now are rumors."

"What kind of rumors?"

Winstead stood and stretched his back. "One thing for certain, with the setup they have right now, they're doing a lot more than just spying on the Internet. If you want to know more, take that plane ride." He scribbled a phone number on a piece of paper and handed it to Kate. "Call this number. The man's name is Ed Turner, runs a floatplane service out of Lake Hood. He's busy this time of year, but tell him I sent you."

Winstead saw them to the door and shook their hands. He smiled. "Goes without saying. We never had this conversation."

19

Outside the geophysics building, Kate waited as David keyed the number for Turner Flying Service. He spoke for a minute and snapped the phone shut. "He can fly us out to Denali around noon tomorrow."

"Good. Great. I'll check the cameras, make sure the batteries are charged."

David glanced at his watch as they walked toward the Explorer. "It's five-thirty. How about dinner, maybe a walk up that hiking trail?"

Kate's stomach growled at the mention of food. "I'm starved. My appetite's still on Colorado time."

* * *

Pelican's Restaurant, one block from the hotel, promised the best seafood in Anchorage, plus a view of the inlet. An ancient oak bar, embellished with a mounted swordfish vaulting its ornate mirror, commandeered one wall. Above the fish, an arched sign boasted twenty-seven varieties of beer.

They ordered two of the house specialties: salmon and steamed crab. Halfway through her second glass of wine, Kate frowned and said, "I feel guilty."

"Why?"

"Because I'm enjoying this." She glanced up at him. "I feel alive again. Here. With you."

"There's nothing wrong with enjoying yourself. You only go around once."

"I believe in reincarnation."

"Remember any prior lives?"

"No."

"Then reincarnation seems irrelevant."

She laughed. "Let's argue philosophy some other time." She sipped her wine and thought for a moment. "If ARC is as big as Winstead says it is, why haven't we seen photos? Why hasn't news leaked out?"

David leaned toward her. "Since the Alliance rose to power, and especially since Cerberus was proposed, the media in this country have been, essentially, controlled. Look at how they censored Constellation, at what's happening to Alex and your own television station. *You're* the one, Kate, to blow the lid off this thing." He paused. "We've been lucky, so far. But we mustn't forget we're in their back yard."

"Hiding in plain sight."

"Exactly."

* * *

The Tony Knowles Coastal Trail began at Elderberry Park, about a hundred yards from a tiny inlet off the Knik Arm, close to their hotel. A riot of flowers surrounded the park and burst in brilliant clusters along the trail. Kate and David followed the blacktop path southwest, toward Westchester Lagoon, and started across a wooden bridge spanning Chester Creek. "A creek in Alaska would be called a river in Colorado," Kate said. They paused, leaning against the railing, watching crystal waters glide silently beneath an unsullied sky. "I could get used to this," she added.

David smiled. "It's great in August, with sixteen hours of sunlight, but you get the flip side in winter." He slipped his arm around her shoulders, let it slide toward her waist. Kate placed her hand over his. Her pulse quickened. After a moment, David pulled his arm free and tapped his watch. "Time to phone home." He took her by the hand and they walked back toward City Center.

In the hotel room, David unlocked the laptop and logged on. Kate stood behind him, squinting at the screen. An answer was waiting for them on the bulletin board: *All's well here. Have fun.* David typed, *More tomorrow*, and sent the message.

Kate placed her hands on his shoulders, a movement both involuntary and deliberate. "I hate not being able to just pick up the phone and call."

"Can't take the chance." He logged off and closed the computer. "We have a long day tomorrow." He stood and faced her, then pulled her arms back up, placing them again on his shoulders. She folded her hands behind his neck and tugged him gently down. David hesitated for a moment, then drew her in, held her tight against his body, and pressed his mouth over hers.

They made love, she urgently, without guilt, surrendering to feelings and desires sublimated and buried by years of loss and grief. They showered afterward, and as he climbed into bed, she said "Here, next to me."

David moved close. Despite the late sunlight that rimmed the heavy curtains, and David's warm presence, a chill seemed to infiltrate the atmosphere. She had not told anyone of the hallucination she suffered two nights earlier, when she, David, Mark, and Alex had been attacked inside her home, when the death-fax hit her. In addition to the serpent-like monster that coalesced from Mark's crushed guitar, she had seen men—apparitions—creeping from the dark corners of the garage, stalking after her with arms raised before them like zombies, with their bugging, blood-eyes and distended veins…

She wriggled tighter against David's body, shivering.

28

The next morning, Kate emerged from the shower wrapped in a white bathrobe, a dissipating cloud of steam preceding her. David stripped off his sweatshirt. "Did you leave any hot water?"

She put her arms around him and brushed her lips against his. "No. I used all of it," she teased, then whispered, "Thank you for last night."

He ran his fingers through her still damp hair and kissed her.

They dressed in jeans, light sweaters, and windbreakers. After a hotel breakfast of fruit and toast, they returned to the room. David called Turner, spoke for a moment, and hung up. He turned to Kate. "We're still on." He shook his head, grinning.

"What?"

"Turner wants us to pick up a bucket of fried chicken. Says we'll have lunch on the trip."

Kate made a face. Pitching around in a small plane, gnawing greasy fried chicken; the thought alone made her queasy. "He want fries with that?"

*   *   *

They arrived at the Lake Hood Seaplane Base at noon and drove down the peninsula that angled into the lake from the north. Dozens of floating aircraft were nosed into shallow docking slips cut into the wooded shoreline, and engines droned as planes landed or lifted off from the lake's scalloped surface. The Chugach Mountains rose blue in the distance, their tops shrouded in low clouds. David parked beside a small wooden sign reading "Turner Flying Service." They hefted the camera gear and Turner's chicken lunch and followed a leaf-strewn trail to the water's edge.

Two men stood beside a high-winged, yellow floatplane tethered in its slip. One of the men waved and smiled. He was big, heavy-boned, with medium-length gray hair. He wore a baseball cap and a maroon polo shirt embroidered with the company logo. In a clear, resonant voice, he introduced himself as Ed Turner. "This is Will Kirkland," he said, facing the other man. "He's the second half of our business."

Kirkland was young, average build, and wore an outfit similar to Turner's. "I just flew some fishermen up to Talkeetna," Kirkland said. "Denali was cloudy, but you might get a break in an hour or so. If you're lucky, the clouds'll lift just enough for flat lighting."

Kate set the camera case down. "Sounds like you're into photography."

"A little. I took some shots of ARC myself, but they're worthless. Nobody's got decent pictures of it. Can't get close enough."

"We'd like to keep this quiet," David said.

Turner snorted. "Sure, if you want. But everybody *hates* ARC, especially pilots, and most of 'em have publicly cussed the damned thing."

"Why are the pilots angry?" Kate asked.

Turner shook his head. "Sometimes their signal blanks our radios for damned near a hundred mile radius."

"And it's not just the planes," Kirkland added. "*Every* radio. There's no way in or out of some places except by plane—no telephone either. Radios are a matter of life and death for some of these people."

"How often do they transmit?" David asked.

"A lot. The signal varies. Sometimes it's really strong."

"They've been transmitting low power for a couple of days now," Turner said. "You'll hear it when you're close."

David lowered his voice. "Any rumors about people being hurt?"

There was a long pause. "Rumors," Turner said. "We think they shot down a planeload of photographers about a year ago. They crashed just outside the boundary. Killed everyone on board. No one ever figured out what happened." Turner looked at the camera gear. "Hope you have a good telephoto lens, because we'll be keeping well outside that boundary."

Kate picked up an aluminum case. "Best in the business."

Turner nodded. "Let's go."

David hoisted himself into the plane's back seat along with the cameras. Kirkland helped Kate onto the starboard float and into the passenger seat. She was relieved when he stowed the chicken out of sight in an aft compartment. Turner made his final inspection and climbed aboard. Kirkland unhooked the tethers and pushed the plane from the slip. Grasping the wing, he turned the plane around, handling it as easily as a toy.

"You folks been in a floatplane before?" Turner asked.

"Light planes and helicopters," Kate said.

He turned to David. "How about you, sir?"

"All kinds. I was in the Navy."

"Yeah? I was a Marine. Flew A-6s in 'Nam." Turner glanced right, left, and punched the start button. The engine coughed and roared, the propeller fanning a puff of black exhaust past the windshield. He steered up the narrow channel toward open water. A quarter of a mile ahead, another floatplane gracefully lifted off in a spray of silver. Turner revved twice and taxied downwind to the takeoff point. He scanned the instruments, nosed the plane into the wind, and throttled up.

The aircraft accelerated smoothly across the lake's surface, small waves drumming against the aluminum floats, the sound increasing in pitch. Turner adjusted a control and pushed the steering yoke forward and back. The plane's speed increased, and in a short distance the lake fell away beneath them. Kate expected more buffeting, remembering her experience with other small aircraft, but takeoff was rock steady and the plane climbed as if it were on rails.

Turner shouted over the droning engine. "This plane's a DeHavilland Beaver. It's Canadian built. Best floatplane you can buy."

"How long will it take to get there?" Kate asked.

"We'll probably make eighty knots ground speed. I'd say around an hour and twenty minutes."

Kate looked behind her. "David, let's get out the Sony and long lens."

David removed the digital video camera, took a thousand-millimeter reflector lens from another case, and locked it onto the camera with a twisting motion. The powerful lens was larger than the camera and required a pistol grip so it could be hand-held. Kate took the assembly and tried holding focus on the mountains below. The image in the camera's viewfinder danced wildly. Shooting ARC was going to be difficult.

"How close can you get?" David asked Turner.

"About twenty-five klicks. They'll harass us when we get to thirty. We go an inch inside the boundary and they can legally shoot us down."

Turner leveled the floatplane. Below, a river wended southward, silver against dark green tundra. Purple-gray mountains of the Alaska Range swept in a crescent before them. Dead ahead, Denali's frozen white mass pierced the clouds.

"We're over the Iditarod Trail," Turner said. "It's eleven-hundred miles long."

The black thread of a highway slanted into view from the east and bent north, hugging the river. Kate recorded a few images at high resolution and played the results on the camera's view screen. Digital image stabilization wouldn't be good enough. She placed the camera in her lap and rubbed her temples. Trying to focus on the palsied terrain had given her a headache.

Turner lapsed into tourist monologue, describing towns, facts about the river, mountains. They climbed to five thousand feet and angled westward, away from the highway. A network of twisting rivers, alternating dark blue and silver, interlaced on their right. The tundra gave way to gray mountains. Denali loomed before them, massive and white. "See the mountains near the base?" Turner asked.

A cluster of dark peaks spiked up at Denali's foot. Kate swung the fat telephoto lens around, trying to locate the mountains. Just as Kirkland predicted, the clouds had lifted and now hovered in a thin veil above them. An image wandered in and out of the viewfinder. "There's a mountain with circles around it," she said.

"That's it. That's ARC. We're twenty miles from the boundary."

Kate pressed her eye to the camera. Dozens of concentric gray circles, intersected by radial lines, ringed a lone, cone-shaped mountain thrusting from the tundra. She lost the image, found it again. *Spider web*, she thought, like a giant spider web. And the black mountain in the center is the spider. Kate rested the camera in her lap. They'd have to get closer.

"Well, right on cue," Turner said. He pointed to his headphones. "They're sending a warning." After he listened for a moment, he spoke into the headset. Kate couldn't understand his words.

Turner shook his head. "I told them we'd stay way outside the limit. But I don't trust these assholes." He glanced at Kate. "Pardon the expression, Ma'am."

"No pardon needed," she said, amused.

"We'll get another warning around eighteen miles out—plus maybe a visit."

David said, "Put it on speaker so we can record it."

"Okay, boss," Turner flipped a switch on the dash and peeled off the headphones.

Two minutes later, the speaker rasped: *This is a warning. You are within three miles of a restricted area. Do not cross the air boundary or you will be met with lethal force. We repeat—*

David held up the tape recorder. "Got it."

Kate ran tape and audio, focusing first on the overhead speaker, then pulling back to reveal Turner as he transmitted a reply. She tilted up and zoomed, capturing a distant image of the dark mountain through the front windshield.

Turner pulled the throttle back and began a slow left turn. He leveled the plane. "Slide the window open. Can you get a shot?"

David grasped the handle and pulled the trapezoidal window back. Frigid air rushed in. Kate tried to get a fix on the target. "The angle's wrong. Can you tilt to the right?"

Turner rolled the plane a few degrees. "Hold it," Kate said. She panned from right to left, glimpsing the mountain as it flashed through the viewfinder. "This isn't working." She made three more pans, each at a different rate.

Turner banked to the left. "We're getting too close. I'll come back around. On my signal, I'll bring the nose up and kill the engine. Just before we stall, you'll have no vibration and very little air speed, but you'll have to act fast." He brought the plane into position. *"Now,"* he shouted. The engine chugged and stopped. The nose lifted and the plane hovered, weightless for an instant.

Kate pushed the camera to the window opening. She found the river and quickly panned left until the mountain came into view. She was able to hold the shot this time. At thirty-two frames per second, she should get several decent images, but she'd have to view them on the laptop to see any detail.

The plane yielded to gravity and fell off to the right. She felt a brief wave of nausea as weightlessness played with her gut. Turner fired the engine up and the Beaver pulled out of its stall. She heard David clicking away behind her with the motor drive.

Kate pulled her eye from the camera. "I think I got it."

"Good," David said. "Because we have company at nine

o'clock."

Turner stared out the left window. "Oh, shit."

Kate craned her neck, straining to see. Coming up fast was a black helicopter.

"Looks like a Blackhawk," said David. He sighted through the zoom lens. "He's armed, so don't piss him off."

"Friggin' assholes." Turner tilted the Beaver and carved away from the mountain. The helicopter closed. Turner grabbed the mike and transmitted his identity. "Call off your helicopter. We are outside your perimeter and are leaving. Repeat; call off your helicopter. We are leaving." The transmission was met by a blast of static from the speaker. "Damn!"

The helicopter, its aft door open, buzzed parallel to the Beaver's right side.

"There's a guy with binoculars," David said.

"Don't let 'em see your cameras," Turner shouted.

Kate leaned back into the dark cockpit, but kept recording. The powerful lens brought the chopper up close. She glimpsed a man in a blue jumpsuit, then lost the image as the helicopter lifted and turned away from them, angling back toward the mountain.

"That was just bullshit." Turner said, his face flushed. "That was illegal as hell. If I thought it would do any good, I'd sic the FAA on 'em."

"They didn't have any markings," David said.

"Let's take a break," Turner said angrily. They flew south, then banked westward, following the thread of a winding, silver river. Trees bristled from the tundra. A long, narrow lake came into view. Turner reduced air speed and they dropped, wind whistling softly past the fuselage. The aircraft touched the lake's glassy surface in a smooth transition from air to water, and the Beaver again became a boat with wings.

Turner cruised toward the south shoreline and cut the engine. The craft nudged against the grassy beach, sliding beneath the dappled shade of spruce and aspen. The two men tethered the plane and helped Kate onto the shore. She walked into the woods and stretched, glad for the feel of firm ground.

They set up folding chairs on a patch of coarse sand warmed by the sun. Turner brought the chicken and soft drinks out of the cargo compartment, along with a can of mosquito repellant.

Denali dominated the opposite horizon, its white summit rising above the trees, reflecting across the lake's mirrored surface. Alaska was, as someone had said, larger than human dimension.

Guilt pricked at Kate's heart again: she was having the time of her life.

*   *   *

Air traffic was heavy, and they had to circle twice before landing at Lake Hood. Kirkland met them at the beach and helped tie the plane up and unload the camera gear. David asked about the cost for the trip. "Nada. Nothing," Turner said. "You guys go after "em. You help close those ARC bastards down and you'll have free floatplane and fishing guide service the rest of your lives."

David shook his hand. "Semper Fi."

"See, ya, Navy," Turner said; then he added: "You guys be very, very careful."

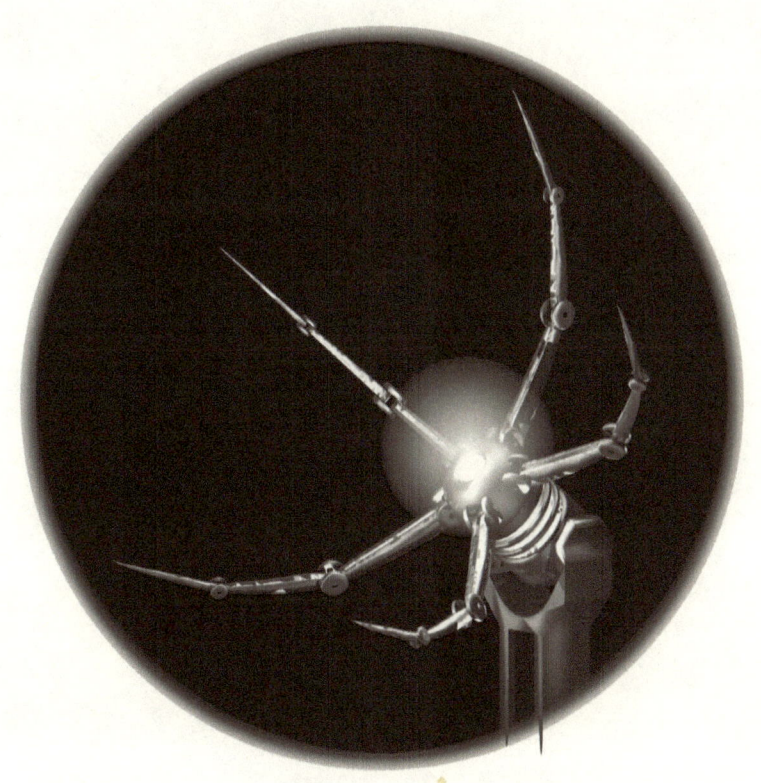

PART TWO

SPIDER

21

Kate tapped her foot impatiently as the Sony funneled the last of its images into to the laptop. David dimmed the room lights and sat down beside her. She switched the camera off and clicked playback. "Here goes."

Mountains jiggled and blurred across the monitor. "Almost worthless," she said. Then the dark thread of a river snaked into view. The image vibrated, briefly stabilized, horizon tilting, dropping, and for a brief instant panned smoothly across the dark mountain. She paused playback, freezing the frame.

An icy serpent wriggled down her spine. Jointed metallic spars, or beams, jutted from the mountain's conical slope, angling out like the jointed legs of a spider. Hundreds of amber-colored domes erupted from the mountain's base and spiraled outward in concentric bands, giving the appearance of a gigantic web.

Partly lost in shadow, an enormous arched door gaped like a devouring mouth in the southeastern side. Domes clustered above, simulating multiple arachnid eyes. Kate twisted her face in revulsion. "My God."

"Enlarge this area," David said, pointing.

She dragged the mouse and clicked. Two domes filled the screen.

David leaned forward. "They're geodesic, like huge radomes. They obviously house the antennas. Must be a couple hundred feet in diameter." Kate widened the image and David pointed to one of the metal legs. "Now enlarge this."

Parallel bundles of gray pipes flicked onscreen. "These are probably waveguides feeding power to the antennas," he said. "They extend out for maybe a half mile, then drop down and branch off. Amazing."

Kate returned the image to its original size, revealing the entire mountain and the spider web of domes encircling it.

David shook his head in disbelief. "Like Turner said, that ring of antennas must be ten miles across."

She enlarged the mountain and pointed to the enormous opening that yawned in the southeastern face. "They didn't fool around when they made the front door, either." A wide road, choked with trucks and heavy equipment, spanned the river and vanished into the mountain's beckoning maw. Square, multi-story structures squatted in clusters on either side of the road. "It's as big as a small city."

"Looks like manufacturing. They probably built sections of the transmitter in these buildings."

The video loped forward frame by frame. An airport with a tower and hangars flashed on. She enlarged a section of the runway. "Those are F-16s," David said. "Jetliners, choppers, plus a cargo jet—quite an operation."

She continued playback. The black helicopter that had confronted them twisted across the screen in erratic flight. An enlarged frame showed a man inside the aft compartment wearing a dark jumpsuit with an emblem over the breast.

"That's not military issue," David muttered. "Strange."

Kate fed a CD into the burner. "I'll make copies."

After she finished, David jacked the computer into the phone line and logged onto the bulletin board. "Message from Alex. This time it's encrypted." He inserted the decryption disc into the computer.

The message formed: *Mr. Starr says contact him.* An email address followed.

David raised his eyebrows. "'Starr'—our codename for Constellation. Alex made a breakthrough." He encrypted a message and sent it: *Someone gave me your number. Said we have a common problem.*

A reply came back almost immediately; they wanted a meeting and gave an address on the Kenai Peninsula. David looked up at Kate. "We're set for seven o'clock this evening."

* * *

They left at six o'clock and followed the Seward Highway east along the Turnagain Arm, then southwest onto the Kenai Peninsula. The Hope Cutoff took them north. After several miles, they turned onto a narrow gravel road that wound into the mountains.

The road terminated in a pine woods before a rambling two-story lodge built of massive logs. Smaller cabins nestled nearby, some in green clearings, others on rocky hilltops overlooking a wide valley and the silver thread of a river to the west. An occasional totem pole jutted from a hillock or leaned beside a pathway.

They left the Explorer beside a dozen other vehicles in the parking area and walked toward the lodge. Children played hide and seek among the tumbled boulders and stands of pines that comprised the main yard. A shaded hiking trail branched off to the left, twisting its way toward the mountain's summit.

"David," Kate said in a pleading voice. "When this is all over, can we *move* here?"

He laughed. "Kate, you said *we*."

She fluttered her eyelids in feigned innocence. "Why, yes. I suppose I did say *we*—it just slipped out." She hooked her arm around his and smiled. "But I meant it."

A large door of planks reinforced with iron bands opened into a vast common area, a larger version of the Thompson ranch house. Heavy beams crisscrossed two stories above, and an enormous stone fireplace occupied half the wall forty feet to their right. Chairs, sedans, sofas, and rustic tables rested in comfortable groupings on native rugs. Scrimshaw and artifacts nested beside books on rows of wooden shelving. Several young couples sat at a round table near the massive fireplace, chatting and laughing over drinks.

A young woman carrying a serving tray approached.

"We're looking for Ben," David said.

She pointed to a staircase rising beside the fireplace. "Upstairs and all the way back."

They walked up the stairs to a long hallway. A door stood open at the far end. Inside, three men were hunched over a small conference table, two of them nodding over a laptop computer. The third, an older, heavyset man with a full head of white hair, read from a notepad. David rapped on the doorframe and the man looked up. He had the rounded, crinkled features of a Native Alaskan.

"Come in," he said, extending his hand. "I'm Ben." The voice was soft, with a slight accent. "These are my associates, Gary and Peter." The two men stood. Gary was perhaps in his forties, deeply tanned, with brown hair chopped into a military-style flattop. He had a pug nose and a rough-looking face—not ugly, not handsome. Kate thought he resembled a well-groomed boxer. Peter had a youthful face unsullied by exposure to sunlight, and a closely shaved head. Earrings glinted from both ears. Kate immediately pegged him as a programmer or hacker.

"My friends are using pseudonyms as a precaution," Ben continued. "I hope you don't mind."

Kate suddenly realized a fourth person was in the room with them—an old man sitting quietly in a darkened corner.

Ben smiled and gestured toward the elderly man, who slowly rose from the shadows and advanced with the aid of a carved wooden staff. He came into the light, and Kate saw an impressively weathered face framed by a thick silver mane that fell across his shoulders and chest. A yellowed scrimshaw talisman swung from his neck by a leather cord.

"This is my uncle," Ben said. "He is called Grey Wolf, and I'm afraid he speaks no English."

Grey Wolf smiled and nodded. He gave Kate a lingering stare that she found unnerving.

Ben sensed her discomfort. "Grey Wolf is a shaman. He insisted on being here today. Regardless of what you might think of such things, he's really been quite helpful in guiding us. He has a very heightened"—he paused—"intuition."

Keeping his eyes on Kate, Grey Wolf leaned toward his nephew and spoke softly in his native tongue, which to Kate sounded like a clicking mishmash of K's and Q's and U's. Grey Wolf then returned to his corner, where he sat with his gnarled hands folded over the ornate, balled end of the staff.

Kate and David took seats across the table from the three men. Ben gazed down at his notepad for a moment, then looked somberly up. "Constellation was organized almost two years ago. It is devoted to exposing and shutting down the ARC project. I joined after our clan was nearly wiped out by them. It seems we were making too much noise about ARC encroachment into our land."

David leaned forward. "Wiped out?"

"Yes. I am of the Kalluk clan of Athabascan Indians. As I said, my uncle is a shaman, and he is highly respected among the tribes. During a peaceful night, while he was meditating on a ridge above our village, he saw the ionization beam kill a hundred and fifty of our people, including his granddaughter and great grandson."

Kate gasped. "My God."

"We have no proof, only my uncle's testimony. ARC burned and buried the village. It's inside their perimeter now."

David said, "You mentioned an ionization beam."

"Yes. It was dark and the beam was visible."

"So they really are using microwaves as a weapon."

"Yes, yes. I thought you already knew that."

"How did all of this get past the government?" Kate asked. "And how did they get so many people—scientists—to work for them?"

Gary responded. "It's what you would call a runaway technology. It started out as a system to control communications. Dr. Larry Sondheim, the U.S. Deputy Director for Science and Technology, is in charge of Project Four Fifty One, the new NSA intelligence gathering network. He got Joseph Krohner and his company, Elektrum, contracted to build the original system. Krohner's an engineer, keeps a low profile, originally from Slovenia, naturalized U.S. Citizen. He formed EleKtrum about ten years ago.

"His company designed a lot of electronic hardware for the military over the years. If you add up all of his personal holdings, he's way up there on the wealth scale. Anyway, Krohner got more funding through research grants and defense contracts, plus a lot of black project money. But the technology he's using is so advanced only a handful of people understand it. The government lost control. Congressional oversight is a joke, because Krohner fooled everyone, including the shadow government—the CIA, NSA, FBI, and so forth. He simply sneaked his weapons technology in, like hiding an atomic bomb in a crate of hand grenades."

Peter added, "ARC has hundreds of scientists, thousands of workers, and a security force the size of a small army. But most of the employees don't know what the project is really about. Some of the top research guys are there for the science alone, like at Los Alamos during the development of the atomic bomb. And for a lot of workers, it's just a good paying job."

"What sort of beast is ARC," asked David. "I thought it was military."

Gary grunted. "It's a typical military-contracted, corporate-managed operation, similar to General Dynamics or Lockheed Martin, with a healthy dose of Area 51 thrown in. But in this case, with the exception of General Greggson, the military is clueless, doesn't know what Krohner's doing—how far he's taken the technology.

Ben said, "President Williamson is very concerned, and he's threatened a full investigation if EleKtrum isn't more forthcoming. But it may already be too late." He folded his arms on the table and leaned toward David. "If ARC isn't shut down—*soon*—they will rule the world with the push of a button."

"What do you mean?"

Ben nodded to Peter, and a screen on the opposite wall flashed with a cross section of the project. The scale was astounding: an entire mountain hollowed out, with an enormous central shaft that ran from beneath the mountain's roots to its flattened top like the conduit of a volcano.

"The power plant is here," Ben said, using a pointer. "Transmitters are in this huge chamber. Command center just above it. The communications and control systems include *four acres* of new generation Cray supercomputers. They can monitor or jam virtually any communications anywhere in the world, including the Internet—which means Cerberus is a reality, not just a concept."

Several parts of the cross section were shaded gray. "We don't know anything about these areas. There's heavy work all along this south side that might be part of the weapons system." A geodesic dome appeared. "As you have seen, these domes extend around the mountain. Some are on the mountain itself. There's a monstrously huge one on the top."

"We've never seen the antennas themselves," Gary said. "They probably combine parabolic and phased array systems that can handle tremendous power over a wide frequency range. We think they have variable focus and can be used independently or together."

Another drawing: the earth, with a beam of radio waves impinging on the ionosphere. "The antennas transmit polarized microwave radiation that heats a region of the ionosphere and induces a rotational effect. This creates a radio frequency mirror. They can tilt the mirror, reflect RF energy from it anywhere on the planet, and with extremely low losses."

Kate asked, "How do you know all this?"

"We have contacts in the government and within the project itself," Ben answered. He gave a sardonic smile. "And like your friend Alex, we do a bit of hacking." He nodded in Peter's direction. "That's how we verified who you are. Even so, it's difficult to find out much about ARC because it's so compartmentalized."

David asked, "How much power can they beam through that ion mirror?"

"I don't know."

"Could they destroy an airplane?"

"They could probably kill an entire city."

Kate went rigid as the thought burned through her mind. "Then it's true," she said with quiet fury. "They brought the plane down." She stared at the table, jaw set, feeling the heat rise into her face and eyes.

Ben's voice softened. "Rumors about the project are especially common among military personnel, partly because of General Greggson's involvement, and we know your husband had been actively investigating ARC. It's possible he was killed for this, along with Senator Travis."

"Two birds with one zap," Peter said tactlessly.

David said, "But they'd require gigawatts, maybe even several terrawatts."

Ben tapped his pen lightly against the table. "The ARC power plant is nuclear."

"We're up against formidable odds," Gary said. "Senator Hurwitz, General Greggson, and the Moral Alliance are behind the project. Thanks to Hurwitz, the Senate just voted to continue funding." He sat back in his chair. "We need hard evidence—proof. We need to know their timetable, what they're planning, and about some additional secret technology they've been developing."

There was a long silence. "I'll help," said Kate, her voice low and firm. "But all I have so far is some shaky video and scary experiences."

"I'll make you a proposition," Ben said. "It's a long shot, and terribly dangerous. But if you want the story of the century, I believe there's a way."

"How?"

"We can get you inside."

22

Two days later, Kate waited nervously in the All-Alaska Executive Personnel reception area, absently teasing her now very short, very blond hair. A fabricated résumé was inside the folder beside her, as well as a top secret clearance, all verifiable by computer, thanks to Constellation's network of advanced programmers and hackers. Of course, her new ID, credit card, and bank account were also phony. Strangely enough, she was actually starting to feel comfortable being Ms. Donna Reston from Minnesota.

"We have friends on the inside," Ben had said, speaking of the ARC Project. "With luck, we might get you hired as a video editor. We know there's an opening in their media department that documents the project, and you might have access to sensitive data. Maybe you'll be the one to find the hard evidence we need." To David he had said: "We need someone to access those manufacturing facilities outside the mountain, see what they're mass producing. You might get on as outside security. They tend to hire thugs, extremists, people on the lam. We can give you a record, say, a couple of felonious assaults. It might help if you visited a particular bar they frequent on weekends. They've been known to hire people right off the street if they have the right, um, character."

"Ms. Reston," the secretary said. "Ms. Prayter can see you now."

Kate grabbed her portfolio and walked into the employment counselor's office. Geraldine Prayter looked up from her gray metal desk and waved Kate to a chair. The counselor had mousy, brown-going-gray hair. Bifocals perched precariously on the end of a beaked nose. Kate could picture her working the return desk of a public library.

The woman looked over Kate's résumé and pursed her lips like she'd sucked a lemon. "Tell me about your experience in video production."

"I've worked as an independent contractor," Kate replied, smiling. "I've produced several industrials and, ah, some political videos. I'm really quite familiar with digital cameras and editing systems."

Prayter appraised Kate over the top of her glasses, her mouth sucking at another lemon, then read through the fake résumé. She seemed impressed by the top secret clearance, which meant Kate supposedly already had an extensive background check. She asked about "Ms. Reston's" motives for moving to Alaska from Minnesota, and whether she would be interested in working at "a facility outside Anchorage." Seemingly satisfied with Kate's answers, she announced that the interview was over.

Kate surprised David, who was dozing behind the wheel of the Explorer. "I guess it looks good," she said, aware of the apprehension in her voice. "She'll let me know about an editing job in a day or two. I'm sure she means ARC."

David tapped the steering wheel. "What bothers me is that I won't be there with you." He started the engine and pulled away from the curb. "Well," he said, "In a few hours, I make my debut as a working class hero down at the Kodiak Bar."

"Seems like a really stupid way to find a job."

"It makes some sense. As Ben said, they hire thugs for patrol personnel. They hang out at the bar. It's worth a shot."

"If Ben hadn't suggested it, I'd say it was a complete waste of time." She grinned. "So, we're bar-hopping tonight. What do I wear?"

*   *   *

The Kodiak Bar, a windowless cinderblock with its name etched in dying neon, looked as if it had been ripped from a decaying neighborhood in Lubbock, Texas. David shoved open the bruised metal door. Inside, twangy country and western yodeled from rattling speakers, the bass kicked up to overdrive. Kate held her breath in a reflexive attempt to save her lungs from the thick nicotine atmosphere.

She thought about Bob Hope: an interviewer had asked how the comedian coped with LA smog. *Heck*, he had quipped. *I don't trust air I can't see.* He'd trust this air so much he'd loan it money.

Moth-eaten hunting trophies hung above the bar like props in a cheap horror movie, their features underlit by a row of garish beer signs. Rough laughter and the click of pool balls punctuated Conway Twitty's latest hit.

David leaned close to her ear. "Buffy, do you think they serve Perrier?"

Kate whispered back, "I ain't here for no sarsaparilla!"

Laughter, edged with derision, drifted from a table across the room. Too many eyes watched them.

Four barstools stood empty, as if reserved for honored patrons. Kate and David chose seats in the middle, Kate sitting at David's left. They ordered beers. David made a show of affection, wrapping his arm around her and whispering into her ear.

"Oh, my." Kate fluttered her eyelids. "You can be *so* trailer park."

"Not too loud," David scolded.

Halfway through their second beer—and, Kate thought, enough Twitty to last a lifetime—the pool game broke up in a calamity of barked obscenities and guffaws. Bets were settled. The players wandered into the bar. A skinny man with a short mustache and greasy hair slouched onto the barstool beside Kate. He wore a dark shirt with a stylized "E" embroidered above the pocket. Obviously the winner of the last game of eight ball, the man flashed a wad of bills and cast a leering, yellow-toothed grin at her. The bartender slapped a glass of whiskey before him.

Another E-Shirt, a squat, brawny man with a rolling gut that eclipsed his engraved silver belt buckle, heaved himself onto the stool beside David. He thrust his elbows onto the bar and looked toward the skinny one.

"Hey," he said, making a smoking motion. Skinny pulled a semi-crushed pack of Marlboros from his shirt pocket and tossed it over David and Kate. The big man caught the pack and removed two cigarettes. He stuffed one in his mouth and stuck the other behind his ear, then lit up and tossed the pack back.

David looked idly ahead, nursing his beer. Fats took a long drag and exhaled a stream of smoke toward David and Kate. The room's noise level dropped noticeably.

Kate tried to hide her nervousness by placing her hand on David's shoulder and turning toward him to speak. When she turned back, Skinny nodded at her, his wide grin exposing more discolored enamel. He held out the pack of cigarettes.

"No, I—" Kate stammered.

David's hand seized the pack before Skinny could retract it. "Thanks." The grin vanished. David shook out a cigarette, tossed the pack back, and rotated to the right. Fats glowered at him.

David held out the cigarette. "Got a light?"

The man's face contorted into a belligerent sneer. "Naw," he rumbled. " I don't—"

But David had already snatched the lighter.

"Hey, I didn't say you could—"

David jetted smoke into the big man's face, and Kate could see the circuits in Fats's head seizing up like an outdated microprocessor crunching numbers for an experiment in plasma physics.

She jumped as Skinny's fingers crawled across her shoulder. "Little lady," he said in an east-Texas oilfield drawl. "Why don't you come with me. Things here might git just a little rough..."

"She's with me," came David's stern voice.

Kate shook the hand off as if it were a tarantula. "Buzz off!" she heard herself say. But her mouth was dry and the words didn't quite form properly; she might have said something more severe. The bartender moved casually away.

"Such language from a lady," the man said. His displaced hand hooked around her neck, tugging her off balance. She stiffened, pulling away. *David—do something*! Skinny suddenly released her and tumbled from the stool. David had seized his hand and was twisting it severely backward.

"Aaaagh! Sonuvabitch!" the man croaked.

"I said she's with *me*. Got it?" David said calmly.

"Leggoame, asshole," the man spat.

"Leggoahim, asshole," Fats thundered, rising behind David.

"Apologize to the lady," David demanded.

Skinny dropped to his knees. "Aaaagh!"

Fats snaked a thick arm around David's neck and jerked backward. Skinny tugged free and staggered to his feet, working his injured hand. His mouth drew open in a rage of misshapen teeth. Bending quickly down, he thrust his hand to his boot and drew out a switchblade that snicked open and flashed in the neon haze.

Kate was on her feet. She snatched a beer bottle and cocked her arm, but the man turned and crouched toward her.

"Naw," boomed Fatso. "Before we fuck your pretty little girl and cut up your sorry sack of shit ass, who are you and what're you doin' here?"

"Just looking for a job," David gurgled.

"He's lookin' for a *job!*" Fats guffawed, shaking scattered laughter from the tables. "They ain't no jobs here, pussy, they're all full up."

David pulled his windpipe free and said quietly, "I'll make an opening." His right leg shot backward, his heel impacting Fat's groin with a linebacker-on-downfield-runner crack. The man grunted and sagged, hands clamped over his crotch like a six-year-old stifling an overfull bladder.

David's uppercut caught Fat's jaw before he could complete his first moan. The big man arced backward and crashed headfirst onto a loaded table, catapulting a fusillade of spewing bottles toward the rafters. Patrons scattered, ducking a downpour of glass and brew.

"David!" Kate cried.

Skinny had frozen into a crouching position like a battery-operated sumo wrestler whose gears had suddenly jammed. Gnashing his teeth, he suddenly re-animated. David pivoted away as the switchblade sliced air at chest level. Skinny gained confidence and advanced. His fatal error was repeating his first move. David's right foot was already rushing upward as the knife began its arc. The booted heel again found its target and crunched into the man's solar plexus, lifting him off the floor. Skinny dropped to his knees, clutching his chest and gasping.

David advanced. "Drop the knife." But Skinny seemed preoccupied with the task of breathing. "Drop the knife or I'll take your head off." The blade clattered to the floor and David kicked it away.

Background conversation and laughter rose to normal. *Fine,* Kate thought, *just another fun evening at the Kodiak Bar.*

David entwined his arm around Kate's and escorted her toward the door. "C'mon, Buffy, time to leave the party."

They exited into clear, bright, Alaska night, a fog of tobacco smoke escaping with them. A man followed them out. "Sir," he said, holding out a white business card. "Mister Wofford said to give this to you. If you're really interested in a job." David took the card and the man retreated back into the Kodiak's grimy entrance.

Kate read: *Bruce Wofford. Security Division, EleKtrum Corporation.*

The Explorer was in a metered parking area a hundred yards from the Kodiak. They climbed in and shut the doors. Kate looked at David. "You were magnificent back there. I was scared to death."

David took her hand. "You're shaking."

"It's just the adrenaline."

"You did pretty well yourself, Lady. You were about to clobber that guy with a beer bottle."

"I got to maintain my image, don't I?" Kate replied in a hick drawl. She paused a moment and cast him a questioning look. "What *else* did you do in the Navy, besides tune radios, Mr. Communications Officer?"

David started the engine. "Taught martial arts to SEALS," he said almost shyly. He turned the Explorer into the street and they headed west toward the hotel.

He glanced at Kate. "You need another drink."

"Yes."

"And some time in the hot tub."

"Yes."

"And someone to massage your shoulders."

"Yes."

"And mad, passionate, love."

"*Oh yes.*"

23

Buddy lifted his head, listening. A dark undertone disturbed the night's vibration. He let out a quiet huff, followed by a low growl.

* * *

Mark rushed into wakefulness from a deep sleep. "Buddy," he mumbled, reaching over the side of the bed. "What is it, fella?" He stroked the retriever's side, feeling tenseness in the dog's body. Another growl rumbled against his fingers.

Buddy trotted to the window and pressed his nose to the screen, staring southward, the direction of the front gate. Mark sat up and glanced across the dark bedroom toward Alex. He could just make out his dim shape beneath the covers.

He walked up quietly beside Buddy and looked out, listening before the open window. The earth was still damp from a late afternoon shower, and the rich scent of woods and pasture drifted on the cold night air. Except for the soft chirp of a solitary cricket, he heard no sound. Buddy growled again, louder.

Mark felt along the bedside table and found the two-way radio. He switched it on and quickly reduced the volume as loud static crackled into the room. The noise suddenly ceased, overridden by a screeching cry that turned his spine to ice. It was the same tortured sound his computer had made just before they experienced the terrifying hallucinations. His mother had named that sound the *Death Fax*.

He pressed the transmit button: "Jared, Carlos—anybody—do

you hear me?" The Death Fax raged in response. He fumbled for the flashlight, knocked something over.

Alex's sleep-laden voice came from behind. "What's going on?"

Footsteps thumped on the stairs. Someone was climbing, using a flashlight instead of the stairwell lights. Hermano appeared at the door. "Señors, keep your lights turned off and stay inside."

"Where's my grandfather?" Mark demanded.

"He and Carlos go to the gate to check it out." Hermano made a guiding motion with his flashlight. "Come down. Jared said everyone stay together."

Worried voices sounded from below.

"I've got to warn my grandfather."

"Stay inside, Señor. They know how to take care."

There was no time to explain about death faxes and hallucinations, or to argue about leaving the house. His grandfather didn't understand what could really happen, how much danger they were in.

Hermano clumped back down the stairs. Mark dressed quickly. He attached the walkie-talkie to his belt, grabbed the flashlight, and pulled his jacket from the closet. *The night-vision binoculars.* If he ever needed them, now was the time. He snatched the NVDs from his duffel and slung them around his neck.

"What're you doing?" Alex asked, tugging on his jeans.

"Finding my grandfather."

"Man, you can't go out there. They'll kill you."

"My grandfather will probably kill me too."

"Doesn't make sense—"

"Look, Alex, don't tell them, at least until I get going. And keep Buddy with you."

Alex sighed and nodded.

"Buddy, *stay,*" Mark commanded. The dog sat and whined, a worried look on his expressive face. Mark ducked from the room, closing the door quickly before Buddy's instincts overrode his master's orders.

The ranch hands would be guarding the front and rear entrances, but Mark knew another way out. He rushed to the end of the hall and tried the door to the little-used back deck. It was unlocked. He slipped through and picked his way across the plank floor, dodging the heavy Adirondack chairs and tables. Below and to his left, near the back door, Hermano and another man talked quietly. The stairs leading to the yard were solid—no creaking to give him away.

He jumped off the bottom step and jogged across the damp grass toward the creek. The sloping bank would hide him until he reached the barn. Behind him, Buddy's anxious barking had already begun.

Beneath the bridge, he switched on the two-way and tried again to contact his grandfather, turning the volume up against the creek's rushing chatter. Only static droned forth. Any vehicles he could steal were at the bunkhouses, too far away, and David Hightower's Bronco was locked in the tractor shed. He switched the radio off and darted up the embankment toward the barn.

He skirted the yellow circle of light thrown by the pole-mounted lamp and ran toward the building's north entrance. A padlock hung from the sliding doors. He tried the small entrance. It swung open, and he slipped inside and snapped on the flashlight. Horses stomped and snorted at the intrusion.

He led Maggie out of her stall and saddled her in the semi-darkness, feeling time passing like a messenger of doom. He needed a weapon. Frantically, he played the flashlight's beam along the wall. Cold steel glinted back: the old double-barreled twelve-gauge, kept for an emergency.

He lifted the shotgun from its rack and broke it open. The brassy ends of two shells reflected from the chambers. He snapped the gun shut and jammed it into a leather scabbard he lifted from the rack. He ran back toward Maggie. *Calm down. You'll spook the horse.*

He quickly tied the scabbard to the saddle rings and led Maggie to the door. The horse balked before the narrow opening. Mark walked through first, gently tugging and calling her, and she suddenly rushed through, as if goaded from behind.

He mounted and pointed her toward the creek; now it didn't matter if the guards saw him. Maggie slowed at the bridge and trotted carefully across, her hooves thumping hollowly against the wooden planks. As she stepped onto the road, Mark spotted the trail leading off to the right. He tugged the reins and spurred the horse at a gallop into the woods.

The cheap nightscope would be impossible to use atop a racing horse, and charging through the black woods brought images of smashing into trees or being clubbed to the ground by low hanging limbs. But Maggie knew the trail well, and she sped through the woods as if chasing across a meadow of spring grass, her hooves drumming against the soft earth.

Mark pressed low in the saddle, his face near the horse's mane, the animal's bobbing neck and head stretching out before him like the long nose of a fighter plane. The position was uncomfortable and precarious, but branches crowded close, and even in his lowered posture he felt the sting of pine boughs raking his back.

At last they broke free of the woods, and he reined Maggie to a halt. The shortcut had brought them within a quarter mile of the front gate. Twenty feet below, the entrance road carved a gray arc around them. He dismounted, led Maggie a few paces back, and tied her to a sapling. The horse's rapid breath left wisps of silver drifting in the cold night air.

He trotted a short distance uphill, stumbling over loose rocks and fallen limbs, then settled behind a boulder and pulled the NVDs from beneath his jacket. He switched them on. *How old are the batteries?*

He inhaled deeply to slow his pulse and brought the binoculars up. The world became an alien green landscape of amplified light. As he focused on the road below, a sound broke the quiet: the low rumble of an engine and the crunch of tires on gravel. A shadow materialized from the right, something swimming slowly around the bend toward him, hunting the dark pool of night.

Another shadow appeared, drifting behind the first. Two vehicles cruising with their headlights off: the first a van, the second a Humvee. Mark's breath caught as the vehicles drew even with him. Unblinking points of light glowed from inside the dark cabs, moving right and left, staring through the windows like the eyes of fiendish ghosts. *Infrared—they've got night goggles with infrared.* A sound emanated from the van, a strange whine that eerily rose and fell.

Mark shrank behind the boulder, his thoughts racing. The van had gotten past the guards at the gate. Had his grandfather been there? He switched on the walkie-talkie again, dialing the volume up slowly. The pulsing static was severe, but there was no fax-like screech.

He flicked the radio off, then inched around the boulder for another look. The van had turned, was facing him, the ghost eyes piercing the windshield, searching…. In a panic, he jumped to his feet and bolted for the woods. He tripped, stifling a shout as his hands and elbows banged painfully against loose rock, the dangling binoculars making a metallic rattle beneath his chest. He froze, listening, panting, hoping he hadn't cried out. No sounds of pursuit, just the motors and the generator-whine. At least he was still hidden.

More sounds: another motor, tires over gravel—this time from the direction of the ranch. He fumbled for the NVDs and sat up. Two hundred yards away, a vehicle cruised slowly around the curve. It was one of the ranch trucks, probably his grandfather's, and they were rolling straight into a trap.

He stood and vaulted across the jumble of rocks toward Maggie, his right knee telegraphing sharp jabs of pain. He untied the horse and swung into the saddle. The fastest way down was through a short, steep minefield of boulders.

He turned Maggie toward the drop and urged her forward. She shook her head and snorted disapproval, but obeyed, picking her way down. He leaned back as the horse went over the edge, the animal's massive shoulders and haunches pumping down the slope. They came to a sliding stop at the bottom, and he found himself looking up from a wide ditch that was much deeper than it had looked through the binoculars. The van's motor revved, and the generator sound grew louder.

Standing high in the stirrups, he saw the van looming just to his right, its big panoramic window pointing at the curve where his grandfather's truck would appear. He spurred Maggie as the ranch truck approached. In a moment, they would be exposed. He yelled. The truck jerked to a stop. The passenger door flew open and a man tumbled out, hands pressed against his head.

Maggie's hooves scrabbled against the road's gravel surface, her rear legs thrashing upward against the incline's loose rock. Mark's right hand arched back and seized the shotgun as the horse lurched over the rise. He urged her forward again, and she stormed between the truck and van.

A sudden shriek blasted inside Mark's head—just like the night he suffered the hallucinations at home. But neither the heat, nor the mental scream, nor the birth of bloodcurdling illusions held any terror. He swept the shotgun to the right. And in the fraction of a second when he rushed before the van's dark window, as reality departed his mind, he squeezed both triggers.

24

Mark struggled onto his side as a bright glare flooded his vision—*headlights*. Shadowy silhouettes cut across the beams, rushing toward him. He groped frantically for the shotgun. *They're coming for me*!

He staggered to his feet. The ground tilted. Hands grasped him, pulled him to a standing position.

"Mark, son, you alright?"

The world slowly stabilized, and he looked dumbly up. Two shapes swam into focus—his grandfather and Carlos. His last memory was of charging across the road atop the horse. He had fired the shotgun at the gray van, hadn't he? Then everything had dissolved to black.

He looked anxiously along the dark road. "Where's the van—and the Humvee?" His voice sounded strange and hoarse in his ears.

"They're gone," Jared replied. "High-tailed it after you fired Ol' Betsy at 'em."

Mark peered beyond the mask of light thrown by the headlights. "What about Maggie?"

Carlos pointed. "Over there." The horse stood by the side of the road, her reins tangled in a small pine. "She's a little spooked, but she's okay."

Mark stiffened as headlights bobbed from the direction of the gate. A pickup rattled up beside them and stopped. José climbed slowly from the cab, followed by Miguel.

"Any sign of our visitors?" Jared asked as the men strode up.

"They left in a hurry." Miguel's voice sounded thick, as if cotton were stuffed into his mouth.

As the two ranch hands entered the light, Mark noticed José holding a bloody rag to his face. Both men looked as if they had been in a fight.

"What happened to you guys?" Carlos asked.

"They knocked us around…wanted to find that Alex kid. But we didn't tell 'em anything."

"Yeah. It was real weird," José said. "We started seeing things, like we just ate a truckload of peyote. Then we sort of passed out. And when we came around, these guys were sitting there. Started asking questions…" He brought the rag to his face again.

Mark became aware of his own pain. Every bone in his body ached.

"We'll get you to a doctor," his grandfather said.

Miguel shook his head. "No."

"We'll be all right." José probed his injured jaw with his finger.

Jared was silent for a moment. "I'm calling the sheriff," he said, guiding Mark toward the truck. "We need some help."

*   *   *

The guard was doubled, and men were posted at the ranch house entrances. Miguel and José insisted on riding the fences, saying they were itching to get their hands on the people who had roughed them up. Sitting in a chair against the wall, rifle across his lap, Hermano kept a vigil outside Mark's bedroom door.

After being fussed over by his grandmother and probed with questions from Alex, Mark washed the blood and filth from his body and went back to bed. The night had returned to its prior quiet, and he felt safer with the additional security.

But now, dreaming in the late hours, burning with the memory of the night's events…

He runs, hand in hand with his mother across an open field, pushing against a howling wind driven by dark clouds boiling in a lowering sky. The air reeks of ozone. Electricity flickers and worms its way through a heavy, roiling wall of gray. Beyond the stormswept field, blackened buildings rise in agony above a raging fire.

He looks into the storm's furnace, and fingers of ice stroke his nerves. Lightning strobes and cracks as *IT* comes, gliding ponderously through the pulsing thunderhead—a great, naked Eye that rolls and glares this way and that.

Its throbbing veins wriggle beyond its glistening surface, transforming into long, branching streamers of purple-orange electricity that stab down like skeletal claws, shocking the buildings and stinging the ground.

If he and his mother cannot find what they seek— the hidden power in an unposed riddle, a hidden answer—it will be upon them. Even now it is turning their way.

He feels the vibration of its coming—

Mark bolted upright. He was certain he had screamed aloud, but Alex was still sleeping peacefully in the opposite bed, cocooned inside the patchwork quilt. Only Buddy seemed aware. The dog had raised his head and was studying him with intense, golden eyes— eyes that probably saw more than anyone could ever guess.

Soaked again by nightmare sweat, Mark stripped off the damp T-shirt and lay back down. He pulled the covers up, trying to shake the malevolent shadows of dread and foreboding that stalked him night after night. He thought he was coming unhinged.

*   *   *

He awoke as someone gently shook his shoulder. Morning sun cast yellow rays into the bedroom, and his grandfather was sitting on the edge of the bed, a half-smile partly hidden beneath his mustache.

"Feeling okay?" he asked.

"Yeah. I'm fine. Really."

Jared's expression became serious. "You were supposed to remain in the house last night."

"But if I hadn't come…"

His grandfather held up a hand. "Then things might have been a lot worse." He was silent for a moment. "Carlos and I owe you a load of thanks, Mark. You did a very brave thing." He ran his fingers through his salt and pepper hair and made a sour face. "Now I know how it feels to be zapped by that—whatever that thing is." He cast a stern look at Mark. "But if something like this happens again, I want you to promise you'll do as I say."

"All right."

His grandfather stood. "Looks like a storm's moving in, so relax today. Recuperate."

"Like I said, I'm fine."

Jared smiled. "You know," he said as he turned to leave, "you have a lot of your father in you."

25

The shuttle banked right, and the Dark Mountain, surrounded by its vast web of death-dealing antennas, crept into view. Kate stared at the hideous mass of granite and steel and shivered. She turned away from the window and glanced at the other passengers: ordinary people, bound for their day jobs at the ARC Project.

How ironic that she and David had put their lives in peril photographing the mountain a few days earlier, and now she would actually be entering the place—no cameras allowed.

Her position as assistant video editor would begin this morning. With luck, she'd manage to steal incriminating data. More likely, she'd end up floating in the North Atlantic, her veins popping from her skin and her eyes bulging like a dead salmon's.

She thought of David. He would shortly be taking a different shuttle flight, beginning his job as an ARC security guard trainee. She had no idea if they would see each other inside the gargantuan facility, or how they would smuggle data out.

She turned again toward the window. As the shuttle descended, hundreds of the enormous geodesic domes housing the antennas rose to meet them. Great bundles of gray metal tubes, the "spider legs" she and David had seen in her video, erupted from the mountainside, shot straight out for what seemed like a mile, and dropped down to domed concrete structures hunching up from the ground. Smaller tubes fanned out from the concrete enclosures and ran above the roads—spider web over spider web.

The plane touched down and taxied past jumbo-jet sized hangars. Executive jets, helicopters, and light planes lined the tarmac near the glass and concrete terminal.

They disembarked and passed through closely monitored search stations inside the terminal, where X-ray machines and other instruments scanned their belongings and, Kate thought, probably their bodies. Armed guards directed her and the other new hires through a set of sliding doors to an outside waiting area. A few minutes later, they boarded a twenty-passenger van and drove onto a wide blacktop road leading toward the mountain.

Row upon row of the towering geodesic domes passed by, curving into the distance. A maze of interconnecting tubes stretched overhead like prison-cell bars, casting slanted shadows across their path. An occasional Humvee cruised past, occupied by stern-looking men in blue uniforms.

The Dark Mountain loomed ahead.

The road slanted up between mounds of granite rubble and stopped before the massive steel door recessed into the mountainside. Rust bled from the rivets around its perimeter, staining its circular face. As the van approached, a rectangular slit appeared at the door's foot, and a section slid soundlessly back and up—a door within a door—admitting them into the mountain's dark interior.

Kate gasped. Through the van's windshield she saw a vast, circular cavern, its black granite walls rising beyond her field of vision. A gigantic cylinder of polished metal climbed from a shaft in the cavern's center and thrust upward, disappearing into distant gloom. The van turned left onto a road hugging the wall and pulled into a parking area overhanging the cavern floor some two hundred feet below. The passengers disembarked and walked to the railing, where warm, humid air blew upward, smelling of oil and chemicals.

Kate swept her gaze across the enormous space. Oversized elevators crawled up and down steel tracks, moving through pockets of light cast by rows of construction lamps. Arc welders flashed and crackled from scaffolding high above, miniature lightning storms hurling cascades of molten metal through the shadowed void.

She felt, as well as heard, a slow, rhythmic thrumming that rolled and thumped through the tenebrous chamber like a heartbeat. Columns of steam boiled up through glowing gratings in the distant floor, the vapor lit from within by a red glare that expanded and faded with the cadent rumble.

"Hi everyone," came a cheerful voice. A young woman carrying a clipboard and wearing a blue blazer motioned the group together. "My name is Mindy. I just want to see if we're all here before we go to the administration center." She sounded like a cheerleader at a college football game stirring up the crowd for another round of "Go team, go…" She called out their names, checking them off the list. "Please stay right with me. There are a lot of restricted areas, and we need to pick up your badges."

Mindy led them along the marked walkway toward a normal-sized door set into the granite. Kate glanced back at the enormous chamber and sucked in a deep breath to steady her pounding heart; not only had she met the enemy, she had jumped down its throat.

The door hissed shut behind her.

*   *   *

During orientation, she learned that ARC was divided into vast, excavated sections within the mountain, just as Ben had shown during the meeting with Constellation. Manufacturing and some employee housing were in the outside facilities. The video production offices, where she would be working, were inside the mountain on the same level as administration and personnel. Most of the other areas were off limits, and she was told nothing about them.

She received her photo I.D. badge: Code Green, a low-level clearance. Code Black was the highest, giving the holder access to the entire mountain. She followed a woman from Personnel down a featureless corridor, and they stopped before one of the numbered steel doors. "Let's try your badge," the woman said.

Kate swiped the plastic rectangle across the electronic reader and the door clicked open. She entered the Video Production and Interactive Media Department.

The clatter of keyboards emanated from the dozen or so cubicles in the dimly lit space. The air felt cold compared to the cavern's smothering atmosphere. Kate walked down a carpeted corridor leading to a row of offices. Sounds of animated conversation came through an open door. A man stormed out as she approached. "Excuse me," he said brusquely, brushing past.

A short, stocky woman stood in the middle of the cluttered room, staring at a fat notebook. Kate knocked, and the woman looked up sharply with frowning, dark eyes. "Yes?"

"I'm Ka—," Kate caught herself. *God, I can't make* that *mistake!* "I'm Donna Reston, the new assistant editor."

The woman's frown disappeared, replaced by a tight-lipped smile. "I'm Carla Torrance," she said with a Valley-Girl tinged accent. She swept a curl of mousy brown hair from her forehead and offered her hand. "I'm the producer. Glad you're here. We have a lot of work to do."

Kate smiled and accepted the handshake.

"Come on," Carla said. "I'll introduce you to the editor."

They entered a gray room filled with racks of video equipment and an elaborate digital editing system. A skeletally thin man with a shaved head turned away from a pair of glowing monitors and stood.

"This is Skip Rowan," Carla said. "He'll give you your assignments."

Rowan held out a large, bony hand and smiled.

Carla turned and walked away, peeling back notebook pages. "We have a production meeting in an hour," she said without looking back.

Skip shrugged. "Don't mind her. She's always like that. Probably because we're always behind schedule."

He introduced Kate to her own, smaller editing station in the adjacent conference room. "It's temporary," he said. "We don't have space to put you anywhere else."

"It's fine," Kate said, sitting down.

Skip handed her a script. "I need you to read this and make a shot list, then assemble the stills and clips." He typed a command and a list came up. "The computers are networked, and scripts, documentary footage, graphics, and so forth are in the master file. You can access most of what you need, but if you find something requiring a higher clearance, tell me and maybe I can get it for you."

Skip left her alone. The room was quiet except for the low vibration that seemed to permeate the mountain. She opened the script and read. The video was a propaganda piece, probably destined for primetime TV. It hyped the ARC project as a wonderful tool that could not only protect the Internet, but also disrupt enemy communications in time of war. Hurwitz, Greggson, and Crotty were portrayed as crusading heroes. Of course, it said nothing about ARC's lethal capabilities—or that these crusading heroes murdered people.

She heard voices outside. The hour had fled, and it was already time for the meeting. She stood and met the production team as they filed into the room: two writers, two graphic artists, three programmers, and a cinematographer. Carla served as producer and director.

They sat at the round table and discussed assignments and deadlines. Two documentaries were underway: the one Kate was working on, intended for the general public, and a classified presentation Carla had nearly finished. A possible bonus: Carla would be taping glamour shots of the antennas this afternoon. Kate wanted in on this, but she said nothing, not wanting to seem too eager.

At noon they rode up two floors to a spacious cafeteria with counters offering everything from sandwiches to elaborate plate lunches. Kate chose soup and a salad, the butterflies teasing her stomach having curbed her appetite, and engaged in idle chat with her coworkers. They seemed like decent people, and under other circumstances she might have enjoyed working with them. Did any of them know the truth about ARC? She steered the conversation away from personal questions and instead toward the nature of their current projects, deadlines, hardware, and software.

After lunch, she copied the clips and stills for the documentary onto a CD-ROM and walked to the editing room. An animated graphic for EleKtrum Corporation was rotating on Skip Rowan's monitor, the stylized E forming and superimposing over a sphere that represented the earth.

She handed him the CD. Still watching the screen, Rowan accepted the disc and placed it in the drawer, where it joined a haphazard pile of others. "Okay, thanks," he said in a monotone.

Kate nodded at the monitor. "Is this the documentary?"

"Yeah, I'll show you what we've got so far."

He scrolled to the beginning and started playback. A three-dimensional A-R-C rotated on a blue screen. Letters dropped in, completing the title: "Auroral Research Center." A blank screen came next—space reserved for Hurwitz's speech—then a simple animated drawing of the ARC installation.

Kate was amazed. A presentation this amateurish wouldn't pass Production 101 in film school. She fished for an opportunity. "Do we have the industrial footage yet?"

"Carla's shooting the antenna scenes today. I've got some stills…" He rummaged through the pile of CDs, found a disc and downloaded the file: underlit, poorly framed shots of unidentifiable electronic apparatus. "Not very good, are they?"

"I can shoot better," Kate said. "And I can light a scene ten times better."

"You know lighting?"

"Cameras too."

Rowan thought for a moment. "Let me talk to Carla." He punched a number. A few minutes later, Kate was set; she would join the shoot: glamour shots of the antennas in an hour.

"It would help me plan lighting if I knew what the antennas looked like, size, that sort of thing," she told Rowan.

He glanced at her green security badge. "The data's inside a file that requires a higher clearance. I'll get it for you."

She stepped politely away so he could enter the access code without her observing. But she managed to glimpse a heading: *Library*, she thought it said. A drawer slid back. *He must be reading a number off a list*. His keyboard clacked for a moment, and he turned to her. "It's ready now, just look for a file named Antennas."

She thanked him, returned to her computer, and accessed the file. The photos appeared: poor quality exterior shots of the domes, and more fuzzy close-ups. She pressed her lips together in a tight smile.

She could make herself useful here, maybe get access to classified data. She left the room to select lighting equipment for the shoot.

* * *

Kate emerged from an elevator into the heat and gloom of the great cavern. An electric shuttle took her, Carla, and the cinematographer to an exposed cargo elevator resting on the floor two hundred yards away. A small tractor pulling a trailer laden with video and lighting equipment rattled onto the platform, disconnected its load, and drove off.

Kate and her coworkers stepped onto the elevator, and two men banged safety railings into place around its edge. A motor whined, and they accelerated upward. Kate looked down. Far below, the red glow still pulsed from the shaft in the chamber's center, its powerful vibration throbbing and reverberating above the ambient noise.

They passed level after level, layers of rough metamorphic rock scrolling past in a black, crooked smear. The platform jerked to a stop below an enormous ring encircling the central shaft. Kate counted eight equally-spaced tubes that radiated from the ring and pierced the chamber walls. She estimated they had climbed more than five hundred feet above the cavern floor, and there were still uncounted levels fading dizzily into the gloom above.

The platform gate swung open, and they stepped off and clattered along an expanded-metal walkway bolted into to the granite wall. Air rushed upward in a hot, howling wind that snatched at their clothing and shredded speech. Kate stayed away from the walkway's edge and its inadequate railing.

Carla shouted over the noise. "This antenna is shut down, but be sure to inspect your badges every half hour or so. Remember, the little square panel will turn black if you're overexposed."

Great, Kate thought. *What does* overexposed *really mean? Is it like in a nuclear plant, where a badge tells you why you're barfing and your hair's falling out in big chunks?*

Carla paused before a hangar-sized door and swiped her badge across the security lock. Riding on tracks recessed into the floor and ceiling, the steel door split and rumbled apart, its two sections parting like jaws. Air funneled into the widening maw with a long, deep moan.

Carla led them through the opening and down a broad tunnel, their footsteps echoing hollowly from the surrounding rock. They finally passed through another door and stepped beneath the curved ceiling of a vast geodesic dome. The translucent panels comprising the structure glowed a dull amber, probably, Kate thought, from sunlight impinging upon the opposite side.

In the dome's center loomed an enormous, dark mass. A machine. The antenna. *No. Not an antenna, a grasping metal claw, with long, spidery fingers opened wide and rigid, raking the ether.* Kate and the others approached the dome's far end, and as the light crept behind them they could see the apparatus more clearly. Cold crawled through Kate's veins. *There you are—there you are—you big, ugly son of a bitch.*

She knew, beyond instinct, the thing before her, or one of its clones, had killed her husband and everyone aboard the plane he piloted. This horrid-looking, so-called antenna was one of the slaughtering organs of the monstrous machine inside the mountain, a steel beast that dispensed lethal doses of microwave radiation. *How many more would it kill—had it killed?*

A technician in a blue jump suit was talking. "… made of a titanium composite, and can rotate almost instantly on an X-Y axis. The 'fingers'—that's what we call them—articulate to change focus. They take the place of the fixed parabolic reflector you see in a typical microwave antenna."

"Let's see it in motion," Carla said, moving her hand in a circle. "We'll get the whole antenna, then some close ups."

The technician climbed a few steps to a control panel. "Keep behind the red line," he cautioned.

Kate backed behind the narrow stripe painted on the concrete floor. Massive hydraulics droned, and the machine's eight long, skeletal fingers clenched inward, folding tightly around a central cone, where the "palm" would be, then flexed instantly outward and back—a threatening, snatching motion. Kate instinctively stepped away.

An electric motor growled with ferocious power, and the digits gimbaled through a ninety-degree arc with terrifying speed. The antenna instantly reversed direction and, with a great *whoosh*, rotated back, creating a small windstorm. It reminded Kate of standing too close to a thundering locomotive.

The technician brought the antenna to a halt. Grips entered the tunnel, towing the lighting gear on rattling carts. They weren't real grips, Kate knew, just a couple of hard hats sent to muscle the equipment around. She had to show them how to erect the C-stands, attach the lights, run the cable.

Carla chose a camera position twenty feet up on a pneumatic scaffold, and Kate placed floodlights around the antenna's base to lighten shaded areas. The cinematographer shot seven different angles as the antenna swept through various patterns. They wrapped at six o'clock and soon were in the editing room reviewing footage.

Although she was tired, desperate for David's company, and worried about Mark and her parents, Kate volunteered to stay late and copy the culled shots onto a disc. She would have the production office to herself. And maybe a chance to access the confidential files. Carla logged her in for the evening and left.

First, she needed something to eat. She found her way to the cafeteria and selected soup and a sandwich. The room was practically deserted. She sat at a table in the corner and stretched, trying to release some of the debilitating tension that had seized her. Her thoughts wandered to David—

Sudden loud voices yanked her back. Two men had entered: one wore a business suit; the other, a very large, bald man, wore a white lab coat. They grabbed snacks and drinks and walked beyond a partition into an area reserved for executives. They hadn't noticed her, and that was fine with Kate. She merely wanted to eat in peace and remain undiscovered.

Then she began to pick out pieces of their conversation: "reduced average gain…override the neural pathways…induced seizure… cerebral hemispheres."

One voice was droning and pedantic, like a bored history teacher driving a classroom of eighth graders into a coma. The other was *lispy*—not effeminate—*hissy*, reptilian, with drawn-out s's. It carried a disturbing force. Their words occasionally became sharp, argumentative. Kate lost interest in her sandwich. She got up quietly and carried her tray to a table near the partition.

The man with the pedantic voice was speaking. "… long term effects. Increase the amplitude and risk detection. We've already discussed that. I say give it more time."

The other voice hissed, "I demand another test group. I can prove the new sequence works faster." There was a rustle of paper. "I stimulated cognitive aberration and deep paranoia with fifty milligauss in under eight hours, with no discernable edema."

"What about the mortality studies?"

The hissing voice lisped through a mouthful of chips he masticated as loudly as a gravel truck. "Stimpfulated fibrilathion at three-hundred methers with a ten kilowatt pulse—twice the range of the present Scanners."

"Good."

Kate cocked her head. Scanners. Did he say *Scanners*?

The lispy one noisily slurped a drink and continued. "But if they want guarantees, they better let me have another large scale test, and soon."

"I'll talk to Krohner myself. Send me the data tonight."

Chairs scraped against the floor. They were leaving. Not wanting to be seen, Kate got up and walked quickly toward the tray return and tossed the remains of her dinner in the trash. She turned and almost collided with a white lab coat. She exhaled a brief "Oh," that was more like a squeak.

"Welll," came the serpent voice. Kate looked up, intending to apologize, but the words jammed in her throat. A pair of oversized eyeballs leered down at her. They rolled and goggled as if detached from their sockets, their movement exaggerated and magnified by thick lenses set in big, round wireframe glasses. The man had a huge body and a small, bald head.

"Ms. Reston, Ms. Donna Reston," the man said, reading her I.D. badge. The pronunciation sounded *Mizz Resston*.

"I'm sorry. I was just leaving," Kate managed. She stepped back and started around the man, but he moved sideways and blocked her.

"Oh, that'ss perfectly all right." The goggle-eyes roamed over her body.

Kate shuddered. His androgynous face was round and hairless, the skin pasty, almost albino white. His lips were fat and discolored, as if he had been on the losing end of a fistfight. The man's I.D. badge had a black border, the top security clearance. The photograph did not improve his appearance: *Dr. Malcolm Fechter.*

Kate smiled nervously. "Dr. ah…Fechter. Hello." She offered her hand.

Fechter seized it in a large, ham-handed embrace, rolling and squeezing it instead of shaking. His bulbous stare traveled down to her hand, then back to her eyes. When he blinked, it was like snapping the shutters of a Klieg light. He held her hand far too long.

"You're new here. What do you do, Donna?"

"I work in the video production department." Kate hoped her revulsion didn't show. "I'm an editor, but I really do a little of everything."

"Good, very good." The sibilant voice became soft, almost mesmerizing. "And what are you working on now?"

The man in the suit stood nearby, rocking on the balls of his feet. "Malcolm, we have to go," he said impatiently.

Kate stammered. "I'm not really sure if I should say what I'm working on. No offense—"

Fechter replied as if he were complimenting a six-year-old for having drawn a picture of a horse in art class. "Oh, *very* good. And who might your supervisor be?"

"Carla Torrance."

The eyes rolled. The shutter-eyelids blinked. "It's been sssoo very nice meeting you, Donna."

Kate forced another smile. She noticed small red blotches and smears on Fechter's white coat. *Blood?* As he turned to leave, an odor swirled in the disturbed air—a biological smell. *What is it: kennel, zoo?*

She lingered at the soft drink machine, hoping she wouldn't end up in the elevator with the two men. *God, this place is a nightmare.* She made her way back to the editing room, regretting having worked late. She was exhausted, and her nerves were frayed. *Just get the job done and get out.*

It took an hour to cull and copy the day's shots. She labeled the disc and placed it on top of Rowan's desk. She glanced around the room, listened for approaching footsteps, then felt beneath his desk drawer and pulled out the sliding shelf. The codes, a list of acronyms and ten-digit numbers, were taped to the rear of the shelf. *Some security.*

She sat down and accessed the network. *Here's where my palms start to sweat.* She found *Library: Video/Graphics* and clicked. It asked for a code. *Hurry!* In half an hour, she'd have to catch the last shuttle back to Anchorage.

Maybe Rowan had the main code written somewhere. She flipped up the bottom of the list. Sure enough, there was another number. She tried it and the folder opened, revealing a file labeled *Index.* An alphabetized list of subjects appeared. Where to go? She scrolled rapidly down; it was mostly technical data she didn't understand. Remembering the discussion she overheard in the cafeteria, she looked for *Scanner.* She found it and opened the file.

Thumbnail shots of a gray panel van appeared. Interior shots showed electronic gear. An icy hand stroked the back of her neck: *a van like this was outside my house the night we had the hallucinations.* No time to peruse the file. She copied it to a disc.

Another quick look: she typed in "Malcolm Fechter." A file came up. She glanced quickly down the list, clicked on "Laboratory." Photo thumbnails of video clips appeared: experiments on animals, a rhesus monkey strapped to a steel chair. She played the clip: Fechter adjusted a miniature version of the antenna they had videotaped earlier. He pointed it at a rhesus from about fifty feet away. The antenna began to rotate. The monkey screeched and thrashed. A screen, a hospital monitor, showed phosphorescent tracings going crazy. The rhesus screamed hideously, then went rigid and slumped. The tracings flatlined.

Another scene, another monkey. This time, the creature stiffened immediately, its head thrown back, body jerking against the restraints. The tracings were practically off the scale. A close up of the monkey's head: the pitiable eyes turning white, blood bubbling from its nose.

Kate staggered to her feet, knocking the chair back. The room tilted, bile rising in her throat. *This is what you did to my husband, you* monsters! She leaned against the desk with one arm, her other across her chest. *Stay calm! The security camera is behind you.* She forced herself back to the computer. Hands shaking, she copied the file to another disc, exited the network, and returned the screen to the editing program.

Back in the conference room, she secreted the discs at the bottom of a stack of blanks, hoping she'd find a way to sneak them out later. No more time, the shuttle would be stopping any minute outside the administration center. She grabbed her purse and coat and ran down the hall to the elevator.

26

Gray clouds descended Pikes Peak like a fleet of attacking Zeppelins, deepening the morning chill and stirring a stiff breeze. Mark and Alex zipped up their windbreakers and walked across the yard toward the barn. Alex tapped the boom box cradled under Mark's left arm. "Got any CDs?" Mark turned the stereo on and a mellow Beatles tune wafted from the speakers. Alex wrinkled his nose. "Elevator music. Got anything *hard*? Metal, punk…"

Mark knew just the song. He held the box up, punched in another track, and turned the volume up. Alex listened for a moment, his head of spiked hair bobbing. "Oh, *yeah*—that rocks! What is that?"

"Helter Skelter."

"Who did that?"

Mark couldn't believe Alex didn't know. "Beatles, man."

"They got any more?"

"A couple."

"Can I borrow your blasterbox?"

"Better use the headphones, or Professor O'Hanlon will throw you out the window."

Alex accepted the box and donned the earbuds. He continued toward the barn, his torso pumping to the beat. "Rocks, man, really *rocks*."

They found O'Hanlon on the second level, hunched over the big control panel. He looked up. "Well, it's about time."

Alex tugged the headphones from his ears. "Give us a break. Mark played commando all night."

O'Hanlon glanced at Mark. "I heard about what you did. You're a brave man, and I'm thankful everyone's okay."

Alex gave Mark's shoulder a light punch. "Tough guy."

Mark shrugged. He wished everyone would forget about his so-called heroics and shut up.

O'Hanlon plucked a manual from a shelf beside the console and opened it. "We're testing some of the motor drives and relays today. I want both of you to act as observers in case anything goes wrong." He settled into the chair and faced the controls. "We might as well start right here." He threw a switch, and indicator lamps dotting the control panel's ebony surface winked on. Another switch snapped. The brass globe beyond the console hummed and rotated a half turn on its gimbals. Bands of tiny red lights raced silently around its surface and intersected in the middle of an area marked "Indian Ocean."

"Did you figure out what that's for?" Mark asked.

O'Hanlon nodded. "Tesla called it a node finder. It shows where the radio signal will go." He pointed to two knobs. "You set the coordinates—longitude and latitude—here.

Alex shook his head. "That's impossible. There's no antenna array. You can't beam a signal without a directional system. And even if you had one, you couldn't send it to a precise point on the other side of the world."

O'Hanlon stared at Alex, eyebrows raised. "You have a surprising understanding of electronics for such a young man."

Alex's eyes shifted to the floor. Compliments must be rare for him, Mark thought. Besides, they didn't fit his renegade-hacker image. But he could tell O'Hanlon's remark had been appreciated.

"Tesla probably used the same mysterious method to send energy to the train," O'Hanlon continued. "I don't understand how he accomplished that, either. However, he was a genius in using resonance. Maybe it has something to do with that."

"What's resonance?" Mark asked.

O'Hanlon turned to him. "Resonance is sympathetic vibration. For example, if you place two guitars close together and play an 'A' string on one guitar, the 'A' string on the other guitar will vibrate. An opera singer can shatter a wine glass if her voice reaches the glass's natural resonant frequency. In radio, it means that one circuit is in tune with another.

"Tesla discovered the earth has an electrical resonant frequency of eight hertz." He gestured to the control console. "Hence the prominence of the numeral eight on that big dial in the center. Maybe Tesla used resonance somehow to guide the signal or to form nodes at specific locations." He swept his hand out toward the transmitter. "This machine uses an ingenious combination of quarter-wavelength resonant coils to create millions of volts of high frequency energy. That voltage appears on the big torus overhead, which acts, in part, as a top-loaded antenna."

Mark glanced at Alex. "That's exactly what I thought."

"Totally."

O'Hanlon chuckled. "Well, we don't have to understand everything in order to perform the tests."

*   *   *

O'Hanlon assigned Mark and Alex areas of the Magnifying Transmitter to observe as he activated parts of the system. Mark took his position beside the huge primary coil, Alex by the rotary spark gap.

"I'm resetting the longitude and latitude," O'Hanlon shouted.

Mark could hear a faint hum and click as the brass globe locked into a new position. The room suddenly became alive with the snapping of relays and the whirring of motors. Above his head, copper spheres and inductors shifted like celestial bodies in a clockwork solar system. Gears began to grind, and Mark watched as the huge primary coil creaked ponderously upward, edging closer to the secondary. After a moment, the noise and motion ceased.

"Take cover," O'Hanlon shouted. "I'm starting the rotary gap."

Standing on a platform supported by four high-voltage insulators, the rotary spark gap dominated the northwest corner of the room, its two enormous motor-driven disks bristling with spiked electrodes. Thick black cables radiated from the apparatus in precise, parallel lines and passed overhead, routing to other components. Mark joined Alex behind one of the power transformers. The heavy steel box would shield them in case the disks shattered or anything else let go.

"The rotary gap is crucial," Alex explained. "When the transmitter is switched on—which he is not going to do right now—voltage builds up on the capacitors and fires through the rotary spark gap into the coils. It's a primitive way of creating electrical oscillations."

A relay snapped and the rotary gap began to turn with a low whirring sound. The two great disks gathered speed, the purring of the electrodes climbing to harmonic, high-pitched notes. The sound reminded Mark of the big saw blade he had seen at a lumber mill just before it made contact with a log—a powerful, insistent vibration filled with a sense of impending danger. The disks required several minutes to wind down after O'Hanlon shut the power off.

"Steady as a rock," Alex shouted.

"Good," returned O'Hanlon. "That leaves just a few more tests."

*   *   *

A sudden sound rolled against the barn's ancient walls. Thunder. O'Hanlon listened for a moment, then shouted. "Stay away from the coils, fellows. I don't know how this machine will react in a thunderstorm." He muttered to himself. "It's probably safer in here than…"

He stopped in mid-sentence. Clacking sounds emanated from below like an invasion of giant crickets. Relays were triggering. The indicator on one of the large dials began rhythmically sweeping back and forth. Motors hummed, and the coils and spheres shifted.

O'Hanlon stared at the transmitter for a moment, then whispered in amazement: "It's adjusting in response to the storm." He switched the power off and the activity stopped. He spread his hands on the console and sighed loudly, staring at the controls, then finally looked up and shouted. "Testing is over for a while, gentlemen."

Rain beat a light patter against the roof as O'Hanlon walked into the office. He lowered a stack of manuals onto his desk, sat down, and began reading. There had to be a reason why the control relays activated during the thunderstorm.

Below, someone strummed a guitar. A second guitar began, then a harmonica, then a chorus: *Ayyy Yayyy Yay yayyyy. Ayyy Yayyy con Dios.* A dog—no—*two* dogs howled. The guitars abruptly stopped as Jared's voice called out: "Fellas, if we can get a couple of coyotes to join in, you'll really round out your harmony."

O'Hanlon laughed and closed his manual with a snap. No more studying today, at least until the Mexican band finished. He wandered to the railing and looked down. The musicians started wailing away again. Mark and Jose strummed the guitars and sang, while Buddy and Higgins supplied additional vocals.

Alex came up beside him, his voice rising above the melodic strains of *La Cucaracha.* "Professor O'Hanlon, if Tesla built all of this before the vacuum tube was invented, then what are those big glass cylinders near the rotary gap?"

O'Hanlon was pleased to field an intelligent question, albeit a difficult one. "I've wondered about those myself. Tesla called them circuit controllers, and I assume they act as voltage limiters or sensitive relays."

"They glowed when you turned on the rotary spark gap."

O'Hanlon frowned. "That's curious." He thought for a moment, then grabbed the wiring schematics and headed for the stairs. "Let's have a look."

*   *   *

Ten massive glass tubes stood like sentinels near the rotary spark gap, fat copper cables snaking in from overhead and attaching to studs protruding from their domed ends. O'Hanlon reached out and touched a gleaming tube, then snatched his hand quickly away. "It's still warm."

He leaned forward and peered through the smoky glass at the unusual arrangement of metal elements inside. "I will admit, the electrode arrangement looks somewhat similar to a conventional vacuum tube." Unfolding the schematics, he traced the cable pathways with his finger. "They're connected to the second power transformer and the spark gap…" A sudden realization flashed through his mind. The wiring configuration suggested one thing, and if it were true, another incredible discovery would be added to the growing list of impossibilities. He turned and strode rapidly toward the stairs. "Follow me."

O'Hanlon stopped beside the control panel, grabbed a flashlight from the shelf, and dropped to his knees. Alex knelt beside him. The flashlight beam illuminated the inside of a large metal box covered with screened cooling vents. A row of glass tubes, much smaller than the ones behind the rotary gap, glittered back. "I don't believe it," O'Hanlon gasped. "Shielded wires run from the tubes to a set of jacks on the control panel. Know what I think this is?"

Alex shrugged.

"An audio amplifier…"

"And the box downstairs is a modulator," Alex blurted. "I'll bet Tesla designed this thing to transmit *voice*."

O'Hanlon stood. "But think of the implications. The vacuum tube wasn't even invented until 1906. Practical voice broadcasting didn't happen until around 1915."

"One way to find out," Alex said. He walked to the railing and shouted.

The music ceased.

"Mark, Bring your ghetto blaster up here."

"Awww, man, just when we were startin' to *wail*."

Mark appeared a few minutes later. "I was recording, you know."

O'Hanlon quickly attached the stereo's output to the jacks on the console. He flipped several switches, and the tubes in the black box glowed a faint orange.

Alex rushed toward the stairs. "When I tell you, turn it on."

Mark turned to O'Hanlon. "This isn't going to blow up my stereo is it?"

"We'll find out."

Alex shouted, and Mark punched the stereo's play button. After a moment, a strange humming issued from below. Alex whooped. "All riiight!"

O'Hanlon followed Mark downstairs. Alex was watching a large solenoid attached to a mechanism on the spark gap. The assembly pistoned and vibrated in a faithful, mechanical reproduction of their recorded song.

"It is a modulator," Alex beamed. "It means the Magnifying Transmitter can broadcast audio. If we applied full power, I'll bet you could pick it up on your dentures in Timbuktu."

O'Hanlon watched in stunned silence as the system oscillated to the music. It was unbelievable, shocking. If the vacuum tubes were truly made by Tesla, they predated DeForest's crude but epochal invention by at least fifteen years.

He finally spoke. "This is a magnificent find, but I'm afraid we can't use it."

"Why not?" Mark asked.

"Because there's no harmonic suppression. It would swamp every AM band for miles around, maybe even FM."

Alex said, "We could try it at low power first."

O'Hanlon nodded. "Maybe later. Let's concentrate on finishing the tests. Then we'll turn on the high voltage."

Alex's eyes gleamed. "Yeah, then we'll see some *real* fireworks."

The tape finished and the room fell silent, the echoes lingering. The rain had stopped and capricious rays of yellow sunlight slanted through the high windows. O'Hanlon looked around at the big coils and patted his beard thoughtfully. Privately, he harbored a growing apprehension about the machine. It was full of anomalies and strange physics he didn't understand.

Yeah, then we'll see some real *fireworks*.

27

The antenna moved menacingly. The talking heads talked, smiled, gestured. Skip looked up from the monitor. "Good work, Kate. You can edit this whole segment."

She smiled, pretending to be pleased. She prayed no one would discover she had accessed classified files. She and David had argued about it last night. He had admonished her for digging into the files so soon, saying that security programs would log every keystroke she made. He decided their mission was in danger, that this was their last day at ARC. He had insisted they leave Alaska immediately.

But Kate had snapped back at him, saying that if things were too tough for him, he could run. She had immediately apologized. He was right. She had acted too quickly. But she desperately wanted more information. She had to link the deaths to ARC, Hurwitz, Krohner, and Greggson, and she *had* to get the data out. She and David compromised: they would stay for a week, carefully gathering information, and search for a way to smuggle data from the mountain. Then they'd make a break for Colorado Springs.

"Carla wants you on another shoot this afternoon," Skip continued.

"Of what?"

"She didn't say." He paused. "Now that you're here, things are moving faster. But don't expect to hear any compliments, she's not one to dish them out."

*   *   *

Carla buzzed Kate at her desk just before the noon break. "We'll be shooting the central computer system at one-thirty. It's a big area, so bring all the lights."

Kate thought for a moment. "We'll probably need to supplement with construction lights. We can adjust the color later."

"Fine."

Shortly after lunch, Kate and the production team rode across the dark cavern floor in a shuttle, passing within a hundred feet of the huge central shaft and the steaming grate that surrounded it. A pulsating crimson light leaped from the depths, fanned through the grate to the cavern walls, and clawed the shaft in slashing, angular patterns. The powerful vibration from its source shook the granite beneath them and penetrated into the vehicle itself.

They rounded the enormous cylinder, and Kate stiffened as she saw three vehicles queued up beyond the rising shroud of steam— gray vans with dark panoramic windows in their sides. *Scanners.*

A door in the cavern wall rolled up, and as the lead van drove through, she caught a glimpse of a room filled with electronic equipment. A fourth van entered the lineup. How many of those things were there? Dozens—hundreds? What was inside them? What could they really do? All that information might be on the CDs she had made, but she might never get them outside the facility. She touched the security badge clipped to her blouse. The area she was traveling through was beyond her clearance. David would kill her when he found out, but she knew what her next bit of espionage would be.

A trip into a tunnel and up three flights on a cargo elevator brought them to the central data processing room. "Room" was a gross understatement. The Cray computers were in a space bigger than a football field. *Hollywood itself couldn't light this properly.*

Carla opted for timed-exposure still shots and footage of a small area of the computer system. It was amazing, Kate thought as she adjusted the lights, how visually dull one of mankind's greatest technological wonders could be—row after row of charcoal-gray boxes five feet tall and three feet wide.

Six o'clock approached. They would have to complete shooting tomorrow, having taken most of their time running cable and setting up lights. Kate volunteered for another late evening.

*   *   *

She cautiously checked the cafeteria to make sure Malcom Fechter wasn't there, grabbed a sandwich, and hurried back to her office. Fifteen minutes later, she rode the elevator down to the main cavern floor and turned left onto the elevated walkway ringing the wall. The Scanners she had seen earlier had been parked about eight-hundred feet away. She nodded as she passed various personnel: technicians, laborers, and some sullen security guards who seemed to scrutinize her badge as they walked by.

Pedestrian traffic thinned, and she finally saw the ghost-gray form of a Scanner on the floor below. It faced the door in the cavern wall, evidently waiting its turn to drive through. A flashing sign on the stairway warned: *Blue Security Only Beyond this Point*. She was forbidden to enter. She glanced around to make sure no one was watching and walked boldly past the winking light and down the steps. As she approached the van, she felt the heart-pounding exhilaration borne from a mix of terror and anticipation, a reaction that always occurred when she defied logic and took risks in pursuit of a story.

The cab looked empty. She opened the passenger door, climbed in, and squeezed between the seats into the cargo area. On her left, a pedestal chair faced an electronic console resembling a radar set. Beyond that was a conical enclosure of perforated metal, its wide end attached to the van's wall. She edged closer and peered through the holes. A chill slithered up her back; inside the metal cage, the black, spindly fingers of a claw antenna, a miniature version of the ones surrounding the mountain, spread wide before the van's panoramic window.

Kate almost cried out when the driver-side door suddenly opened. She dropped down and balled herself into the shadows as a man climbed behind the steering wheel and started the engine.

The overhead door in the cavern wall rumbled open and the van drove through it into brighter light. Finding herself now exposed, Kate crawled past the antenna and wriggled into a small space between the metal cage and a black box that rose to the vehicle's roof. Through the one-way panoramic window, she glimpsed humanoid figures, like test dummies, arranged at various distances throughout the deep chamber.

The van stopped. She squinted through the cage's metal perforations and watched as the driver climbed into the back and sat at the control console. She held her breath. *If he looks directly at me, I'm dead.*

He flipped switches and the panel lights winked on with a hum. The screen lit, washing the van's interior in a green glow. Kate stifled a cry as the box she had jammed herself against made a droning sound and shuddered against her body. *It must be some kind of generator.*

She heard the man say, "Neural detection sequence," and then call out distance and degrees. An eerie pulsing sound filled the van. It had the cadence of a human heartbeat, but with an electronic overtone. Were they able to locate humans by detecting their victim's beating hearts? The thought made her flesh crawl.

Inches away, the antenna adjusted with a sudden clench and began to slowly rotate—not like a typical radar antenna, but around its central axis like the blades of a fan. The man at the controls calmly said, "Attack sequence. Zero degrees, fifty meters," and the generator sound dropped in pitch, as if it were delivering power to a load.

A voice crackled through a speaker: "Kill confirmed. Go forty-five degrees, fifty meters." The antenna adjusted, and the "Kills" were repeated through 270 degrees of sweep and at different distances. *They're testing and calibrating,* Kate thought. The Scanners could apparently locate their human quarry with the neural detectors and then zap them at distances up to a hundred meters.

The man climbed back into the driver's seat and drove the van into another chamber. He climbed out, banging the door shut behind him. An overhead door closed, and Kate was left alone in quiet semi-darkness. She crawled forward and looked through the front window. Rows of vans and trucks of all sizes stretched ahead. *A parking lot for Scanners.* She climbed quietly out through the passenger door and rushed to an elevator on her left. She entered and punched *J*, the level of the video production offices, and gasped with relief when she stepped out into a hallway open to her security clearance.

A few minutes later, she dropped into her chair in the editing room, shaking, heart still racing. Even as she congratulated herself for having successfully completed her spy mission, she felt guilty and foolish. She had taken an unacceptable risk for very little gain. Her breathing finally slowed, the rush fading. Now she would play it safe, do her job and attract no attention, concentrate on finding a way to get the CDs to the outside world.

She knew that was a lie.

28

The wraparound console, with its rows of flickering video monitors, hovered like an electronic storm above the black marble floor. The rough granite walls climbed twenty feet to a ceiling of luminescent panels that cast a dim, shadowless light throughout the room. Other than the distant drone of the mountain's systems, the only sounds were the soft hiss of ventilation fans and the leathered creak of the swivel chair.

From this quiet workstation, Joseph Krohner could access every surveillance camera, computer, and electronic system in the project. Tapping into Cerberus's omniscient cybernetic probes, he could eavesdrop on communications and Internet traffic around the globe, interrupting or disrupting them as he pleased.

On a central LCD screen, he watched a heavy apparatus being slowly lowered onto its concrete pad inside an antenna dome. The apparatus was a special modulator—a product of Malcolm Fechter's research—that when activated could twist the antenna's powerful microwave signals into a mind-shattering beam similar to those emitted by the truck-mounted Scanners.

ARC's current weaponry could kill or destroy, but this new technology would allow its transmitters to project widely dispersed, non-lethal electromagnetic radiation that would eventually seize the minds of entire continents.

One of the monitors emitted a series of beeps. He leaned toward it: Security Breach. Krohner frowned as he read the data. Two infiltrators had been discovered. One, a female working in the video production office, had accessed highly-classified data. The computers had matched her photograph and voice print with those of a television anchor from Colorado Springs—none other than the widow of one Jack McCullough, whom ARC had eliminated two years ago, along with Senator Jeff Travis. The other infiltrator, a man hired as outside security, was apparently her partner. A detail had already been sent to arrest him. Special handling was planned for both of them.

Constellation, Krohner thought, his frown deepening. This had to be their work—that troublesome gaggle of hackers and Indians. They had stayed one jump ahead of Cerberus, had disseminated potentially damaging information. If they could insinuate spies into sensitive areas of the operation, what else could they manage?

Krohner would find out. He would take pleasure in hearing details of the two intruders' interrogation, as guided by the perversely sadistic genius of Dr. Malcolm Fechter.

29

With some trepidation, Kate had told David of her snooping inside the Scanner. She had expected him to blow his stack. Instead, he looked at her in exasperation and quietly said, "Do you have some kind of death wish? If we're caught...." He didn't finish the statement. She had agreed. She now concentrated on finding a way to smuggle out the stolen CDs. Without them, everything they had seen was hearsay, their mission a failure.

This morning, as she sat at the editing console, she reviewed her options. Sneaking a disc through security would be virtually impossible; the system could detect such media with special electronic scanners. She had no access to an outside phone line to upload the data, and no opportunity to secrete the CDs on a vehicle or person leaving the mountain, where they could retrieve them later. She couldn't go outside the mountain herself without being searched. There was one possibility: the high security personnel, the ones with the black ID cards, had direct lines to the Internet. But the only black-card holder she knew was the frighteningly strange and repulsive Dr. Malcolm Fechter.

She rifled through the stack of CDs on the storage shelf. The two she had hidden were still there, but she had to find a safer place for them. She casually removed them and walked to her computer, stealthily dropping them into her purse as she sat down.

She stared at the monitor. Could she fortify herself and contact Fechter, create some ruse to enter his office, get to his computer? No.

Too dangerous. Impossible. Another plan: she would skip lunch, and when the office was clear she would study the files she had stolen, try to remember the details, make notes, sketches. It would be better than nothing—or should she try Fechter after all?

At 10:30, her phone rang, and the decision was made for her: "Is this Mss. Donna Resston?"

Kate's breath caught in her throat. "Yes—Dr. Fechter—what can I do for you?"

"I understand you are accomplished in video and photography," came the soft, lisping voice. "I need your talents in recording some of my work."

Her mind raced. She winged it. "Why, ah, I'm on a project now. I'll need the producer's approval—"

"That will not be necessary. Bring video and lighting equipment. I will send someone for you in, say, an hour?"

"I suppose," she said weakly.

"Very well. I look forward to seeing you again, Mss. Resston."

Ice spiders crept across her flesh. *Okay, Ms. Investigative Reporter. Buckle your seat belt.*

She packed a video camera, tapes, and a small lighting kit, then spent the rest of the hour psyching herself up. At exactly 11:30 she heard a man speaking to her boss, Carla. The voice was odd, slow, every word carefully measured. "I'm here to escort Ms. Donna Reston to Dr. Malcolm Fechter."

A moment later, he entered the conference room. He was big, powerfully built, with a scalp-hugging burr cut. He wore the ubiquitous blue EleKtrum jump suit. His face was expressionless. Kate stood up and extended her hand. "Hi, I'm Donna Reston."

He grasped her hand mechanically. "Gart Morgan." He made no eye contact.

Kate hoped he didn't notice how nervous she was, but considering his demeanor, she wasn't sure he cared. She hoisted the camera bag over her shoulder. He grabbed the lighting kit by the handle and started out the door. "Please follow me, Ms. Reston."

They entered an elevator. Gart passed a card over the magnetic reader and pushed a button. They began descending.

He stared straight ahead, silent. Kate pushed her luck. "Do you work for Dr. Fechter?"

"I'm sorry, Ms. Reston, I can't answer any questions."

"Thought that might be the case," she mumbled.

His expression didn't change.

The doors opened onto a wide tunnel bored through the dark granite. Warm, moist air moaned along the corridor, tugging at her blouse and bleached hair. The mountain's thrumming heartbeat pounded louder.

They turned right, following the serpentine tunnel counterclockwise. Pervasive gloom sucked up the feeble light cast by rows of rectangular lamps dotting the walls. Pipes and conduit ran overhead, some gray, some glistening and silvery, and branched off here and there, curving smoothly into a wall or through the floor.

A yellow and black shuttle waited in an alcove to their right. Gart loaded the camera gear and slid into the driver's seat. "Please get in, Ms. Reston."

The motor whined, and they pulled into the tunnel, the tires humming loudly over the rough-textured floor. Numbered steel doors of various sizes appeared at regular intervals on both sides of the tunnel, each equipped with a magnetic card reader. Jiggling headlights appeared ahead, and a cart towing a trailer loaded with steel cylinders rattled past them. The other driver held up his hand. Gart returned the gesture without looking up.

Kate estimated they had driven about a quarter of a mile when they slowed and pulled into another alcove. They got out and he handed her the camera bag.

The door was on the right: D-60. Gart used his card and the door parted elevator style. Kate squinted at the bright, white room beyond. A haggard woman in a white uniform slouched behind a wraparound desk, staring at a monitor. She glanced at them briefly, then picked up a telephone. After a brief conversation, she mumbled, "It will be a few minutes."

Gart gestured to some chairs. "Sit here."

Kate put the camera bag down and sat. *What, no out of date Sports Illustrated?*

Gart sat down two chairs away, head forward, hands on his knees. Conversation was, no doubt, out of the question.

The woman's telephone beeped. "You can go in now."

A door to the left of the desk unlocked with a buzzing sound and slid open. Kate lifted the camera bag and followed Gart into a chamber no bigger than an elevator—an airlock? The door behind them closed while another opened into a sterile white hallway. *Nightmare Black or Mortuary White—decorator colors for ARC Mountain.*

The odor hit Kate like a solid wave: part zoo, part chemical, part something else. She stifled her gag reflex. Gart walked ahead, and Kate followed. A row of reinforced windows on her right looked into a wide room. Dogs, monkeys and other animals occupied cruelly small cages, some of the creatures curled into tight balls of fur, others staring sadly. An occasional cry pierced the thick glass.

Instrument trays and a stainless steel table glinted from an open area. Sinks, cabinets, and chemicals lined the wall. Kate half expected to see humans suspended in glass cylinders full of amber fluid, with wires and tubing snaking from their craniums...

Gart pushed a door open and they entered a large chamber. In the center of the room rested an operating table, its white covering starkly reflecting the bluish glare from the overhead lamps.

Kate's eyes were drawn to a dark corner, to a tall glass cylinder glowing beneath the narrow beam of a spotlight. She stared in horrified fascination at its fluid-suspended contents—the branching ivory tendrils of an exsected human nervous system. Thousands of the white strands crawled from the still-intact spinal cord and interlaced in a ghoulish outline of limbs, torso, and head. Eyeballs, still tethered to the optic nerve and brain, stared in lidless indifference from the frontal lobes.

Bell jars displayed masses of convoluted gray flesh: the brains of animals and humans. X-rays, CT-Scans, and transparencies of skulls and organs glowed from wall-mounted light boxes.

Kate looked to the right. A cone of light enclosed an angular stainless steel chair like the one she had seen in the classified video clip, the one with clamps and straps that had restrained monkeys while Fechter tortured their brains with radio waves. Only this one was different. It was larger.

A claw antenna, perhaps two feet in diameter, pointed at the steel chair. A thick black cable snaked from its bulbous back and entered a metal cabinet cluttered with knobs and switches. Near the cabinet's top, a large panel emitted a green phosphorescence.

Behind the chair, black pyramids of a flat-black material, like spikes of a giant meat tenderizer, studded the wall. Electronic equipment crowded the shelves: black and gray boxes with dials, lights, and wires. Stands held metal disks, parabolic reflectors, cones, and strange geometric shapes. A motor quietly purred. Something softly bubbled. Something faintly hissed.

Doors beyond the operating table slid apart.

Dr. Malcolm Fechter, sheathed in his stained white lab coat, stood in the dark opening, motionless, as if he were a wax museum's prize monster and the curtains had just parted to reveal him to a gasping crowd.

His lips separated and drew back, exposing teeth in a mockery of a grin. Huge body, small, bald head, with gimlet eyes magnified by round, thick lenses—*Ghoul*. Fechter lurched through the door. *Lurched*. He walked ponderously, his upper body rocking, swaying his center of gravity from side to side.

"Ahhh, Donna," he said without moving his lips.

Every fiber of Kate's being said *run!*—out the door, into the tunnel, to the shuttle, to the surface—

"Hello, Dr. Fechter," she said, forcing her lips into a trembling smile. She looked around the room, gesturing with her left hand. "This is a, um, fascinating laboratory. It is a laboratory?"

Fechter spread his hands on the operating table and looked down at it, his eyes sweeping its length. His gaze continued upward until it fixed on Kate. "Of course, yess, it is a laboratory."

"Well, then," she said lightly. "Where do you want me to set up?"

Fechter walk-lurched to the antenna. "Here," he said pointing to the floor. "I want you to record an experiment."

Kate began attaching the camera to the tripod head. Her hands shook, rattling the locking mechanism. "When we finish recording, do you want me to take the cartridge back to editing, or leave it here?"

"You can leave it with me."

Kate locked the camera down, gathered the tripod's legs together, and carried the assembly to the spot Fechter had indicated.

"Dr. Fechter, it would help if I knew the purpose of the video."

"The purpose is to record an experiment accurately."

"Have you considered a complete documentary about you and—"

"Donna, my dear," he replied, his voice carrying an edge of irritation. "I merely wish to record an experiment. If it goes well, we may talk about a documentary."

"Okay, what are we lighting?"

"Thiss," he said, pointing to the chair.

Kate spread the tripod's legs, leveled the camera, and panned it toward the chair. Fechter watched her closely.

"I need to set up some lighting."

"Of coursse."

Gart unloaded the lights and stands. Kate assembled three of the units, arranged them around the chair, and plugged them into nearby outlets. She switched the lights on and adjusted the barn doors, going back and forth to check the image through the camera's viewfinder. Fechter finally stopped watching Kate and began adjusting controls on the metal cabinet.

"I'll need to set up a soft light to eliminate some of the shadows."

Fechter looked up from behind the cabinet. "No." Light from the console's screen reflected from his thick lenses, veiling the Ping-Pong ball eyes with translucent neon green. "What you have is quite adequate."

"Then we're ready."

Fechter walked to the camera and put a spectacled eye to the viewfinder. He toyed with the zoom. "I need someone to stand in for a moment—do you mind, Donna?"

"Wh—what. You mean sit down?"

Fechter looked at her. His mouth stretched again into a rictus-grin. "Yess. Just for a moment."

Gart edged closer to her. She began to circle away from him.

"Let Gart stand in, I can adjust the lights—"

Fechter rotated his eyes toward his assistant and gave a brief nod.

Kate dodged to the right, but Fechter was instantly away from the cabinet, cutting her off. Panicked, she turned and swept a light stand across Gart's path. It shattered at his feet, the bulb exploding with a pop and spray of sparks.

Fechter stretched toward her. She reached into the cluttered instruments on the counter and seized a sharp, triangular metal object on a short stand. A wire ran from the device to a heavy instrument, and when she swung, it sent a row of electronics crashing to the floor.

Fechter made an angry, grunting sound and seized her blouse. She swung again and a gash appeared on his left cheek. His glasses spun to the floor. He clawed at his face and brayed. He was even more hideous without the thick lenses; his eyes did indeed bulge, and they were framed by sockets the color of a fresh bruise.

Kate raised her weapon again, but Gart was on her, pinning her arms and pulling her backward off her feet. Fechter found his glasses. He stood, seething, mopping the blood from his slashed face. He bent and seized Kate's legs. She fought and writhed as they lugged her, stumbling, over broken glass and jumbled instruments.

They threw her onto the chair. A metal edge painfully struck her ribs, cut her arm. She screamed and swung at the men with tightly curled fists. Steel clamps seized her wrists. A strap tightened around her chest, then her legs, constricting her like a death-row inmate in an electric chair.

She sobbed. "Please. Let me go. Why are you doing this?"

"Don't be afraid. Gart has been through my little procedure, and he's just fine, aren't you, Gart?"

A mechanical voice replied, "Yes."

She could see nothing; the two remaining spotlights blinded her. Then Fechter's sweating visage pierced the gauze of light. He had applied a thick bandage to his wound, and it glistened with red ooze.

"I don't want to hurt you—*Kaate*."

His words stabbed like blades. An emergency voice blared in the back of her brain: *All is lost...All is lost...*

"You know my name—how?"

"Computers tell us much, *Kaate*. Soon you will tell us more." He drew closer. "Soon, you will do whatever I wish."

The hideous face grazed her own. It tilted right and left while snuffling noises rose from the back of his throat. The fat lips parted. His tongue darted out, releasing moist, fetid breath. Kate jerked her head to the left, felt his plump fingers seize her chin. He squeezed, trying to force her face toward his own. She suddenly complied, snapping her head right, smashing her forehead into his temple. He hissed and disappeared behind the lights. Beyond the curtain of brightness, she could see the claw antenna begin to rotate.

She jerked against the restraints and screamed. "You murdering son of a bitch. I'll kill you—I'll kill you—I swear to God." She ceased struggling, panting.

"Funny," Fechter lisped. His voice was almost gleeful. "That's exactly what Gart said."

30

An inferno of pain burned through her body. The room tilted, spun. She convulsed against the restraints, slamming the clamps against their pins. Her back bucked and heaved until she thought her spine would crack. Then the pain faded and she could only feel-hear an undulating vibration. Intertwined was a voice, a soft, hypnotic murmur: *hear me, do as my voice commands*—obey. She drifted. The voice became part of her very soul…

Different voices now—

"Kate! Kate!"

A crash. She felt herself being lifted, carried. Lights flashing by. Something cold on her face, her arms. She tried to focus. A man pressed close to her—*David*! She tried to lift her arms—she was strapped. No. Her limbs simply wouldn't respond.

"She's coming around."

She moved, numbly at first, then with greater control. Her senses began to reassemble in random bits and pieces, returning like frightened rabbits creeping back to a burrow ravaged by snakes. Her entire body throbbed with pain.

David's arms enfolded her, brought her into a sitting position. "Kate. Thank God."

She felt the soft bench beneath her, welcomed the darkness; then she realized she was moving. Lights sped by. They were in a shuttle, racing within a tunnel. David hugged her tightly. "I thought for a minute I'd lost you."

She could barely feel her tears.

"Here it is," said the driver. They slowed and pulled into an alcove. "Think she can walk?"

With help from David and the other man, she stood shakily and took a few drunken steps.

An electric motor whined. Headlights oscillated along the granite wall. "Someone's coming."

The two men grabbed her beneath the arms and jogged toward an opening just beyond the alcove. A red light glared above the archway.

"My purse," she panted. "It has the CDs."

"Got it," David said.

Steps led steeply down. Grasping the railings, they dragged Kate to the bottom, stumbling some twenty feet to a steel door. The other man swiped a badge across the magnetic reader, and the door clicked open.

They stepped onto a catwalk inside a dark shaft of indiscernible height. Overbearing sound assaulted her ears—the same pulsating thrum Kate had heard when she first entered the mountain. The walk curved around an enormous metal sphere dotted with circular windows that flickered red, the glare throbbing in sync with the powerful internal vibration. The rays speared the humid atmosphere, reflecting in crimson pinpoints from the faceted granite walls. They must be very near, she thought, to the pounding heart of the Dark Mountain.

They turned left, and she looked at the man who was helping David carry her along. He was as tall as David, but heavier, rough looking... She suddenly recognized him—one of the Constellation members she and David had met on the Kenai Peninsula, with Ben. "Gary?" she asked, incredulous.

"His real name is Greg Illiani," David said.

The man smiled briefly and nodded. "I'll explain later."

They paused by one of the windows. Looking inside the sphere, Kate could see a glowing red substance racing brightly past, spinning about its vertical axis like a circle of fire. It hovered, gently rising and falling, buoyed by some invisible force.

"Plasma." David said, his voice filled with awe. "A controlled plasma. Why? What would they use that for?"

Barely visible through the red glow, a series of parallel rings rose from the depths of a long conduit entering the bottom of the sphere. A column of plasma accelerated in pulses through the rings, streaming in a bright, fluid arc into the spinning circle. Tendrils split from the whirling mass and swept into another tube that entered from above.

Illiani motioned impatiently, and they started forward again.

Kate's equilibrium returned, but she felt totally drained. "No, stop, please," she begged.

David propped her against the railing. "We can carry you."

"I just need to catch my breath. Thirsty. God, my body hurts." She gave a short laugh, grimaced. "I need a sauna."

"When we get out of this," David said, "I'll buy you a sauna, and hire a masseuse and a chiropractor."

Illiani jabbed a finger upward, frowning. Dark shapes moved along the catwalk above.

They pulled Kate from the railing, and started forward again. An endless belt of metal steps—a vertical escalator—circulated through a hole in the floor. Greg dropped through the opening first, hopping onto a descending step and grabbing the support bar. He swung onto another catwalk below and looked up, signaling "all clear."

"Can you do it?" David whispered.

"Fine time to ask—"

Kate swung her left foot unsteadily out, missed the step, made contact with the next one. David gave her a gentle push toward the bar, and she clutched it tightly as she dropped through the hole. Vertigo returned. She closed her eyes. *Where do I step off—where do I step off?*

Arms shot around her waist and jerked. She collapsed backward, landing on Illiani. David was there an instant later, pulling her up. Illiani motioned them toward an arched opening. It led down a long tunnel in which passageways and doors intersected at odd angles.

The first room roared with machinery: powerful electric motors turning shafts, driving pumps, blowers. Another space, big as a warehouse, opened a hundred feet farther down. It smelled of oil and hot metal. A massive chain swung from a crane riding steel beams far above, its massive hook grappling an enormous, partly-gutted electrical machine.

David motioned Kate to stay hidden while he and Illiani scouted the space. She collapsed onto the floor, back propped against a crate. The pain in her joints and muscles had subsided a little, but a headache was building—a whopper. She rubbed her temples.

David returned and handed her a paper cup filled with water. "Nobody's here now," he said in a low voice. He looked at her intently, his brow furrowed with concern.

"I'll be okay," Kate said, gulping the water. "David, if they know about me, they know about my family."

He gently squeezed her hand. "Jared's a smart man. He'll take care of them."

She looked around the dismal room, hearing the mountain's disturbing heart pumping in the background. "How do we find the exit to this hell-hole?"

"Any way we can."

Illiani appeared. "I found these." He thrust a bundle of clothing forward: blue workman's trousers, heavy denim shirt, sweat stained cap. "Hope they fit."

Behind the crate, she hastily tried on the trousers. They were too big, but she managed to hold them up with the belt from her skirt. The shirt fit over her blouse, bulky but manageable. She looked over the top of the crate. "How did you find me?" she asked as she adjusted her costume.

"It was luck," David answered. "They discovered who I was. Greg was part of the arresting squad."

Kate cast an alarmed glance at Illiani, but David held his hand up. "Greg and I punched a couple of guys out, then Greg got me inside the mountain."

"I don't understand."

Illiani smiled. "I'm with the FBI."

Kate's mouth dropped open in surprise.

"ARC is under investigation," he continued. "I was working undercover as outside security. When I found out they 'made' David, I knew they'd be coming after you, too."

"Greg stole a black security badge." David said. "That got us inside. We did a lot of bluffing, found your office. Your boss told us where you were, but nobody knew where Fechter's lab was. We took the elevator down, bumped into an orderly who clued us in."

Illiani said, "We intimidated that surly nurse in the reception room, and she opened the doors. The first thing we saw was Fechter hunkered over some machine, and you strapped down in a chair. Your boyfriend took care of the other man. We grabbed you and took off."

"What about Fechter?" Kate asked.

"He escaped." Illiani screwed up his face. "Man, is he one *ugly* sucker."

Kate hid her purse in a zippered canvas tool bag David found and pressed the greasy mechanic's cap over her head. She stepped from behind the crate. "Well. Rosie the Riveter."

David wrapped his arm around her waist, kissed her cheek. "Okay, Rosie, let's book."

Illiani cracked the door and peered into the tunnel. The sphere's pulsating drone intertwined with the rapid *thump, thump, thump* from the machinery room. They turned right, following the dim tunnel to a pair of swinging doors. Dark granite and the smell of machinery gave way to white tile and strong antiseptic.

David pivoted as an elevator on their left chimed. He tugged Kate, and they fled around a curve and paused before a double door, listening. The elevator opened and they heard voices, footsteps, and the rattle-squeak of something being wheeled in their direction.

The doors behind them swung wide with a push. Kate gasped; the room was like Fechter's horrid laboratory. A stainless steel table stood in the room's center. A nearby cart displayed knives, saws. An overhead vent hovered above the table beside a multi-reflector light. "Autopsy," she whispered.

The clattering wheels approached. They raced toward the end of the room and paused before a wide door with a small, round window.

David pushed the latch and they stepped into cold and darkness. Rows of stainless steel drawers glimmered dully. A morgue. No exit.

Kate looked back through the window as a gurney banged through the autopsy room door, pushed by two men in green scrubs. They parked the gurney and wrestled a limber body onto the steel table.

A woman entered—heavy, big as a large man, with broad shoulders, a square jaw, and a wide, frog-like mouth. Her brown-gray hair was knotted into a tight bun held in place by a black hairnet. She pulled on a white scrub hat, struggled into an operating gown, and yanked on elbow-length rubber gloves, thrusting her hands into the latex with an angry, jabbing motion. She snapped on the overhead light and pulled a microphone into position. The men spoke briefly with her, then turned and left.

"She's starting," Kate whispered, her words misting in the frigid air.

Illiani muttered, "That could take hours."

Shivering, Kate knelt and crawled beside one of the stainless steel drawers. Taking a penlight from her purse, she directed just enough light between her fingers to read the tag: *01649: Big Creek, 4-March, 1998.* She crawled farther. Halfway down the row, she found *01703: Flt. 948.* Her heart froze. This was Jack's death-flight. She pressed the latch and tugged. The heavy drawer slid out quietly, exposing a white-sheeted mass inside. Beads of cold sweat dampened the back of her neck.

She peeled the sheet back, played the penlight over the exposed face beneath. The ghastly, pop-eyed remains grinned back like a prop from a Halloween haunted house. The choking sound she made startled the men, who rushed to her side. She crabbed away from the body, hand clamped over her mouth.

David took the penlight and looked. "From the plane crash," he whispered. He opened drawers, drew back the sheets. Each corpse had a reddish, puckered incision across the forehead, just above the eyes, that traveled past the ears and circled behind the head—the top of the skull had been removed and replaced. Kate had seen enough. David wrapped his arm around her, and she turned her head against his shoulder.

A high-pitched whine sounded faintly through the morgue door; the big woman had switched on an electric saw. Bending over the body, her massive shoulders hunched, she lowered the instrument to her subject's head. The dentist-drill whine dipped in pitch and a reddish mist painted her face shield and the front of her operating gown. Vapors and wisps of smoke rose to the overhead vent.

David signaled Illiani, who nodded. He cast a confident glance at Kate, then quietly opened the door and stepped out.

The big woman jerked her head up, staring at the three through her grisly visor. She flicked the saw off, and the whine began to slow.

"What is it? Who are you people?" she demanded in a grating voice.

"We need your cooperation, Ma'am," David said, advancing slowly.

"There's a security problem." Illiani said.

Kate read the woman's badge: *Dr. Gretchen Hilde.*

Gretchen tore off her visor and backed away. "You're *outside* security. You shouldn't even be in here."

"Please put the saw down," David said softly.

"Dr. Hilde," said Illiani, "We can do this the easy way or the hard way—"

The frog-mouth drew back in a snarl. "*Fuck* you!" The saw jumped to life as she cocked it above her shoulder.

Kate took a reflexive step back. Repugnant as the woman was, when she was enraged, with that huge mouth and reddish gums, she made a quantum leap in *ugly*. If Fechter had a sister, Kate thought, Gretchen would be the one.

The woman bared her teeth, twisting the bone saw before her. The instrument's cord was plugged into the table; no one could yank it free without coming within Gretchen's reach. One good swipe and you lost a hand, severed a row of tendons, cut an artery—

David shouted above the keening saw. "Gretchen, we won't hurt you—"

She began a metallic, inhuman screech that sent Kate's hands to her ears. Still wailing, Gretchen thrust the saw toward David's throat, jerking it viciously back and forth. His right foot shot up. There was a *ping* as the saw bounced off the far wall.

Gretchen's ululation became a startled *aaagh!* Both men rushed her, grabbing for her arms. To Kate's amazement, the woman charged, dragging the men with her. *Dammit, David, no time for chivalry, punch her lights out!*

Without thinking, Kate threw herself across Gretchen's path. They all fell in a heap. Gretchen came up clawing and screaming. Her huge fist caught Illiani squarely on the jaw, stunning him. She swung again, hit Kate a glancing blow, knocking her cap off and spilling her blond hair.

She stared at Kate. "*You!*" she bellowed, and drew her fist back for another blow. David clamped his arms around her, pinning her elbows. But she lunged backward, ramming him into the autopsy table, crashing the instruments to the floor, knocking the corpse askew. David lost his footing and released his hold. Gretchen whirled, snatched two fat knives from the counter, and charged, chopping the air like an insane machine with piston-driven blades. David advanced, readying another strike.

In mid-chop, Gretchen suddenly turned and bolted for the door. She paused before Kate and raised a knife, her face a grotesque mask of hatred.

Kate was staring into the eyes of another ARC-spawned monster, a hideous member of the apparatus that had murdered Jack and took pleasure in torture and ruin. The sudden emotion commanded her muscles, and as Gretchen tensed to bring the knife down, Kate's adrenaline-powered right fist rocketed upward.

Her tightened knuckles intercepted Gretchen squarely below the mandible. The impact produced a *crack* that stung Kate's forearm and sent Gretchen's head snapping backward. The knives clattered away as the woman staggered against the countertop. She slid to the floor and sat, slack-jawed. Blood oozed from her mouth and dribbled down her scrubs, mingling with corpse-spatter.

"Jesus," said David, staring at the woman. He looked at Kate.

"You okay?"

Kate nodded, rubbing her bruised hand. "You should have hit her."

"I'm not used to hitting women." He looked again at the stunned Gretchen. "Remind me never to practice on *you*."

They bound Gretchen with cord ripped from the telephone, gagged the toad-mouth with surgical tape, and dragged her behind a counter.

They ransacked the room, searching for a map, but found nothing. They would have to feel their way blindly through the Dark Mountain's labyrinthine interior. They pushed through the doors and headed left, racing for stairs, a lift, anything leading to the outside world.

31

Ten feet above the floor, Mark balanced atop the domed cap of the power transformer and carefully maneuvered a brass rod onto a high-voltage terminal. Alex tightened the assembly with a wrench. An identical rod rose from the transformer's second terminal, three feet to Mark's left. Together, the rods formed a tall V.

O'Hanlon's voice came from below. "Make sure they're good and tight, men,"

Mark looked forward to this short-circuit test of the transformer. It was the last major component they would check before powering up the Magnifying Transmitter. He followed Alex down the ladder and turned to the Professor. "What's next?"

O'Hanlon walked to a nearby switch panel. "The circuit breakers." He pressed a button and a muffled thunk shook a riveted steel tank resting outside the generator room. "Now we set the power level." He grasped a control lever protruding from a cast iron apparatus bolted to the floor and swung it a short distance to the right. "We're set at ten percent power."

He lifted a hinged cover, exposing a red pushbutton. "Stay behind me, and don't touch anything metallic."

Mark looked up at the transformer's finned bulk, the brass V rising from its top like a pair of giant TV rabbit ears.

Alex grinned. "This is the hot juice, man—a million watts of raw, unadulterated AC. It could blow you into bloody vapors in a microsecond."

"All right," O'Hanlon said, his finger poised above the button. "Here goes."

The relay fired with a loud *bang*. A powerful hum vibrated the air as a fat python of electricity shot across the V-shaped gap and writhed upward, stretching and coiling from rod to rod. The convoluted tube of energy lingered and twisted between the gap's up-thrust ends and snapped free, launching a translucent flame that rose toward the ceiling and faded into distorting waves of heat.

O'Hanlon allowed this display to repeat three times and released the button.

"Whoa," Alex whooped. "I can still feel the heat radiating down."

O'Hanlon rotated the control back to zero and smiled. "Looks like the transformer is good. At least for a million watts."

"We used about ten million watt-seconds," Alex said. "Guess *that'll* show up on your electric bill."

"When do we go full power?" Mark asked.

"Unfortunately, we can't," O'Hanlon replied. "It would melt the rods." He lifted a manual from a nearby workbench. "I'll disconnect the circuit so you can remove the electrodes. After that, take a break. I'm going to review some of the wiring."

* * *

Later, Mark entered O'Hanlon's empty office and crossed to the window. He could hear the clatter of a keyboard coming from the adjoining storeroom, where Alex had had set up his laptop and a phone line.

Mark sat on the window seat and gazed out at the ranch house and the green stretch of woods beyond. Things were too crazy. Too *dangerous*. The last encoded message from his mother said she was actually working inside the ARC project. Mark knew if they discovered her they would kill her, or worse. Those same people wanted Alex so badly they had attacked the ranch. They'd try again. And what about the gray van? What was its range? Could it zap them in their beds at night? The sheriff and a deputy had investigated the attack, but the lawmen seemed as much confused as helpful. Mark took some comfort in knowing they now patrolled past the ranch every few hours, but he was still uneasy.

He drummed his fingers against the window seat's wooden edge. Maybe he'd play his guitar, or saddle a couple of horses and teach Alex how to ride.

Suddenly, an image flashed into his mind: the grounds and ranch house covered in snow, viewed from the window. And he recalled the faint, waxy smell of crayons. Why was he thinking of *crayons*? Then it came to him. He must have been four or five years old. It was winter, and he had been at this same window with a coloring book. He remembered a wooden lid that opened into a box, his secret hiding place. He stood, lifted the seat padding, and found it: a brass handle. He pulled and the ancient lid creaked open.

The crayons were still there in the shallow tray, along with some yellowed paper displaying the work of a child artist: purple cows and green chickens. Mark picked up the masterpieces. So he really had been in this room, once upon a time. He thumbed through the pages and paused. Some were extremely old, covered with notes and mathematical equations.

One page held a curious set of drawings. The first was of a large numeral 8. The second was a skillful drawing of a dragon biting at its own tail. Its wings resembled curved lightning bolts. The caption beneath said, "Ouroboros." The third drawing was a figure eight resting on its side, the symbol for infinity. *Tesla Doodles*, he thought.

He heard barking and a squeal of laughter. He glanced out the window. Buddy flashed across the lawn and intercepted a Frisbee, Higgins in close pursuit. Enrica—the pretty little daughter of one of the ranch hands—ran after the dogs in a ridiculous game of chase, with Buddy prancing in the lead, the red Frisbee clamped in his mouth. Mark chuckled. He unlatched the window and raised it, surprised that it moved so smoothly in its hundred year-old frame.

"Enrica," he shouted. The girl and both dogs stopped and looked up at him. "Hold the Frisbee with the left side down. And put more spin on it."

"Mark," she shouted back. "I just can't throw it right, and Buddy doesn't care, anyway."

As if to prove her statement, both dogs backed off, wagging and barking for the next wobbly throw. After a few more tosses, Enrica abandoned the game and walked away.

Mark looked toward the corral, where Miguél and José leaned against the fence, rifles at their sides. No one was allowed outside unguarded, not until the "situation" was resolved. He shut the window, took out his wallet, and withdrew a warped photo that had been taken three years ago: his father and him astride their mountain bikes at the base of the Lost Canyon Trail. Buddy was in the photo too, ready to run with his pack. The rims of his eyes began to burn, and he quickly slid the photo back.

There was a scrabbling sound on the wooden floor, and Buddy trotted into the office and rushed to Mark, who scratched him behind the ears and ruffled his fur. The dog jumped up, placing his big paws on the window seat.

Mark snatched the papers. "Don't mess these up." Buddy dropped back to the floor and began snuffling around the room. Mark eyed the drawings again. Written in bold, flourishing letters, below the rendering of Ouroboros, was a series of confusing words. He read them out loud: "Synchronous, Terrestrial, Or-tho-dro-mous, Resonant, Magnifier, and Dipolar Rotating Antenna—Geo-Orthogonal Node."

The acronym leaped out at him: S.T.O.R.M.D.R.A.G.O.N.

He wondered if it would be a good name for a band. *Stormdragon.* Nah—sounded like a Chinese restaurant. He stacked the strange drawings on O'Hanlon's desk and left a note with the acronym on top, then placed the coloring book back inside the window box and shut the lid.

As he turned to leave, the phone rang. It was his grandfather. His voice sounded urgent. "Mark, get Alex and meet me outside. Quick."

"What's going on?"

"Just get movin'."

* * *

Mark's grandfather strode rapidly up the walk, talking as he approached. His voice was calm but firm. "Fellas, the FBI is headed up here from the gate. They're after Alex. Ride to Roberto's camp on the north ridge and lay low until I contact you."

Alex burst through the door, cradling the laptop from his makeshift office. Mark waved to him and they jogged off toward the corral. With Carlos and Jesús helping, they saddled the horses in minutes. Mark swung onto Maggie while Carlos helped a nervous Alex onto a gentle chestnut gelding. Jesús opened the corral's west gate.

"FBI's already here," Jesús said as he mounted his horse. "Jared's letting them into the house."

They rode west into the foothills, following a narrow trail that climbed between boulders and around islands of pine and aspen. The trail was old, trodden deep and smooth over the decades by horses and wildlife. Carlos led, followed by Alex, Mark, and Jesús. Buddy and Higgins tagged along, dodging playfully through the woods, pulled this way and that by the irresistible evidence of squirrels and rabbits.

Mark rode smoothly as his horse lunged up the slope. Alex bounced in the saddle like a puppet on a jackhammer. "Stand up in the stirrups and lean forward," Mark shouted. "Keep your butt off the saddle." Alex followed Mark's suggestion and looked back, grinning. After a few lessons, Mark thought, Alex might actually learn how to ride.

They descended a barren furrow, dislodging hissing micro-land-slides of rock and sand. A wide hollow appeared, its smooth walls of fawn-colored boulders precisely mated. The riders dismounted and tied their horses to a rough hitching post of fallen logs, then walked up a wooded path to a clearing, where a solitary platoon of lightning-torn pines guarded the hill's rocky crown.

They were at the top of the sandstone rise known as Spy Knob, so-called because it commanded a view of the entire ranch. The Poacher's Gate was below and northwest, hidden by thick woods. To the south, the reservoir and Lookout could be glimpsed, but Mark kept his eyes facing east, toward the ranch house and barn.

They almost stumbled over Roberto, who was crouching behind a tumble of boulders, a pair of binoculars pressed to his eyes. His arm shot out, motioning for them to stay hidden. "Uh, oh," he said. "They're headed for the barn." After ten minutes of silence, he lowered the binoculars and shrugged in surprise. "The FBI guys just drove off."

*   *   *

Mark's grandfather, riding his black stallion, appeared fifteen minutes later. He dismounted, tied his horse to the makeshift hitching post, and called the small group together. He stood at base of the cliff, his gaze lingering on Alex. "The FBI wants to know how Alex hacked into Cerberus, what he found out, and who attacked us. They said if we cooperate, they'll send a few men to help guard us, and they won't prosecute Alex for hacking."

Mark asked, "How did they find out about Alex?"

"Through their usual channels—apparently not through Cerberus."

"Did they see the transmitter?"

Jared nodded. "They didn't know what to make of it. They wondered if the attackers might be after it. I told them no." He was silent for a moment. "I told them there's a leak in their communications, but they already know they've got a problem."

"What do they want from us?" asked Carlos.

"Business as usual. But they want to interview all of us."

"You don't really trust them, do you?" asked Mark.

"Not a hundred percent. But I think they were shooting straight with me." He looked around the group. "I think we should cooperate. I couldn't speak for you, Alex, but I believe you'll be a lot safer if you stay here and work with them."

Alex thought for a minute, his face grim. "I'll stay. It makes sense."

Mark's grandfather walked to him and extended his hand. "We'll help you, Alex, whatever happens."

32

Kate tightened her grip on the naked steel rungs and looked down at the landing far below. Jutting into the cavern's throat, its outline illuminated by a single red light, the narrow shelf hovered over an infinite well of darkness. Enormous pipes, bleeding with condensation, rose vibrating and thrumming from the depths and climbed past her into shadowed heights.

The muscles in her forearms began to cramp; she desperately needed to relax her hands. But there was nothing to lean against. The thin, angular bars she clutched were welded to the curved skin of a vertical pipe, sticking out into open space like the skeletal vertebrae of a prehistoric beast.

It seemed as though they had been running and climbing forever, crawling through the Dark Mountain's intricate bowels, dodging the ARC patrols. Trying to avoid detection, they had become trapped inside the huge maintenance shaft and were now forced to make this precarious climb to the next level.

The enfolding darkness tugged at her, trying to drag her backward into the abyss. Looking down triggered another wave of vertigo. She squeezed her eyes shut, but the effect worsened. The shaft seemed to tilt as if it were rotating on a giant pivot. Up became down. Her balance shifted—*No!*

She hugged the rungs, opened her eyes. The world slowly stabilized. She dared another glance down. David was just below, his face silhouetted by the distant red light. She could feel him smiling confidently back, urging her on. She climbed again, hands and legs searing with fatigue.

Illiani's voice came from above. "We're at the catwalk."

"Thank God," Kate panted. She heard him grunt as he heaved himself onto a metal surface.

"Just a little farther," he called down.

Kate grabbed the next rung, but as she tried to step up, her right foot skidded on the slick surface. With frightening suddenness, both feet swung into empty space. She panicked as she felt the rungs stealing from her grasp.

David's arm shot around her waist and pulled her back. "I have you," he said calmly. But he was breathing hard, his voice strained. Her feet banged hollowly against the pipe, then found the rungs. She felt Illiani's hand grasp her forearm. He lifted as David pushed.

A moment later, she struggled up through the rough steel opening and collapsed onto the catwalk, gasping. David followed and dropped down beside her. Stifling a flood of tears, she reached out and hugged him.

"Damn it," she croaked. "So much for the Warrior Princess image."

David wrapped his arms around her. "You're exhausted. We're all tired."

"And hungry," Illiani muttered. He turned and followed the catwalk to an opening in the wall.

Kate dabbed her eyes with the sleeve of her jumpsuit. "I can't climb anymore," she said miserably. "Go on without me,"

"I didn't even *hear* that."

Illiani returned. "There's a stairway down, through the wall."

They discussed their options: if they didn't find a viable exit soon, they'd return to the main level and try to fake their way past the guards. One thing was very clear: they couldn't go on much longer.

Light beams suddenly pierced the darkness. Men were on the landing below, their shouts drowned by the din from the pipes. David and Illiani leapt to their feet and grabbed Kate beneath the arms. Discs of light chased after them as they ran for the opening in the wall.

They stumbled down a steep, low stairway and stopped before a door. Illiani opened it cautiously, and they stepped into a wide, smooth, well-lit tunnel.

A claxon suddenly blared, and a calm female voice echoed from multiple loudspeakers: "Code Yellow. Code Yellow. All personnel report to stations." They paused, listening. Kate thought the entire mountain was being summoned to locate them.

"Strange," Illiani said. "That's a perimeter defense alert,"

Somewhere ahead, around the curve, doors opened. Footsteps approached. There was conversation, a brief laugh. Kate tensed to run.

David caught her arm "Follow me. Act normal."

Normal, she thought, *is scared out of my wits*.

They walked rapidly toward the voices. Four men in business suits appeared, ambling unconcernedly. The two groups passed each other and nodded. Kate affected as much of a masculine posture as possible and shielded her face beneath her cap. By now, everyone must know ARC security was looking for two men and a blond woman.

The claxon and voice sounded again; then the tunnel was quiet. As they moved forward, Kate noticed artwork and photographs hanging from the painted walls. They slowed their pace.

"Must be near the executive offices," Illiani said.

"The brass probably has an express elevator from the operations center to the top," David said. "Got to be more than one way up."

A hundred yards ahead, the tunnel ended. On the left wall, a door responded to Illiani's card and hissed open. The space beyond held a polished marble conference table and a video projection system. Sunlight streamed in through a long slit of a window set deeply into the opposite wall.

Illiani moved through the room, checking the work stations. David insisted that Kate sit down. He held her hand, studied her face. "We'll get out of this."

She smiled back, and he walked off to join Illiani. She glanced around. There were flip charts, computers, and a sophisticated digital projector. This was a high-level meeting room. She nudged the mouse on the computer beside her. The screen saver disappeared and a 3-D

CAD drawing of some complex apparatus popped on screen. Turning to the cabinet nearby, she rifled through storage cases, grabbed CDs, and threw them into the zippered bag.

David rushed back. "We're in luck," he said breathlessly. "There's a door to the outside."

Illiani shouted, "Hurry. A chopper's coming in."

David snatched a white technician's coat off a rack and helped Kate into it. "It'll be cold outside."

She looked toward the ceiling as she threaded her arms into the sleeves. "David!" she said, nodding upward. A mirrored security-cam blister stared from the ceiling.

"Just keep moving, and hope no one's watching."

As they brushed past the conference table, Kate swept the CDs stacked beside the projector into the bag with the others—might as well load up with all they could get.

A steel doorway stood at the end of a short corridor, and Kate could hear the faint droning of a helicopter. She ducked and covered her ears as David leveled his pistol and fired two shots into the lock mechanism. In the confined space, the discharges sounded like bombs.

The men rammed their shoulders against the door and the latch clanked free, allowing them into a small alcove. The remaining door was unlocked. Warm air rushed out with a sigh as Illiani pushed it open. They stepped through.

A concrete path ran off to the right, leading to steps that marched up the mountain in a jagged switchback. Somewhere above, the helicopter sounded as if it were flying in a circular pattern. They stepped onto the walkway and Kate squinted in the sunlight, shivering delightedly as a cold wind swirled by. Perhaps the hardest task lay ahead, but they were at least free from the Dark Mountain's nightmarish catacombs.

A frightening but familiar sound suddenly vibrated beneath her feet. She looked over the railing. A geodesic shape squatted on a concrete pad not far below. An antenna dome. Its threatening, low-pitched growl meant the claw antenna inside was in motion, sweeping along its axes, focusing on targets. Then a new sound came, one she could almost feel—a high-pitched sizzle, almost a crackle, as if an electric charge pierced the surrounding air.

She stood back from the railing. David and Illiani were looking out over the plains, listening to other sounds: the distant shriek of jet engines, and dull booms like thumps from a thickly padded drum. Miles away, to the south, columns of dark smoke curled from the ground.

Turning, Illiani pointed to a row of windows glinting along the walkway, each one a frowning horizontal slit recessed into the granite. He waved them on, and they crept forward, bending low to avoid being seen.

The metal stairs began, angling steeply to the right. David and Illiani pulled Kate swiftly up the narrow steps. She paused on the third landing to catch her breath.

Below stretched the Black Mountain's spider-web network of roads and domes. Looking west, the veined tributaries of a river reflected silver, swollen with meltwater from the glittering face of a snowcapped mountain. Perhaps fifteen miles north, Denali's radiant white mass pushed through the clouds.

Kate signaled she was ready to continue, and they climbed the final switchback to a landing some twenty feet below the uppermost ledge. The helicopter's drone steadied and began dropping in pitch.

David crawled up the last few steps, moved off the path to the right, and hid behind a ragged pile of tailings torn from the overhead cliffs. He peered momentarily between gaps in the heavy rubble, then motioned for the others to come forward.

Kate crept up beside him and looked through a narrow crack. Some seventy-five feet away, a sleek helicopter sat on a circular landing pad carved into the mountainside, its twin turbines maintaining a steady whine. U.S. Army insignia appeared faintly over brown and black camouflage paint.

Two men faced the helicopter. One was tall, very slender, wearing a dark business suit. He stood with his arms crossed in front of him, the tails of his coat snapping in the downwash from the rotor blades. The other man wore a lab coat beneath an open parka. Kate shuddered. Could it be Fechter? No. The man she was observing looked too...

normal.

The chopper's rear door opened and two men in camouflage stepped out. They carried side arms and walkie-talkies. Next came four Army officers, who ducked beneath the blades and stood beside the two civilians. Another officer climbed from the forward cabin.

"A four-star," David whispered.

Illiani squinted. "Who is that?"

"Looks like General Greggson."

Holding his hat in place, the general walked briskly from the chopper and charged through double doors recessed into the cliff face. The others turned and dropped in step behind him.

The two remaining soldiers stationed themselves near the chopper and assumed positions of alert boredom. The engines whined down and the rotors slowed and stopped. The pilot climbed out and headed for the doors.

"Damn," Illiani said through his teeth. "There goes our ride."

"No," David said. "It's perfect."

"What do you mean?"

"It's a Blackhawk. I can fly it."

* * *

Kate stepped boldly onto the helipad, following David and Illiani. She should be nervous carrying out this dangerous charade, but after the last few hours, it seemed like a walk in the park. Her main concern now was whether the vertigo would return and her legs would buckle beneath her.

The two soldiers focused on them, but remained at ease. As she walked closer, Kate could make out their insignia: one was a sergeant, the other a first lieutenant.

"That's close enough," the lieutenant shouted firmly, holding up a hand.

David and Illiani acknowledged with a wave, but drew closer together. Behind David's back, tucked into the elastic belt of his jump suit, were his and Illiani's semiautomatics.

Illiani's hand casually reached out and jerked a pistol free. He immediately dropped to his knee and swung the weapon up. "Freeze!

Nobody moves and nobody gets hurt."

David grabbed the remaining pistol and assumed a firing stance.

"Shit!" the lieutenant spat. "You guys are making a *big* mistake."

"Weapons on the ground!"

The men slowly unholstered their pistols and lowered them to the tarmac. David pointed. "Head for the rocks and start climbing."

The two soldiers hesitated, then jogged to the rim of the landing pad, slipped over, and dropped out of sight.

David opened the Blackhawk's flight deck door and shoved Kate into the copilot's seat. He handed the confiscated pistols to her and started around the aircraft's nose. Kate slid the guns into the canvas bag's side compartment and zipped it up. Illiani climbed in behind her.

She glanced through the right window. ARC guardsmen were swarming onto the helipad, weapons drawn. "David, *hurry!*" she screamed.

He vaulted into the pilot's seat and jerked Kate's safety harness over her chest. She shoved his hand away. "I can figure it out—just get us out of here." She stared at the guards as she fumbled with the harness. The leader held up a hand and shouted something to the man immediately behind him, who spoke into a radio. The group hesitated, as if awaiting instructions.

Kate cast an anxious glance at David. His hands were racing over the console. He hesitated, seemingly at a loss, then toggled two switches. There was a deep-throated moan followed by a rushing whine as the twin jet engines inhaled and started building rpm.

She looked outside. The commander had taken a step toward the chopper and was shouting, making quick slicing motions across his throat with his right hand. The engines masked his voice.

The four big rotor blades began accelerating in a wide, wicked circle, and in seconds were throwing gale force winds at the guards. The fuselage rocked as the turbines whined higher. The lead guard squinted against the wind, then stepped backward and barked orders. The men spread out and aimed their weapons.

Kate reflexively ducked and covered her head as a volley of bullets pocked the windows and spanked against the helicopter's fuselage.

"David!"

Wind and jet noise suddenly roared inside the cabin. Kate looked back; Illiani had racked the window open and was swinging the Blackhawk's big machine gun around on its pintle. There was a staccato roar, and a wide swath of pavement in front of the guards exploded in a fan of splintered concrete.

Her body pressed into the seat as the ground dropped away. David pushed the control stick in front of the seat, the ship's nose dropped, and they accelerated south, the helipad slipping away beneath them.

Illiani jammed the window shut.

"That got their attention," David said.

"Nothing like a seven point six-five millimeter."

They veered west, the helicopter rising and falling like a small boat cruising storm swells.

Kate felt her stomach churn. "I thought you said you could fly this thing," she shouted over the engine noise.

"I didn't say I could fly it *well*," David yelled back.

The chopper began to pitch sharply and bounce, and Kate gripped the edge of her seat as if the nylon harness needed assistance holding her in. She looked down and gasped; they were directly over one of the mountain's giant exhaust stacks. Boiling clouds of steam belched from the black maw and rose to engulf them.

She pictured them falling through the gaping hole, caroming against the walls, crashing into the nuclear reactor's superheated furnace. For a panicked instant, she could see nothing through the windshield but silver-gray; then blue sky opened as suddenly as if they had left a tunnel. The turbulence dropped.

"Hold on," David shouted. "Starting contour flying."

Dear God, Kate thought, *if that's any worse, I'd rather jump.*

He pushed a lever on the left of the pilot's seat, and they dropped, skimming over the top of an antenna dome.

"Where are you *going*?" Kate shrieked.

"Gotta stay low. So they can't use their weapons."

The helicopter bucked to the left, then swung back to level flight. David stared ahead, locked in concentration. Another antenna dome flashed by. The flight became a torturous roller coaster ride as the Blackhawk plunged down cliffs and dodged thrusting granite outcrops.

One of the huge structures feeding microwave energy to the ARC antennas stretched hundreds of feet above them. Kate imagined the jointed girders shuddering into motion, flexing, ripping the Dark Mountain from the ground, and the complete mass stalking after them like the giant arachnid it resembled.

Level ground rose to meet them as they reached the plateau, and they raced low over a service road, soaring between domes, barely clearing the tubes branching between antennas. The domes ended and the helicopter sliced between rows of rectangular buildings, their gray facades flashing past in a sullen blur. David banked the helicopter sharply to the right as they shot into a wide road intersection, and they accelerated eastward, straight down the middle of Main Street. The bridge and the smaller mountain, with its mile-long entrance tunnel, rushed toward them.

Humvees and trucks choked the road, thick as freeway traffic. David pulled the chopper's nose up and angled right, skirting the smaller mountain's southern flank, then climbed steeply over a landscape of storage tanks and steaming towers. A short stretch of bare tundra flicked by, and the river was suddenly below them, rushing white and turbulent. They slowed to an unsteady hover.

"Why are we stopping?" Kate shouted.

"Hang on."

He eased the craft forward and rotated to the right, parallel with the river, and dropped down. The gap was wide where they entered the gorge, but narrowed a short distance ahead. David slowed their descent and pushed the Blackhawk forward. They hugged the river as it snaked southward, fighting sudden wind gusts twisting off the cliffs. The river straightened, and the rushing current became torpid, curling back into a green backwater. David tugged on the headphones. After a moment, he gritted his teeth. "Christ."

"What is it?" Kate asked.

He slowed the chopper and spun it around. Less than a quarter of a mile away, two black helicopters raced toward them. Pylons stuck out from their fuselages like short, stubby wings, each bulking with fat weapons pods.

David began rotating the chopper back. "Greg," he shouted. "We've got two Apaches on our tail."

"So *fly* this sonuvabitch, man."

"Hold on to your ass. We're about to party."

As he spoke, David shoved a lever forward. The turbines whined, and the Blackhawk accelerated down the river.

White geysers flashed from the water. "Chain guns," David yelled.

Kate felt her body press hard into the seat as they slapped into a steep left turn, following the curving canyon wall. The river immediately wound right and David pitched the big chopper again on its side, narrowly missing the cliff. The canyon straightened and broadened into a wide corridor, the rocky landscape dissolving into woods.

Loud *bangs* and a metallic gnashing, like an eighteen-wheeler stripping its gears, blasted through the cabin. The Blackhawk lurched to the right, spinning in a cloud of dense smoke. Kate bent forward, hands clamped over her mouth, as the engines stuttered and the ship's nose wavered toward the shoreline and a tiny mound of black beach.

An Apache flashed by, circled wide and hovered, facing them, squaring-off like an angry pit bull. The second Apache cruised nearby, and Kate could see the man in the rear jabbing his finger downward.

David stared at the other machine. "We can't even *fly* anymore, you son of—"

A bright flash engulfed the cockpit, followed by a rocking blast. Fragments peened against the fuselage like wind-driven hailstones. Kate blinked and stared; a cloud of smoke drifted where the first Apache had been. Metallic debris was still raining down when the second Apache peeled off in a steep left turn. A sudden, sleek shape flashed by the Blackhawk's right side, followed by another on the left.

Illiani yelled, "What the hell—"

"Comanches," David shouted. "They're Comanches."

"Ours or theirs?"

A dull thump rocked them from behind—another explosion. Shrapnel pelted the fuselage and fanned into the water below.

"Ours," David said perfunctorily.

To Kate's utter amazement, he started laughing.

"What?"

"Those were *Comanches*. The most advanced chopper we've got."

"Comanches," Kate said. "I thought they were Apaches."

"Nope, wrong tribe." He laughed again.

Comanches, Apaches, thought Kate. *We're smoking, falling apart above a river, helicopters with Indian names shooting at us, and our pilot is laughing his head off.* Where's the cavalry? Despite herself, she smiled. She would have sworn that laughter cured all ills, if her hands hadn't started shaking and she could have stemmed the trickle of blood that started suddenly from her nose.

The intermittent whine above the cockpit decreased in pitch.

"Oh, shit," David said. "We lost the engines."

Kate looked down. They must be several hundred feet above the river. The shoreline was what—three hundred feet? Did helicopters fall when the engines stopped? She didn't think so. They glided or something.

David became fixated, working the controls, staring at the gauges, glancing at the too-distant beach. His face wore another look—exhaustion. She wanted to speak to him, offer words of support, but she saw his frown, the grimace as his lips drew tight around his teeth. The rotor speed increased as they floated downward; then the stripped-gear sound crunched and vibrated with renewed force.

"Damn!"

Now they were a hundred feet above the sluggish river. How deep was the water? A metallic *bang* shuddered through the Blackhawk and they spun wildly, slamming Kate forward against the harness, the sky and river a tumbling blur. Her chest tightened.

They were falling.

33

Kate choked and instinctively flailed her arms, attempting to bring her head above the freezing water.

"Hold on," came the rasping voice. "We're almost there." It was David. His arm was beneath her chin, tugging her as he swam. Finally, he grasped her around the waist, and her numbed feet touched the river's boulder-paved bottom.

"We made it," he panted as they stumbled onto the rocky beach.

She flinched apprehensively as a shadow glided overhead—a helicopter—fanning her already freezing body with spray and wind. Instead of strafing them, the machine slowed and settled onto the tiny beach. The engines whined down and the big rotor began to slow. Another helicopter droned, circling some distance away.

David guided her to a sunlit patch of sand and peeled the soaked technician's coat from her body. She sat cross-legged on dry gravel and propped her back against the smooth, round surface of a boulder, feeling its heat ease into her back. David knelt beside her, his face white with cold. Illiani shivered nearby, watching the helicopter.

She closed her eyes and said a brief prayer; at least they were on solid ground. She jerked into a sitting position. "Oh, *God*, where's the bag with the CDs?"

David frowned. "Here, Kate. Right here." He pried the fingers of her right hand from their frozen grip around the bag's strap. She leaned back against the boulder and chuckled through chattering teeth. He kneaded her hand and forearm, trying to encourage circulation.

Kate glanced at the helicopter that had just landed. It was one of the Comanches—very different from the Blackhawks: long, and narrow, futuristic looking, with no conspicuous guns or protrusions. The canopy slid back and the man in the rear seat jumped down and trudged their way. He was wearing a blue flight jacket with U.S.A.F. insignia. He carried a pistol. "I'm Captain James Lowell. Somebody explain what's going on here."

David turned to him. "Thanks for getting the Apaches off our tail."

"They were I.D.'d as hostile aircraft. The question is where *you* fit into the picture."

"We'll talk, but this woman needs help. We've got to get her warmed up, some medical attention…"

"So enlighten me. We'll do what we can."

Illiani broke in. "Captain Lowell, I'm Greg Illiani, special agent, FBI. We've been gathering intel under cover. We escaped. The Apaches were trying to bring us down."

"We stole the Blackhawk." David said. "It had just dropped off some Army brass. One of them looked like General Thad Greggson."

Kate glanced toward the crashed helicopter. It was mostly submerged, its bent rotor blades clawing above the river's surface like the fingers of a drowning man.

"Greggson's a fugitive now," Captain Lowell said. "The Armed Forces have been directed to capture him and shut ARC down."

His partner approached with a small nylon bag that he opened and handed to David. Inside were rations, matches, and a first aid kit. The orbiting Comanche streaked past them, continuing its wide circle.

Lowell continued. "There's a fishing cabin or something about a mile down river. I'll try to get a medevac team to lift you out. It'll take a while. I can't radio because they're jamming the frequencies."

He turned to leave.

"Captain," David said.

Lowell paused and looked back.

"ARC can do a lot more than just knock your communications out. They've got a microwave weapon that can fry you in seconds."

Lowell nodded grimly. "We know." He trudged back to the Comanche.

*   *   *

Heat and energy bled painfully from her body and swirled away on the river's bone-freezing current. They had walked nearly a mile before spotting the cabin on the opposite shore, and now they waded across in sluggish, waist deep water. They slogged up a gravel embankment toward the log shack.

The door creaked open on rusted hinges, revealing a single decrepit room. Sunlight streamed through the front window and made a bright rectangle on the wooden floor. Something small scurried and disappeared through a knothole. David helped Kate into a rickety wooden chair. He brushed back her damp blond hair and kissed her forehead. She shook uncontrollably. *I've never been so cold.*

The men gathered dry sticks and limbs, broke them into bite-size pieces, and stacked them inside a fractured, pot-bellied stove. Illiani held a trembling match to the kindling, and in a few minutes the old stove began to radiate warmth.

A sudden knocking pulled Kate from a dreamlike trance. David was still standing, holding her upright in the chair. Her right hand held his, her cheek resting against his forearm. Illiani was on his feet instantly, drawing his pistol, peering through the small front window. David slipped his own weapon free as the FBI agent cautiously opened the door.

Framed by bright sunlight, an old man in a sealskin parka stood at the entrance, a worn brown knapsack strapped to his back. His features were those of an Athabascan Indian. "Who are you, and why are you here?" He asked in a soft voice.

"Well," Illiani growled, "We've just been through hell, and we're not here by choice."

The man scowled. "You work for the ARC."

"No. We *escaped* from ARC."

Illiani nodded toward Kate. "This woman is injured. We need to get her to a hospital."

The old man held up his right hand, and Kate craned her neck to see what was happening. Four Indians with rifles appeared, flanking yet an older man, who had long white hair and a deeply weathered face. He advanced slowly, his steps aided by a carved wooden staff.

"Don't be alarmed," the first man said. He turned and spoke to his armed companions, who nodded and walked a short distance away. The elder man came to the door and looked inside. His gaze rested on Kate, and his expression was one, she thought, of recognition.

"Grey Wolf!" she said, as the memory of her meeting with Ben and Greg on the Kenai Peninsula flashed into her mind. Why was he here, so close to the ARC project?

Illiani clasped the old man's hand, smiling. "Grey Wolf, indeed." He turned back to the other Indian.

"My name is Ketuk," the Indian said, offering his hand. "And I see you already know my uncle."

Illiani invited the two inside.

Grey Wolf placed a wrinkled hand gently over her forehead, his brow furrowed with concern, the serene brown eyes seeming to read something as he gazed at her. The old man radiated kindness and concern—and a curious energy.

Ketuk watched for a moment, then said, "Grey Wolf wants to know what happened to her."

"They tortured her," David said. "She's physically exhausted."

"What, specifically, did they do to her?"

Annoyance crept into David's voice. "Specifically, they strapped her to a chair and beamed her with microwave radiation."

Ketuk turned to Grey Wolf and, after a brief conversation in their native tongue, said, "She most likely has a swelling of the brain. You would call it cerebral edema."

Kate shot the man a puzzled expression. The Indian smiled faintly. "My Ph.D. is in biology, Alaska University. My uncle is a shaman, and although he is not a doctor by western standards, you would be wise to take his advice."

"Can you help get her to a hospital?" David asked.

"Let her rest for an hour to regain strength. My truck is a mile from here, and the path is very rough. Meanwhile, Grey Wolf will prepare a medicine that should help."

The Indians left and returned a short time later with a handful of bark and small, clover-shaped leaves that Grey Wolf boiled in a tin cup. The odor reminded Kate of freshly cut grass. She screwed her face up at the taste and coughed.

They broke open a plastic bag of military rations, which the Indians augmented with strips of dried fish and herbs from their packs. Kate eagerly drank a cup of soup the shaman concocted. She began to feel stronger.

Ketuk's men fashioned a stretcher from pine limbs and a blanket taken from one of the packs. Two of the men would guide Kate and the others to their truck, then take them to the nearest town, fifty miles away. Nothing was said of the Comanche pilot's offer to send help; no one knew if he had notified a medevac team, or even if he had survived the confrontation with ARC.

* * *

The trail began behind the cabin and climbed up a gravel embankment toward a stretch of shaded woods. Two of the younger Indians carried Kate on the stretcher, and Ketuk and Grey Wolf walked for a distance with them. They paused midway into the woods, and Kate climbed from the stretcher, testing her legs.

David turned to Ketuk. "Where are you going from here?"

Ketuk pointed north, to a gray mountain rising east of the river.

"That is where our village stood before ARC destroyed it. That is where Grey Wolf will return to meditate, to the place where he witnessed the destruction of our clan."

"That's close to ARC. You know of the danger."

"Too well." He drew close. Grey Wolf stood to one side, his hands folded over the staff, watching with an enigmatic smile. Ketuk leaned forward and lowered his voice, giving Kate and David an intense look. "Grey Wolf says that a great conflict will soon take place. Many will die, and much will ride upon the actions of a few. Both of you will play an important part in this. He says to hurry to your destination. The time is drawing near."

Kate nodded and looked again into the old man's kindly eyes. She didn't believe in shamans, prophecies, or any such nonsense. Although there was something about Grey Wolf…

David said, "Thanks for your help, Ketuk, Grey Wolf. Watch out for yourselves."

Ketuk nodded. "You, too, my friend."

* * *

After a stumbling climb over loose gravel and river stones, they finally came onto a furrowed landscape carpeted with low bushes and dotted with stunted, weather-beaten pines. David and Illiani took their turn at the stretcher and followed their guides along a trail only the native Alaskans could read. The temperature rose; instead of fighting hypothermia, they began to sweat.

A battered pickup appeared about a quarter of a mile away, parked at the end of a dirt road that looked almost as rough as the terrain they had just walked.

"Helicopter," Illiani said. "Looks like a Huey." All heads turned toward the northwest. Kate glimpsed a dark shape cruising slowly southward just above the trees, following the river.

"Red Cross," David said. "That's our ride."

The helicopter lifted and began a wide circle, then slowly thumped toward them. It hovered for a moment, then lowered to the ground, raising a storm of red-brown grit. Two men wearing Red Cross jumpsuits climbed out and jogged beneath the blades toward them. David and Illiani spoke with the men for a moment and returned to Kate.

"They're headed back to Elmendorf," David shouted. "There's room for all of us."

They thanked Grey Wolf's men and climbed aboard. Kate looked around as she strapped herself into a seat between David and Illiani. She counted eight injured; the Huey appeared to be filled to capacity.

The turbine's whine increased in pitch and the helicopter lifted off. Kate looked north. The columns of black smoke they had seen hours before had dissipated, but ARC, several miles away, still loomed large and threatening. The helicopter turned southward, settling into a steady drone.

As sleep tugged at her consciousness, an image formed of invisible filaments cast through the air, seizing the helicopter in a prehensile grip, drawing them back to the Dark Mountain—a spider-shape that watched them as they flew.

34

Urgency in someone's voice shocked her awake. A crewman was staring wide-eyed through the helicopter's left window. Kate looked out and saw smoke and flames billowing upward. She could make out an airfield, hangars, and buildings through the dark haze. Burning aircraft blotted the debris-scattered runway.

"God*damn*!" the man said. "Can you believe this shit? Something blew away half the air base."

A tan brick building swung into view. Kate could see ambulances with flashing lights jamming the streets and parking lot as the helicopter dropped toward the rooftop landing pad.

They touched down, and David and Illiani helped the medical team unload the injured below the spinning blades. Freed of its burden, the Huey lifted off and pointed its nose north. As the clatter from the helicopter diminished, explosive *crumps* could be heard rumbling from the air base. Wind drove most of the smoke away from the building, but a powerful, greasy stench permeated the air.

They lowered Kate onto a gurney. "I can stand."

"Not yet," David said as they banged through double doors leading to the elevators. Two floors down, they entered a hallway choked with an overflow of injured, filled with moans and sharp cries of pain. Illiani disappeared down the crowded corridor, sidestepping gurneys and blanketed bodies.

A harried medic with a clipboard approached Kate. "What's the problem here?"

David explained: "Exhaustion, exposure, possible cerebral edema."

"From a blow to the head?"

"Microwave radiation."

The man looked perplexed.

"I think you'll find a lot of your patients with similar symptoms."

The doctor flicked a penlight across Kate's eyes.

"I'm okay," she said wearily.

"Any headache, nausea?"

"Not right now."

The doctor jotted notes as he spoke. "The area hospitals are taking our overflow. You should check into one of them for observation. We only have space for serious injuries."

He handed her his recommendations and moved on.

"Grey Wolf's remedy must be working," Kate said to David. "I'm feeling much better."

Illiani returned, shouldering through the confusion. "There's hundreds of people. A lot of 'em dead." Lowering his voice, he said with a grimace, "They're like the cadavers we saw inside the mountain."

David helped Kate to her feet.

"Sir," a commanding voice said. "Please come with us." Two Air Force Security guards motioned for them to follow.

They threaded single file around the injured, and Kate looked down in horror as a man lying on a gurney convulsed in a spastic intake of air. He rolled his head, exposing liquid, blood-red eyes bulging past the lids. There was absolutely no question about what had happened at the air base.

The guards ushered them into a small office. Kate dropped onto a chair.

"Please remove your firearms and place them on the desk," one of the men said. David and Illiani complied. "And that, sir," he said, pointing to the canvas bag David had slung over his shoulder. He handed it over and the guard frowned as he removed the two pistols they had confiscated on the mountain. He held up one of the CDs.

"What's on these?"

"Important data," replied David.

The door opened and an Air Force officer walked in. He identified himself as Lieutenant Robert Newville. He opened a clipboard. "I need your names, please."

"I can save you a lot of time and trouble—" Illiani began.

"Sir, first I need your names."

"Greg Illiani, Special Agent, FBI."

Newville was unimpressed. "Let me see your ID."

"I'm under cover. I don't have my ID."

Newville turned to Kate. "Your name, ma'am."

"Lieutenant," Illiani raised his voice slightly. "If you value your rank, you will hear me out. *Now*."

"Sir, protocol calls for—"

"You're about to protocol yourself into a court-martial."

The lieutenant gave Illiani a look of harassed indifference. "All right, sir. Talk."

"We have classified data in our possession. Our presence here is a danger to this hospital. We need transportation to Anchorage, ASAP. Give me the phone."

Newville hesitated, then nodded and a guard handed the phone to Illiani. He punched in a long number, waited, shielded the mouthpiece and spoke briefly, then hung up. "Wait a few minutes."

The lieutenant glanced at his watch with bored skepticism. Several minutes passed. The phone rang and he answered. Listening, he raised his eyebrows and straightened. The conversation was short. "Mr. Illiani," Newville said in a conciliatory voice, "I've been ordered to provide transportation for you. If you'll wait here, I'll make arrangements."

David turned to Illiani. "Who the hell did you call?"

"The Director. The FBI links to the Unified Commands, in this case, PACOM. The order was probably routed through the Alaskan Command at Elmendorf, assuming they weren't wiped out by the attack."

Newville returned. He handed back their weapons and the CDs.

"Please follow me. We have a car waiting for you."

*   *   *

The Air Force staff car discharged them a block from the hotel, as requested, and they entered the building through the back. After David retrieved a key in the lobby, they took the stairs to their room on the second floor. The spare clothing was still neatly hung and folded, the laptop and cell phone undisturbed. Apparently, ARC hadn't yet discovered their second home.

Illiani dialed a local shop and ordered a change of clothes.

David opened the computer and launched the Internet browser. Kate's heart sank as she saw *Unable to complete connection* pop onto the screen. "Not a good sign," he muttered. He snapped open the cell phone and keyed a number. After a moment, he said, "Long distance is down."

"Then how did Greg call the Bureau?" Kate asked.

"Most of the commands have hardened landlines. It would take a major blast to knock them out." He punched in a number. "I'm calling Turner's flying service." A moment later he said flatly, "Answering machine."

Baths, food, and a brief rest became priorities.

Kate almost sobbed as she stepped into the warm shower; a few hours earlier, she had doubted she would live to experience this simple luxury again. As the water cascaded across her shoulders, she steadied herself against the wall, sapped by exhaustion and hunger. She dressed in jeans and a gray sweater, then stepped from the bathroom and saw David and Illiani huddled over the computer.

The television was on, the sound turned low. A news channel was covering the *Disaster at Elmendorf.* Eyewitnesses told of a bright purple glow over the airfield and loud explosions like sonic booms. Hundreds of deaths, untold millions in damage. Stay tuned.

David looked up from the laptop. "You should see this." He scrolled through an endless chain of drawings, maps, plans, and diagrams. "All this is from just one CD. We haven't even looked at the others."

Illiani pressed his lips together in a wry smile. "It's the mother lode. Enough to put Hurwitz and his buddies away for the rest of their lives."

"And another thing," David said, squeezing her hand and smiling. "You look great."

She smiled back.

David showered and emerged from the bath wearing jeans and a navy blue mock-turtle. Room service arrived, and the three pounced on their first true meal in nearly fourteen hours.

Illiani ate while standing, peering through the curtains. David annihilated a roast beef sandwich and took a long swallow of Canadian beer. He placed his bottle on the table and looked up. "What tricks does the Bureau have for getting us out of here?"

Illiani let the curtain drop back into place and sat down. "Unfortunately, none. I'm avoiding the Anchorage field office anyway. Don't know who I can trust."

"When the Arconians figure out we have these CDs, they'll rip this burg apart."

"The 'Arconians' will be watching everything. Air traffic, the highways out of Anchorage, car rentals—"

"We have a car here."

Illiani registered surprise. "Here?"

"Rented it under a different alias. I doubt they've traced it."

Propped up in bed, Kate finished her sandwich and attacked an apple. "There must be some way we can find Constellation."

David inserted another CD into the computer. "Right now, I think Turner is our best bet. If he'll fly us as far as, say, Juneau, we could hire another plane and hedgehop into Colorado Springs in a couple of days." He tapped a key and sat back. "Greg, check this out." Illiani looked over his shoulder. "ARC can intercept all satellite and land-based microwave relay signals."

Illiani straightened. "Jesus. They're getting what the NSA has plus every phone call on the planet."

"Yeah. The only conversation they can't hear is between a couple of kids with tin cans and a string."

"Their computers probably scan for key words, maybe even voice prints. That means…"

"They could have traced us to Elmendorf, and maybe the hotel."

Illiani glanced at his watch. "We've been here too long anyway. They're probably searching the—"

There was a knock on the door. Kate coughed, almost choking on a bite of apple. Illiani pulled his pistol and squinted through the security peephole. "It's just my clothes."

Fifteen minutes later, he had showered and dressed in jeans and a flannel shirt. David and Kate crammed their gear and the CDs into two backpacks. Both men wore pistols beneath their jackets.

The Explorer was still in the hotel's underground parking lot. Illiani groped around the vehicle, checking for homing devices and other unwelcome attachments while David walked through the garage. No one seemed to be watching.

"Looks clean," Illiani said.

David slid behind the wheel and started the engine. They reached the top of the ramp just as a sedan screeched to a stop beneath the carport on their right. Two men in blue jumpsuits bolted from the doors and rushed for the hotel's main entrance. David turned left and accelerated toward the Minnesota Bypass.

Kate picked up the cell phone. "We have a voice message."

"Try it," David said.

She punched the number. The recorded voice had an Indian huff: "Hello, this is Ben. Glad you're back. You should ship your package by air. I suggest you take it to Ed for fastest service. Hurry, or you may miss the delivery date." Kate repeated the message and added, "At least we're pointed in the right direction."

A barricade stifled traffic on Floatplane Drive. A black Humvee was parked beside the flashing lights, and four blue-clad men with M-16s walked from car to car, peering into the windows

Kate frowned. "ARC security guards."

David screeched into a tight U-turn, drove down a side street, and parked beside a row of cars in a lakeside picnic area. He turned to Kate. "It's about a mile to Turner's dock. Feel like a hike?"

She smiled. "Sure."

"There's plenty of cover. Keep some distance between us."

They shouldered their packs and single-filed along the shoreline. As they drew even with the barricade, they glimpsed the Humvee through the trees about a hundred yards up the embankment. A bullhorn blasted out: "Stop for a brief inspection. Have your driver's license ready."

David dropped back to Kate. She was breathing hard. "How are you doing?"

"Are you kidding? Piece of cake." She stopped and tugged on his sleeve. "David!" she whispered.

Two blue-suits, M-16s across their shoulders, appeared just beyond a cluster of trees. David pulled Kate off the trail. She glanced back; Illiani had disappeared.

"Whoa! Wait a minute." One of the guards was walking toward them. Kate feigned wide-eyed surprise. The second guard flipped a cigarette away and fell in behind his partner. His radio squawked unintelligibly.

"What is it, officers?" David asked in a concerned voice.

"Let's see some ID. It's for security." The man studied David's face closely, then stared at Kate.

The second guard licked his lips, his eyes wandering over her body. David produced his fake driver's license. The guard glanced at it for a moment, then handed it back, bringing the muzzle of his rifle up at the same time. The second guard followed his motion. "Turn around and head toward the road," he barked.

"Change of plans, gentlemen," a low voice growled. Illiani stepped from behind the screening cluster of oaks. He pulled the slide back on his Glock with a conspicuous *click*. The guards froze.

David palmed his own pistol and pointed back down the trail. "Walk."

After a short march, an empty clearing with a picnic table appeared. David halted the men when the trees fully shielded them, and Illiani collected the rifles and radios. "Look, now," the first guard snarled. "You don't want to fuck with—"

David's fist shot upward, and the man's jaw made a cracking

sound as his head snapped back. He dropped to the ground and lay still. In a simultaneous motion, Illiani knocked the second guard flat. They bound the unconscious men with laces from their boots and dragged them beneath the table.

David stood. "That'll buy us half an hour."

Illiani examined his right hand and balled it into a fist. "Ow. Happens every time…"

"You need to come up like this and rotate," David said, making a fist and punching it upward.

"Please!" Kate hissed. "We don't have time for this." She glanced nervously back toward the barricade.

David heaved the rifles into the lake and they marched toward Turner's docking area, staying as close to the trees as possible. Floatplanes packed the shoreline, most of them with men standing alongside like racecar drivers awaiting the call to start engines. Kate noticed only a few planes were landing. None were taking off.

Ed Turner was pacing back and forth beside his yellow Beaver, talking excitedly into a cell phone. He looked up as they approached, his face brightening as he saw them. "Come on," he said, striding up. "We've only got a few minutes. ARC is closing everything down. Got to leave right now or lose our chance."

Fifty yards to the right, a Cessna's engine fired; on the left, a red Beaver started up. Kate noticed propellers beginning to turn all along the shoreline as more and more engines joined in a growling chorus.

Turner hurried back toward the plane. "Get in, I'll explain on the way."

Kate climbed into the middle row of seats, and Illiani entered from the opposite side to buckle in beside her. Turner swung behind the steering yoke. The engine coughed to life as David pulled himself into the forward passenger seat. He turned around and extended his hand toward Kate. Her fingers entwined with his and she nodded, a determined smile crossing her face.

Turner taxied toward open water, following the Cessna and red Beaver. Throughout Lake Hood, Kate could see floatplanes nosing away from the beaches and funneling to multiple takeoff zones.

Turner switched the radio on and a voice rasped through the droning static...*severe action. For security purposes, all aircraft must land immediately or face severe action...*

"It's on every channel," Turner said. "Started about an hour ago." He pointed the aircraft into the wind, adjusted flaps, and shoved the throttle forward. The Cessna and the other Beaver were already airborne, and Turner followed, rising swiftly into blue sky. They banked eastward, and the Chugach Mountains swung into view, gray-green above the white expanse of the Columbia Glacier.

"Look," shouted Kate. "They're all taking off." Below them, a cloud of floatplanes climbed skyward.

Turner's grin widened. "Yeah, baby! Every plane on Lake Hood."

"You planned this?" David asked.

"It was kind of spontaneous. What are they gonna do, knock us *all* out of the sky?"

David shot a knowing glance at Kate and Illiani. "They could do that."

Turner banked left, putting more distance between his plane and the Cessna. "Yeah, but we got a secret weapon. Constellation has a man inside the mountain who's gonna do something to the computers. Knock 'em offline."

Illiani leaned forward. "You got a bogey at eight o'clock."

Kate turned. The wasp-shape of an Apache attack helicopter crept into view.

"Oh, shit," Turner said. How fast are those things?"

David answered. "About a hundred and fifty."

Turner edged the throttle up. "We can't outrun 'em."

A new message grated over the speaker: *All aircraft must land immediately. If you do not comply, you will be fired upon...*

As if following a carefully choreographed plan, the swarm of floatplanes diverged and headed in different directions. Several swooped close to the helicopter.

"The chopper's falling back," Illiani said.

...warning. This is your final warning...

"They'll use the ARC weapon—"

"Dive," David yelled. "Evade their radar."

Turner shoved the yoke forward and the Beaver dropped, arcing toward a glacier's white expanse.

...*This is your final warning...* the radio erupted in a warbling screech. Smoke curled into the cockpit.

"No!" Kate screamed.

Ahead of the Cessna on their right, a yellow-violet flame sizzled brightly in the air and ballooned to monstrous size. Kate watched in horror as the guttering plasma swallowed the other plane. Like bones in a reversed X-ray, the Cessna's fuselage shone darkly through the fireball's overpowering glare. The plane exploded in a nova of white sparks.

The horizon spun as Turner banked left and shoved the Beaver into a hard dive. A shrapnel-laden concussion shocked the plane into a roll and blasted shards of the starboard windshield into the cockpit. Turner wrestled the sputtering aircraft back into level flight.

Kate swept away something thin and jagged embedded in her right cheek, the wind forcing a thread of blood across her ear. She stared dumbly at her reddened hands, then wiped them against her jeans. David touched her shoulder. She looked up and saw his face was peppered with crimson. The engine noise and keening wind ripped his words away.

The cabin blazed anew with violet light as another fireball shimmered before them.

She stared into its alien eye, for that is what it resembled. It was roughly spherical, and its ragged violet shell flashed and flickered around the yellow-orange core. From this roiling nucleus writhed branching shafts of electricity that snaked outward and lashed into thin air like animated veins. It made a crackling, tearing sound, permeated with a hum like a shorted transformer.

So, that's *how it looks,* Kate thought.—*what Jack and the others saw the night ARC killed them. Now I'm about to die in the same way.* Fear yielded to anguish and anger: she would never avenge her husband, never expose the monsters behind ARC. *This is how it ends—*

She screamed as the thundering mass of energy filled the windscreen. She threw her arms protectively across her face, bracing for the searing heat to come. Then the light faltered, fluttered, and dissolved away into blue sky. The plane danced through shock waves of expanding air. Metal shrieked and chattered.

Then calm.

Turner leveled the craft and pulled the throttle back. The wind noise diminished. He glanced at his three passengers. "I thought we were toast," he said, his voice shaking. "Thought we were gonna fly apart." He reached out with an unsteady hand and reverently patted the dashboard. "But she held together, by Jesus."

Kate stared tensely ahead, terrified that the hideous light would reappear. David and Illiani craned their necks, scanning the sky. Finally, David exhaled, puffing out his cheeks. "Looks like your friends came through."

"Pulled the plug," Illiani said.

The cockpit smoke began to dissipate, blown through the shattered window, but the engine spat and stuttered. Turner flipped a few switches. "Instruments are out, engine's—no telling what's wrong. I know where we can land for repairs, if we can make it."

"Sure we'll make it," David said. "It's a Beaver, best floatplane made."

Turner grinned. "Damn right. Now let's get out of here before they turn that frickin' ray gun back on."

35

Senator Sam Hurwitz was furious. The timeline had been slammed forward. The president had acted much sooner than Sam expected, because of leaks, spies, failure to totally block the Internet—and *Constellation*.

He ticked his chair back and forth like a metronome, glowering into space. He was prepared to deal with the situation, so long as Crotty could get his Alliance drones to show up and Greggson didn't fall all over his ass at the crucial moment. But he had to act before Justice decided there was enough evidence to arrest *him*, *Hurwitz*. The phone beeped. He punched in the scramble code and jerked up the receiver.

"The committee's running hard on this, Sam," said Moral Alliance chairman Frederick Crotty. "We have the equipment, but getting things into place will be tough. This is such short notice…"

Hurwitz replied in his most empathetic voice. "Yeah, I appreciate your predicament, Fred, but you gotta' realize we have no choice. It's an emergency. Tell your people the time is at hand. We have an opportunity to implement Phase One ahead of schedule."

"Consider it done, Sam. But, now, this thing with General Greggson—it looks B-A-D."

Hurwitz hunched over the phone, ejecting a cloud of Cuba's finest. "Fred, don't forget how much *power* we'll have…" He paused and clenched his fist, almost crushing the cigar. "When I'm finished, we're all gonna look like goddamn heroes."

"Right, Sam."

"I need a show of support."

"Right."

"I want you there right beside me."

"I'll be there, Sam. I'll get back to you after the squads report in."

Hurwitz dropped the phone back into its cradle. Things might go smoothly, even without Greggson there. A lot depended on whether the president ordered a full-scale attack against ARC before tomorrow evening. He had to give the prez credit. He didn't think Williamson had the balls to act. But all Hurwitz *really* needed was enough people to show up for the cameras. At least the rally would look convincing.

He pushed his chair back and propped his legs on the desk, one hand behind his head, the other casually cradling the remains of his cigar. The time he had spent in politics and in the field had prepared him well. It was all about dominance, one species over another, and within that species, dominance by a few. Now the biggest big-game hunt of all time was about to start, and Hurwitz was Top Gun.

36

A rectangle of daylight gleamed brightly through the small access hatch in the barn's roof. Carlos's head appeared in the opening. He cupped his hands and shouted down: "Try it again."

O'Hanlon swiveled his chair beside the control console and threw a switch. A motor hummed. Gears squealed somewhere in the rafters and ground to a crunching halt.

"Whoa, it's still stuck," Carlos yelled.

O'Hanlon turned the switch off and looked up into the dark cavity beneath the cupola. Sections of the roof were designed to slide apart, giving the Magnifying Transmitter's big torus access to open sky, and after more than a hundred years of non-use, it wasn't surprising that some of the wheels had frozen.

"They're all free but this one," Carlos's voice echoed. "Let's give the oil a chance to work."

O'Hanlon watched as Carlos scrambled through the hatch, walked along a heavy wooden purlin, and backed down the ladder to the landing. Rock music and the clinking of tools came from below. O'Hanlon walked to the railing and looked down. "How's the wiring coming?"

The music volume dropped. Alex and Mark answered simultaneously, "Almost finished."

Two of the transmitter's old capacitors had been leaking insulating oil. The new units the boys were installing took up half the space the original four-foot monsters required, but they were vastly better.

O'Hanlon wondered what additional miracles Tesla might have achieved if he had been provided modern components.

He returned to the console and for the fifth time read the transmitter's checklist. They couldn't afford mistakes when they energized the machine with more than a million watts. Not *this* machine.

Carlos walked up beside him, wiping his hands on a rag. "Once the roof opens up, you'll turn the transmitter on, right?"

"Tomorrow, if you can fix that wheel."

Carlos nodded. "I'll try again in an hour. If I can't unstick it, I'll have to saw it off and hunt for a new one."

"Before we test, we'll need to move the livestock away, maybe into the west pasture."

"Just give me an hour's notice." Carlos stuffed the rag into his back pocket and headed for the stairway.

O'Hanlon sat back and sighed. Tesla's agreement required ultimately testing the transmitter at full power, and if the system failed at such a level, well…

His mind filled with horrifying images of electricity lashing from the big coils and striking down him or one of the boys. Arc-overs could turn the barn into a conflagration, and if a capacitor blew, it would go like a bomb. The manuals hinted at "gravest danger" should the system be operated improperly.

He thought of the odd sketches Mark had found, the ones he had labeled STORMDRAGON, and mentally again scrutinized each yellowed page. Why did Tesla combine drawings of the figure 8, the symbol for infinity, and Ouroboros? The "8" he thought he understood. It was the theoretical electrical resonant frequency of the earth, discovered by Tesla decades before modern science proved him correct. But where did *infinity* fit in? What about Ouroboros, the mythological serpent that "eateth of its own tail?" He wished he had the third manual.

* * *

Mark tugged the socket wrench, tightening the heavy cable onto the capacitor's high voltage terminal. He stood back, admiring the completed job. The new capacitors, housed in gray plastic boxes, looked cheap beside the varnished oak exteriors of the originals. He absently rubbed his nose, leaving behind a dark stripe of grease. Alex tossed him a rag, and he swiped it across the smudge. He gestured toward the huge coils in the barn's center. "When we turn this thing on, it's supposed to make giant bolts of electricity, isn't it?"

Alex shook his head. "Couldn't even guess. It's essentially some kind of Tesla Coil. The one at the science museum is about six feet tall and does an eight-footer with an input of around six kilowatts. The relationship's not linear, but this machine is forty feet tall, and has a ten-million watt input. But it's a lot more complicated, and with that resonant third coil…" He shrugged.

Stormdragon. Silly as the acronym was, Mark supposed the big machine could be likened to a dragon. A dragon that would rise after a hundred-year sleep to roar and spout electric fire.

"Well, let's see," came the Professor's voice. He was walking slowly along the row of capacitors, running his hand over the cables. He stopped beside the new units and tugged the connections, then looked at the test meter attached across the bus.

Alex tapped the digital readout. "Twenty microfarads. Right on the money."

"Good. If we're off more than ten percent, we'll have serious problems."

"Mark, you better come see this," a man's voice echoed down. It was FBI agent Charles Holt, who was standing at the railing above, just outside O'Hanlon's office.

Mark rushed up the stairs, with Alex close at his heels. Holt and another agent, Terrence Crowell, were seated side by side in Alex's makeshift office in the storeroom, staring at the glowing screens of two laptop computers. During the short time the agents had been on the ranch, Mark had grown to like them. Holt was the youngest, a computer expert who enjoyed video games. Crowell was big, extremely muscular, and had a British accent. His nickname was Crow, which fit, because he was black. They turned as Mark approached.

Holt punched a key and moved aside, giving Mark a better view of the monitor.

A news headline blinked on.

Explosions Rock Elmendorf Air Base
200 Feared Dead
Severed Communications Delay News

Images of burning aircraft and buildings began to form. Mark's anxiety ramped up as he read the text.

At least thirty aircraft blew up on the runway yesterday afternoon at Elmendorf Air Force Base outside Anchorage, Alaska. Two hundred are feared dead, and more than 300 have been injured. The blasts leveled more than a dozen structures on the base and shook buildings as far as two miles away.

Strong radio interference, said to be originating from ARC, or the Auroral Research Center, has hampered attempts to get news from the region.

Another headline appeared, along with a photo of General Thad Greggson.

Greggson Charged/Missing

Sources say U.S. Chief of Staff, Thad Greggson, who is sought by the FBI, was last seen boarding a helicopter at Elmendorf Air Force Base several hours before the base was destroyed by a series of major explosions.

Greggson, along with four of his staff members, were charged two days ago with misappropriation of funds, conspiracy to commit fraud, and theft of military equipment. Sources believe Greggson has gone into hiding at the top-secret Auroral Research Center, located between Anchorage and Fairbanks. Attorney General Trey Morrison said more charges may be filed against Greggson tomorrow, and that federal warrants have been issued for his arrest.

Mark frowned. His mother was already a day late posting a

message, and now Alaska was turning into a war zone. "What does this mean?" he asked the agents.

Holt shoved the chair back and stood. "It means we better watch the evening news." He headed for the door, then paused. "I'll see what I can find out."

Mark paced. "Man, this *sucks*."

"Your mom will be okay." Alex said. "She's smart. And she's got Mr. Hightower with her."

"What makes it bad is waiting."

They were silent for a moment. Crow finally spoke, his deep voice filling the room. "Charles will call you as soon as he learns anything."

"We could ride horses," Alex suggested, a note of optimism in his voice.

Mark looked at him for a moment. "Yeah," he said. "That's what we'll do."

Crow made a rumble of disappointment. "Man, I hate horses."

*　　*　　*

Mark urged his mount up the last few yards of the Z-shaped switchback leading to Spy Knob's summit. He halted and gazed westward through a ridge of upended rock. The clouds had been gathering all afternoon, and now a thunderstorm snarled along the foothills, chilling the air. Silver threads of lightning darted against the distant mountains, and rain drifted in long gray strands, thinning to a gunmetal haze.

Hooves sounded behind him as Carlos came up the trail on his palomino. He reined his horse alongside Mark. "Up here you're just a lightning rod, you know."

Mark glanced again at the lowering clouds.

After a moment, Alex and Crow joined them. The hill's narrow, boulder-strewn top was getting crowded.

Mark remembered a summer of years ago, when he and his father were overtaken at the Lookout by a thunderstorm. They had parked their bikes and scrambled below the big rock ledge, watching moisture slant down and evaporate before touching the earth. "It's called *virga*," his father had said. "When the rain evaporates before it reaches the ground."

"Airplane," Carlos said, pointing southwest.

The mutter of a single engine fought through the hiss of rising wind. As Mark looked up, a shaft of sunlight lanced through the clouds and spotlighted a small, yellow plane flying low before the advancing wall of gray.

The plane banked to the right and began dropping toward the east pasture. Mark's radio squawked. One of the ranch hands was speaking: "...small, and real low. I think it's going to land."

His grandfather's voice came next. "Land? Where?"

"In the stock pond."

"The *stock pond*?"

"Sí. It has—*como se dice*—pontoons."

37

Lightning flared, and the plane pitched in the growing turbulence. Kate ignored the storm, focusing instead on the familiar terrain below. They had flown into Colorado Springs from the north, staying outside the air traffic control zones for NORAD and Peterson Air Force Base. Now they approached Pikes Peak, angling deeper into the foothills.

Her spirits soared as the ranch came into view. She could plainly see the two small lakes, the house, barn, and the train track's silvery loop. Horses grazed in the pastures, and she thought she saw riders on the big hill in the west woods. David looked back at her from the copilot's seat and smiled. She had finally made it home.

"There's the stock pond," she said, pointing toward the pasture.

"I see it," Turner replied. "We'll go straight in. Storm's coming up fast."

The seven-acre pond seemed large when on the ground, but from the air it appeared a mere puddle, impossibly small to land upon. Kate held her breath as the Beaver dropped toward the dark patch of water.

The buffeting increased as they skimmed the treetops and dropped low over the field, leveling for touchdown. The shoreline flashed below and Turner cut the throttle. Wavelets rattled against the pontoons as they made sudden contact with the lake's surface. The western shoreline rushed to meet them. Almost immediately they nosed into the embankment, the aluminum floats making a hollow scraping noise against the gravel.

Turner cut the engine, and Kate heaved a sigh of relief, a broad smile breaking across her face. The three men jumped ashore carrying nylon rope and steel anchor posts. As they hammered the rods into the ground and attached the tethering lines, Kate grabbed the two aluminum attaché cases holding the CDs and laptop. She stepped onto the starboard pontoon and paused, inhaling the rain-washed scent of pine and mountains.

"Kate!" she heard a shout and looked up to see a truck bumping across the pasture toward them. Miguel waved from the cab, grinning. She waved back, jumped into knee-deep water, and slogged to the beach.

Her father's truck pulled up a moment later. The doors flew open, and Mark rushed to her side. She dropped the attaché cases and wrapped him in a hug, finally breaking into tears.

"Hello, darlin'," came her father's deep voice. "You sure know how to make a dramatic entrance."

Her mother was next, hugging her, fretting about the bandage on her cheek, and commenting on her bleached blond hair. Buddy and Higgins were suddenly dancing at her feet. She bent down to pet the dogs and received a face full of whiskers and wet licks. David, Illiani, and Turner walked up the embankment, and her father turned to greet them.

Her mother called out, "Let's get everyone inside, Jared. This storm's about to hit."

Hailstones and rain lashed the truck as they drove back across the pasture, but the clouds parted the moment they reached the house, and evening sunlight swept across the hills and valley in ragged bands of gold. Kate stepped out, her feet crunching on a thin layer of hail. A rainbow arched over the foothills, one end melding with the shadows of Pikes Peak, the other bowing toward Colorado Springs.

No place on earth, she thought, *is more beautiful than this.*

*   *   *

Almost in a daze, Kate pulled her chair up to the long dining table with the others. She looked around the room; it seemed as if she had been away for years. Less than two days ago, she had been battling for her life inside ARC's ghastly maze. Now she was with her family in the safest and most peaceful environment she had ever known.

Her mother ministered to her guests in her traditional way—with mounds of food. María placed heaping platters on the table while Kate and her companions told about their escape.

After the harrowing attack above Lake Hood, they had limped into Tatitlek, north of Juneau, where Turner managed to replace the floatplane's burned-out instruments and repair the damaged ignition system. David had tried to send an encoded message, but found the ARC microwave beam had destroyed the laptop's circuits.

After leaving Tatitlek, they followed the coastline as far as Washington and then hedgehopped through Oregon, Idaho and Utah, always fearful that ARC would discover them. At each stop, Turner had insisted on taking them farther.

Her father nodded at Turner and said, "I owe you a great deal for having brought my daughter and Mr. Hightower back alive. You're welcome stay here as long as you like."

"Thanks," Turner replied. "But I'll be leaving for San Diego first thing in the morning. Got an uncle there I'll visit until this thing blows over. Besides, the bad guys are hunting for you, and a yellow floatplane is hard to miss."

Everyone filed into the den after the evening meal, including Professor O'Hanlon and FBI agents Holt and Crow. Kate noticed Mark frowning at her as she sat beside him. "What's wrong?"

"Mom," he answered softly, the blue eyes full of sympathy. "You look like you've lost an awful lot of weight."

She winked at him. "Thanks, pal. That's the nicest thing anyone ever said to me."

Jared sat on his barstool beside the fireplace, a booted foot hiked onto the chair's lower brace. "I know you're exhausted," he began, "but we've got some business that can't wait." He folded his arms and looked at David. "Why don't you tell us what you and Kate found out."

David swept his gaze around the room. He leaned forward. "ARC may be the most formidable weapon ever built. We think it can quickly destroy targets anywhere on the planet. From what we've seen, those targets could be anything from a single aircraft to an entire city."

O'Hanlon gave an incredulous look. "How?"

"Microwaves, and loads of power. Special antennas control the focus and direction of microwave radiation. They cycle low-energy microwaves to induce a rotating disc of charged particles in the ionosphere. This creates a high efficiency radio-frequency mirror over sixty miles up. They can tilt the mirror and bounce powerful beams off it. Microwaves from the first mirror can create another mirror, and so on, meaning they can direct the energy almost anywhere."

"A death-ray from the sky," Alex said ominously.

"That's pretty accurate."

The group fell silent.

Kate wrapped her arms around her knees. "They have another technology," she said quietly.

David placed his hand on her arm. "You don't have to talk about that."

"It's okay." She paused for a moment. "They have a portable machine. It puts out a radio beam that affects the mind." A shadow crept across her face. "There's a man—a Dr. Fechter—working for them. He used one of those machines on me. If David and Greg hadn't come at the last moment…" She shuddered. She heard a sharp intake of breath, and glanced at Mark. His mouth had dropped open, and he stared at her, a look of anger and horror on his face. She gave him a reassuring smile.

Illiani spoke: "The gray vans. They call them *Scanners*. I saw hundreds, including bigger ones, being built in a plant outside the mountain,."

"They have electronic gear," Kate added, "and those claw-shaped antennas inside, just behind the side windows."

David said, "They plan to disperse them around the country, use them for crowd control, assassinations. Apparently, a Scanner can focus its beam on someone, or a small group, and screw up their minds, or kill them."

O'Hanlon said, "If that's true, perhaps ARC has the same

capability, on a huge scale. Perhaps they could mentally disable an army, or…"

David interrupted: "According to the CDs we found, they're developing a technique to induce mental states, like fear or passivity, in large populations."

"We just learned the president may launch a full-scale attack against the project," Charles Holt said, "possibly by tomorrow afternoon."

Mark said, "If they attack, maybe they'll forget about us."

"Don't count on it. You know too much."

"Well, if this weapon is so great, why don't they just use it on us *now*?" Alex asked.

Holt shot him a wry glance. "Maybe they want you *alive*."

The thought sent a chill through Kate.

Her father turned to Alex. "Anything new from Constellation?"

"Yeah. Mostly what you already know. ARC blew up the Air Force base, and they shot down some planes that were after General Greggson."

O'Hanlon's face was grim. "We'll postpone testing the Magnifying Transmitter until all this has settled down."

"But we might as well continue with preparations," Jared said. He looked at Kate. "And you can start writing your documentary."

She shook her head. "We're taking this straight to Channel Twelve."

"That's not a good idea."

"Daddy," Kate said firmly, "The story has to be aired *now*."

Crow's deep voice boomed out. "That would be very unsafe, Ma'am."

"Look. I'd like nothing better than to stay with my family and be 'safe', but you have no idea how powerful, and evil, these people are. Look at what they did to Elmendorf. What if they can't be defeated? This may be our last chance to get the truth out."

"She's right," David said. "If we waste time, everything Kate went through—that we *all* went through—will be meaningless."

Jared looked down, his jaw working. Finally, he looked at David.

"I assume you'll be going with her?"

"Of course. Both Greg and me."

"Agents Crowell and Masters will be available too," Holt said. "That makes five."

Almost six, Kate thought, considering Crow's size.

Jared fixed his eyes on her, then gave a slight nod. "Do what you must, Darlin'."

The meeting broke up and the participants drifted to their respective bedrooms. Kate's father hugged her. "I'm pretty old fashioned," he said with a kindly smile. "But it would be all right with me if you and David wanted to share the downstairs guest room."

She kissed him on the cheek. "Good night, Daddy."

*   *   *

Kate slipped through the mountain of warm, jasmine-scented suds and stretched out in the oversized tub. Bubble baths, a luxury in which she rarely indulged at home, were her personal tradition when she stayed at the ranch. As she soaked, inhaling the herbal aroma, the layers of physical and psychic filth heaped upon her inside the Dark Mountain seemed to dissolve and sigh away like exorcised demons.

She finally stepped from the tub, dried, and buttoned on a soft flannel nightgown. She walked quietly across the room and slid beneath the covers of the ancient four-poster bed. David mumbled a few incoherent words as she drew close and folded her arm around him.

And so she slept, with the warmth of his body joining her own. Her dreams, when they came, were distant and vague, only hinting at a darkness that coiled and swirled at the edge of her mind.

38

The next morning, Kate, David, and half the ranch personnel watched Ed Turner's yellow floatplane lift off into a crisp blue sky. He circled once, rocked his wings in a goodbye, and pointed west.

"We owe him our lives," Kate said to David as they walked back to the Jeep.

"We'll see him again," he said, smiling. "I intend to collect on his promise for some free fishing."

* * *

The elevator doors slid apart and Kate, followed by David and Illiani, stepped into the Channel 12 lobby. The two men wore jeans and windbreakers and carried aluminum attaché cases. Kate, her hair dyed back to its normal glossy black, wore a dark news broadcaster's outfit. They swept past the reception desk and down the hall to Randall Mason's office. She knocked on the door and stepped inside.

The station manager looked up from his desk and blinked, pen frozen in midair. "Kate," he said. His voice sounded tight, as if she'd caught him with his pants around his knees. He stared at her bandaged face. "What happened to you?"

"I'll explain later." She nodded for David and Illiani to enter. "Randall, I'd like you to meet two friends."

Mason stood as the men entered, and shook hands. He registered surprise when he learned one of her entourage was an FBI agent.

"Randall," Kate said, fixing him with a stare. "I want you to see this."

David slid a laptop onto Mason's desk as she spoke. Behind him, Illiani closed the office door.

Mason seemed uncomfortable. "Sure," he said, his eyes darting to each of his visitors, then to the laptop.

Kate tapped a key and a video clip of Sam Hurwitz began: *"The ARC Project is destined to become the cornerstone of this nation's defense system—"*

She hit the key again. An aerial shot of the ARC installation flashed on, then a claw antenna, a schematic of the microwave system, animal experiments, and a plan for invisibly controlling or killing individuals and large populations.

Mason looked up. "Where did you get—?"

Kate's voice dropped in pitch. "Inside the project." She leaned forward, her hands on his desk. "ARC is no innocent research center, Randall. It's a weapon. A *huge* weapon. And they're already using it *against this country*."

They're the ones who destroyed Elmendorf Air Force Base. They've killed hundreds of innocent people, including senators. Edwards for one." Her voice hardened. "They used it to bring down my husband's plane two years ago."

She paused, straightened. "And there's more. They can affect people's minds. Burn the intelligence right out of them, make zombies of them. They can jam communications, blow away our defenses. If we don't get this story out *today*, Hurwitz, Krohner, and Greggson will rule this planet."

Mason stared at Kate. "I need corroborating—"

Kate almost shouted. "We don't have *time*." She held her hands out. "Think about it, Randall. You know me. This is real. We have to act *now*."

Mason glanced at Illiani. "Why don't you let the FBI handle it?"

"Because," Illiani said, "ARC has better eavesdropping capabilities than the NSA. If we tried to reach the Bureau, they'd know."

"Well, won't they stop us if we try to broadcast?" Mason asked.

David stepped forward. "We're certain of it. But if we transmit before they clamp down, we accomplish our purpose. Every news organization in the world will pick it up."

Kate cocked her head and gave Mason a wry look. "Besides, this is the scoop of the century. Are you going to let it slip away?" Mason chewed his lip. Kate could imagine the conflict raging inside the pudgy cranium: security versus truth.

"They'll fire me," he said quietly.

"They're *murderers*," she fired back. "We risked our lives for this, Randall, and we're placing our lives on the line *here*. Unless the public learns the truth, your job won't matter anyway."

Mason stared at her for a long moment, his fearful expression slowly hardening into resolve. "How soon can you have this ready?"

She closed the laptop. "First part, seven o'clock. I'll need the full time slot, and I'll need Gil's help."

"The president is preempting at seven."

"Then make it six-thirty. And not a word to anyone."

"Don't forget about Angela. She'll call TriConn. They own the station. They're Moral Alliance advocates."

"Can't we keep Angela away?"

Mason snorted. "Maybe if you stuff her in a broom closet."

Kate smiled thinly. The idea had some merit. She shrugged. "We'll deal with it when it happens."

"Then go for it."

* * *

Gil Henderson was hanging up the telephone when they hustled through the control room doors. "Kate, hey!" He stood and hugged her. She went through another round of introductions. "FBI?" Gil said as he shook Illiani's hand. He glanced back at Kate. "What the hell kind of video did you bring *back*, anyway?"

She handed him four CDs. "Load these." She turned to David and pointed to a CD burner. "Can you make copies?"

"Good as done." He pulled up a chair and began loading discs into the machine.

Illiani wandered around the editing room, peering at the equipment as if he expected to find hidden cameras or bugs.

"Oh, man, coool!" came Gil's exuberant voice as the editing monitors lit with images from the CDs.

"Back that one up," Kate said, pointing. "Here's where I want to start—" She jumped as the doors banged open and Angela, blond hair swirling behind her, raged into the room. She tramped to the editing bay and glared down at Gil.

"What is this shit?" she shouted. "I *anchor* this station, and you are *not* bumping me."

Gil's gaze lingered on the monitors for a moment before he turned to face her. "Angela," he said calmly, holding up a placating hand. "Bear with us. We've got to run with this—"

She jerked her head toward Kate, screwing up her face as if she had just seen a cockroach crawl onto the editing console. "Last time I saw *you*, you were doing stories about *parking lots*."

Kate said nothing. Gil stood and folded his arms. "Angela, I'm sorry, but you'll just have to back off on this one."

"We'll see about that."

She looked hard at the monitors, her scowl morphing into a petulant smile, then spun around and stormed out.

"Good ol' Angela," Gil muttered.

Kate sighed. "She's probably on the phone to TriConn already."

"By the time they take legal action, we'll have this thing in the can."

"It's not *legal* action I'm worried about." Kate thought for a moment. "Let's get the Avid from my office. If we set it up here, we can work a lot faster."

"All right," Gil said, "But if we don't get started *now*, it'll be moot."

As if to underscore his words, the evening news teaser began: Greggson's image, the burning Elmendorf Air Force Base, a distant aerial shot of ARC: Details at six.

The phone buzzed. Gil lifted the receiver. "That was Mason. Angela just called TriConn."

David and Illiani carted the Avid editing system into the cramped control room. A small table pirated from a nearby cubicle supported the two monitors and keyboard, while the computer and hard drives rested on the floor. With help from Gil, they quickly wired the system and connected it and the laptop to the network.

Kate culled scenes from the CDs at random, downloading them to Gil, who began assembling them into a broadcast-quality version that included fades, dissolves, and color-corrected images. Normally, Kate would need a week to analyze and log all the data, assemble a shot list, write the script, pull the shots, and edit. She had a few hours.

Less than half the information on the CDs had been explored, and David used the laptop to continue searching. When he found something of interest, he shot it to Kate through the network. She fretted as she frantically worked the Avid; without time to properly organize the scenes, linearity was impossible. The show was being thrown together like a patchwork quilt.

Illiani prowled restlessly through the offices and grounds, checking every few minutes with Crow and Masters, who were stationed outside the building. At one o'clock, he brought sandwiches from the deli and distributed the food in the editing room. "Angela left an hour ago," he reported. "Mason said she waltzed out with a smug look on her puss."

"Here!" David said abruptly. He held his hand up and beckoned, not taking his eyes from the laptop. Kate and Illiani peered over his shoulder.

"This is filed under an operation they codenamed 'Scepter.'" He slugged back a swallow of soft drink and cleared his throat. "Here's a plan of the White House. These lines radiate from the West Wing, the Oval Office, and the president's bedroom. They run to locations on Pennsylvania Avenue, and each line shows distance in meters.

"There's a similar plan for the vice president, the Speaker of the House, and the secretary of defense." He scrolled to a chart showing dates and times. "Plus a timetable. And *this*." He punched up the next image and pointed. "This shows power levels, frequencies, and distance against a percentage of lethality."

"What do you make of it?" Kate asked.

David's head snapped up. "A coup. They plan to kill them—all four." He turned around in his chair and faced her and Illiani, holding up his hands for emphasis. "Hurwitz is president pro tem of the Senate, third in the line of succession. He'll take over as president. He'll appoint Greggson as secretary of defense, and ARC and the Moral Alliance will effectively become the government. And the timetable is set for *today*."

Illiani scooped up a stack of the duplicated CDs and started for the door. "I'll be back."

"What's up?" David asked.

Illiani turned around. "Something I should've done much earlier—have Crow take these to NORAD. They have a secure landline to the White House."

Kate nodded and turned to Gil. "Do we have the CNN satellite feed from D.C.?"

"Yeah." Gil punched the channels in. Three monitors lit with raw, unedited video. "These are the setup transmissions from the White House and from…" He paused, looking at the screens. "The Hurwitz rally at the Lincoln Memorial."

"That's what I want." She looked closely at the center monitor: Microphone in hand, a female reporter stood before a stage that had been erected on the broad Lincoln Memorial grounds. A backdrop bearing the Moral Alliance emblem was rising into place behind the tall black cabinets of a massive speaker system.

Glancing down at her notes from time to time, the reporter continued her delivery:

…an emergency rally this afternoon, here at the Lincoln Memorial. Moral Alliance leader Frederick Crotty said the rally has been called to protest President Williamson's campaign to shut down the ARC, or Auroral Research Center, and to condemn his recent attempt to arrest General Thad Greggson." She looked off to her left. *And the crowds are pouring in.*

The camera followed her gaze and panned out toward the reflecting pool, where waves of people marched across the lawn, hundreds holding aloft placards and signs reading *Free Greggson* and *Save the ARC*.

The announcer returned:

Senator Sam Hurwitz said he will attend the rally in support of the Moral Alliance. President Williamson has scheduled a press conference this evening to explain why he has taken action against ARC and to justify the charges against General Greggson. The stage is set, literally, for a political showdown.

The reporter paused for a moment, as if listening to some off-camera conversation. The camera again panned across the grounds.

"There!" Kate said. "Record that."

"Got it."

"Play back, slow."

The image reversed, then crept forward. People underwater-walked across the grounds, cars inched along the boulevard. A camera truck entered the frame, its satellite dish pointing skyward.

"Stop. Enlarge the truck."

The image was soft, but Kate could make out the detail well enough.

"David…"

"Yeah, I see it."

Splashed across the bobtail truck's white side was the ostentatious, powder-blue and gold emblem of the Moral Alliance. An elevation boom and several small vertical antennas poked from the truck's roof. What had caught Kate's eye was the satellite antenna. Instead of the ubiquitous parabolic dish, the antenna atop the truck had the jointed digits of a claw.

39

The heavy steel doors unlocked with an explosive *chank* and growled open, admitting Joseph Krohner into the vast, semidark space deep within the mountain. Inside the great room, white-coated technicians labored on tiered levels before banks of glowing meters, screens, and beeping control stations.

Sound from the mountain's myriad systems droned through the heavily shielded walls and merged into a throbbing, discordant murmur. To Krohner, it was the anthem of ultimate power.

Heads turned as he stepped through the door, but he acknowledged no one. He angled right and walked stiffly along the raised walkway toward the room's center. He stopped at the base of a circular platform. Resting at its top was the Throne, the integrated chair and electronic console that placed the entire ARC system at his command. He climbed the steps, eased himself into the leather seat, and pressed a footswitch. Hydraulics hummed, and the chair began to rise.

He stopped high above the floor and looked down through the slanted glass walls into the enormous cavern below. Ten-thousand transmitting modules—gleaming black monoliths ten feet square and thirty feet tall—marched in serried rows across the vast chamber like an army of giant robots.

Tubular waveguides coiled from the dark behemoths and funneled upward to feed the massive antenna array surrounding the mountain. Amber light beaming through narrow slits near the top of each module proclaimed that unit ready and on standby.

A panoramic display as large as a motion picture screen hovered above the protective glass walls. Krohner stabbed a button, and a homolosine projection of the world swam into view, the grid lines and geopolitical zones traced in glimmering neon. Three-dimensional animations of the planet, overlaid with translucent, multi-hued renderings of the ionosphere and magnetosphere, flanked the central image. The animations continually updated, altering like storm clouds on a weather map.

Krohner tugged on a headset, twisted the microphone close to his mouth, and spoke quietly. "Display attack coordinates."

A swarm of glowing dots raced across the world map: red for nuclear missile sites, yellow for military airfields. The heaviest concentration of targets blinked from the United States.

"Display defense screen," Krohner commanded.

The map disappeared, replaced by a rotating, three-dimensional image of the ARC installation. A translucent dome enveloped the mountain and antennas, its undulating surface a complex, intersecting pattern of shimmering circles.

Krohner permitted himself a slight smile. The Kill Screen was working perfectly. Nothing could pass the invisible shell without being incinerated. And from behind this impenetrable field of destruction, he could launch searing beams against any threat, anywhere in the world.

The Kill Screen concept was simple: a rapidly rotating microwave beam projected from the mountain completely surrounded ARC for a distance of twenty miles horizontally and sixty miles vertically. Anything from a bird to a bullet to a Stealth Bomber penetrating the sweep region would disturb the field. In a microsecond, the beam's energy level would ramp up and destroy the intruding object. The system was quite automatic, totally impervious, and could be sustained indefinitely.

Then he thought about the three individuals who had escaped with the top-secret CDs, and the smile vanished. These people, the female TV reporter and her two male cohorts, had penetrated his high-security fortress and stolen from him. *Unacceptable. Unforgivable.*

He toggled to a map of the U.S., zoomed in to Colorado Springs, and nudged a pair of black crosshairs over the city block where the TV station—Channel 12—was located. In less than five minutes, he could reduce the area to cinders. But, for the present, he would restrain himself. Let them handle it locally, *quietly*. If that failed, he would eliminate the thieves himself, using somewhat stronger measures.

Only hours earlier, ARC security had arrested another infiltrator. A Constellation spy. The man had altered the ARC targeting program, temporarily disabling the primary ARC weapon and allowing aircraft to escape from Anchorage. The twisted smile returned. Fechter had the man now and would make an example of him—a mindless automaton—if he left the man any brain cells at all.

Krohner settled back into the padded leather chair and watched transmitter performance readouts scroll past. He was now at one with the most powerful weapon ever conceived. The nuclear generating plant could pump out an unprecedented one hundred trillion watts. In pulse mode, the peak transmitter output could reach a staggering one hundred petawatts—a thousand trillion. With the antennas directed and focused, ARC could deliver as much destructive energy as a nuclear bomb.

But ARC would soon be far more than a cataclysmic weapon. It would be a new paradigm, a system that would ultimately allow the influence and control of virtually every mind on the planet. Orwell's *1984*, Huxley's *Brave New World,* were nothing compared to what ARC would accomplish in the very near future.

ARC was virtually undefeatable. All weapons systems checked.

Nothing could stop them now—nothing.

Charles Holt, whom Mark now regarded as his own personal FBI agent, strode alongside as he walked to the barn. Mark shook his head. "This just doesn't make sense."

"What doesn't?"

"How could they build ARC, and the president not even know what it could do?"

Holt shrugged. "Eternal vigilance is the price of liberty, and we weren't vigilant."

"It's hard to be vigilant if it's all secret."

"Good point." Holt thought for a moment. "I guess the wild card in this case is technology."

"What do you mean?"

"I think they had such advanced technology it was easy to hide things from us. We lost control because nobody understood the science, what they were actually doing."

They entered the barn and found Alex standing beside the tarp-shrouded train. A box of electronic instruments rested at his feet. "Let's uncover it," he said. "O'Hanlon wants me to run some tests."

Mark grasped the section of tarp covering the rear car and yanked it up. A gray blur suddenly shot from the dark interior and launched off his shoulder. Mark ducked, flinging his arms over his head, and made a startled cry.

Alex laughed. "It was a *raccoon*, man, just a raccoon."

Mark watched as a ringed tail disappeared into the hay bales stacked beyond the train. He dusted himself off. "I knew that." He glanced back at Holt, who was tucking his pistol back into his shoulder holster. His eyes met Mark's, and the agent smiled sheepishly.

"Well," Alex said, bringing his hands together in a mild clap. "Let's hope the little beggar doesn't have his whole family in there."

Mark peeked cautiously inside the car. White cotton padding erupted through the shredded upholstery and lay in a snowy pile on the floorboard. "Aw," he moaned, "it's ruined."

They peeled the tarp back and pushed the train outside into bright sunlight. Holt walked around the machine, shaking his head and staring. "I can't believe this thing was designed a hundred years ago."

Mark and the FBI agent attacked the destroyed seats with a shop vacuum and a broom while Alex probed behind the dashboard, checking for damaged wires. Mark swiped perspiration from his brow with the back of his hand. It was a typical Colorado Springs summer day: no wind, and a bright sun in a flawless blue sky. He glanced across the field toward the shaded pines. "Why don't we take it into the woods. It'll be cooler."

Alex looked up, his face also gleaming with sweat. "Yeah, I suppose that would work." He looked at his watch. "Call your grandfather, and let's hustle. It's close to lunch."

* * *

Jared walked in, running a kerchief across his forehead. He inspected the train transmitter and nodded. "I set the power at twenty five percent. You're ready to go."

Holt came up beside Alex as he lowered his test instruments and tools into the rear car. "You say this thing actually runs on *radio waves*?"

Alex gestured toward the barn. "From that transmitter near the door."

Holt shook his head again. As he stepped into the first car, Buddy suddenly rocketed past him and jumped into the seat. Chuckling, the agent sat down beside him. Mark and Alex took their positions in the cockpit and threw the switches. The train's motor buzzed and hummed, the couplers clanked, and they rolled away from the barn and past the corral.

They climbed the hill at twenty-five miles per hour and hit thirty on the way down. Mark coaxed the machine to forty on the straight run across the meadow, then nudged Alex. "Look at the speed."

"See if it'll do fifty."

Mark grasped the brass throttle lever and ticked it forward. The motor's whirring sound smoothly increased in pitch, and he felt the train tugging him along faster, the wheels making that cool, metallic purr against the tracks. This machine *wanted* to accelerate. They were rocking along now, gliding across the meadow, the wind whistling past the tall antenna. He watched the approaching woods through the round windshield and was tempted to pour more energy to the motor, but curves lay ahead and he wanted to avoid an unplanned detour into an aspen.

He looked back. Buddy was sitting upright, sniffing the breeze, ears flying straight out like a pair of wings. Holt gave a "thumbs up."

"Better back off," Alex said.

Mark looked at the speedometer; its black needle was edging past fifty miles an hour. He pulled the throttle back and they coasted into the woods and rolled to a gentle stop beneath a canopy of pine branches. The temperature felt twenty degrees cooler. Small boulders shouldered above a thick carpet of pine needles, and the creek could be heard burbling on its way to the stock pond. Alex keyed the walkie-talkie and told Mark's grandfather he could shut down the transmitter.

Holt stepped from the car, smoothing his hair back into place.

"How fast can this thing go?"

Mark shrugged. "We don't know,"

"We did fifty with the transmitter set at twenty five percent," Alex said, lifting his instruments from the car. "So I have to leave the rest to your imagination."

Holt bent down and peered beneath the engine. "You sure the power doesn't come in over the rails?"

Alex folded back the access panel. "Nope. Radio. The rails only ground the system. We don't understand how it works, that's why we're running tests." He reached inside the cylindrical compartment and began attaching wires. "Mark," he called out. "Turn the limiter and throttle to maximum."

Mark made the adjustments, knowing that without power being transmitted, the train's motor would remain at rest.

A voice crackled over the radios. "This is Gamma. We've got a helicopter coming in. Looks like he's checking us out."

"That's near the Poacher's Gate," Mark said. He walked to the edge of the woods and squinted into the foothills. Echoing softly at first, then louder, was the heavy beat of rotor blades. A dark shape appeared above the distant tree line, circling slowly in their direction.

"Stay hidden," Holt said." He jogged back toward the train.

Mark flattened against the big pine and Buddy stood at his side, letting out a nervous growl. Downwash from the rotor blades thrashed the treetops as the chopper drifted in low, and Mark could see distorting heat waves from the exhaust and hear the loud rush and whine of the turbines.

A large cylinder, like the searchlights he had seen on police helicopters, pointed down from the helicopter's nose. He stared at the fuselage as the chopper passed overhead, thinking he might glimpse Colorado State Troopers or some other insignia. But there were no markings at all. Other than the searchlight, the only distinguishing feature was its color—black.

41

The camera pushed in for a closeup as Kate finished her narration. She hadn't wasted time in the makeup room, or even brushed her hair into place. She had videotaped her report straight from the trenches: bruised, scratched, battered, seen-it-all, barely-escaped-alive, walked-the-walk and talked-the-talk. She had delivered the no-bullshit bottom line. She glanced at herself in the monitor. *I look like hell.*

In an impossibly short time, she and Gil had taped a bombshell investigative report that implicated Greggson, Hurwitz, Crotty, Krohner, and others in murder and a conspiracy to assassinate the country's top leaders. They had exposed ARC for what it really was—a demonic, brain-burning, murdering, war machine designed for world domination.

She heaved a sigh and glanced up at the control room window. An admiring smile had broken across David's face. He clapped his hands in silent applause. Gil gestured thumbs-up. "Perfect," his voice came over the intercom.

Kate gave a wave of her hand. "Thanks." She unclipped the microphone and stood up. "And thank you, Bob," she said, turning to the cameraman.

He smiled and nodded. "Great work, Kate. You filling in for Angela?"

"No," she said emphatically. She stepped down from the set and focused her attention on the news monitor. The networks were still reporting long-distance telephone and radio breakdowns across the country due to satellite problems and unexplained burnouts of land-based systems. No one knew how extensive the problem was. There was no quick way to find out.

She turned and almost bumped into David.

"Impressive." He paused, looking at her as if he had more to say. But she read it in his eyes, realized he was holding her hands. He simply blurted out "I love you." She blinked hard. A boyish smile broke across his face. "Nobody ever accused me of having tact, or social grace. Or timing."

Kate slipped her hand gently behind his neck, drew close, and kissed him. "I think your timing is perfect." She turned toward the control room, looked back at him, and pulled her hand slowly free. "Now let's finish this thing."

Gil and Illiani were grinning when she and David entered the control room.

"Nice performance," said Illiani.

"Thanks," she replied.

"Good job on the report, too," he said, glancing at her sideways.

She shot him a twisted grin and turned to the studio monitor. The last seconds of her tape were playing. The title, *ARC—Archenemy*, glowed in neon-red letters over a series of dissolves: Elmendorf Air Force base in flames, the assassination plan, a Scanner, ARC Mountain, a claw antenna pointing menacingly at the sky.

Gil popped a cassette from the duplicator and grabbed another off the console. Handing them to Kate, he said, "Here's two Beta copies. The VHS and DVD versions will be ready in a few minutes. It's ready to broadcast. Just say the word."

Randall Mason burst into the room. "I watched it in my office." He looked at Kate and nodded, triumph and pride etched into his face. "It's a goddamn blockbuster."

Illiani stood. "Randall, you and your staff should leave the building. The communications blackout is just foreplay. When this hits the air, the shit will hit the fan."

Mason hesitated. Finally, he said, "I'm staying." He gave Kate an admiring smile and left the control room.

David packed the CDs and tapes into the two aluminum attaché cases and snapped the lids shut. He handed a case to Illiani and looked at Kate. "After the broadcast, we're out of here."

She glanced through the control room window. Mason, Weatherman Fred, the station engineer, and most of the staff had entered the newsroom set and were dragging chairs in front of the monitors.

Mason's voice came over the intercom. "We're all staying, Kate." He glanced around the set for a moment, then made a circular motion with his finger. "Roll the piece."

David nodded and looked at Gil. "Do it."

Gil turned back to the console and punched a button. The commercial that had been playing went black. The Channel 12 logo flashed onto the monitors accompanied by staccato "breaking news" music the station used for urgent broadcasts. A crisp male voice began: *We interrupt this program to bring you a Channel Twelve special report.* The segment started with a slow zoom to Kate seated in the news anchor's chair.

This is Kate McCullough, reporting from the Channel Twelve newsroom. After a harrowing week inside the ARC, or the Auroral Research Center, in Alaska, this reporter has discovered a terrifying and deadly secret.

She clasped her hands on the desk and looked straight into the camera.

ARC is a weapon that is being used against the people of the United States. This weapon has killed hundreds of innocent people, including U.S. Senators Edwards and Travis.

"I have proof that General Thad Greggson, Chairman, Joint Chiefs of Staff; Samuel Hurwitz, president pro tem of the Senate; Joseph Krohner, president of Elektrum Corporation; and Frederic Crotty, leader of the Moral Alliance, have conspired to murder President Williamson and overthrow our government—

*   *   *

Inside the control room, Kate wheeled around as running footsteps echoed from the hallway. Illiani jerked his pistol from its holster and flattened against the wall just inside the open door. Masters, the remaining FBI agent, was jogging toward them. "They're here," he shouted.

"Where?" Illiani demanded.

"Parking lot," he said breathlessly. "An eighteen wheeler. A big— *thing*—came out the top." He held his hand up, making a claw.

David shouted, "Out! Everyone out!"

Noise suddenly roared through the speakers. The console lights sparked and glared. No screeching, fax-like sound came this time, but instead a shuddering, humming rush: air, metal, and flesh tortured from a hideously powerful blast of energy. As pain burned through Kate's head, an image of Fechter flashed into her mind; *hovering over her, torturing—*

Gil shot back from the console as if stabbed by an electric shock. The windows flashed orange. Kate snapped her head up and stared into the newsroom as screams penetrated the thick glass. Sparks were spraying from the metal news desk and from the cameras, lights, chairs, and cables.

Mason spun around and crashed against the center window, mouth gaping, hands clawing at his face. Behind him, Weatherman Fred and his companions twisted and jerked as gouts of yellow flame jetted from fissures erupting across their bodies.

Kate reeled, her legs buckling. David's hand tightened around her wrist. He pulled her up and dragged her, stumbling, through the threshold. The monitors exploded behind them in rapid succession, casting razored shards of glass across their backs and into the hallway.

Above their heads, lights arced and snapped in a singeing cascade. Kate glanced back: beyond Gil's swaying figure, the control room flashed yellow-white, assaulted electronics strobing and squealing like an insane disco. Smoke boiled into the hallway, succeeded by a sheet of orange flame that leapt up and raced across the ceiling.

The overhead sprinklers released a sudden downpour just as David yanked the stairwell door open. He thrust Kate through. "Go on," he yelled. She felt her way down a few steps and waited. Illiani and Masters rushed through the gloom and onto the stairs beside her.

Kate croaked, "Where's Gil?"

"Go with Greg," David shouted. "I'll get him." He turned and disappeared through a wall of black smoke, his calls diminished by the roar and hiss of flames and water.

Hours seemed to pass. Smoke thickened. Water rushed down the stairs in a stepped waterfall. Just as Kate began to panic, David lunged through the door, dragging Gil, and leaned against the railing, coughing and gulping air.

Kate rushed to his side, then gaped at the editor's prostrate figure. "Gil!" she cried, grasping his hand. "Oh God." His skin had blistered and peeled back like torn wallpaper; his eyes bulged past their lids, gelatinous, oozing red. David knelt and placed two fingers over Gil's carotid artery.

Kate murmured, "Is he...?"

"I can't tell." David looked up at Masters. "We've got to get him—" a loud *whump* came from the level below, followed by a hollow rumbling. Smoke and heat funneled up, turning the stairwell into a suffocating chimney.

David lifted Gil onto his shoulder and carried him down to the first floor landing, where Illiani was peering through a crack in the door. Angry shouts came from the other side. "ARC guards in the lobby," Illiani said tensely.

"That's our only way out," Kate said, pressing her eye to the opening.

"Greg," said David, his voice hoarse. "You and Masters take Gil." He pulled his pistol free and chambered a round, then gave Kate and Illiani a lopsided grin. "I'm getting tired of these blue-suited assholes."

"Yeah," growled Illiani, as he and Masters drew their weapons. "The Arconians are really beginning to piss me off."

David grasped the doorknob and looked reassuringly at Kate, then he draped his right arm over her shoulder and swung the door open.

A man in a business suit was shouting angrily at a guardsman. "… Goddamned building's on fire, for Chrissake. Let us out *now*—" The guard, a big, swarthy man with greasy black hair, swept the barrel of his rifle across the man's face, sending him to the floor. A woman screamed.

"Step forward and show your IDs," the guard barked at the crowd jamming the lobby. Three more guards backed up his command, blocking the front exit, holding their rifles at the ready.

Kate and David staggered forward, leading a column of swirling smoke. Masters and Illiani, who supported Gil's limp form between them, followed closely. The guard spotted them. "You!" he bellowed. "Hold it right there." He bulled through the crowd and stopped before Kate. David's head lolled as if he could barely remain conscious.

"Show your IDs," the guard demanded.

Kate begged, "Please, they're seriously hurt—"

"Drop him," the guard spat through gritted teeth, "or I'll kill him." He jerked the muzzle of his rifle back and forth.

"All right," Kate replied.

As she bent to release David, his head snapped up and his right hand slipped from behind her back, bringing forth the concealed pistol. The guard stared at the weapon as if it were a coiled rattlesnake. "Drop it," David said icily.

The guard swung the barrel toward him, and David parried the muzzle with a hooking motion. There was a deafening blast as it discharged. Kate balled her fists and screamed, her voice cut off as David squeezed two rounds from the pistol. A look of horror and anger swept across the guard's face as he stared down at his ruined chest. He staggered backward and crashed to the floor.

Galvanized by the explosions, the crowd screamed and surged in a panicked rush for the doors. The three remaining guards responded with a fusillade of indiscriminate, full-automatic rifle bursts, blasting a shower of glass and brick from the walls.

People buckled as they crossed the line of fire. David, Illiani, and Masters knelt and brought their pistols up. Two guards fell. The third dropped his rifle and thrust his hands into the air. "Don't shoot! Don't shoot!"

The last of the fleeing hostages bolted through the doors. Moans from the wounded joined the wails of distant sirens in the suddenly quiet room. Tendrils of blood crept through the debris, the stench from the firefight mingling with the acrid odor of smoke.

Kate wrapped her arms around David. She thought she should have been hardened by her experiences inside ARC, but she was sickened and horrified by the carnage. David hugged her. "Go on," he said gently. "See to Gil." He pulled away and began collecting weapons from the fallen guards.

Kate bent over Gil and grimaced; the brightly-lit lobby revealed his ruined face and eyes far too clearly.

Beside her, Masters pushed the captured guard against the wall. "How many outside?" he hissed, pressing his pistol under the man's nose.

"Eight more," Kate heard the guard stammer. "Plus the truck."

Illiani rushed to the front windows, his feet crunching over fragments of glass and brick. Kate looked past him. An unmarked tractor-trailer was parked parallel to the building, less than a hundred yards away. No antenna was showing. He shouted, "That truck. Is that a Scanner, or whatever the hell you call it?"

"Yeah," the guard stammered. "It's a Jumbo."

"Is that what burned this building?"

"Y-yeah," came the nasal reply.

"Jumbo, huh?" Illiani muttered. "How clever."

Glass crashed somewhere above, and a rumbling shook the building. Water began seeping down the walls and splattering from the overhead light fixtures. Kate looked up. "We have to get these people out. Gil may still be alive…"

"Our priorities are you and the data," David said as he used a necktie to tourniquet a man's shattered arm.

The wail of sirens grew louder. "Help's on the way," Illiani said.

David stood. "Take them outside." He turned to Masters. "Put our ARC buddy to work."

"Oh, shit," Illiani hissed. "More Arconians."

Three black Humvees raced across the parking lot and braked beside the eighteen-wheeler. ARC guards bolted from the vehicles and jogged toward the building, their rifles held at a diagonal. David snatched an M-16 from the floor. "Stay down," he warned Kate. He bent low and ran up beside Illiani.

Beyond the tractor-trailer, a riot of red and blue flashed as police cruisers and emergency vehicles accelerated down the street, their sirens rising in a whooping crescendo. The guards hesitated, then fled back to the Humvees. Six police cars roared into the parking lot and stopped in a disordered phalanx before the tractor-trailer.

A mix of uniformed police and black-clad S.W.A.T. team members launched from the cars and hunkered into protective positions, using the vehicles as shields. As the ARC guardsmen crouched behind the Humvees, a megaphone appeared above the door of the lead police car, and an amplified voice blared, "Drop your weapons—"

The shriek of sirens and the blatting of air horns rose above the megaphone as an ambulance and two fire trucks wound through the parking lot and halted before the lobby. Firemen scrambled from the trucks as the paramedics began unfolding a gurney.

Carrying Gil, Kate and David met the paramedics at the entrance. She looked up to see a police helicopter circling overhead. "Christ a'mighty," Illiani muttered as he held the door open. "This is gonna be one helluva cluster-fuck."

"Oh, man," said a young paramedic as he glanced inside. "How many—"

"Six." David said, lowering Gil onto the gurney. "Load this man up and get out *fast*." The man stared at David for a moment, then wheeled Gil toward the ambulance.

Boots pounded against the pavement and a group of firemen rushed past them into the building. Smoke shadows drifted across the parking lot toward the knots of gawkers who had collected on the street and in front of the shops. Something on the second floor made a heavy *crunch*.

The ambulance ignited its flashers and siren and sped away. A police car screeched to a stop in its place, and a sergeant and his partner climbed out and trotted toward the entrance. They spotted the rifles David and Illiani had slung across their shoulders and halted.

Masters appeared, prodding the captured guard with the snout of his pistol and flashing FBI credentials in his free hand. "They're with me," he said, nodding at David and Illiani. "But you can arrest this asshole for murder." He shoved the guard toward the police car.

The sergeant backed up a step, looking confused. "Everyone stay where you are. I need statements…"

Thumping noises and a sharp moan of hydraulics pierced the ambient noise. Kate jerked her head toward the eighteen-wheeler. A cavity had opened in the trailer's top section and a fat, black stalk began telescoping skyward. Diesel smoke snorted from twin exhaust ports rising from the trailer's rear quarter. The stalk switchbladed apart with frightening speed, its long, jointed members unfolding like the legs of an agitated spider.

Kate's blood froze—*the claw antenna*. The segmented digits assumed a parabolic shape some twenty feet in diameter, then flexed and curled, as if searching for an optimum focus. A truncated cone in the center of the antenna pistoned obscenely forward and back.

David pushed her shoulder. "Run! Get behind the building and keep running!" She hesitated, looking back at him. "Now!" he commanded. "Meet us—" A crackle of gunfire swept away his words. He motioned sharply for her to go and ducked back inside.

Kate ran to the corner of the building and fumbled open a gate set into a long hedge. Beyond was a landscaped walkway that wound between the Forest Park Building and the shopping center.

A knot of people stood behind a mound just off the flagstone walk, staring in terrified fascination at the firefight. *Fools*. She started to yell at them, tell them to run while they could, but instead she turned and looked back—to see her nightmares revisited.

The claw antenna tilted downward. The air before it hummed, shimmered violet. Screaming began: police officers writhing and falling as flames ripped from their bodies. A woman beside her wailed and backed away, her fingers clawing at her cheeks. "My God, my

God—his *head*!"

David, where in God's name are you?

Stumbling in horror, the people turned and fled, some charging through the door of an adjacent shop, others racing for the back gate. Pivoting smoothly up, the antenna flexed and pointed. Air glimmered again and the circling helicopter's jet engine faltered. The antenna tracked the chopper as it pitched on its side and arced toward the ground. With a loud whump, the fuel tank ruptured and spewed flames across the fuselage. The helicopter plummeted into the middle of the street, and with a window-rattling crash splashed fiery debris into yards crowded with screaming onlookers. The rotor blades detached as a unit and thrashed into a row of parked cars, ripping through metal like an axe through tin foil.

David, where—

Tires yowling and smoking against the pavement, the Humvees slammed aside the police cars blocking their path. As the tractor-trailer rig crept toward the gap, the antenna pivoted down. The claw flexed wider and began a counterclockwise sweep across the shopping center.

Violet air shivered and hummed. As if bombs were detonated in a carefully timed progression, the windows of each storefront blew outward in a series of crystal showers. People screamed and twisted, falling, thrashing—*igniting*—as if thrown before the raging heat of a blast furnace

It's coming this way. Run, Kate, you idiot.

There were shouts, and suddenly David careened through the gate, followed by Illiani and Masters. She charged with the men toward the rear of the building, the shattering glass, screams of pain, nearly upon them. The angry humming of a million wasps assaulted the air, and a blowtorch heat raked her back. Muscles jerking in a Saint Vitus' dance, she pitched headlong onto the flagstone.

Even as she fell, the back of her mind registered new sounds: a short, hissing whine that rose in pitch, followed by an earth-shaking blast, then silence.

*   *   *

She had blacked out. Her first sensation was deep, searing pain radiating from her back; then a throbbing from scraped hands and knees. She pushed into a sitting position and winced, her blouse grating against her back like sandpaper on an open wound. As she tried to stand, the ground tilted and a wave of nausea tightened her insides. She sank back to the ground. David was sitting to her right, the side of his face scratched and bleeding. "Are you okay?" he asked, his voice slow and thick.

She gave a thin smile. "I hurt."

Suddenly aware of the sounds around them, they glanced apprehensively toward the parking lot. The tractor-trailer and its black antenna had moved closer. Kate tensed to stand and run. But the antenna was motionless, canted to one side, black smoke issuing from the partly obscured trailer.

She heard the hiss of high-pressure water and the rapid purr of a motor. Men shouted—firemen? A movement caught her eye: Illiani and Masters rising unsteadily to their feet.

"Damn," said Illiani, his fingers gingerly probing the back of his neck. "I feel like a baked potato."

David stood and walked stiffly to Kate. He pulled her to her feet. She stared at the ground behind him; the aluminum attaché cases were still there, dented but intact.

"You risked your life for those?" she asked.

He glanced at the two cases. "Of course I did. You think I could leave them?"

"Hear that?" asked Illiani.

Drawing closer was the heavy drone of a powerful engine and the unmistakable squeak and clank of steel treads. The three men shuffled cautiously to the hedge and paused, peering over its top.

David looked back at Kate. "Come see."

She drew close to the hedge. Beneath the lopsided antenna, smoke vented from a great ragged hole in the tractor-trailer. She looked beyond the destroyed truck to the far end of the parking lot. Rolling toward them was an enormous, tank-like vehicle, with a gun the size of a telephone pole protruding from its turret.

"Somebody called out the National Guard," David said.

"That's a self-propelled howitzer," said Illiani. "Surprised they didn't take out the whole block."

Kate looked toward the mangled tractor-trailer. Bullet-riddled police cars and Humvees smoked and steamed, debris spotting the ground around them. Beyond the wreckage, some twenty soldiers in full battle dress were marching ARC guardsmen across the pavement toward a waiting personnel carrier. Throughout the shopping center, squads of camouflage-clad soldiers searched along the damaged stores and tended the injured. Ambulances were arriving, as well as additional police.

Three soldiers approached.

"Be cool," said Illiani. "Let me do the talking."

A lieutenant stepped forward. "All of you please step outside.'

Illiani was first through the gate. He identified himself and Masters as FBI agents, explaining that David and Kate were under their protection.

The soldier recognized their names. "Please follow me—"

"Yo, Illiani, Masters," a voice boomed excitedly over the sound of the fire truck pumping unit. It was Crow. He strode up and clamped Illiani in a bear hug.

"Ow!" Illiani pulled free. "Take it easy. I've been fricasseed by that goddammed machine." He winced and nodded toward the tractor-trailer.

Crow confined his enthusiasm to handshakes, his smile changing to a look of concern. "Kate, David, Masters. Man, am I glad to see you guys alive. You hurt? You need a doctor?"

"What about the CDs?" Illiani asked.

Crow shook his head. "Thought I was a goner. They chased my ass all over the damned county. Couldn't get to NORAD, so I shook 'em and detoured to Fort Carson. They got a hard line to NORAD. Put the CDs on a fast uplink and sent all of 'em to DC.

"I told the commander at Carson about the situation. Told them you'd probably be under attack. The president himself ordered the Guard out." He turned and looked back at the Forest Park building.

"What about the others?"

Illiani's face became grave. "They didn't make it, Crow. And if it weren't for you, we'd be charcoal with the rest of them."

"Yeah, well, the president better kick ass real soon, 'cause if he doesn't..." Crow looked off into space and shook his head.

"Communications still out?" asked David.

"Yeah, phone, radio. Everything but the line at NORAD." He paused for a moment. "The local guard is under orders to protect our carcasses, so they'll probably want us at Carson ASAP."

"No way," said Kate. "We're going home. Tell the commander he'll have to do his protecting at the ranch."

"All right," said Crow, nodding toward an Army Humvee parked in the middle of the lot. "We can try. Let's pay the man a visit."

Kate looked back at the smoldering remains of the Forest Park Building. Water jetted from the boom of a hook and ladder truck and arched into the building's collapsed roof, drowning the blaze that had gutted the second story. She thought of Randall Mason, Weatherman Fred, and the others; of the hideous way they had died, of their ruined bodies lying beneath the rubble. Silently, she cursed Hurwitz, Greggson, and Krohner. *Monsters*. She dreaded what was to come. ARC would hit them again—harder.

42

A great cheer washed over the Lincoln Memorial as Moral Alliance leader Frederick Crotty, his luxuriant gray hair swept up and back in a parody of a revival preacher, stepped before the microphone. He waved for silence and waited as the noise dropped to a low murmur. "Brothers and sisters," his voice boomed from the four towers of high-wattage speakers. "We are here to give our support to a man who will fight for our interests, fight for our country, fight for justice, and *fight for morality*!" The clamor swelled.

Through the window of his dressing room, Hurwitz watched the sea of zealots swelling before the stage. He laughed inwardly as Crotty played them with his quasi-religious histrionics. The crowd wasn't as big as he would have liked, but thirty thousand wasn't bad, considering they'd had such short notice, and Crotty was good at firing the morons up.

Hurwitz rotated his wide shoulders away from the scene, tossed his speech on the desk, and settled into his chair with a grunt. It was good the technicians had time to install the special effects. Manipulating the masses required well-orchestrated showbiz basics, plus a heavy dose of symbolism. Of course, once the ARC project reached its final development, such finesse would be unnecessary. Populations would be controlled—not cajoled, guided, or persuaded, but *controlled*—as easily as roasting a turkey in a microwave. He chuckled at the analogy.

An aide knocked on the open door and approached. He held out a sheet of paper. "Senator, this is from General Greggson. It's about Colorado Springs. We took some casualties."

Hurwitz frowned and snatched the paper. "How the hell—" He scanned the page. "Someone called out the *National Guard*?"

"Yes sir."

Hurwitz looked up accusingly. "What about the CDs?"

"That's all the information I have, sir."

"Greggson let the goddamned cat out of the bag. This was supposed to be a covert..." Hurwitz stared at the page again, venting his wrath on the message with a bomb of cigar ash. "I don't have time for this shit. I gotta get on that stage in a minute and blow smoke up everybody's ass." Another rabid cheer invaded the room. "Call Greggson. Tell him I don't care if he burns the whole goddamned town. Those CDs—and the people who stole them—are *not* to survive."

"Yes sir."

Hurwitz heaved himself from the chair and snatched up his speech. "Meanwhile," he said evenly, "we stay on schedule with Scepter."

"Yes sir." The aide turned quickly and left.

Hurwitz sucked the remaining life out of his cigar and nosed it into the ashtray. After a final glance through the window, he hiked up his pants, turned, and walked out the door.

The crowd roared as Crotty spun from the microphone and raised his arms, commanding the ignition of two great Statue of Liberty-styled torches thrusting above the proscenium arch. With flashing, pyrotechnic *booms*, twenty-foot flames jetted forth, juxtaposing over twin Moral Alliance shields suspended above the stage wings. To the crowd's frenzied response, Senator Sam Hurwitz strode into the spotlight and warmly embraced Crotty, who obsequiously bowed and offered him the stage.

Grim-faced, eyes straight and storming, Hurwitz bear-walked to the podium and stepped onto the foot-tall platform that allowed him to reach the microphone. He raised an open palm, then lowered it, fading the crowd's din as if he were turning down the volume on a radio. Bending forward, arms locked straight against the sides of the podium, he swept his gaze dramatically from one end of the throng to the other.

"Brothers and sisters," he began. "Six years ago, the United States Congress approved funding for a project called the Auroral Research Center, or ARC. This project was designed to protect our country from terrorism, biological or chemical warfare, military invasion, attacks against our computer networks—or a*ny action* against the American people.

"The ARC gives us protection by allowing us to monitor communications worldwide and, if necessary, to manage *specific* communications *if* they pose a threat to our country.

"President Troy Williamson is attempting to shut down the ARC, to *kill* this magnificent, unrivaled, technological wonder, this multifaceted shield of protection, and to prosecute one of its chief visionaries, General Thad Greggson." He paused for effect. "Such actions, Mr. President, are tantamount to *treason*." Hurwitz slammed his fist down beside the microphone, sending forth a bass-drum boom that echoed throughout the Memorial.

"*Destroy the ARC?*" Hurwitz belted out the question. He paused, rose to his full height, and drove every angry word with a sharp finger-jab at his own chest: "*I-will-not-let-that-happen.*"

The crowd's roar crested and crashed over the Memorial grounds like storm surf against a granite cliff. Television cameras dollied and panned. Hurwitz stepped back from the podium, both arms raised, palms outstretched. Crotty strode to his side and seized his right arm, forcing it higher—a referee posing the winner of a prizefight.

43

Buddy lay on the Indian rug in the living room, his eyes following Mark as he walked anxiously back and forth in front of the big fireplace. Gramps and another man were also present. They had been staring at the television and muttering for a long time. Mark and Gramps were upset. Buddy sighed. Now was not a good time to play Frisbee.

* * *

Mark stopped pacing and glanced at the television for the hundredth time. The message was still there: "Standby for an important news event." It had popped on nearly an hour ago, obliterating his mother's broadcast. All the other channels carried the same message. The phone lines were still dead, and the radios offered nothing but static.

His grandfather sat nearby, silent and stony-faced. Suddenly he rose and turned to the FBI agent lounging beside him on the leather couch. "We've been on our butts long enough. Let's you and me round up a few men and pay a visit to Channel Twelve."

"I knew you'd say that," the agent said, unfolding his legs and standing. "It's my duty to advise against it. But if I were in your place, I'd do the same thing."

Mark didn't ask if he could come. After the black helicopter had cruised overhead that day, he and the rest of the transmitter crew were under strict orders to remain inside. And inside he'd stay, while the real adults took all the risks and he wasted time playing video games with Alex.

A voice suddenly blared from the television, and the three of them turned in unison to stare. "Ladies and gentlemen. We are broadcasting live from the Lincoln Memorial in Washington, D.C…"

The test pattern was gone, replaced by a wide shot of a large, dramatically-lit stage with enormous Moral Alliance logos suspended high above it. Hand-held signs reading "Save the ARC" and "Senator Sam for President" bounced and rocked within a sea of wildly cheering people.

Jared stared at the screen incredulously. "What the hell is *this*?"

"It's that Crotty guy," Mark said, flicking the remote. It was the same on every channel: Frederick Crotty strutting on stage, praising Senator Sam Hurwitz, yelling at the crowd to "Save the ARC."

"Well, that does it," Jared said, seizing his hat. "There's a rat in the woodpile big as Denver. I'm goin' after my little girl."

Buddy's head jerked up. He made a sharp *wuff* and trotted to the door, where he froze, head cocked to one side.

"Hear that?" the agent asked.

It was the low beat of an approaching helicopter. Buddy's tail began to tick-tock in half-committed wags. Mark slipped restraining fingers around the dog's collar while his grandfather and the agent strode into the yard and scanned overhead. Near the barn, Carlos was calming two agitated horses, while Higgins postured outside the corral, barking. The chopper was coming in really close this time.

urwitz and Crotty stumped off stage, buoyed by the crowd's feverish chanting: *Hur-witz, Hur-witz...*

The senator nudged Crotty. "Like a coupl'a rock stars—hah?"

Crotty nodded and grinned back. He teased an embroidered handkerchief from his coat pocket and delicately patted the sweat from his brow. An aide suddenly thrust a cell phone into Hurwitz's hand. The aide wasn't smiling. Hurwitz held the phone to his ear and turned away from the noise.

"Somebody tipped off the president," came the anxious voice. "Secret Service is all over the place. Hustled him into the tunnels. Totally out of range."

"God*dammit*," Hurwitz spat. He gestured wildly with his free hand. "What the *hell's* goin' on? What's the status?"

"Operation Scepter is cancelled, sir. It's too risky. We think you and Mr. Crotty should leave immediately—"

Hurwitz parted the curtain and stared. Sure enough, a line of flashing lights was snaking onto 23rd Street, racing his way. He gritted his teeth and turned to the aide. "Get my briefcase," he snapped. "Call the chopper." He moved toward the exit and jerked a finger at Crotty. "Let's get the hell outta' here."

* * *

The helicopter, painted in Moral Alliance powder blue and gold, was idling two hundred feet behind the stage, its rotor blades stirring the grass. Hurwitz ran across the lawn as fast as his splay-footed gait would take him. Crotty, already inside, motioned frantically for him to hurry.

"Screw you, you little puff-haired weasel," Hurwitz mumbled under his breath. He finally reached the door, paused, choking from the aerobics-induced asthma attack, and heaved himself into a seat. The aide rushed beneath the blades and thrust a heavy black briefcase onto his lap.

"Get all this on tape," Hurwitz wheezed, waving at the stage. The aide nodded and slammed the cabin door.

Police swarmed across the grounds as the chopper lifted off. Crotty looked mortified. He shook his head. "How could this happen?" he puled. "What will happen to us now?"

Hurwitz glared at him and fumbled for his inhaler. When his respiration finally slowed, he turned toward the copilot and shouted gruffly, "Get me Greggson." The exhalation triggered a fit of coughing, which he muffled with a handkerchief.

He fumed. The spoilers had to be those nobodies from Colorado Springs. This time, he'd make certain they were out of the picture. This time, he wasn't just being pragmatic.

He wanted revenge.

The helicopter clattered in from the northeast and lowered boldly to the ground between the house and barn, stirring a whirlwind of loose hay and dust. Mark could make out U.S. Army markings against the desert camouflage. *You'd better be friendly*, he thought, *because at least five guns are probably pointed at you right now*. Buddy wrenched from his grasp and darted across the yard, racing straight for the machine. Mark charged after him. "Buddy. *No!*"

The chopper doors swung open. Dark shapes dropped to the ground and forged through the swirling dust, bending low beneath the whirling blades. Mark's panic changed to elation as his mother, then David, Illiani, Holt, and Crow materialized, but his smile faded as he drew close. The group was grimy and bloodied. Even from ten feet away they smelled of smoke.

"Mom, are you okay?" he asked as his mother knelt and ruffled Buddy's fur.

She stood and let out a sharp "Ouch" as Mark hugged her. He flinched and backed away.

"I'm fine," she said with a tired smile. "Just a little roughed up."

Mark's grandfather hugged her gingerly, then held her at arm's length. "You really all right?"

"Promise."

Mark shielded his eyes as the chopper rose. It crossed over the pasture, gaining altitude, and spun southward. As the noise subsided, he noticed two men, Army officers, talking with David and the FBI agents. One of the men identified himself as Major Newcastle.

"We'll provide as many men as we can spare," the major was saying. "But right now, with no communications, it's a total snafu. I urge you to reconsider going to Fort Carson or NORAD."

"You'd never make it," came Crow's deep voice. "They have the roads guarded, and *they* have communications. We don't. They've got Humvees, automatic weapons, and those damn Scanners."

"The ranch is defensible," Mark's grandfather said. "Deploy your men here. We can use runners between the outposts for communications, and lights to signal if there's an attack. I can brief you with some maps."

Newcastle seemed to mull over the idea.

The ranch house door banged open and an FBI agent rushed out. "Greggson just declared martial law. They raided the Alliance rally—"

"Whoa, slow down," David interrupted. Take it from the top."

From the corner of his eye, Mark noticed O'Hanlon and Alex ambling toward them.

The agent continued. "Cops busted the Alliance rally. Knocked 'em off the air. Then Greggson comes on. Says he's declared a national emergency and is assuming command."

David turned to the officers. "You take orders from Greggson?"

"No," Newcastle replied. "But if Greggson controls communications, he could command most of the Armed Forces."

"How thorough is the blackout?"

"Total—every frequency."

"A transmitter with enough power could punch through."

"You find something with that much power, you let me know," Newcastle muttered.

O'Hanlon stepped forward and cleared his throat. "Gentlemen," he said, "there may be a way."

* * *

Mark watched as Newcastle eyed the Magnifying Transmitter. The major stepped back from the railing and shook his head. "Impressive, but this thing's an antique. Couldn't even get a signal across town."

"Oh, yeah," David said, his eyes gleaming. "It could do *that* alright." He turned to O'Hanlon, who was standing beside the control console. "Have you tested it?"

O'Hanlon swept his hand toward the roof. "Assuming we can get that hatch open, we could do a test transmission within an hour."

David looked up at the big torus looming silver-gray in the shadows. "I don't understand how you could beam the signal without a huge antenna system."

"I don't understand it yet myself, but this device was designed by an extraordinary genius."

Major Newcastle glanced at his watch and shrugged impatiently. "I'll be at the front gate." He turned to leave, then added in a skeptical tone, "Let me know if you have any luck."

O'Hanlon sat down. "I suppose this is rather futile."

"It's worth a try," David said. He shifted against the railing. "But keep in mind, if this transmitter actually works, General Greggson will notice, and he's not going to be pleased."

O'Hanlon nodded and smoothed his beard. He sighed. "Yes."

David gave the professor a pat on the shoulder, then looked at Mark as he turned to leave. "I'll check on your mother, then see how the major's doing at the front gate."

"Mark," O'Hanlon said. "See if you can find Carlos. Tell him it's time to get the livestock moved away from the barn."

He nodded and started for the stairs. O'Hanlon's voice followed him. "And come right back. The hatch is still stuck. You'll have to do some climbing."

*   *   *

O'Hanlon sat at the control console, transmitter checklist in hand, feeling as if he'd been thrust into a dream—*or a nightmare*. Jared walked up to him and held out a thin, leather-bound document.

"What's this?"

"The third manual," Jared said, sitting against the railing. "I know it's breaking the rules, but this is an emergency."

Their voices echoed in the quiet building, words oddly distorted by the acoustic interplay of conflicting surfaces. The sun painted the windows a hazy magenta as it crept behind the mountains, and the barn creaked and popped as the outside temperature began to drop.

O'Hanlon turned the document over in his hands. It was like the first two manuals, bound in smooth leather. But this one had only a few pages, and a heavy strap and lock held the covers tightly shut. His fingers touched a raised pattern on the front. He looked at the embossed area, tilting the manual into the light. A puzzled smile crossed his face.

"What is it?" Jared asked.

O'Hanlon held the manual up and tapped a finger on the pattern. "This design. It was on a paper I saw in the office, one that Mark found. A drawing I think Tesla made."

"Looks like a dragon."

"Ouroboros."

"Hm?"

"An ancient symbol. A serpent that eats its own tail. Symbolizes creation, life, death, infinity. Sometimes it forms a circle, sometimes a figure eight, like this one—infinity."

"They say Tesla had a sense of humor." Jared fished in his pocket and held out a brass key. "The instructions for using this are on the back of the manual."

O'Hanlon turned the manual over, unsnapped a concealed

compartment, and studied the single parchment page inside. He reached down and inserted the key into a slot beside the master switch, then hesitated. "Turning this key is supposed to reveal numbers to the combination lock on the manual. But why the elaborate steps? Why would Tesla insist this manual be read after the machine is tested?"

Jared shrugged. "Tesla was pretty adamant about having his instructions followed."

O'Hanlon removed the key without turning it and held it up. "Leave this with me, Jared. I need to think about this. Unless we follow the specified procedures, this key could trigger something— something we might not want."

"I suppose we could cut the lock off."

O'Hanlon looked at the manual, running his hand over the patterned cover. "No. That's too obvious. If it were that simple, Tesla wouldn't have bothered with it." He laid the manual on the console. "I'll see if we can rush through the testing. Then we'll open it up. He heaved a long sigh. "Problem is, we're running out of time."

46

David was pulling on a black T-shirt as Kate opened the bedroom door. She caught a glimpse of reddened and blistered skin. "Let me see," she said, lifting his shirt. She winced at the crimson swath the Scanner had made across his back. "Worst case of sunburn I ever saw."

"Forgot my sunblock."

She removed her top and he examined her back. "Two-tone: pink and very pink."

She showered quickly, the water stinging like hot pellets where the microwave beam had burned her flesh. David waited for her to emerge and gently rubbed lotion onto the affected area.

"I could sleep for a week," she said, nodding as his fingers worked across her shoulders.

"So, start right now."

"No, I'm coming with you."

David stood and slid a pistol into the holster strapped to his waist. He looked at her and nodded. "You've earned that much."

She pulled on a dark blue sweater and walked into the closet. She found what she was looking for—the second holster and pistol. She secured them to her belt and stepped back into the bedroom.

"That's a nine-millimeter Glock," David said. "You know how to use it?"

She palmed the weapon, ejected and checked the magazine, jammed it back into the receiver, and stuffed it into the holster. She put her hands on her hips and cocked her head to one side.

A lopsided grin broke across David's face. "Very sexy."

* * *

They found Illiani standing beside the tractor shed. "Well," he said, looking them over, "if it ain't the Bobbsy Twins."

Kate stared back at Illiani. He had changed into borrowed clothing: jeans and a gray sweatshirt. He also wore a pistol. "More like the Three Stooges."

The Bronco started immediately, the severed tailpipe emitting a loud rumble.

Illiani's voice came from the back seat. "Ah. Civilian transportation."

"Don't get too comfortable," David said. "Rides rougher than a Humvee."

"Don't care if I never see one again."

They crossed the bridge and cruised noisily up the gravel drive. A fading sun painted the treetops red and lit drifting tufts of high clouds brilliant orange. On the right, Pikes Peak and the surrounding foothills had dimmed to frowning shadows.

Illiani tugged the walkie-talkie from his belt and turned up the volume. Kate wrinkled her nose at the buzzing static. "Radio's still screwed."

"Keep the squelch light," David said. "It'll be an early warning system in case they get cute with microwaves again." He swung to the right, making room for a pickup headed the opposite direction. "Changing of the guard," he said, returning a wave.

They drove down the last hill toward the ranch entrance. Two camouflaged Army Humvees huddled side by side in a graveled space just inside the gate. A squad of soldiers was unloading weapons and boxes from the vehicles, stacking them in a row beside the fence. David parked and the three climbed out.

Major Newcastle squinted into the twilight as they approached and pointed. "Chopper. I caught a glimpse. It's not ours."

Barely audible above the soughing of the nearby woods was a helicopter's low, rhythmic beat.

"Maybe recon," David offered.

"Something's up, sir," came a soldier's voice. He held his radio out and turned up the volume: garbled voices blended with the static. "They're on military frequency. They're close."

"You have anyone down there?" David asked the major, nodding toward the blacktop road that curved into the darkening canyon.

Newcastle shook his head. "This is all I got."

David turned toward the Bronco. "We'll scout a mile or so." He paused and looked back. "Maybe it's time you got your men under cover."

The major shot David an annoyed glance and tapped his forehead in a mock salute. "Yes Sir."

A ranch hand unchained the gate and let them through. They coasted downhill for a mile and pulled off to the right, where a jutting cliff allowed a view across the gorge. David killed the engine, and they walked to the metal guardrail.

Twilight's shadow filled the valley, and a chill was creeping in where sunlight had fled. Across the gorge came the murmur of engines laboring uphill, headlights floating around a distant curve. Kate's heart raced as the vehicles came into view: two Humvees leading two large vans, followed by two more Humvees—all black.

"Shit," Illiani muttered, his shoulders slumping. "And I wanted to watch *Wheel of Fortune*."

David held binoculars to his eyes. "The Humvees have machine guns."

"That ain't all," Illiani said.

Kate heard and saw it before Illiani finished his statement: a black helicopter pacing the convoy, bringing up the rear. Its navigation lights were off. As it lifted and arced away from the canyon, she noticed a fat cylinder resembling a searchlight dangling from its nose.

"Let's get the lead out," David shouted, jogging for the Bronco. "They'll be at the gate in five minutes."

Kate slid into the passenger seat as David cranked the starter. The muffler-deprived engine roared and they skidded onto the road and made a screeching U-turn uphill. Kate looked through the rear window. Headlights slithered along the cliff walls behind them as the Humvees entered the last switchback.

47

Mark yanked the knotted rope around his waist and stepped through the access hatch into purple twilight. The day's heat had collected in the barn's upper story, and he was thankful to be outside in cooler air. He was fifty feet off the ground, but looking down toward the yard and corral, it seemed like a hundred.

Kneeling at the roof's peak, he looked over his shoulder toward Colorado Springs. A galaxy of yellow lights glittered across the valley, the headlamps and taillights of cars crawling along the roads and highways like a million phosphorescent ants. It seemed weird that, despite the communications blackout, the attack on Channel 12, and everything else that had been going on, the town looked perfectly normal.

Alex's voice drifted up through the hatch. "Hurry, it's getting dark. If you can't do it, I will."

"I can do it," Mark shouted back. "I don't have arcophobia, you know."

"That's *acro*phobia."

"Whatever."

Riding on steel tracks twenty feet ahead was the sliding roof section with its rusted wheel still frozen in place. Mark straddled the roof and scooted forward, the asphalt shingles rasping against his jeans like sandpaper.

He stopped beside the wheel, pulled a socket wrench from his tool belt, and slipped it onto the axle nut. Bracing his feet against the sliding section's wooden edge, he pushed until the wrench bit painfully into his hand. But the nut seemed to have found a permanent home.

Frustrated, he stood and balanced his right foot atop the handle. He steadied himself, tensing to press down, hoping his weight would provide enough force to break the nut free. He froze as a flash of light caught his eye. He turned northward and stared in disbelief as a glowing violet shaft dropped from the darkening sky and wavered over the Air Force Academy. A yellow flame suddenly jetted from within the beam's path and spiraled down, dragging a dark tail of smoke. Mark sucked in a sharp breath. *That was a plane*!

Moments later, two heavy *booms* rolled along the hills. Buddy, who had been waiting patiently on the second landing, began barking anxiously. Signal lights winked from the lookout post on Spy Knob. Urgent shouts sounded from the ranch house.

"Mark, forget it," Alex yelled. "Get your ass back inside."

"Just give me a minute." He stepped down hard on the wrench, but the tool popped free with a *clink*, the sudden loss of resistance throwing him off balance. With a yelp, he crashed onto his back and plummeted in a free fall down the steep incline. The tether snapped taut around his midsection, punching the air from his lungs and swinging him in a tumbling arc across the roof. He came to a stop some twenty feet below the access hatch. Panting, he flattened against the shingles, a fierce stinging radiating from his elbows and cheek. He probed his throbbing jaw gently, wondering how much skin he'd left behind on the gritty shingles.

Buddy's frantic barking joined Alex's shout: "Mark. You okay? What happened?"

"I'm all right," Mark yelled back, his words edged with frustration and self-derision. He was disgusted with himself. "Give me a second."

A sudden flurry of aerial cracks and booms quickened his pulse. He brought himself to a low crouch, seized the rope, and began hoisting himself up hand over fist, his feet scrabbling for purchase against the roof's steep pitch. He reached the hatch and swung his legs into the opening, puffing out a long sigh. He looked northward again.

Bands of light curled and flickered over the Academy, the ground below scintillating red and orange. Here and there the swirling light coalesced and darted down, sparks and flashes erupting beneath like tinder before a blowtorch. Fires jumped from the Academy grounds in spreading yellow clusters. Fear knotted Mark's gut as his mind replayed a recent nightmare: a malevolent *Eye* that crept through an ominous storm…

He tore his gaze away and lowered himself through the hatch onto the big beam that ran beside the torus. He untied the rope from his waist with a few quick jerks and backed down the ladder. Buddy gruffed and jumped up, pawing at him as his feet met the landing.

Alex began coiling the rope. "What's *happening* out there?"

"It's the Air Force Academy," Mark said, hearing the awe in his own voice. "Some kind of ray is hitting it. It's on fire."

"It's those freakin' ARC bastards. I bet Peterson and Fort Hood are getting it too."

"Boys, come down," O'Hanlon called from the first landing, his voice tense.

Mark met the professor near the control console and repeated what he had seen.

"My God," O'Hanlon said, shaking his head. "Then it's true…" He looked at Mark. "Did you get the wheel loose?"

He held his hands out in a shrug. "I don't know. Something broke. I lost the wrench."

The Professor nodded. He thought for a moment. "Get the flashlights. We'll try to break it open."

Mark ran to O'Hanlon's office and snatched the flashlights from a shelf beside the door. He was startled by Alex's voice coming from the window. "Flashes are all around," he said, moving his hand in a circle.

"We gotta' help Professor—"

"Listen!"

Mark rushed to the window and peered into the deepening gloom. From the direction of the front gate came the sharp rattle of gunfire.

48

Sam Hurwitz paced angrily across the heavy Persian carpet, sucking his last Havana down to a drooping white ash. He glanced at Frederick Crotty, who was enthroned behind his gilded, frou-frou, Louis XIV desk in his gilded, frou-frou Louis XIV chair, wearing a pinched expression and waving a limp-wristed hand against the drifting strata of cigar smoke.

Hurwitz stopped and glared around the room. Here he was, the next President of the United States, soon-to-be Commander of the Entire World, stuck in Crotty's office in Memphis—home of gospel music, Elvis, and the Moral Alliance's bastardized, pink, frou-frou, Graeco-Roman headquarters.

The phone beeped and Crotty answered. He held the phone out. "It's General Greggson," he said, not changing his dour expression.

Hurwitz snatched the receiver and snarled, "Get me outta this goddamned poof-palace so I can do some good."

Crotty glowered at him.

"You're damned lucky you got that far," Greggson's voice snarled back. "In case you didn't know, we're countering an air attack. We have an escalating situation—"

"The president—" Hurwitz began.

"We'll *get* the president. Give us a chance. You do *your* job. We'll do ours."

Hurwitz banged the phone back into the cradle and stormed from the room. This was the worst possible scenario. They had planned for it, but it would get messy; there would be heavy casualties and a decimated national defense system.

He paused in the hallway and absently patted his empty coat pocket for another cigar. On top of everything else, he'd have to bum cigarettes off someone. That is, if anyone smoked in this faggot-ward. He walked toward the media production section. He'd get prettied-up, then tape his statement to be televised as soon as the president was dead and the situation under control.

He felt his nerves calming to a dull roar. They'd still pull the whole thing off. Everyone would soon learn just how powerful the ARC weapon was. And those people in Colorado Springs: at first he'd wanted them dead, now he hoped they would be taken alive. He'd like to watch that creep, Malcolm Fechter, play with them.

Anyway, things were moving. So what if the body count was high. Soon enough he'd be in charge. No stopping what he'd set into motion years ago.

No stopping the leviathan called ARC.

49

The console lights winked on with a click and a hum. O'Hanlon's emotions were at war. He had dreamed about testing the Magnifying Transmitter; listening to its singular sound, watching the mechanical systems, measuring the electrical field, observing the spark gap, coils, torus. Would it radiate energy invisibly, glow, discharge enormous bolts of lightning—or would it self-destruct and kill them all? Switching the Magnifying Transmitter on should be the zenith of his career. Given the present circumstances, it more likely would be a disaster.

There was no time to follow proper procedure. He needed days, if not weeks. But the enemy was at the gate; he must throw the ancient machine precipitously into operation, and safety out the window. His eyes strayed to the Ouroboros Manual. Opening it prematurely might have serious repercussions.

Of course, even the smallest, most insignificant element could thwart their efforts; if the roof section wouldn't slide open, the operation was doomed anyway. Maybe that would be best. They could resume work later, when the world was more stable—assuming they were still alive.

Mark and Alex rushed up breathlessly, their words tumbling out.

"They're shooting…"

"At the front gate…"

"Automatic gunfire…"

Doors banged below. There were running footsteps, a frantic voice calling out. "Mark, Dr. O'Hanlon, everyone, come down…" It was Mark's grandmother. She bounded up the steps.

"Come on." She motioned urgently. "The generator room. It's the safest place."

O'Hanlon sighed. "Go on, boys."

"But…no," Mark stammered. "We gotta send the message…"

Jenny rushed toward him, panic etched into her face. "No! Come with me right now."

Jared had walked up the stairs behind her, and he came to her side. "It's okay, Jen," he said softly. "You take care of yourself. Let these men do their work."

"Jared," she said, her voice low and angry. "You know what those people do…"

"If they break through, I don't think we'll be much safer down there. And if this machine can get a message out, and we can save lives, we're morally bound to try."

His grandmother was silent for a long moment; then she turned to O'Hanlon and the others, her eyes pleading. At length, she nodded. "All right. Go on." Her face softened into a teasing, hopeful smile. "But I'll be back to make sure you don't mess up."

Crumps and booms like distant artillery rumbled in from the north and east. The windows flickered yellow, purple.

"We're locking the doors," Charles Holt shouted from below.

"All right, men," O'Hanlon said, swiveling to face the control panel. "Take your positions." To himself, he murmured, "Let's see if we can raise the *Titanic*."

50

Acrid gunsmoke hung in the quiet woods that only minutes ago had exploded with machine gun fire. Crouching low, David thrust his fist up, signaling halt. Kate sank to the ground beside him and peered through the thin stand of pine. In the fading light, she could see the ARC convoy parked on the road ahead, stretched out like a great dark serpent.

A short time earlier, two of the black Humvees had raced to the gate, wildly raked the entrance with machine gun fire, and retreated. Now the vehicles waited down the road, apparently biding their time before launching another assault. The ARC forces had large caliber machine guns, a helicopter, and, of course, the Scanners. Kate, David, and Illiani had planned a desperate move to even the odds.

David had refused to allow Kate on this suicide mission, but she had been adamant. No way was she going to let the murdering bastards past the gate.

"Two Humvees up front," David whispered. "Two Scanners—big vans with antennas on top—two more Humvees at the rear. Maybe fifteen, twenty men."

Illiani inched up close. "What are they doing?"

David motioned for quiet. "Listen." From the road, a faint humming repeatedly rose and fell. "One of those damned antennas sweeping back and forth."

"They're going to burn us out, just like Forest Park," said Illiani. "Let's not give 'em a chance."

Crouching, they jogged toward the rear of the convoy and lay prone twenty feet from a gully, its dark gash separating the road from the woods. The rearmost Humvee loomed a hundred yards to their right. An ARC soldier leaned against the vehicle, sweeping the woods with his nightscope. Kate's anxiety surged. In minutes, it would be too dark to see with the naked eye. ARC would have total advantage.

"Hurry," David whispered, motioning them forward.

They belly-crawled under the wooden fence where it crossed a depression, scrabbled on their elbows across ten feet of bruising rocks, and dropped over the gully's edge.

The dry, sandy earth muffled their footsteps as they trudged uphill toward the convoy. *I'm running on adrenaline alone*, Kate thought as she tried to slow her breathing and calm the periodic shaking that seized her hands and legs.

Fifty feet from the rear Humvee, they stopped and looked above the gully's rim. The ARC soldier was facing the front of the column. From somewhere inside the Scanners came a phased whine that slowly climbed in pitch and amplitude.

"Generators," David whispered. "They're powering up the antennas."

Kate's chest tightened: the claw antenna stopped its radar-like oscillations, and its jointed digits began to clench in and out, adjusting its shape. The assembly began rotating around its axis. A moment later, the second Scanner's antenna began to turn.

The ARC soldier walked toward the head of the column and disappeared into one of the vehicles. There was a crackle of radios, shouted commands. Engines revved, doors slammed.

A sizzling hum suddenly emanated from the Scanners, and a neon-purple haze danced in front of the antennas. A moment later, gunshots reverberated from the ranch entrance. Through the din, Kate thought she could hear men screaming.

"Go!" David shouted, churning up the embankment.

The leading Humvees were beginning to move, pulling onto the road. David sprinted to the rear vehicle, jerked the driver's door open, and pointed the Glock. "Out! Out! Get out!"

Kate could see the driver staring back through night-vision goggles, his mouth open in a startled "O." She cradled her pistol and aimed at the vehicle's dark interior.

"Now!" Illiani's voice roared from the vehicle's right side.

Four ARC soldiers scrambled out and sprawled face down on the pavement. David and Illiani snatched up the pistols and NVDs. There was a squealing of tires, shouts. Kate looked up. A Humvee was turning around.

David hooked Kate's arm. "Inside, quick."

She and Illiani dove into the vehicle's rear compartment. David slid into the driver's seat and hit the accelerator. Kate groped for the seat belt, found it, and began stabbing the buckle blindly against the connector.

"Here," Illiani said, thrusting a pair of NVDs onto her lap.

She held them to her eyes, looked up, and saw the returning Humvee pull across their path. A man shouldered through the vehicle's open roof and grabbed for the pintle-mounted machine gun.

David accelerated straight for them, swerved, and slammed into the Humvee's left rear. The target vehicle skidded counterclockwise, tires screaming against the asphalt. He jerked the wheel to the right, and they raced past.

Kate prayed the machine gunner was shaken up enough to allow them time—

A *thunk, thunk, thunk* hammered across the Humvee's side, and the rear windshield disintegrated in a blinding spray. Through tears and grit, she saw flashes spitting from the rammed vehicle's gun. *We're dead unless—*

A staccato outburst raged from overhead—Illiani, standing in the gunner's hatch, returning fire with the machine gun. Silence. David slowed.

"Hah! Nailed the sonofabitch," Illiani yelled.

"Hit the Scanners—"

Illiani's gun roared again. Kate saw the lead Scanner's windshield flicker orange as the rounds met the truck's body. David suddenly swung his arm around and gave Illiani a quick jab.

"What?"

"Humvees twelve o'clock."

Kate pivoted to look uphill. The remaining two Humvees had penetrated the ranch gate, a quarter mile ahead. Now they charged back onto the road, turning straight for them.

Green flames flared in Kate's NVDs. Bullets thwacked and hammered. The front windshield sprayed inward, a sandstorm stinging her face. She shook powdered glass from her hair. Illiani suddenly collapsed beside her.

"I'm hit," he panted. "Run, get out of here—"

David looked back. "Greg!"

Kate pushed Illiani into a sitting position and tugged the seat buckle around his waist. "It's my leg," he groaned.

Ahead, a Scanner was backing away from the line of fire. In moments, it would bring its antenna into play. David gunned the Humvee and they surged ahead, the gully's dark mouth racing toward them.

They dropped in at an angle, skidding down, bouncing, then leveling as the wheels banged onto both sides of the narrow depression. Kate thanked God for the Humvee's high clearance as they skimmed and chattered over rocks big enough to gut the undercarriage of every SUV on the market.

A hailstorm of rocks and gravel pounded the Humvee as the big tires clawed their way up the gully's far side. The vehicle launched off the top, bounced across a short level space, and disintegrated the fence in a blaze of flying splinters. They accelerated into the woods, jitterbugging past trees like a high-speed run through a funhouse. The engine exhaled a cloud of oily smoke and they clattered to a stop. David turned. "Greg?"

"Damn," came the strained reply. "You drive like a New York cabby on speed."

"I just hate a bitchy fare."

Kate drew the goggles to her eyes and looked toward the road. Past the gully, she could see a Scanner and two Humvees pulling uphill, headed for the gate. "Damn it," she said through gritted teeth. "We only got half of them."

"They chasing us?" Illiani asked.

David swept the NVDs in an arc. "Five on foot."

They tugged Illiani through the door, and with the agent's arms draped over their shoulders, hobbled behind a rock outcropping a hundred feet from the smoking Humvee. They lowered Illiani to the ground and tightened his belt above the seeping hole in his right leg.

Not good, Kate thought. *Greg wounded; a Scanner and two Humvees headed for the ranch; an unknown number of allied casualties; and five men in pursuit of us.*

"Stay here," David said. "Take care of Greg."

Kate looked up at him. Even in the failing light, she thought she saw a strange gleam in his eyes and an odd little half-smile. He was silent for a moment, looking down at her. Then he bent and touched his lips briefly to her mouth. "Time to get rough."

PART THREE

OUROBOROS

51

O' Hanlon snapped a switch, listened to the motor wind up, and grimaced as the roof section made a grinding, screeching sound. Overhead, gears wrenched to a stop. He toggled the switch back, briefly throwing the motor into reverse, taking pressure off the system. Mark and Alex moaned in disappointment. If the section wouldn't open, there was no hope of using the transmitter.

"Third time in a row," Mark said.

Alex walked to the railing and aimed a flashlight into the darkness above the rafters. "I think it moved a little."

The Professor glanced at Mark, who was staring southward, frowning. The boy was worried about his mother. She and David Hightower should have returned from the gate by now, and sporadic gunfire had been echoing from that direction for the last half-hour.

He looked back at the console, his hand hovering over the controls. He wondered how many times he could force the jammed section without breaking the mechanism. He sucked in a deep breath. "Here we go again," he muttered, and toggled the switch.

The motor hummed, engaged the gears, and groaned against the load. A loud cracking sound issued from the cupola, and something bounced off the torus, pinged off one of the coils and crashed onto the floor. Then there was a long, agonized squeal like a train pulling into a station. Splinters and dust rained into the barn. A gap appeared above the torus and widened. The roof section slowly grated to the end of its track and stopped, leaving a thirty-foot square of black sky and diamond stars. Cool night air drifted down through rising heat.

"All *riiight*," voiced the boys.

O'Hanlon puffed out his cheeks in a sigh of relief. And anticipation. He glanced at the checklist, even though he had committed it to memory, and closed another switch: STEP NUMBER TWO. Somewhere in the bowels of the transmitter a heavy motor whined and gathered speed. Hidden gears turned with a rhythmic grind and squeak.

The Professor's jaw dropped as the big torus, riding atop a narrow, telescoping tower of steel and glass, rose ponderously through the opening. It made a ratcheting sound that reminded him of the lift mechanism of a roller coaster. Passing the roofline, it headed for the sky like a silver airship. The torus elevated some forty feet above the barn and stopped with a heavy *clunk*. He stared, spellbound, at the intricate, fragile-looking structure that protruded through the roof.

Alex shouted, "Yeah! Totally awesome!"

Violet light suddenly glared through the roof opening and snuffed out. Another *boom* growled along the hills. *It's coming closer*. Buddy, who had been nervously pacing around Mark, looked southward and whined.

O'Hanlon turned back to the control panel and snapped another switch: STEP THREE. The big brass globe on his left lit up with hundreds of pinpoint lights. "Get the atlas," he said, pointing to a heavy volume on the shelf. "Find the latitude and longitude for Washington, D.C. After that, we'll try to locate the major air bases."

Alex tugged the book free and fumbled through the pages. "Got it," he said, his finger resting on a map. "North thirty-eight degrees, west seventy-seven degrees. That's as close as I can get with this old book."

O'Hanlon entered the coordinates with two dials, and the globe hummed, spun on its axis, and clicked to a stop. Glittering bands of light moved across its surface, finally intersecting at the meandering boundary between Virginia and Maryland.

From the gate, gunshots popped and rattled.

Mark looked at O'Hanlon, his expression desperate. "That microwave beam is coming down all over Colorado Springs. *All over.*"

"All we can do is send a message."

Mark balled his fists. *ARC, the phony research center, supposed to help defend the USA. Instead they were traitors*, he thought—*monsters and traitors*. Had ARC's vile purple rays already found his house, his friends, killed his girlfriend, Andrea?

A fat lot of good sending messages would do. He wanted a weapon, a gun. Anything he could fight back with, even if it was futile. But here they sat in an old barn with a big, musty, untested machine an obscure scientist invented over a hundred years ago.

What they needed was their own death ray.

Then a revelation hit with such sudden clarity he almost staggered. It was as if his mind suddenly looked out over the Magnifying Transmitter and witnessed the machine in operation, saw the invisible electromagnetic field as it crashed from coil to coil, gathering voltage. He pictured its resonant energy vibrating between earth and sky as wave after synchronous wave raced around the planet and back, building up in a sympathetic dance of power. *That* was Tesla's genius—the transmitter was in tune with the earth itself.

The truth was right in front of them. The machine was designed send energy any place on the planet without wires, and *without any loss of power.*

"Professor O'Hanlon," he said with sudden intensity. O'Hanlon turned, his eyes connecting with Mark's.

Mark held his hands out, palms up. "The Magnifying Transmitter is supposed to send power to any place on earth *without loss*, right?"

"That's what the manual said."

"What if we beamed it straight at ARC?"

The others stared at him.

"At full power," he continued, cocking his head. "All ten gazillion watts—straight at them."

Bands of purple, orange, and yellow painted the sky beyond the roof hatch. There was a loud hum followed by a sharp crackle like lightning splitting the clouds. Then a thudding boom rocked the barn.

More shouts, someone running across the wooden floor below. Holt's voice. "They're coming across the bridge. Turn the lights off and stay quiet." He continued on toward the barn's south entrance.

O'Hanlon gave a dismayed sigh and switched the wall sconces off, casting the barn into darkness. The control panel's large, luminous dials provided enough light for the small group to see each other. Beyond the console, the brass globe's tiny lamps threw faint, glittering patterns against the nearby coils, reflecting from the glass insulators and polished copper like frozen fireflies.

Alex broke the silence. "If this transmitter can actually converge power at a location with minimal attenuation…"

The professor raked his fingers through his beard and frowned, staring into space. "Our maximum input power is ten million watts." He shifted his gaze back to Mark. "To do any real damage to a facility the size of ARC, I'm afraid it *would* take a 'gazillion' watts."

"But…" Alex began.

O'Hanlon held up a silencing hand and looked at Mark, his expression that of a teacher impressed with a student's brilliant, unorthodox solution to a difficult math problem. He swung around and faced the transmitter, the light from the instruments highlighting his cheeks and beard and throwing the hollows of his eyes into shadow. After a long moment, he rotated back. The frown was replaced by a mischievous smile. "We might do nothing more than get their attention, but…" He shrugged. "Maybe it's worth a try."

Mark and Alex grinned at each other, an unspoken *yes!* flashing between them.

"We'll start with a short transmission at low power," O'Hanlon continued. "I'll increase it if everything checks." He swiveled to face Alex. "You have copies of the ARC CDs on your computer, is that correct?"

Alex nodded. "Yeah."

"See if you two can find ARC's precise location. We'll try to determine the coordinates."

"I have an atlas program too," Alex added. "It gives longitude and latitude for everyplace in the world."

As they turned to leave, Mark commanded Buddy to stay, and the dog reluctantly obeyed, sitting tensely beside the console.

"Fellows," O'Hanlon said. "Keep a low profile. And keep quiet."

O'Hanlon stood and pushed his chair away from the console. He grasped a control handle attached to the massive variable transformer rising through the floor. A dial on the instrument bore numbers from zero to one hundred. He pulled the clamshell release lever and rotated the handle to the "10" position, the device making a clacking sound as it ticked off the power stops: STEP NUMBER FOUR. He found his hands were shaking. *Dear God, I hope we're doing the right thing.*

* * *

Mark and Alex crept into the dark office and quietly closed the door. A strobe of violet light defined the open window as another microwave beam seared the sky. Crouching, Alex crept into the storeroom. Mark circled around the desk, dropped to his knees, and cautiously looked out the window. He froze.

Parked below were two black Humvees, both with machine guns mounted on top, and a big, dark-colored van. He could barely make out two shapes running toward the house. A crunch of footsteps came from immediately below, whispered commands, a light clink of metal on metal. Atop the van a strangely-shaped antenna, little more than a shadow in the dim light, hummed slowly back and forth. Where were the FBI agents and ranch hands? He left the window and hurried into the storeroom. Alex's face glowed in the computer's pale light.

"Hurry up," Mark whispered.

"Give me a minute, will you." Alex inserted a CD into the slot, manipulated the mouse. He wrote something down on a notepad. "Got it."

They returned to the control console just as Mark's grandfather rushed up the steps. "Come down. They're right outside." He paused and looked sadly at O'Hanlon. "Sorry, Professor, looks like we're out of time."

"Where are they?"

"On the tracks out front," Mark said. He angrily pounded his fist into his palm. "Wish I could run over 'em with the train."

There was a moment of silence, then Alex spoke, his eyes wide. "Maybe we could."

"What do you mean?" Jared asked.

"I left the train's receiver on. The power setting is wide open, and the brake is off. You could run it from inside the barn…"

Jared looked silently at Alex. He grinned.

52

Kate watched as David slipped into the blackness beyond the rock outcrop. The woods had become too dark to see well, even with the NVDs. The ARC microwave weapon discharged again, briefly lighting the sky and pummeling the air with thunder.

She looked toward the road, two hundred yards away. The stealthy, dark shapes of men glided from the shadows and drifted into a dim clearing. She counted five individuals. Two split off and disappeared back into the woods. She resisted an urge to call out to David. "Not fair," she said under her breath. "Five against one."

A quiet chuckle from Illiani startled her. She glanced down at him, perplexed.

"You're right," he whispered. "It's not fair—to the Arconians."

Kate looked back at the three advancing men. They were headed straight for the abandoned Humvee. She ran her fingers over the pistol at her side. In a few minutes, the men would be at the vehicle. Then they would search beyond. One seemed to be pointing at the rock outcrop even now, as if they could home in on her thoughts. The men suddenly stopped, turned toward the woods, and brought their rifles up. She jumped as a loud burst of automatic gunfire shattered the quiet.

"Stay down," Illiani said sharply.

She was unaware that she had risen from behind the rock and had stepped into plain view. She dropped back and peered once more into the clearing. Only one man was visible. He rose from a bent position, lifting something from the ground. Then he began walking straight for the rock outcrop.

"One of them is coming this way," she whispered to Illiani. She tugged the pistol free.

The man passed the Humvee and stopped. Her hand shaking, Kate leveled the Glock.

"Kate," the man said.

"David!" Kate jumped from behind the rock. "There are five of them," she stammered.

He shrugged off a heavy bulk strapped around his shoulder and held it out. "I know."

Kate looked and saw five M-16 rifles dangling from their straps. "Oh."

They knelt beside Illiani, and David directed a thin beam from the flashlight across the agent's leg. Kate winced as she saw blood welling from the jagged hole in his lower thigh.

"Shrapnel," David said, tugging the tourniquet tighter. "Looks like it missed the femoral artery."

Illiani gave a grunt of pain. "Lucky me."

David ejected and pocketed the magazines from two of the rifles, tossed the weapons aside, and slung the three remaining M-16s over his shoulder. He lifted Illiani to his feet "Hang on, pal."

They headed west, Illiani hobbling between Kate and David, his arms hooked across their shoulders. Kate relied on David's guidance. She couldn't get the NVDs to stay on her head, and they bounced uselessly around her neck. Without them, the woods were dark as a cave, the trees black against slate-gray. The only light came from stars filtering through a heavy canopy of pine boughs and the ARC weapon's occasional, lambent flare. She had to step carefully to avoid fallen limbs and rocks.

"How can we possibly stop them…" she said, grunting as she struggled with Illiani's weight.

"We play it by ear," David replied. "And hope they're concentrating on the ranch."

They walked on in silence. After a few minutes, Kate began to stumble.

"I've got to rest," she panted.

David shifted the agent's weight onto himself. "The Bronco's not far."

Kate didn't answer. Her emotions were flying into overdrive. She leaned against a tree and tried to calm herself. *I'd be hyperventilating if I didn't need the oxygen so badly anyway*. She wanted to drop Illiani and run for the Bronco, race to the house. Her family couldn't defend against the Humvees *and* Scanner.

But they couldn't leave Greg behind to bleed to death. She pulled Illiani's arm across her shoulder and they set off again.

"Here it is," David finally said, slowing.

Kate could barely make out the Bronco's dark shape in the clearing. David opened the rear compartment and lifted Illiani inside. The agent lay with his injured leg propped against the top of the fender well. David covered him with his jacket and slid into the driver's seat. He handed Kate one of the rifles.

"Cock it like this," he said, pulling a tab straight back and releasing it. He pointed to two small levers. "Safety is here. This one switches from single to full auto." He started the engine. The muffler-free tailpipe was shockingly loud.

As David backed onto the gravel road, Kate struggled with the ill-fitting NVDs. She finally got the straps tightened. At last, she could see and have both hands free. She looked behind; there was no sign they were being followed. An ambush could occur at any moment, but that was a chance they would have to take. They climbed the final hill, and David pulled off the road about a hundred feet from the crest. With luck, the creek had masked their engine noise.

"Go on," Illiani said as they turned to look at him. He patted the M-16 by his side. "Got all the help I need."

David yanked the bulb from the overhead courtesy light and opened the door. Kate grabbed her rifle and followed him up the road. At the hill's crown, they paused and looked down. Kate had never seen the ranch so dark before. There had always been lights outside the barn and a few windows lit. Now the property was an eerie black stain against the backdrop of fires and lights of Colorado Springs.

To the north, flames rose from the Academy, and her breath caught in her throat as she saw the spectral beams slanting down from space. *Dear God, they're destroying the entire town.*

"There," David said, pointing. "Just beyond the bridge."

Kate could make out the angular shadow-shapes of the two Humvees and the van, parked about a hundred feet from the barn. The sight nearly drove reason from her mind. She tugged David's arm and whispered urgently. "There's a way across."

With Kate leading, they jogged through the woods, heading down and to the right. She stumbled twice, the night vision goggles skewing her perception. It was like trying to run while looking through the viewfinder of a jiggling video camera.

The sound of rushing water grew louder, and the creek's dark furrow appeared. She searched along the bank and they waded in, picking their way over the rounded river stones. The cold water rose to her knees, threatening to tear her feet away and sweep her downstream.

They reached the other side, and with David beside her, she climbed up and looked over the embankment toward the dark bulk of the Scanner and Humvees. The vehicles rested on the train tracks where they curved toward the barn. Machine gunners, their upper torsos rising through the roofs of the Humvees, searched the woods and road with NVDs.

Kate's eyes moved past the vehicles to the barn. She gasped. The cupola had split apart, the two sections having moved toward opposite ends of the roof. Through the wide gap rose a long, slender tower. At its top rode the torus, its silvery form looking as anachronistic above the old building as a satellite dish on the Tower of London. *They did it*! She wanted to cheer, but at the same time wondered desperately if anyone inside the barn was still alive.

She looked back at the Scanner, and her veins turned to ice. The claw antenna now pointed at the barn and was swiveling back and forth. She tensed, pulling up the M-16. David's restraining hand settled on her shoulder.

"Not yet," he whispered.

She looked again and saw three hunched figures running toward the house, each carrying a rifle.

"The Scanner's our priority," David said. "We have to get closer."

They ducked below the creek's boulder-strewn bank and scrambled upstream toward the bridge.

gent Charles Holt jerked the NVDs from his eyes, his whispered voice filled with urgency. "The antenna's turning this way."

Jared nodded, and they ducked back inside the barn's north entrance and ran to the train's transmitting console. If the plan worked, and the train created a diversion, Holt, Crow, and he would pump as many rounds as they could into the Humvees and Scanner. O'Hanlon would switch on the Magnifying Transmitter, and Mark and the others would escape out the north door and head for Spy Knob, where María and several of the men had gone.

Jared gritted his teeth as he turned the power switch on. He had to remain calm, fight the urge to run out and blast away at the aggressors, whose main goal seemed to be the torture and murder of his family and friends. In particular, he wanted to settle the score with the Scanner. The accursed machine could somehow ferret out his men and disable or kill them with its microwave device. If he couldn't pull off the diversion, he and his family were as good as dead.

Using one hand, he shielded the flashlight, squeezing the beam to the smallest illumination needed to see the train tranmitter's controls. He rotated the wheel-shaped power regulator to twenty percent. If he went to fifty percent, he guessed the train would hit sixty miles an hour, maybe more. He planned to gradually increase the power, keeping the train's speed down until it passed the curve, then he'd pour the coals to it. He gave Holt a final glance, then hit the *Transmit* switch.

* * *

Mark and Alex crept to the office window and stared into the dark woods beyond the house. Unable to see the train, Mark listened and finally heard two faint metallic clanks he thought must be the couplers grabbing as the engine lurched forward.

He looked down at the three vehicles parked below. The Scanner was squarely over the tracks and was the farthest from the barn. The closest Humvee was partly on the tracks, the other barely touching a rail.

Then the strange antenna captured his attention. It suddenly ceased sweeping back and forth and pointed toward the barn's lower story. It adjusted its shape and began rotating like a slow-motion propeller. From inside the van came a rising, generator-like whine.

* * *

Jared played the flashlight beam across the train's transmitting console. The gauges read normal, the transmitter circuits humming away. The train should be carving through the woods by now, about to enter the quarter mile of straight track that angled toward the barn.

He held his breath and reached for the power regulator. A sudden disorienting heat stabbed at his mind. *The Scanner—*

He turned. The flashlight dropped from his enervated hand. In the pale reflected light, he saw Holt drop his rifle and stagger forward, hands pressed against his temples. Jared lurched backward and spun uncontrollably across the transmitter console, his forearm sweeping across the controls. He sank down, clutching wildly for any solid object. He seized the power wheel, and as the world went black, twisted it to maximum.

* * *

Mark heard the whirring of the train's motor and the steely cry of the wheels against the rails.

"It's coming!" Alex whispered.

But it seemed unbelievably loud. And another sound accompanied it: a wild, urgent, deep-throated moan, like a big-block racecar engine with the throttle cracked wide open. This would surely get the enemy's attention.

He glanced at the Scanner; the antenna was tilting up. It pointed at him, started rotating. Alex jumped to his feet and jerked Mark's collar. "*Run!*"

*   *   *

Kate pulled herself even with the bridge and looked cautiously at the Scanner. The claw antenna had tilted up and was aiming at the barn's upper story. It began to rotate. A mix of panic and anger shocked her nervous system.

David raised his rifle. "On my count…"

She flicked the M-16's safety off and switched to full automatic. As she rose, she reflexively jerked her head toward an onrushing sound—coming from the right—a metallic ringing and a powerful, climbing, gear-against-gear whirring that tingled her spine and bristled the hairs on the back of her neck. She jerked the NVDs from her eyes and almost fell backward as she saw it: a great, roaring firebrand that screamed through the woods, its comet-tail of flame throwing the trees into black silhouettes and sweeping long, branching patterns of yellow and orange across the grounds.

"Great God," she gasped as it hurtled toward them. "It's the *train*!

Wind-blasted flames jetted from the cowling, engulfed the engine, and flared back in a blazing sheet that covered the machine's wheels and cars and lashed into the surrounding woods, torching the undergrowth and the low-hanging boughs of pines. It screamed fast—*faster*. The whistle cracked the air; the headlamp glared like a lightning bolt—a full metal jacket fireball from Hell. *Aye, Captain Nemo, we have ramming speed—*

"Get down!" David yelled, seizing her arm.

But Kate was unable to tear her eyes away.

The train thundered past in a superheated blur that singed her hair and pulled her breath away. With a titanic *crash* it broadsided the van and catapulted it into a high spinning arc over the remaining two vehicles. The airborne van's fuel tank exploded with a loud *thump* and disgorged a sheet of searing napalm across the rearward Humvee.

Encased in fire, the vehicle shot from the tracks in reverse, the machine gunner a wildly-animated scarecrow of flame.

Kate and David turned and fled toward the house as the fire-shrouded machine accelerated toward them. The vehicle rammed into a bridge support, rocked sideways over the steep embankment, and with a great rending and screeching of metal clattered over the boulders toward the creek below.

The remaining Humvee spewed gravel as it lurched forward, but the airborne van plunged earthward and hammered dead center into the escaping machine. Metal clapped and banged; flames and sparks mushroomed out and up as the vehicles spun into a twisted sculpture of steel and fire.

Machine guns barked. Bullets whined past Kate's ear, and David yelped and dropped to the ground.

She snapped the NVDs back into place and stared at the two men firing at them. They were advancing from the house, their own infrared NVDs glowing like headlamps, guns spouting daggers of green flame. Then, with almost unemotional detachment, as if she were seated comfortably in a movie theater watching herself as a character in an action thriller, she swung the M-16 smoothly up from her side, grasped the forward stock with her left hand and, screaming, pulled the trigger against the guard. The muzzle spouted a long, flaring green torch that she swept back and forth before the two aggressors, the ejected shell casings a curving brass ladder in the staccato glare.

The rifle and her voice became silent, their ammunition spent. She held her pose, looking past the smoking barrel, seeing nothing but fire-kindled sky above the woods. The dispassionate part of her mind wondered how many holes she might have punched through her parent's house.

David's moan brought her to his side.

* * *

O'Hanlon ran toward the office and abruptly stopped as Mark and Alex tumbled through the door. His first horrified reaction was that the boys had been injured, but they were laughing, punching each other, high-fiving and whooping it up like delirious eight-year olds.

"Majorly awesome—"

"Destructo derby—"

"Totally *annihilated*—"

Buddy joined in, tail wagging, paws thumping the floor as he pranced.

If Mark was happy, he was happy.

Sidestepping the victory dance, O'Hanlon crept into the office, inched along the south wall, and peered through the window at the destroyed vehicles below. He jumped back, his heart skipping a beat when several loud pops exploded through the burning wreckage. *It's the ammunition burning*, he thought. No signs of life. Where were Jared, Holt, and the others?

A dull *boom* rolled through the barn. ARC was at it again.

He retreated from the office and closed the door. The boys had calmed, but their eyes glittered like wolf pups anticipating the hunt. The good guys had beaten the bad guys. Time for the next battle. *To a child, everything is possible.*

O'Hanlon swiftly returned to the Magnifying Transmitter console. He glanced at the checklist, reached for the controls, and turned a lever marked *Node Deflectors*—STEP NUMBER FIVE.

Fifteen feet below the roof opening, at the base of the mobius coil, two long metal arms capped with aluminum spheres began to contra-rotate. They increased in speed, whooshing and thumping—a downbeat for the coming symphony.

O'Hanlon glanced around the room, trying to anchor himself in the present reality, and gave the boys a lingering look. He turned back to the console, set his jaw, and snapped another switch. A rising, high-pitched whine joined the thrumming background as the rotary spark gap's twin disks began to howl—STEP NUMBER SIX.

Heart pounding, feeling as if he were about to jump from the Golden Gate Bridge without a parachute, O'Hanlon grasped the big ebony-handled Transmit switch with both hands and pulled it swiftly down. The handle's thick copper blades chunked smoothly into their respective slots, completing the circuit to the giant relay that would activate the power transformer and send its high voltage current surging into the Magnifying Transmitter.

*   *   *

Nothing on the planet could have prepared Mark for the forthcoming roar of electrical energy—a raw, buzz-saw blast that bellowed up and shook the air like an orchestra of Gatling guns. It carried with it a major undertone, the intermingled sounds punching out a chord he thought every mega-power rock band in the world would kill to own.

The torus hissed and crackled, sheathing itself in a blue-violet glow veined with white electric darts that danced and stuttered from the aluminum skin like lightning in a hyperactive thunderstorm. The spark gap screamed and roared and snapped arc-welder bright sparks between its spinning electrodes, throwing the coils, transformers, and insulators into scintillating extremes of light and shadow.

The needles of instruments showing voltage and current vibrated and jumped. At the top of the console, the indicator of the big dial labeled *Resonance* wavered around the numeral 8. Mark watched O'Hanlon grasp the power lever and pull it to his right, attempting to increase the input.

But the lever balked and O'Hanlon pulled his hands away. He stared at the apparatus, a look of worried confusion on his face, and shouted, "Something's wrong."

54

Joseph Krohner's eyes focused on the warning screen just as a voice sounded in his headphones.

"Sir, some of the antennas have developed a problem."

"Explain."

"Ninety-six antennas experienced a high standing wave ratio for nearly a minute. They automatically kicked off-line. We're running diagnostics."

"I want the problem found—quickly."

"Of course, sir, but there's more."

"Tell me."

"A burst—one minute long—of very strong, extremely low frequency occurred at the same moment we detected the anomalous SWR. The ELF may have been responsible, may have produced a high voltage corona—"

"What was the transmission source?"

"We don't know yet, we're concentrating—"

"I can't afford systems failures. Report to me as soon as you know more."

"Yes sir."

Krohner frowned. He leaned forward in the chair and prodded his chin with a forefinger. Ninety-six antennas affected. Not enough to hurt the operation, but it eroded margin. More troubling was the potential cause. A counterweapon? Impossible. ARC tapped into every espionage organization and black ops division in the world. If anything existed, they would have known about it. It couldn't be the system itself. All critical elements—transmitting modules, wave guides, antennas, computers—were constantly monitored and checked.

He called up the image of Colorado Springs on the main grid and studied the transmission levels and targets. Shifting red disks indicated areas of the city undergoing destructive microwave bombardment. He tapped a few keys and the red targets disappeared. "Standby" flashed across the status screen. Colorado Springs could wait until the system was at one-hundred percent. He had bigger fish to fry.

He glanced at the conflict data. A squadron of stealth aircraft had evaded the ARC radar system and was meeting a fiery end as they closed on the Kill Screen. In return, ARC was incinerating every major air base in North America. Vandenberg, Edwards, and Travis were already obliterated. Now ARC was concentrating on the more distant bases.

Greggson was furious about the destruction, but Krohner had to protect the installation at any cost. Let Greggson fume. He didn't realize he was no longer in command—didn't realize his life and mind were forfeit as soon as his usefulness had run its course. As for Hurwitz and Crotty, the Attorney General's arrest orders had removed from Krohner the burden of taking them out himself.

The headphones intruded. "Dr. Krohner."

"Yes."

"The antennas are functioning normally. We found nothing wrong. We can load them to full capacity."

"Do it. But I want to know if the signal appears again. And I want to know where it's coming from."

Krohner pressed the joystick button and watched as the red spots again bled onto the map grid. He leaned back in his chair, crossed his arms over his chest, and smirked. *I wouldn't want to be living in Colorado Springs right now.*

55

O'Hanlon yanked the black handle up, instantly killing the power. The glow shrouding the torus flickered out, the hiss and crackle of high voltage electricity fading to silence. He snapped more switches, and the rotary spark gap wound down in a diminishing purr. The node deflectors coasted and creaked to a halt. Only the pungent smell of ozone and hot metal lingered.

"Oh wow," Mark murmured.

Alex gaped at the transmitter in stunned silence.

O'Hanlon backed against the chair and sat down. He felt both elated and drained. The machine had apparently survived the first test, and as soon as his nerves settled, he'd investigate the problem with the power control. He sniffed. The odor of burning rubber and plastic had begun to filter in from the wrecked vehicles outside. He didn't want to think about what else was burning inside those metal coffins.

"Listen," Mark said. "No more explosions."

O'Hanlon looked up through the roof opening. No violet rays troubled the sky. The night was quiet. Was the lull in the microwave attack a coincidence, or had they actually delivered ARC a sucker punch?

His anxiety quickly returned. Surely they hadn't done any

damage to the huge microwave weapon. Maybe ARC had only stopped attacking Colorado Springs to pinpoint the irritating little signal. Maybe he had just driven a nail into his own coffin.

Flashlight beams jostled below.

"Mark, Dr. O'Hanlon. Anyone?" It was Kate's voice. "We have injuries here."

"Mom!" Mark shouted.

O'Hanlon looked over the railing and saw Kate and David struggling across the floor below, David leaning against her shoulder for support. Braced by Crow, Holt and Jared staggered along behind. O'Hanlon snapped off the console's power, grabbed his flashlight, and followed Mark down the stairs.

They settled the three men onto chairs in the small meeting area and switched on an overhead light. David held a blood-soaked rag to his head. "I'll be alright," he mumbled. "I'm just a little out of it."

Jared and Holt shielded their eyes from the light and looked groggily around the room. Jenny held Jared's hand, tears glistening in her eyes. He brightened a little and placed a reassuring hand on her shoulder. Still animated with excitement, Mark told them about the train and how it had demolished the Scanner and both Humvees.

José and Esteban, along with two FBI agents, rushed into the room. They were grimy and scratched. Jared waved them to the table.

"It's quiet outside, boss," said José. "But..." his face clouded. "They knocked a lot of our guys out cold—maybe some of 'em dead—with that electronic thing." He paused and gave a faint smile. "We saw that stunt with the train."

"There's at least six more of their men out there," said one of the agents.

"What about the front gate?" David asked as Kate tied a makeshift bandage around his head.

"We don't know."

Kate nodded southward. "Greg's been shot. He's in the Bronco just off the first hill."

"We'll get him," Crow responded. He and Esteban turned and headed for the door. José fell in behind them.

A sudden boom shook the building. O'Hanlon's heart sank. "I was naïve to think we had actually stopped them."

"Guess you'd better have another go," Jared said.

"I need more power, but I couldn't move the control lever past ten percent. It has some sort of magnetic lock."

Jared looked at O'Hanlon for a long moment. "I think it's time to open the third manual."

O'Hanlon inserted the key into its slot on the console and turned it with a *click*. Tumblers on one of the big dials rotated and stopped, yielding a four-digit number. He entered the numbers into the lock on the third manual, snapped it open, and tugged the strap loose. There were only three pages. In the wavering beam of Mark's flashlight, he began reading.

The heading, written in precise, heavy script:

WARNING
THE OUROBOROS EFFECT

His eye dropped to the brief paragraphs that followed. After a few minutes, he closed the manual and placed it gently on the console. Now he understood the danger, the penalty for not following Tesla's instructions to the letter.

"What?" Mark asked.

As O'Hanlon opened his mouth to speak, violet light filled the roof opening and flickered out. A moment later, thunder hammered the walls and rattled the windows. From the pasture came the screams of terrified horses.

"There's no time for explanations." He turned and clapped a hand on Mark's shoulder, almost as if saying goodbye to an old friend. "I'm increasing the power, my boy. Tell the others to stand clear."

O'Hanlon faced the console and, following the manual's instructions, snapped a series of switches. With a startling *bang*, the magnetic lock blocking the power control jumped free. He turned around as he heard voices behind him: Jared and Kate.

"I want to see this," Jared said, pulling up a chair. "I've waited a long time."

Alex advanced from the stairs. "Everyone's off the floor."

O'Hanlon smiled weakly and nodded. It was appropriate for all of them to see the big, and maybe final, show. He advanced the power lever to fifty percent, and the barn came alive with the whine of electric motors and squeak and grind of gears. Electrodes, inductors, and spheres altered and repositioned. The machine began its metamorphosis, shifting to accommodate the increased power.

With a sudden shriek and clank of metal, the tower again began extending, the telescoping sections sliding up and locking individually into place. O'Hanlon stared in amazement as the torus climbed up and up, rising to more than a hundred feet above the roof. He gaped at the tall, slender structure. How could such a delicate-looking tower safely support a mass with so much sail area? But there was no time to ponder the physics. He closed a switch marked "Breaker," and the big relay on the main floor slammed shut, the explosive sound vibrating through its steel enclosure.

The rotary spark gap's twin disks screamed up to speed; the node deflectors began to rotate, revving to a steady *whump, whump*.

"Wait!" came Alex's excited voice. O'Hanlon turned and gave him a perplexed stare.

"The modulator—you said it's like a Class-C setup. That means, if you give it audio input, it increases the peak envelope power. Every downbeat of music or shouted word will *double* the instantaneous power output." He cocked his head, his eyes wide with anticipation.

"The boom box is still hooked up," Mark said. "And it has a CD loaded."

O'Hanlon looked at the boys and shrugged. "Sure. Why not."

Mark darted below the console. After a moment, he stood up. "It's playing."

"All right, fellows," O'Hanlon said with a nod. "Let's send them a message."

And with a final glance at the Magnifying Transmitter, he straightened, grasped the black-handled transmit switch, and forced it down.

56

ystems Failure. Krohner bolted upright in the command chair and stared at the readouts scrolling down in columns across the viewscreen. Antennas were failing, waveguides were blowing apart, control systems were going berserk. His eyes bulged. *Impossible! Impossible!*

His chief engineer's panicked voice crackled loudly in the headphones. "Dr. Krohner—"

"Yes, yes, I see it. What the *hell* is going on?"

"The low frequency wave is back again. It's as powerful as an EMP weapon, but nearly constant. It's increasing in intensity—and it's modulated."

An irritating song played in the background, growing louder.

"Turn the goddamned *music* off—"

"But that's *it*, sir. The music's in the wave. It's permeating everything."

Krohner hugged himself, his shoulders hunched forward. He steadied his breathing and glanced through the slanted observation window into the vast chamber below.

Hundreds of the giant microwave transmitting modules had triggered off-line, their green lights switching to red. If this continued much longer, they would lose the Kill Screen, and a missile or stealth aircraft might penetrate their defense grid. What Satan-spawned entity could have developed an electromagnetic pulse weapon of such power?

"Sir?"

Krohner didn't answer.

The voice was silent for a moment, then continued. "We may have located the EMP source."

"For God's sake, *where*?"

"Colorado Springs, sir. But it's hard to say exactly. The wave has an erratic component and the polarization is impossible..."

The accursed music began to override the technician's voice. Krohner snatched the headset free and punched on the speaker. He listened to the raw, buzzing signal that assaulted his stronghold. It carried harmonics like a jamming signal, yet he could clearly discern a melody and lyrics, like a horrible broadcast from some sixties rock station. Now, with each heavy beat and chorus, lights and readouts in the control room flickered and pulsed—

Krohner snapped around in his chair and stared at the engineers frantically working the consoles and screens behind him. Half of them were standing, looking around the room, listening in total confusion. He almost vaulted from the elevated chair as a dozen of the huge microwave modules shorted and blasted white-hot sparks through their cooling vents.

Another heavy chorus of music screamed through the system and a dozen modules ejected smoke, blew out their casings, tripped circuit breakers. He could feel the thunder of their destruction even through the ultra-thick safety glass and buffered control room walls. He glared at the screen. The red target spots began draining from the Colorado Springs grid. Warnings flashed faster than he could read.

They mocked him with idiotic music as they chipped away at his impenetrable, undefeatable redoubt. His mind raced. In all of the southwestern United States, there was only one facility big enough, secret enough, to have hidden a weapon of sufficient power to challenge him.

Krohner stabbed the microphone button, spewing spittle as he snarled his order.

"Initiate an X-V emergency launch. Full charge. He repeated the order, and then rocked forward and back in his elevated throne, arms clamped around his body. *You want to play hard ball? You think I'm an impotent threat with my microwave system that's light-years ahead of every weapon on the planet? Well, as they say*—you ain't seen nothin' yet.

57

In the fading light, Grey Wolf, shaman of the Athabascan clan known as Kalluk, stood on the high rock ledge overlooking the river and cast his gaze westward, toward the Dark Mountain. He cradled the ancient fetish in his left hand, drawing his fingers across its smooth, carved surface.

He chanted—*Agaayuh aatchuiruq afuyautaitchuq nuna*—not for the death of the men inside the mountain, but for peace. He prayed that no more planes would come and be dashed to the ground, that the machinery inside the mountain would cease its evil emanations, that his people could return to their land and the world would be healed.

Suddenly, the angry hissing and crackling sound coming from the mountain changed. Now he could hear a beat, a rhythm, the indistinct words and tonalities of a distant song, as if it were borne on the heat waves of a summer afternoon. It brightened, became more definite. Then he heard it quite plainly. He glanced at his men, who were standing beside him. They cocked their heads in confusion and looked at their shaman, their faces questioning.

Grey Wolf listened for a long moment, eyes cast upward, head nodding to the rhythm.

"Ah," he said at last. "Beatles."

58

Mark stared toward the rafters, awe-stricken, shielding his eyes as blasts of blue-white light flashed and rained through the square opening in the roof. Lightning zigzagged from the elevated torus—not the crackling, snake-like threads generated during the transmitter's first test, but great, furious tree-trunks of electricity that lashed hundreds of feet from the torus' silvery contour and rose thundering into the night sky. The glaring barrage coiled and whipsawed near, then far, the sound rising and falling with its proximity.

The song playing on the stereo went through the mysterious modulator Alex had discovered, and then, through some magical process Mark couldn't begin to comprehend, its sound rode upon the electromagnetic waves sent out by the Magnifying Transmitter. To his astonishment, a faithful reproduction of the song also blasted out from the electrical discharge escaping from the torus, the lightning-spawned music roaring forth like a million Led Zeppelin stage amplifiers turned to ear-splitting maximum overdrive. If anyone in the entire state of Colorado had never before heard *All You Need is Love*, they heard it now.

With startling suddenness, the racket ceased. Lightning branching from the torus stuttered, diminished, and stopped, leaving its echoes tumbling in the hills. The rotary spark gap coasted, whirring down in rpm. O'Hanlon's flashlight beam traveled over the console. "We've lost power," he said, his voice laden with despair. He snapped the switches into the off position.

"Maybe it's the circuit breaker," Mark offered.

"No," said Alex. "The power's out everywhere. You can't see any lights in Colorado Springs, just fires."

Mark switched the stereo to the AM band. "Listen, the radio's back."

...less than a minute ago. First, an update on the Colorado Springs mystery. Traffic in and out of Colorado Springs is still snarled for miles along Highway Twenty Five. There are eyewitness reports of fires, military action, and strange lights over the city. The Office of Emergency Preparedness is urging everyone to stay at home. Stay tuned. As we receive information....

His grandfather plucked the walkie-talkie from his belt and pressed the transmit button. "Hey, you guys hear me? Anybody?"

After a moment, a voice buzzed in reply. "Hey, boss. How about that light show. Everyone okay?"

"Hey Carlos," Jared replied. "Yeah, we're all right. What's going on?"

"We stopped three of those clowns tryin' to come in on dirt bikes. You guys keep your eyes open; I think there's more of 'em."

"Hear anything from Alpha?"

"Nothing, boss."

A hiss of static suddenly grew, obliterating the conversation. Jared adjusted the squelch. "Damn, there it goes again."

Mark switched off the stereo. "There's static on the radio, too."

Crow stumped rapidly up the steps. "Hey," he shouted. "You need to see this."

"What?"

"The sky."

Klaxons blared throughout the Mountain. Krohner switched on the security channels and watched the view screen as hallways filled with engineers, technicians, and workers rushing for doors marked "shelter," some dropping paperwork or personal belongings in their haste.

He stabbed a button and the screen filled with external video images of the ARC project. He leaned forward, staring intently, listening. Blasts of air roared from the five hundred massive hexagonal portals that encircled the mountainside. With a freight-train rumble, they separated from their concrete and steel frames and pulled back into the mountain's dark interior. Steel cylinders groaned and screeched as they pistoned through the holes, telescoping outward section by section, until each extended to a distance of eight-hundred feet.

The enormous geodesic dome resting on the mountain's flattened top split into four sections that pivoted away and lowered, exposing to the sky a great conical mass of steel and carbon-titanium alloy. Powerful hydraulic pumps growled, and eight segmented metal arms unfolded from the cone like scorpions' tails. They curled out and out, and when they finally locked into place, they had formed a claw antenna the diameter of a battleship.

Glowing wire frame schematics of the entire weapon system

hovered in a multicolored holographic projection before Krohner's elevated chair, the animated images indicating the status and position of every major mechanical part and circuit.

One by one, systems icons winked green. Krohner barked a command into the wireless headset: "Start field generators." A moment later, there was a subtle quickening in the low pulse permeating the control room. On the projected schematic, an image representing the steel cylinders blinked from red to green, and a voice crackled, "Vortex is go."

Krohner lowered the chair and leaped onto the floor. He paced back and forth through the hologram, the laser-generated lines tattooing his body in glowing neon. "Containment."

"Containment is go."

He turned and stared at the three dimensional image of the great claw antenna poised on the mountaintop. "Begin plasma injection and automatic sequencing."

After a few moments, the voice confirmed the order had been executed, and a doleful throbbing shuddered through the control room.

Wheeling around to face the wall projection, Krohner focused on the map of Colorado Springs. Black cross hairs crept across the screen and centered over the target.

"Sequencing complete. Ready on your command."

Krohner waited, narrowing his eyes, then said in a cold, dry voice: "Fire the weapon."

Kate stepped outside the barn and gasped: from the Air Force Academy to Peterson Air Force Base to Fort Carson, Colorado Springs was a patchwork crescent of raging fire.

She turned away from the sight and looked toward the barn. High above the dark structure, the torus hovered round and mysterious, its polished sides reflecting ghostly patterns of orange from the burning city.

"See it?" Crow whispered.

Kate shifted her eyes to the right of the torus, to a faint luminous patch swirling in the deep sky. At first glance, the pale spiral appeared like an overlarge moon leering through a veil of high clouds. But a closer observation revealed curling tendrils and a cyclic motion, the interior of the glowing mass rotating faster than the outside. It reminded her of a satellite image of a growing hurricane.

"See what I mean? And that spot in the middle, it's getting bigger—fast."

The coruscating eye was brighter than the rest of the spiral, its color edging toward violet. And it was growing.

"Look's far off, but huge," said Kate. "It's eerie…"

"Yeah. Question is, do we run, head for the hills…"

"Way creepy," came Mark's voice.

Kate spun around. The boys were standing behind her, staring upward.

"Egregious creep-out," said Alex.

"I told you to stay inside," Kate said sharply.

"I just wanted to see—"

"Go back—"

"Uh oh," said Crow.

Kate looked up again. The spiral had enlarged, become brighter. It pulsated like a thunderhead wracked with torrents of lightning. The eye of the spiral grew to searchlight brilliance, its hue now red-orange. Then it moved off-center, enlarging at an accelerated rate. With a shock, Kate realized that it was detached, had dimension of its own—

"It's moving."

"Coming down."

"Like a meteor."

Oh, dear God, it's headed straight for us.

Kate seized Mark's hand and tugged him, running, toward the barn. The ground flickered in a dizzying melee of light and dark. She felt herself stumbling, Mark pulling her to her feet. Shielding her eyes, she saw the fireball descend. It swirled red, yellow, violet, boiling with internal explosions. Lightning coiled from its surface into the clear night sky and arced toward the ground.

It flared solar-bright.

Kate threw her body across Mark, shielding him, bracing against the inevitable; then, through half-lidded eyes she saw long, angular shadows sweep across the ground, felt a shift in the radiated heat.

She stood, shading her eyes with her hand, watching as the flame screamed high over the ranch, hurtling southward, guttering like a spastic sun. It cast an orange-white glare against the hills and dropped silently beyond Pikes Peak.

Crow watched the disappearing light, his face a mask of awe and fear. "It's gonna hit NORAD," he shouted. He turned toward the barn and beckoned frantically. "Get inside."

Kate could hear it coming through the trees as they raced into the barn—a crackling, roaring, magnified torch-sound. The barn's big door slammed against its tracks, a searing wind jetting around the edges. Boards rattled, windows exploded, and the ancient timbers creaked and moaned.

Just as suddenly, the atmosphere reversed, gasping back into the space from which it had come. In the brief silence that followed, Kate heard an ominous, hollow booming coming from the Magnifying Transmitter.

She threw her flashlight beam toward the noise—the support tower swaying from the gale's assault, the telescoping sections tilting and banging against each other like gigantic wind chimes. She looked up, holding her breath, expecting an avalanche of metal to come crashing down on them. But the resilient system held, absorbing the stress, rocking slowly back to center.

As she watched the undulating tower, the roof opening flared red, the light forming a brilliant rectangular beam through the settling dust. Crimson lanced through every crack and gap in sweeping parallel rays. The powerful glare lingered, fluttered, and then receded back into the night.

Kate's mind played an image of the superheated fireball plunging into Cheyenne Mountain, torching away, melting through to NORAD's protected command center deep inside.

Flashlights bobbed. Her father and O'Hanlon intercepted them.

"Run for the generator," Crow shouted, pushing through. "There's gonna be another shockwave."

Crow led, their flashlight beams joining in jittering cones of yellow.

Jenny stood in the generator room doorway. Her jaw trembled, a glint of wetness on her cheeks. She smiled with relief as Kate and the others approached. "Kate, thank God…"

"Back inside, quick." Kate followed her mother into the concrete room. Illiani lay on the floor just inside. David was standing, a steadying arm hooked over the generator's inlet pipe. Jared and

Crow ushered O'Hanlon and the boys inside and pulled the steel door shut with a clang.

Silence.

Then the floor began to move—an unbalanced, queasy motion like an elevator repeatedly dropping and braking.

Kate pressed her hand against the wall, her heart hammering against her ribs. A sound, like rapid thunder tumbling over and over itself, pounded the walls and thumped the ground. Glass broke. A massive, lingering crash came from somewhere outside. Something heavy thudded against the transmitter room's wooden floor.

The violence ceased, and a flurry of echoes rolled through the valley. Water rushed softly in the creek outside. The collective sighs of the room's occupants whispered from the hard, flat walls.

"I'll check," Kate's father said, his voice loud in the new quiet.

"Mr. Thompson," Crow said. "If you don't mind guarding these folks, Charles and I will have a look outside."

The two agents ducked out before Kate's father could reply. She looked through the open door. Above the transmitter, a ragged mouth with rafter teeth grimaced against the night sky. A cold breeze soughed through the jagged opening—the cupola and top half of the roof had been torn off.

She and her father stepped outside the room, their flashlights casting sharp yellow beams through the roiling dust. Shingles and splintered wood lay in jumbled piles across the floor and atop the coils and transformers.

"Oh dear," O'Hanlon mumbled from behind.

Kate directed her flashlight along the tower's slender metal lattice, following it up. The silvery torus still floated high above. "The tower's intact," she said, astonished.

Her father kicked a board aside and walked onto the main floor. "Kate, you and the boys stay back." He played the flashlight around the barn for several minutes and returned. "Except for the roof, I don't see any major damage." He stepped back inside the room and nodded toward David and Illiani. "How are you two doing?"

The agent looked up. "I'm not dead yet," he said thickly.

David waved his free hand dismissively. "Can't see very well, but I can walk."

Kate's father leaned against the wall and massaged the back of his neck. "Question now," he said at last, "is whether we take our chances and head for the hills or stick it out here."

"You heard Carlos," Kate said. "If we leave, we'll be vulnerable."

"They haven't been able to take us, so far. And if they can't deliver for their masters, I think they'll blast the entire ranch."

Mark, kneeling beside Buddy, spoke up. "We could blast *them* again. We stopped them before. Twice. They didn't come back until we lost power."

"In case you didn't notice, the power's still off," Alex said.

Mark stood slowly and clicked on his flashlight. He turned and extended his arm, placing the light beam squarely on the ancient generator. Alex held up his own light and illuminated the instruments clustered on the wide, flat panel.

Kate's father shook his head. "That generator hasn't been run since 1903. The old pipes have holes, and the wooden slats would probably blow out from the water pressure." He swept his hand westward. "On top of that, someone would have to go all the way up to the dam and open the gate."

"I will," Mark said, his voice hard with resolution.

Kate whirled on him. "You will *not*. Even if we did try, they'd drop a fireball right on top of us."

O'Hanlon's pensive voice echoed in the ensuing silence. "The transmitter was at fifty percent when we lost power. Perhaps if we went to one hundred percent...."

"S ir," the senior technician's voice crackled in Krohner's headset. "A field unit in Colorado Springs reported something interesting."

"Go."

"They said electricity was coming off a big tower extending from a barn on the ranch property and jumping into the air. This apparently coincided with the latest attack on this station. I thought you should know."

Krohner ran his hand across his face. He shook his head as if the man had spoken Chinese.

"Repeat what you just said."

The technician did as asked, then added, "They said the electricity stopped when the power went off in Colorado Springs. This also coincided with the attack on this facility. They said there was very loud music—said it seemed to be coming from the tower."

Krohner sat back forcibly in the control chair. "What is the status?"

"The ground units have regrouped—eight on foot plus five motorcycles. The helicopter is due for another overflight."

Krohner folded his arms, then raised a hand and pinched his chin. It was insane to think the fugitives in Colorado Springs possessed the weapon being used against him. But these were the same people who had infiltrated his mountain and stolen top secret data...

Another consideration: the ranch was only a few miles from NORAD. Perhaps it was a secret government project—one ARC had missed. If they had advanced EMP hardware, he wanted it. But he was also afraid of the possible consequences if they were able to repower their weapon.

Krohner made his decision. "Tell the field units to capture the—" He made a wry face. "Barn."

"Yes sir."

"Tell them we will be providing some incentive for the people in the barn to leave."

"Yes sir."

"And I want power diverted for another X-V, targeting the ranch."

There was a pause at the other end. "Sir, what shall I tell the field units...about evacuating?"

Krohner focused on the projection screen, his hands working the keyboard and joystick. "Tell them nothing."

62

Footsteps pounded outside the generator room, a flashlight beam bouncing along the floor ahead of the runner. It was Crow. "Everyone," his deep voice boomed as he burst through the doorway. "Time to run for it."

"What…" Kate began.

"That purple ray," Crow said, bending down and scooping Illiani effortlessly from the floor. "It's coming this way."

"The Jeep's on the north side," Jared said, waving everyone toward the door.

* * *

They paused just outside the barn, and Kate saw a glowing violet curtain slanting down from the sky, creeping toward them like a thunderhead.

"It's coming across the north pasture," she cried.

And where it touched down, trees and grass exploded orange and red, and white, flames fanning instantly toward the sky. Through the NVDs, the beam was a nightmare wall of green fire, the panicked horses racing just ahead of it. Here and there the undulating aurora darted forward and seared across the herd. Gouts of flame erupted from the stricken animals as they fled. Horses screamed and burst into fiery torches, as if kindled from an internal white-hot heat.

Kate staggered. Bullets suddenly pocked and whined against the barn's stone walls. There was a metallic spanking as projectiles impacted the Jeep.

"Damn it!" Crow roared.

"*Inside!*" she heard someone shout.

Hands grasped her shoulder and pulled her back. The door banged shut. She was again surrounded by darkness. Trapped.

"They'll stop the beam. They wouldn't kill their own men," someone yelled.

"The hell they wouldn't," came a reply.

Kate's senses returned and she looked around to see everyone back inside the barn. Silent. Even her father seemed at a loss. O'Hanlon spoke: "The generator room is reinforced. Maybe the metal will help shield—"

"Where's Mark?" Kate snapped, her voice loud, shaking. She felt panic tearing at her sanity.

"Here."

He stood in the corridor that led past the stalls toward the barn's southern end and the tack room, his old mountain bike at his side. A long burst of automatic gunfire rattled outside.

"Mark...Son," Jared said in a coaxing voice. "Come with us..."

"Professor O'Hanlon," Mark said. "Please get the generator ready." Looking down at Buddy, who whined, squirming to get free from Alex's restraining hand, he said, "Stay. And this time I mean it." He tugged a pair of NVDs over his eyes, mounted the bicycle, and disappeared down the dark passage. Buddy barked frantically.

"Mark!" Kate screamed. She took a step toward the corridor, felt her knees buckle. Then her father's arms were around her. She sobbed. "Daddy. It can't end like this."

His calm voice resonated beside her. "Easy, darlin'. David and Jenny need you now. He turned her around to face him. A whimsical little smile broke across his face, pinching the deep wrinkles in the corners of his eyes. "It ain't over 'til it's over."

Adding to the rapid chatter of gunfire was the crack and snarl of motorcycle engines racing across the grounds.

* * *

Kate pulled away from her father and looked at the others. *No*, she thought, *it's not over*. She clicked her flashlight on and located a bridle hanging nearby. No time for a saddle.

She snatched the bridle from the wall and darted for the north entrance.

Her father's voice chased after her. "Kate—*No!*"

"Don't try to stop me," she fired back. And then she was outside the door.

A wind hissed past the barn and across the ground, whipping her hair and stinging her eyes, dragging bits of straw and leaves toward the humming violet beam like sacrificial offerings.

She stood outside the corral, bridle in her left hand, M-16 strapped across her shoulder, snugging the NVDs tight with her free hand. She heard the neighing and screaming of horses, the rumble of their hooves as they fled the killing ray. She placed two fingers to her mouth and blew a shrill, high, wavering note, the wind catching and dissipating the sound. Did she dare hope that Winnie, the spirited chestnut stallion she had groomed and ridden since before Mark was born, would be among the surviving horses, that he would hear and respond as always when she called?

She whistled twice more, pouring forth soul and sound in sustained helpless notes that left her short of breath and tears burning her vision. And still the horses raced past in terror. Despair and fatigue and horror clawed and beckoned, urging surrender to the death that would in minutes be upon them.

Suddenly a dark mass stormed up beside her and stopped in a swirl of dust, snorting and blowing in deep nervous breaths. A velvet muzzle nudged her ear.

Her arms clasped the big stallion's neck. "Winnie! You heard me. You remembered."

She slipped the bridle over his head, jumped from the wooden fence onto his back, and urged him forward. And as if he understood the urgency of the hour, he reared and charged at a pounding gallop into the night.

63

Mark swerved onto the Lost Canyon Trail, the ghost-green image in the NVDs bouncing crazily before his eyes. The ink-black dips and furrows gave no hint of depth, and the bike's front wheel rammed into them, threatening to sling him over the handlebars. He shifted, braked, twisted madly as rocks and limbs rushed suddenly into his path.

The bicycle itself was a problem. He'd grown since he had last ridden it, and the seat was too low. He had to stand when pedaling hard, pitching his weight precariously forward.

He downshifted, pumping for the top of the first steep hill. He knew the path well. It was peppered with loose sandstone and demanded just the right pressure on the rear wheel, or he'd spin out. He crested the rise and braked on its narrow spine. Looking back, he saw the glowing microwave beam creeping across the ranch. Then another light glared, wiggling up the trail behind him, carrying the metallic snarl of a two-stroke engine.

His nerves flew into the red zone: *Dirt bike!*

He pushed the front wheel over the edge and accelerated down into darkness. Shadow trees and boulders whispered by as the bike rattled over the rock-studded trail. He remembered the first ridge; saw its dim shape racing toward him. He yanked the handlebars up as he shot over the top, weightless as the bike left the edge, and slammed down, racing faster.

Impossible! He had to make the precise turn at the bottom of the trail or end up crashing down a steep embankment into the creek. The maneuver required timing, setup. Now he couldn't even see the intersection.

The dirt bike's headlamp licked across ground in front of him, flaring bright green in the NVDs. His memory of the trail had failed. *Where do I turn?Where do I turn...* Then a sudden shape flashed past, rippling through the darkness like a banner—*Buddy*! *Buddy knows the way*—Mark clicked the derailleur into high gear and banked, shooting into the curve, following the dog's lead.

He quickly straightened and shot across the narrow footbridge spanning the creek, then downshifted and began climbing. His breath came in gasps. He chased Buddy around another curve, over the last bridge, and pumped hard along the flat, gaining speed for the final hill.

Light wavered and bounced through the trees ahead. The motorcycle's rasping motor grew louder. He stood on the pedals, his leg muscles beyond pain, losing feeling, collapsing. He had never before made the hill without stopping. Then his father's voice came unbidden: *Come on, Mark, kick in the afterburner*!

He let out a scream. This was no kid's game, no fun ride to the Lookout with his father and mother. The ranch, his family—maybe even the whole country—depended on his singular act. If he failed, he failed on a scale with life and love at one end and torture and death at the other.

Then he was over the top. The dirt bike was grinding up the hill behind him, revving as it crested, tearing at him, and its headlamp blinding-bright in the NVDs. He made an instant, reflexive decision. Instead of heading for the dam, he followed Buddy. Straight for the Lookout.

He tore the goggles off and pedaled hard, forcing his cramping legs to move. As he dove over the small hill—the "hump," as his father had called it—the granite ledge rose into view, a gray tongue jutting out over a void, over Colorado Springs, now a glittering abstract pattern of orange and yellow flame.

He and his father had always approached the Lookout with great caution, braking as they coasted down, skidding, watching the pebbles skitter across its flat surface and disappear over the edge. But now, instead of rolling gently onto the treacherous rock, he twisted to the right, entering the narrow, rough gash that dropped below the ledge.

The front wheel struck something, catapulting him over the handlebars. He folded, tumbling into the rocks, the back of his mind registering the dirt bike's scream as it raced for the ledge.

Dust and blood filled his mouth. Bruised elbows, knees, and ankles pressed painfully against unyielding rock. A star-studded sky spun silently overhead. Buddy anxiously licked his hand, his face, whining.

Mark sat up stiffly, head throbbing, stomach pushing against the back of his throat. He steadied himself and looked down into the blackness below the Lookout. If the motorcycle had gone over the edge, the rider was dead. If he hadn't gone over—Mark was dead.

No dirt bike. No sound.

He stood, crying out as pain knifed from his left foot, frantically groped in the dark for his bike, found it, felt the twisted handlebars and heard the chain clinking loosely from the sprockets. He let it drop, pulled himself up the slope, and began running toward the dam, each step spiking a blinding rush of pain. The small reservoir lay ahead, its calm, jet surface reflecting constellations of stars.

He found the steps leading up to the concrete dam, climbed, and raced along the walkway, swinging himself forward between the metal handrails. The big outlet pipe ran just above the creek's rushing water, lost from view in the black canyon thirty feet below.

The long steel lever that controlled the floodgate jumped through the darkness, nearly striking his chest. To release water into the pipe, he merely had to pull the lever down. He grasped the handle, pausing just long enough to glance toward the barn. The purple ray was creeping closer. *Oh, God! Am I too late? Has it already struck the barn?*

He heaved against the lever. It was rock solid. Pushed harder, felt no movement. His concentration was broken by the chainsaw-crack of another dirt bike laboring up the trail. *Not again!*

A headlight lanced through the trees. A second headlight joined the first. Mark slid beneath the lever, locked his hands around it, and repeatedly jerked down with his entire weight. Tears of desperation streamed down his face, and with each violent tug, he hissed between gnashing teeth: "YOU—GOD—DAMNED—ARC—ASS—HOLES."

A headlight swept across the lake and found him. He yanked with all his might, felt something give. The lever shrieked and swung down, dropping him to the concrete. A shuddering roar vibrated from below as water funneled into the pipe.

Mark stood, gasping, and looked out toward the barn. Casting a defiant stare at the closing violet beam, he murmured, "Comin' at *you*—you bastards."

He didn't even look as the second motorcycle skidded to a stop.

A movement caught his eye—something on the lake's surface—a ghost of a whirlpool, a reflection. He stared up and gasped. In the deep sky there swirled another hurricane-like spiral, a bright globe pulsing in its center. ARC was building another monster fireball, and there was no doubt in his mind where it would go.

64

O' Hanlon grabbed the splintered roof beam and heaved. It crashed to the floor, fanning up a cloud of dust. Working in the glow of a flashlight, he and Alex began dragging fallen rafters away from the Magnifying Transmitter's high voltage coils.

He cast an anxious glance through the ragged hole in the roof. The purple beam still carved across the night sky, moving closer. During brief lulls in the gun battle outside, he could hear it hum and crackle. They had only minutes before the beam reached them, and he expected to hear Jared's voice at any moment, warning them to run for the presumed safety of the generator room.

Coughing dust from his lungs, he grabbed the flashlight and swept its beam across a copper helix. "They're dented," he said, running his hand over an injured section, "but maybe they're still functional."

"That leaves the capacitors and spark gap," Alex said.

"There's no time—"

Jenny's urgent voice cut him off. "Dr. O'Hanlon, something's happening. Come quickly!"

He dodged the pile of debris and ran toward the voice. Jenny was standing beside the generator's steel door, a worried frown creasing her face.

A loud hissing, like the sudden discharge of a high-pressure air tank, emanated from the concrete room. O'Hanlon and Alex rushed inside and stared at the generator. Air was whistling and moaning through the seams in the water inlet pipe. O'Hanlon took a step forward. Then a low rumble began, growing in ferocity until it shook the pipe and vibrated the floor.

"My God!" O'Hanlon said, awed. "Mark's done it." He thrust his flashlight into Alex's hand and approached the valve. "He's opened the floodgate." He grunted as he pulled at the wheel. "Water's coming down the pipe." The valve resisted. Then, with a drawn-out squeak, it broke free. The unfettered air roared and echoed hollowly inside the generator, the rumbling inside the pipe now like a freight train thundering through a mountain tunnel. Whooshes and bangs rattled the machine. The escaping air shrieked.

O'Hanlon stepped back. With a shock, he realized the floodgate had been opened too quickly. As soon as the wall of accelerating water hit the turbine, the sudden pressure would destroy it and the pipe too. "Everybody—get out!"

He and Alex helped David, who was still partly blinded, seize an unhappy Illiani by the arms and begin dragging him across the floor.

"Help me up," Illiani grumbled. "I can stand."

At that moment, the pipe shuddered and boomed. Water blasted through the seams in a liquid scream as the tsunami of water exploded into the turbine.

O'Hanlon stood, frozen in place, expecting a high-pressure blast of icy water to burst from the pipe and blow all of them from the room. But the rumbling continued at a steady rate.

Then another sound began—a massive rotor slowly building speed.

"Quick! Quick!" O'Hanlon shouted. "It's coming on line." They hobbled Illiani outside and dropped him into a chair. A steady whine droned from the room.

"Whoa-ho!" came Alex's voice. "We got electricity."

"Throw the changeover switch on the panel. *Quick*!" O'Hanlon shouted. The boy wordlessly ducked back through the door.

Flashlights jostled behind him.

"That ray—that purple ray—it's almost here," Jenny said in a voice that was half shout, half sob.

O'Hanlon brushed past her and Jared, heading for the stairs. "We have electric power," he yelled back. "Mark opened the gate."

"Oh, thank *God* he made it," he heard Jenny cry.

On the second landing, O'Hanlon ran to the control console and switched on the power. The instruments lit, the big meters indicating full voltage. He prayed the generator could sustain the required current.

He glanced up through the destroyed roof. The murdering beam slanted close, practically filling the opening. Then another glow caught his eye, a great spiral shape rotating in the distant sky, almost obscured by the creeping violet curtain. *This time, they intend to give us the double-whammy.*

O'Hanlon's fingers raced across the controls. He was aware of Alex standing beside him. Let him stay. The generator room's reinforced walls couldn't protect them now anyway.

The node deflectors sprang to life; the spark gap's spinning disks sang their fierce chorus. He reached down and cranked the power handle up to seventy-five percent. The big gears creaked and groaned, adjusting the transmitter's components to the new settings. Outside he heard explosions, saw yellow-orange light leap up from fires, and heard the sizzle and hum of the deadly microwave beam. As his hand grasped the Transmit handle, he saw Alex kneel down and adjust Mark's battery-powered stereo. The boy stood up, an anxious, crooked grin on his face. "I found a better song."

O'Hanlon jammed the big knife switch down.

As the microwave scythe swept toward the barn, as all hope failed, Stormdragon—for the third time in more than a hundred years—thundered to life.

Standing beside the floodgate, Mark listened to water rumbling through the big pipe as it followed the canyon below. He turned to face the men rushing along the walkway toward him. He was too tired to fight, but at least he'd try to delay them shutting off the water. Buddy stood between him and the men, hackles raised, growling. Mark grasped the dog's collar. "Wait, Buddy."

The first man slowed, approaching Mark cautiously, flicking his flashlight over him as if he might have some hidden weapon. The man paused and held the light in Mark's face. "What are you doing up here?" he asked gruffly.

Mark remained silent, squinting at the man defiantly.

"Alright, you little shit," he snarled, taking a step forward. "I don't have time—"

"Hey," yelled another voice.

The man turned around, and the sudden roar of an automatic weapon hammered the air, its flashing muzzle raking back and forth. The flashlight clattered onto the walkway, and in the same instant Mark could see the man's feet swing away from the beam of light and disappear over the handrail. The second man's flashlight spun into the canyon, his airborne body chasing the cartwheeling light. Buddy raced down the walkway toward the third person, the wielder of the gun, barking a greeting, his tail gyrating wildly.

"Mark, are you alright?" It was his mother's voice. She ran up the steps and strode toward him, Buddy trotting at her feet.

Mark was thunderstruck. His emotions suddenly took off; he wanted to shout, laugh, and cry all at the same time. He simply said, "Yeah. Thanks."

Her light probed below the dam. "You opened the gate."

Mark looked down, staring into the canyon. "But I couldn't do it slowly. The water's going to blow out the pipe, or maybe worse."

A popping, crackling sound came from the direction of the barn. Both of them silently turned and watched the descending curtain of death. It was impossible to tell whether it had crept over the barn or not. But it was close, flickering like rays of light slanting through murky water. Mark looked into its depths and shook his head, his fist hammering in frustration at the railing. *Nothing's happening. Maybe the water destroyed the pipes. Maybe the generator doesn't work; maybe they're all dead—*

"Can you ride that dirt bike?" his mother finally asked, a resigned tone in her voice.

"Yeah," Mark responded. Now he felt numb, just wanting to fall in a heap right there on the walkway. He couldn't leave his grandparents, Alex, O'Hanlon and the others, couldn't bear it if they died while he was running away.

"Get moving. Take the back way."

Mark cried out in a pleading voice, "But Mom, I can't—"

The air suddenly cracked with a sound so powerful he involuntarily gasped and ducked behind the railing. *The ray is destroying them!* But as he looked toward the barn, he saw a brilliant, branching river of blue-white lightning coil above the hilltops and lash defiantly against the descending beam. The massive discharge roared, hummed, snapped—the fiery breath of an electric dragon.

And a song burst from the torrent of electricity and thundered out like God, Jesus, and the Archangels got together and threw the world's mightiest rock show.

Mark slowly stood, gaping, staring. He grinned through the tears streaming down his face and thrust up a clenched fist. "*Helter Skelter*!" He turned toward his mother, who stood silently beside him, her mouth open in amazement, head cocked toward the surging display of energy. "*Helter Skelter*," Mark repeated, yelling above the din.

"What?" She shouted back.

"They're still alive." He watched the beam falter before the rising surge of energy, listened to the growing thunder of McCartney and Lennon's classic screamer. *If music makes any difference, this song will smoke their sorry ARC asses.*

He turned, picked up the fallen flashlight, and pointed it into the lake. The beam pierced clear water and revealed the inlet pipe, now only a few feet beneath the surface. A broad whirlpool had formed, the funnel curving down, snatching bits of debris into the pipe's black maw. He frowned. The water level had dropped dramatically. In a minute, they'd lose power. Overhead, the pulsing eye of the spiral flared brighter. If it was like the last fireball, it was moments away from launching.

He looked anxiously toward the barn. *Hurry! You only have seconds before they kill us all.*

K rohner staggered toward the glass wall overlooking the ranks of giant microwave transmitters, his arms outstretched, hands splayed wide and rigid, shoulders hunched in a frozen shrug. Bellowing through every speaker, every console, every electronic circuit—the heavy beat of *insane* rock and roll—

The floor shook as row after row of the huge black modules exploded, vomiting fountains of sparks across the great chamber. Orange and yellow and purple light strobed wildly through the observation panel. Smoke billowed from the self-destructing transmitters faster than the emergency ventilation could pull it out.

"*Kill the power!*" Krohner screamed into the headset.

The steady drone emanating from the chamber ceased. Ten thousand red and green status lights blinked out. Krohner whirled around and raced to the command chair. With the transmitters offline, the mountain was vulnerable to an air attack, and it would come within minutes.

Now he would again divert power to the X-V. He should have employed the plasma weapon immediately after the first EMP attack. It was too large to be affected by an electromagnetic wave; the enemy would have to attack with a pulse a million times more powerful—an absolute impossibility.

He stared at the holographic projection. One by one, the plasma weapon systems blinked green. The wall screen showed the claw antenna atop the mountain, the air around it shimmering yellow-orange as it fed energy into the spiraling ion mirror high above Colorado Springs.

The computer voice fought its way through the wretched static. *Automatic sequencing complete. Ready on your command.*

Still standing, Krohner grasped the joystick, flicked the safety aside, and pressed the button marked *Fire*. His eyes shifted to the remote camera. The glow before the huge antenna intensified, jetting upward like a blowtorch with an infinitely long flame. He could hear its angry rumble even inside the deep, heavily protected control room.

Teeth gnashed, mouth curled in a snarl, he glared at the projected map of Colorado Springs.

In moments, he would have his final revenge.

O'Hanlon stared in stunned disbelief at the electric firestorm thundering from the torus above; the roaring discharge breaking from the terminal must be at least ten feet in diameter and a thousand feet long. With terrifying intensity, it soared and branched against the stars like a crack in the fabric of time.

The frenetic rock song that reproduced itself through the artificially generated lightning shook the building with its pounding bass and hammered his chest with such force he had trouble breathing.

He jerked his hand from the console as sparks of electricity began to snake wickedly from the switches, dials, and metal fastenings. Every conducting object in the barn was spouting threads of electric fire.

A hand on his shoulder startled him. He turned to see Jared's worried face illuminated in the frantic light. Jared cupped his hands and shouted into his ear. "Get below. They're making another one of those fireballs." He pointed upward.

O'Hanlon looked up, but could see only the intense column of electricity lashing against the sky.

Jared shouted again. "The generator's slowing down—you're losing power."

O'Hanlon nodded, and as Jared backed toward the stairs, frantically urging him to come, he reached down and pulled the power lever to one-hundred percent.

The rotary gap exploded in a dazzling shower of white-hot metal. The transmitter shook the floor with such intensity he was afraid the supports would collapse. Molten aluminum cascaded from the tower; blinding electric arcs crashed between the transmitter's giant coils. The capacitors detonated in a series of bomb blasts.

O'Hanlon felt Jared's hands seize his arm. He managed to yank the power switch up, severing the circuit. Nothing happened. The energy continued to build. The great column of lightning brightened, enlarging and engulfing the tower, melting its way down. He stumbled from the console, one arm thrust over his head against the light and heat. As he staggered down the stairs behind Jared, he became aware of another sound entwined with the deafening blast, an insistent melodic hum that soared loud, growing, rising—an overdriven symphony of resonant energy.

Smoke and ozone filled the air. The barn was engulfed in flames. Jared disappeared through the south door, waving him urgently forward. But as O'Hanlon rushed for the exit, a flaming mass crashed down, blocking his path. He jumped back. Pulling his shirt over his mouth, he turned and backtracked toward the generator room. The heat and noise had grown unbearable. Maybe the concrete room would protect him until the fire burned itself out.

He glanced back into the main room as he pushed aside the heavy metal door, but could see nothing now but a brilliant, roaring glare. As he slammed the door behind him, the demonic song seemed to roll over and over, pounding through the walls, the floor—the earth itself—

HELTER SKELTER

The antenna's holographic image wavered and faded. Jagged lines raged across the main screen. The fiendish rock music roared louder through the control room, obliterating communications.

Krohner spun around and glared at the technicians behind him. "Compensate!" he screamed.

The chief engineer jumped up from a console, sweat glistening on his face. He shouted something unintelligible, frowning, shaking his head. The room's lighting flickered to the beat of the music riding the attacking EMP wave.

Krohner ripped the headset from his face and hurled it over the heads of a group of technicians clustered around a console. He couldn't lose control of the weapon at this stage. Trillions of watts were surging through the antenna into the ionosphere, creating a fireball above Colorado Springs about to descend with as much energy as a hydrogen bomb. Beam focus and timing were critical.

He charged across the room and hammered a switch. A door slid open, admitting him to the express elevator. He punched the top button, and the floor pressed against his feet.

The doors parted and Krohner burst into the observation tower atop the mountain. He marched toward the west-facing window. Frantic technicians hunched over the blinking, buzzing consoles lining the octagonal room. Shouts and curses joined the rising cacophony.

"Krohner," a clipped voice shouted. It was General Thad Greggson. "What the hell is this? Communications are shit. You got rock and roll coming out the light sockets. The computers are fucked—"

Krohner stormed past the general, knocking his shoulder aside, maintaining a direct path to the window. He stared out. Five hundred feet away, the projection antenna's outstretched digits were curling inward, changing focus, pulling off-target. He had triggered the "Fire" command minutes ago. The ionospheric fireball should already have plummeted into Colorado Springs. Instead, yellow-orange plasma continued to jet skyward, propelled by the antenna's levitating field.

He shoved a technician who was desperately trying to override the antenna's movements with manual controls. Krohner seized the elevation knob and twisted, listening for a complying drone of hydraulics. But the antenna's erratic behavior continued.

"Shut it off!" he screamed.

"We tried," someone yelled in a panicked voice. "The controls don't respond."

Krohner jerked his finger at two technicians. "You and you. Go down. Shut off the power feed at the plant level. Now!"

As if shocked by a cattle prod, the men turned and rushed toward the elevators. Krohner stared outside. The antenna had tilted away from the horizon and now pointed straight up. His eyes darted to the countdown readout. The numbers flickered in a random pattern, switching on and off with the thundering beat of the hell born music.

When he captured the people responsible for this outrage, he would personally torture them until they were driven insane. He would have Fechter invent new and creative ways to maim and defile—

A siren wailed. Flashing emergency lights triggered across the mountaintop. The shouting voices in the room died, the technicians' frenetic activity stopped. Microwave overdose was imminent. The shouts started again, this time with frightened overtones. People backed from the consoles slowly, and then began rushing toward the elevators. Krohner turned and screamed. "Back to your stations. I'll have your lives for this."

The crowd swept past Greggson, who stood glowering before Krohner. The general mouthed something inaudible, then turned on his heels and strode to a waiting elevator.

Krohner banged through a door onto the catwalk surrounding the tower. The rocket-engine roar from the plasma assaulted his ears; and the rock music—so loud he thought his skull would shatter.

He looked up. In the deep sky overhead, flickering and glaring, edging toward violet, was the fireball.

It began descending.

Krohner staggered back inside the tower. The klaxons still blared, barely audible above the din. This was no malfunction of the alarm system. Stray microwave intensity was building; he could feel the heat, the humming in his head. He rushed to the elevators, punched buttons. Waited.

The claw antenna spewed wriggling shafts of lightning into the air, the discharges dancing playfully at the end of each digit: the enemy's vengeful spirit had come home to taunt him.

The searing pressure inside his head shot up; sparks began breaking from the instruments inside the room. He hammered the elevator buttons, but the doors remained shut.

The music stopped, and the singer belted out a final line—something about having blisters on his fingers. Outside, the sky became bright as the face of the sun.

Krohner clawed at his temples and screamed.

The glaring, blue-white column of electricity thundered upward to an impossible distance, its great, forked branches coiling from the central mass and lashing the black sky, writhing and twisting like liquid lightning.

Mark frowned, puzzled. How could the generator continue producing electricity? The reservoir level had bled down; there was hardly a trickle of water to feed the turbine.

He straddled the dirt bike and kick-started the engine. He had only ridden a motorcycle a few times, but he thought he could handle the machine well enough. His mother had told him to ride to the far side of the hill, to safety. But he was determined instead to follow her back to the barn.

His mother sat astride her horse, rifle strapped to her back, restraining the prancing, jittery animal. She turned to Mark and pointed downhill, shaking her head and shouting. But her words were torn away by the burgeoning roar from below.

Then things happened all at once. Long, thin electric sparks began darting from trees around them, popping the air. Mark's hair suddenly stood on end, as it had at the science museum when they demonstrated the big electrostatic generator.

He looked toward the barn, and his eyes bulged in disbelief—the discharge thundering from the building had detached itself and begun *moving*, swaying and spinning, ghosting uphill like a fiery tornado. Flames burst from trees along its path and curled into the monstrous vortex, merging with the raging electricity in an upward rush. It was following the creek, heading right for them.

His mother whirled the horse around, motioning frantically for Mark to follow. But he pulled alongside, pointed, and gunned the bike toward the Lookout. Buddy leapt ahead, his tail curled between his legs.

As he raced over the hump, Mark felt sharp jolts of electric shock clinch the muscles in his forearms. He ducked low, trying to keep from attracting a stray bolt of lightning.

His headlight found the Lookout and stabbed out toward Colorado Springs, still a glittering pattern of red and yellow flames. He turned right, and the headlight glinted off his mountain bike lying on its side in the rocks below. He shut the engine off and dropped the motorcycle, leaving its headlight pointing down the trail. His mother dismounted, pulled the bridle off Winnie, and slapped the horse's flanks, freeing him. She ran up beside Mark, and they scrambled beneath the overhang to kneel at the same spot he and his father had sheltered in during a storm years before. Buddy pushed up between them, shaking with fear.

The ground shuddered and the air ignited as the maelstrom of electric fire thundered up the mountainside. Yellow light flared against the boulders; shadows trembled and stretched; wind screamed up the cliff face, blasting them with a torrent of sand and gravel. The world suddenly shimmered brilliant blue-white—then snapped to darkness as quickly as if someone had turned off a switch.

A sound followed: a guttural roar that soared on a high note and then slowly dropped to a low rumble, splitting the sky from horizon to horizon. A second of silence: then an earth-hammering *boom* that punched the air from Mark's chest and rocked the massive granite overhang above their heads. The sound rolled and tumbled along the hills, finally dissipating in a sigh of whispered echoes. The clatter of falling rocks rode the fading sound.

"God," Mark's mother whispered at last. She moved her arm from around his shoulder, and he ducked outside the overhang and climbed onto the ledge. Smoke burned his throat. He realized it was coming not only from the smoldering trees above, but from Colorado Springs itself.

The dirt bike was where he had left it, but his mountain bike had disappeared. He glanced at his mother as she struggled up the path below him. Tears pooled in his eyes. How could his family have survived?

They reached the fire-blasted trail and started down toward the barn.

S am Hurwitz glanced at his watch and fumed. He had sent one of the Alliance headquarters staff into Memphis for cigars over an hour ago, and he hadn't returned. The whole friggin' town must have shut down because of the communications blackout.

Despite the lack of acceptable smokes, he was feeling a little more at ease about things. He had just taped a very convincing address to the American people that would air as soon as the president was terminated and ARC had subdued the military.

> *My fellow Americans, it is with a heavy heart that I*
> *must report the death of President Troy Williamson—*

Haw! He poured a second Scotch from the well-stocked bar. Now he was beginning to relax. He settled deeper into the plush chair and eyed the open pack of Camels on the table beside him. Idly, he wondered if he could somehow glue three or more cigarettes together to form an acceptable equivalent of a cigar…

His eye caught a change in the image on the wide-screen TV. The looped piece ARC had been broadcasting for the last three hours had stopped playing, replaced by a test pattern. No big deal.

Then he noticed the test pattern had the call letters of a local station. This wasn't right. They should be receiving only the ARC transmission. He sat up and grabbed the remote. He channel surfed: static, static, more static. He almost dropped his drink. A newscaster was reporting. He punched the sound up.

> ...*total blackout that appears to have occurred nationwide. And just now major news stories are pouring in...*

Hurwitz swallowed with a choke and slammed his drink onto the table.

> ...*confirmed stories that there has been an attempt to assassinate President Troy Williamson, and that a conspiracy to overthrow the U.S. government has been stopped...*

Hurwitz stared at the TV, his mind reeling. He snatched the telephone off the table and stabbed in the satellite-linked number to the ARC switchboard. Only hissing static responded. Footsteps pounded behind him.

"Do you see this? *Do you see this?*" came the shrieking, panicked voice.

Hurwitz turned around and stared at Frederick Crotty. The Moral Alliance leader's prissy, combed and sprayed hairdo stood out from his head in disheveled spikes. His shirttail hung in loose wads over his belt, and his baby-blue silk tie was unknotted and jerked to one side.

"Your plan *failed*," Crotty screeched, the fingers of his right hand snatching at another batch of hair. "We're dead, we're *dead*..."

Hurwitz pried himself from the chair's deep folds and got shakily to his feet.

...U.S. Air Force launched a series of air attacks against the secret ARC transmitting facility in Alaska, and we are just now receiving footage...

Crotty continued. "Well, they're not taking me *alive*..." He tilted his head and stared at Hurwitz. His eyes oscillated, and his voice took an unnerving tone. "You ruined my life—"

...mountain housing the ARC facility blew up, apparently from a problem with one of its own weapons...

The TV image: an intense ball of light shimmered above ARC, then settled onto the mountain—burned *into* the mountain. Flames and black debris blasted out in a great fan, sending a shockwave racing across the ground. The image shook, and a lingering *boom* crumbled in the background.

...monitoring for nuclear radiation...

Crotty continued his insane patter: "The staff's leaving, you know. Security too. They won't get very far, because the police are coming. You can see the lights..."

"The chopper—" Hurwitz said.

"Gone." Crotty's face contorted in disgust. "They're not stupid, you know. Not as stupid as you and your..."

Hurwitz felt a cold sweat creep onto the back of his neck. He came around the chair and faced Crotty. "A car. Where's a car..."

"You're too late. I told everyone to leave."

Hurwitz balled his fists and glared at Crotty. He could hear sirens in the distance. He roared. "You *what*?"

"You're going down; you short, fat, stupid—"

"You little *faggot*." Hurwitz spat. He took a step toward Crotty. "If it wasn't for me, you'd still be hustling morality fliers and blowing altar boys—"

Crotty's eyes bugged out. His hand stopped toying with his hair and swept inside his jacket. Out came a snub-nosed revolver. The sirens drew closer. Hurwitz turned to walk away. "*Fuck* you."

Pain ripped through Hurwitz's left side as the blast shocked his ears. He wheeled around, his hand over a hot, oozing patch just above his belt. He felt himself topple backward and crash against the table. Through a haze of dancing spots, he saw Crotty open his mouth, shove the snub-nosed past his teeth, and pull the trigger.

71

Mark and Kate followed Buddy's lead as they stumbled down the mangled hillside. The charred trail wound before them, the ground and rocks blackened with ash, the trees smoldering shadows. Smoke hung thickly in the low areas, and coals glowed and flickered through the darkness like hellish eyes. Landmarks had been blasted away. Even boulders seemed to have been lifted and tossed from their normal sites.

Through the pall, Mark could see a throbbing red glow rising beyond the tree-shrouded hill. The *ranch is burning*! His anxiety rose to the exploding point. His family had to be alive—*had* to be.

The wooden footbridges had been ripped away from the creek, and they laboriously picked their way across, threading between the boulders rising above the rushing water. If not for Buddy, it would take them all night to find their way down.

At last they approached the gravel road. His mother held up a hand. "Let me check ahead."

"I'm coming with you," Mark said.

She glanced at him for a moment, nodded.

They walked down the remaining few hundred feet of trail and turned left onto the road.

Fear and dismay stabbed Mark's heart; beyond the bridge rose the barn's smoldering shell. It had burned to the ground, leaving only the stone walls of the first story. As he stared at the ruin, a section of framing timbers cracked and folded into the dying blaze, fanning up a storm of sparks. With small comfort, he noticed the ranch house had been spared.

Buddy suddenly stopped, staring toward the bridge's dark silhouette. Kate signaled for Mark to drop down; then she brought up her rifle and crept forward.

Headlights appeared, bobbing toward them. Buddy barked and bounded ahead, his tail elevated for the first time since his confrontation with the ARC thugs.

"Buddy!" Mark shouted. His mother's hand shot out again, gesturing emphatically for him to stay hidden.

The vehicle crossed the bridge, stopped, and the doors flew open as two men stepped onto the gravel. A voice called out. Mark raced into the twin beams of light and almost knocked his grandfather down, wrapping him in a bear hug.

"Daddy!" his mother cried. "Thank God, thank God." She swiped tears from her face. "I was so afraid…" Her arms enfolded them both; then she broke off and hugged the other man—David—with affection Mark had only witnessed between her and his father. Mark looked at his grandfather, who merely smiled.

When the hug-fest was over, Jared said, "Jenny is okay. Alex too. We even got Greg Illiani out before the fire started." A saddened look crossed his face. "Almost everyone's accounted for except Professor O'Hanlon." He looked toward the flames and shook his head.

They rode back to the house and parked beside two ranch pickup trucks. Inside, candles glowed from the tables. Injured men lay on the floor and couches and were tended by Jenny and María. Mark's grandmother spotted him, and he went through another tearful round of hugging.

In the master bedroom, Illiani sat up in bed, propped against a pile of pillows. He was pale but alert. "Bleeding stopped," he said, giving a bored shrug. "Guess I ran out of blood."

An hour later, David, whose eyesight had returned to normal, commanded a three-truck convoy to take Illiani and the other seriously injured into Colorado Springs. Crow and Holt organized patrols to secure the property. Jared started the emergency generator in its shed in the back yard. Much of the house wiring had been shorted out, but Alex rewired some of the circuits, and in less than an hour they had lights in most of the rooms.

Mark began to feel lightheaded. He realized it was past midnight and he hadn't had anything to eat since noon. He was grimy and bloody. His left foot had swollen and painfully refused to bear his weight. Funny, he'd never thought of himself as one of the injured.

María heated a quick meal on the propane-fueled stove. Mark and Alex sat in the dining room and heaped their plates with food. Mark was almost too tired to eat, but once he started, he felt as if he'd never stop.

"What you did—it was totally cool," Alex said, looking up from a plate stacked with roast beef. "You're a hero—seriously."

Mark glanced at his friend, who was filthy with smoke and ash. He himself was probably twice as dirty, and cut and bruised as well. He washed down a bite with a soft drink. "Nope," he said. "If I'm a hero, we're all heroes. Especially my mom." He glanced at Buddy and Higgins. The dogs sat on either side of him, watching eagerly as each morsel traveled from plate to mouth. "Buddy led me to the reservoir. I couldn't have found it without him." He tossed each dog a generous handout.

"Professor O'Hanlon stayed with the transmitter," Alex said. "Kept it running while the rest of us bailed out."

Mark hung his head. "It's a major drag we lost him." Then he looked up. "We should go look for him. Maybe he's out there, hurt or something."

"They're still searching," Alex said. "You can't get close to the barn. It's too hot."

Mark almost choked as a woman's shriek warbled into the room: "Somebody come. Quick!"

They ran to the kitchen, Mark bringing up the rear, hobbling on his injured foot. He saw María standing in the middle of the room, staring at the opened cellar door. "What?" Mark and Alex chorused.

"I wanted to get potatoes, and…there is somebody…"

Ears pricked, the dogs trotted forward and stared into the darkness beyond the stairs. Crow and Holt burst into the kitchen, weapons drawn.

"Hello," came a muffled call. "Can you hear me? Hello."

The dogs' tails began to wag.

The two agents motioned for the boys and María to stand back. Crow aimed his pistol as Holt kicked the door wide. The voice came again, a little louder, but still muffled.

"That sounds like…" Mark began.

"Yeah," said Alex, bewildered.

Holt's flashlight stabbed into the gloom. "Who's there?"

The excited voice came back. "Thank Goodness! Help me out of here!"

Mark followed Alex and the two agents down the stairs into the brick and concrete storage room. He found the overhead light and switched it on. A banging rattled the wine bottles in a wooden rack against the left wall. After a few minutes of fumbling, the FBI agents triggered a release mechanism and the rack grated away from the wall, pivoting on hidden hinges. Air rushed into the opening and a musty smell drifted out, carrying with it the odor of smoke.

A pair of bright eyes blinked out of the darkness, and a flat-black version of Professor Patrick O'Hanlon staggered into the room. He was entirely covered in soot, his hair and beard standing wildly out from his head. His right hand held a penlight; his left grasped the handle of a heavy-looking metal box secured with a fat padlock. He exhaled, and then looked around the room, his face breaking into a minstrel-show grin. "You fellows. You're all okay!"

Mark was stunned. What was this hidden room? *How did O'Hanlon get in there?* They rushed to the professor's side and took his arms, helping him limp forward. Mark looked back. The FBI agents were probing the dark space with their flashlights. He heard the word "tunnel," and it suddenly made sense: O'Hanlon had somehow found a secret passage between the barn and the house, one that saved him from certain death.

"Did everyone else make it out?" The professor asked, handing the box to a perplexed Mark.

They told him everyone in the barn survived. Then they machine-gunned their questions.

"How did you find that tunnel?"

"What happened with the transmitter…why couldn't you shut it off?"

"What's this box?"

O'Hanlon paused at the steps, catching his breath. "All that, fellows, will take a little time to explain."

72

Mark rose slowly into wakefulness, pulling free of dreams filled with fire and screams and torture. His limbs were stiff, his body complaining from a hundred painful insults. His injured foot throbbed. He pushed the covers away and glanced at the clock: almost noon. He could still hear the generator chugging away behind the house; at least they would have hot water and lights.

He limped to the window. A brown dome covered Colorado Springs, and the smell of smoke lingered heavily in the air. How much had ARC destroyed? Was his home still intact, Andrea and his friends still alive? He wouldn't know until they drove into town and saw for themselves. All the ranch electronics—radios, televisions, computers, telephones—had been turned into junk last night by the electrical battle between ARC and the Magnifying Transmitter.

He saw his grandfather walking toward the generator shed, a five gallon can of diesel fuel in each hand, the two dogs tagging along. Buddy had evidently grown tired of waiting for Mark to waken and had left him to his dreams.

He shook Alex awake. They dressed and went onto the front porch, Mark hobbling along with the aid of an old hickory walking stick from his grandfather's closet. He stared at the blackened rubble that was once the barn. A few turns of the transmitter's big secondary coil, smashed during the machine's final agony, curved up from the smoldering ashes like the ribs of a gigantic beast. The tower was almost unrecognizable, shattered, melted, and bent obscenely over the stone shell of the lower story.

The creek still burbled along in its rocky bed as if nothing had happened, but the ground for hundreds of feet on either side of it was ravaged. It was as if an angry god had reached down with a cosmic blowtorch and burned the barn, seared the creek all the way to the Lookout, and held the flame against Spy Knob, blasting and blackening its lightning-wracked crown.

Looking north, he could see the wide band of destruction the ARC beam had wrought. All the way from the fence line to the edge of the bunkhouses, every tree, bush, and blade of grass was burned. Had there not been so much recent moisture, the fire would have raged on and taken the ranch house with it.

In the middle of the field, the backhoe's hydraulic shovel bit the earth. A deep pit had been excavated, and a tractor chugged slowly to its edge, towing a dark mass. With anguish, Mark realized they were burying horses. A few of the surviving animals grazed in the eastern meadow, but the herd was conspicuously smaller. He wondered how many had been killed, and if Maggie had survived.

His gaze fell on the wrecked Humvees and the Scanner, and then quickly darted away.

Alex broke the silence. "That was the most awesome thing I ever saw."

"What?"

"The electricity from the Magnifying Transmitter. It melted down the torus, and then it formed a column and spun right up the creek, roaring and twisting around like a tornado. It must have been way over a thousand feet high, branching out everywhere, all red and violet and yellow. I think it became a DC plasma—some sort of earth-ionosphere short circuit." He pointed. "It got to the top of that hill…"

"Spy Knob."

"Yeah. It grew even bigger. I thought it was the end of us all. Then it went out—*boom*—just like that."

Mark looked at the sky. "At least that microwave beam hasn't come back."

Alex followed his gaze. "Yeah. Maybe we got 'em this time."

The front door swung open and Mark's grandfather came onto the porch. "Guys. Time for a meeting."

* * *

Mark, his mother, and Alex sat on one side of the table, O'Hanlon, Crow, and Holt on the other. The tireless María had set out a feast of chicken, corn, salad, potatoes, and the usual assortment of spicy peppers and garnishes. Mark dug in.

O'Hanlon, who had been silent and grim, smiled when he sat down, and began loading his plate. Liniment glistened from reddened skin on his face and arms, and a thin layer of bandages mummified his hands. He had trimmed out the singed portions of his beard and hair, leaving them as ragged as a moth-eaten rug.

Mark's mother displayed a collection of cuts and bruises on her face and arms. She had lost more weight, and there was a hard gleam in her eye Mark hadn't seen before, one that reminded him of Linda Hamilton from *Terminator II*, or Sigorney Weaver in *Aliens*. She looked—toughened.

A red sling held Charles Holt's arm, and a wide bandage covered Crow's forehead. Everyone had his battle scars.

Jared came in at last and sat down. He swept his gaze around the table, and then finally spoke. "I want to thank everyone for your courage and your sacrifice during the last few days. We were a team. Without the help of everyone in this room, we wouldn't be alive today. I thank God none of you was seriously hurt."

He poured himself a glass of water, then sat upright and smoothed his mustache. He continued: "Four of my men—ranch hands and friends—and every one of the brave soldiers from Fort Hood, were killed last night. Ten others were injured, and David Hightower has taken them into Colorado Springs." His head dropped slightly. "I lost most of my best horses—champions.

"With the transmitter destroyed, the trust fund is gone. We have no way to collect any additional money." He looked at O'Hanlon and gave a wan smile. "I'm sorry things didn't work out they way we'd planned, Patrick." He helped himself to the food.

"It has been an honor working on this project," O'Hanlon replied softly. "It was providence that we had the means to fight back. I assume the Magnifying Transmitter had some impact on the ARC weapon, that we helped stop them. I shudder to think what might have occurred if they had *not* been stopped."

After a brief silence, Alex spoke. "Dr. O'Hanlon, would you explain what happened—how we lost control of the transmitter?"

O'Hanlon's fork, held gingerly between his gauzed fingers, hovered over his plate. He seemed reluctant to sacrifice eating for talking. "Tesla designed the Magnifying Transmitter to send not only radio signals, but *power*, any place in the world. Using principles of terrestrial resonance, he was actually able to send power without loss and without wires—an astounding accomplishment." He took a bite.

"But that doesn't explain the runaway buildup of electricity…"

"The third manual—the Ouroboros Manual—explained that. Tesla made an enormous discovery. He found that if earth-resonant power was maintained and properly directed, once a power threshold was reached, the natural energy stored between the earth and the ionosphere would sustain the output. He called it the Ourboros Effect because, like Ouroboros, it had the appearance of feeding upon itself. Perpetual energy."

Alex gasped. "Free energy?"

"Yes. But there's more. If you allowed the transmitter to pass a second threshold, the energy would increase uncontrollably. That's what happened to us. It gave us the additional power we needed, but it also destroyed the very machine that created it. And it nearly killed us."

Alex put his fork down with a clink. "You mean we just lost a machine that could generate free energy and send it any place in the world—"

"Yes."

Alex sat back in his chair and let out a long sigh.

Holt spoke. "Professor, could you rebuild the transmitter?"

O'Hanlon thought for a minute. "No. I could not. I don't remember enough of the circuitry, and I don't understand how it worked."

"Why did Tesla put a lock on the manual?" Alex asked.

O'Hanlon gave him a wry smile, wiggling the fork back and forth like a miniature baton. "He was testing us. Testing to see if twenty-first century man was sufficiently enlightened to receive such a gift as the Magnifying Transmitter." He paused and looked around the table, his twisted smile deepening.

There was a period of silence. Mark asked, "How did you find the tunnel?"

"When the fire started, I couldn't get out, so I ran into the generator room and slammed the door against the flames. The heat was terrible. I hid behind the generator, hoping its mass would shield me, but the air became toxic. In desperation, I began pulling and pounding at the outlet pipe, hoping I could crawl through it.

"Somewhere, somehow, a panel opened. I almost fell inside. There were steep stairs, and fresh air rushing up. I went down and entered a brick tunnel. I had my penlight, and I started running. I could feel and hear electricity crackling around me.

"The air began to glow. I almost panicked. About halfway to

the house, the electricity subsided. I stopped to catch my breath…
actually; I passed out for a moment. But I found myself in a small
room. There, on a stone shelf against the wall, was the metal box I
gave to Mark."

Mark had forgotten the box. He excused himself, went upstairs,
and retrieved it from his bedroom. He brought it down and handed it
to his grandfather, who looked at it with a whimsical expression. "I
never knew there was a tunnel," he said, shaking his head. He hefted
the box. "After lunch, we'll cut the lock off."

There was another silence.

Alex looked up hopefully. "I need to get home, find out if my
mom's okay."

"Let's wait for a few hours. Give David Hightower a chance to
come back."

Mark's mother spoke. "We don't know what's going on in
Colorado Springs, Alex…"

Crow said, "I'm sure the National Guard has moved in. They'll
have declared martial law."

"A lot of planes have been landing at the Air Force Academy,"
Holt added. "I think help is coming."

Mark looked at O'Hanlon. "How did the music from my boom
box reproduce through the electricity?"

O'Hanlon chewed for a moment, then answered. "The
Magnifying Transmitter used a crude form of amplitude modulation, or AM. The music's audio-frequency vibrations varied the
power delivered to the transmitter, which in turn varied the energy
in the electrical discharge from the torus—in the same way an audio
amplifier varies power in the cone of a speaker. You could say it
actually used the discharge like a giant loudspeaker. At the same
time, it transmitted an amplitude-modulated wave that could be
picked up by any radio." He chuckled. "And, so we've heard, by
virtually *any* electronic apparatus. So that incredibly aggravating
song, um, *Helter Skelter*, might have been heard quite clearly on

radios and televisions around the entire world."

O'Hanlon put down his knife and fork and snickered, then tossed his head back and gave a hearty laugh. Mark stared at him, thinking he'd finally lost it. O'Hanlon had the full attention of everyone around the table. His outburst finally dwindled, and he dabbed the tears from his eyes with his napkin. He looked at everyone as if he were enjoying some private joke.

"Professor O'Hanlon," Mark's mother said, a quizzical half-smile on her face. "What's so funny?"

He held up his hands, palms out, and wiggled his bandaged digits. "Just thinking of the last words of that song," he said with a grin, his teeth white behind his singed beard. "*I got blisters on my fingers!*"

* * *

After lunch, Mark's grandfather got the big bolt cutters from a tool shed behind the house, and they gathered in the main room, standing in a circle around the box. He placed the cutter's jaws over the padlock link and forced the handles together, splitting it with a metallic snap, and then slid the lock free. He pulled back on a lever that kept the box tightly sealed. There was a brief hissing noise as the lid swung open. He reached inside and withdrew a thick sheaf of papers bound with ribbon.

He spread them on the table and read: "Present to Suisse Bank Internationale, Switzerland." A long number followed. The remaining documents were similar.

"Swiss bank accounts," said Holt, smiling.

"Or maybe safety deposit boxes," Crow added.

"That makes sense," Jared said, studying the papers. "According to Tesla's plan, we were supposed to receive a bonus for revealing the transmitter. But we never knew how it would be delivered, or what it would be." He tied the papers and returned them to the box, then looked at O'Hanlon. "If we're lucky, Patrick, your harrowing trip through that tunnel may have bailed us out."

73

That afternoon, Kate walked across the field toward the ranch house, dabbing at her eyes. How many times had she cried in the last few days—the last two years? She had just visited the widows of the two men who had been killed. The women had driven up from Colorado Springs, expecting to find their husbands alive and well. One of the women had become hysterical, the other stoic.

Kate kept her sight on the path ahead. Every place she looked presented scenes of destruction. The train, the barn and its marvelous invention, the meadow and woods and horses, even the trail to the Lookout—her son's fondest memory of his father—all ruined.

Now her thoughts turned to financial survival. Her father's source of income had been destroyed. Her job had evaporated with the destruction of Channel 12. She'd find more work, and she had her story to produce, but these things would take time. Maybe the Swiss bank accounts—if that's what they were—would help them get back on their feet.

A vehicle crunched on the gravel road ahead and she looked up. David had returned. She jogged onto the parking area as he stepped out of the pickup, his head freshly bandaged. He turned and smiled. "The Guard set up a field hospital. They'll transfer Illiani and the others as soon as transportation is available."

He hugged her and drew her around to the truck's rear. In the pickup bed were a television, radios, and other electronic equipment. He handed her a sack. "Extra flashlights and batteries."

With Mark and Alex's help, they carried the equipment in, and David set up the TV and a radio. Jared, O'Hanlon, and the FBI agents gathered around.

David gave a brief rundown of the situation: It would be days before they knew the extent of deaths and injuries, but thousands had been affected in Colorado Springs, and possibly thousands more on military bases across the nation. Denver was unscathed. About a third of Colorado Springs had burned, but David and Kate's homes had been spared. Power and telephones were still inoperative. Alex's mother had been moved to a hospital in Denver.

They quickly discovered the television was useless; the ranch's tall antenna had been ruined the night before, and ARC had destroyed every transmitter in Colorado Springs. The radio, however, could pull in distant stations. Kate thought it was surreal that the usual ads and programs were running, but life went on.

The news: ARC had severely damaged U.S. air bases, killing thousands and destroying billions in resources. The NORAD installation at Cheyenne Mountain had been totally annihilated. Dozens of planes and hundreds of missiles had been shot down during the attack against ARC's mountain fortress, but nothing could penetrate the electronic shield. Then ARC had blown up, apparently consumed by one of its own weapons gone amok.

The Army was busy rounding up the ARC survivors. Kate and the others smiled when they heard that everyone, military and civilians alike, was speculating on the powerful rock music—*Helter Skelter*—that permeated all frequencies worldwide, at the same moment ARC self-destructed.

Senator Hurwitz had been arrested on multiple charges and was recovering from a gunshot wound inflicted by Frederick Crotty, who had blown his head off with the same weapon.

The Moral Alliance was under investigation, and a movement by several prominent senators, with the wholehearted approval of the president, was already underway to promote freedom of the Internet and to scuttle legislation approving Cerberus.

Alex tinkered with a satellite dish, and they finally began receiving TV news broadcasts. Aerial footage of a smoking ARC Mountain, Colorado Springs, and Elmendorf Air Force Base ran constantly in the background as news personalities interviewed everyone from congressmen to inhabitants of Alaska and Colorado Springs.

Kate grew anxious. She was a news anchor with the biggest story, yet she was stuck far from the action. She felt like a racehorse chained at the starting gate while the others charged onto the track.

* * *

After three weeks, FEMA and the Corps of Engineers had Colorado Springs patched back together. Electricity and telephone services were restored. The Army pulled out, martial law was rescinded, and the town began rebuilding itself.

Everyone went home from the ranch. O'Hanlon again took charge of the museum, which had been spared destruction. David returned to his house. Alex would stay with Mark and Kate in Colorado Springs until his mother had recovered. Jared began exploring government loans and haggling with the insurance company, trying to save the ranch.

* * *

Mark's first visit was with Andrea. She led him inside her house, and with wide and tearful eyes told him about the night Colorado Springs had burned. Terrifying lights had come down from the sky, and neighborhoods seemed to randomly burst into flame. No one knew where to run. She and her family huddled in their basement, praying they wouldn't be next.

Then the killing lights had stopped, and when they went cautiously back outside, they saw a huge, bright column of fire darting up from the western hills. The fiery column had started twisting and growing, leaping up into the sky, branching like lightning. *Helter Skelter* blasted down from the heavens as if from an immense celestial rock show. And when Andrea began to think the end of the world was coming, she saw a brilliant flash and a felt a ground-rocking blast of thunder. Then the light was gone. The night had returned to smoke and sirens and the glare from hundreds of fires.

Mark smiled sympathetically as he watched her talk, enjoying the sound of her voice. He thanked God she was alive. And he was tempted to say, "Yeah, it was us who did that, who stopped the bad guys. That was my rock music you heard, coming from our giant, one hundred-year old transmitter in my grandfather's barn. And my mom had gone inside ARC and seen this huge weapon they were going to rule the world with...."

But he decided to remain silent and let it all come out over a period of time.

So he just listened and smiled and nodded.

74

K ate watched her newly edited segment unfold on the monitor. The soundtrack bleated out a recording of the ARC "death fax" signal as the video displayed its unmistakable, jagged waveform. After three weeks of editing, closeting herself in her bedroom-office in Colorado Springs, she was almost finished with *Killer Science—The Story of ARC's Murdering Technology*, the investigative piece she hoped to syndicate.

The segment ended, and she leaned back in the chair and stretched. She had already been approached by several major talk shows, and her agent had pulled in a book deal and a small advance. There were hints that Hollywood might be interested if she stirred up enough public interest. *Yeah, yeah.*

She missed Gil. If he could have helped her, she'd have been finished two weeks ago. But Gil's days as an editor and cameraman were over. Unless they could get his eyesight back...

Buddy's anxious barking intruded on her thoughts; Mark must be home from his visit with Andrea. But he seemed to be taking an unusually long time before letting Buddy into the house. She shook her head, chuckling softly. After all they had been through; Buddy was still terrified of the dog door in the kitchen.

She glanced at the desk clock: almost 6:30. David would be arriving in half an hour to take them all out to dinner. She stood and stretched. Time to get ready.

Then a sound came through the computer's speakers that nearly stopped her heart. Soft. Brief. She stared at the computer, her mind racing. It was the death fax. It could not have come from the video, the segment had played and stopped.

She let out her breath slowly, listening: Buddy's barking, the soft purr of the computer's fans. Then she noticed the dog's bark was not his usual sound of greeting; it was rapid, angry. He began scratching at the kitchen door, whining.

She pulled the Glock from the drawer and walked from the office. She approached the den's closed door and paused. From the other side she thought she heard a thump and a muffled voice. Cold crept across her flesh like the touch of spider webs.

She threw the door open—and felt the ground drop away. In the center of the room stood a big man in a white lab coat, his thick arm around Mark's neck, a fat hand clamped over her son's face—Malcolm Fechter. The bald head, perched incongruously atop his disproportionately broad, bloated body, tilted toward her. The magnified eyes blinked and stared through the Coke-bottle lenses. His lips peeled back in a charnel-house grin.

Kate brought the gun up. Fechter's bulbous eyes widened. "Now, Kaate, I wouldn't be hasssty." He swung Mark into her line of fire. A high-pitched whine drifted from a silver, dish-shaped object cradled in the palm of his free hand.

Kate's voice turned to steel, the words forced through clenched teeth. "Let—him—go."

"Oh, no, Kaate. I want you to watch."

He pressed the silver device against her son's temple. Mark twisted in his grip, forcing out a muffled scream.

"Come any closer," Fechter said, "and his brain will hemorrhage."

Kate's voice crackled like splintered ice. "You won't leave here alive." She stepped sideways, holding the pistol at arm's length, sighting down the barrel.

"I have more weapons than this, Kaaate," he said, pulling the apparatus away from Mark. "I have the—ultimate weapon."

The Glock's barrel aligned on Fechter's head.

He began speaking in a sibilant whisper. "Hear my voice, listen to my voice—*obey*."

Kate suddenly felt doors closing in her mind: first, there was confusion, then relaxation. Her anger dissipated. The tenseness in her body melted away. Now she was ready to listen, to obey.

"Ahhh. You remember our little session in the laboratory. You were a wonderful subject. So interesting to program." He moved toward her, dragging Mark with him.

"Sit down, Kaate."

She dropped into the chair beside the door.

Mark twisted his head away from Fechter's grip. "Mom, *no*—"

She saw her son struggling. But these things were no longer important.

"Kaate," came the Voice. "Drop the gun."

She opened her right hand and felt the pistol slip from her fingers.

"You will remain seated. You will not be able to move. You will be able to hear and see and understand, but you cannot move."

"Yes," she said. Part of her consciousness, the part that was the embodiment of her being, seemed to wake from a deep slumber—she could once again comprehend. Rage took her. She tried to stand, reach for the gun. But her limbs remained frozen. It was as if some nerve-killing agent had been injected into every muscle, completely disconnecting them from her brain. She could only sit and blink and stare.

Her heart trip hammered as her mind and nerves screamed for action. She fought an avalanching overload of fear, hatred, and unbearable frustration. *Think! Logic is all that remains!* Her mind slammed through its neural maze, searching for the key—a word, a phrase—that would break Fechter's mental lock.

Buddy's frantic barking grew louder, more desperate. She heard him scrabbling and scratching at the kitchen door. If only he could get inside, maybe he would distract Fechter enough for Mark to struggle free.

Fechter held the strange silver device outward, and Kate could see its underside pulsing with a soft red light. "Thiss is a wonderful tool," he said. Then he swung the instrument close to Mark's head. He spoke like a TV chef demonstrating the finer points of baking. "Its effectiveness is not so much a matter of power, but of placement and proximity, and"—he paused for emphasis—"modulation." The apparatus made an arc across Mark's head, and he stiffened and screamed.

"Yesss," Fechter said. "See? It can induce pain, spasms, and hallucinations. Or, one little motion and—oops!—there go the piano lessons." He chortled. "It can cause one to vomit, to lose control of one's bladder and bowels, paralyze—even sexually excite." He dragged Mark closer to Kate. "I will demonstrate on your son. Then you and I will enjoy each other—maybe your son too."

Fechter tilted his head as if listening. "The dog. I'll burn his brain until blood squirts from his eyes." He leaned close, his grinning, sweating face a mask of insanity. "You destroyed my life, Kaate McCullough, destroyed years of pricelesss research. Now it is payback time. I think we'll begin."

*   *   *

Buddy slammed against the kitchen door. He could feel the evil Man inside the house, and the Man's presence cast a dark, stinking shadow across his mind.

He eyed the special dog door and rushed to it. He stopped short, whining, terrified. He barked viciously—barked his Great Fierce Bark; spun in a circle; pawed the door; watched it swing partly open and shut. He quaked at the thought of going through—horrible things would happen.

Another scream came from inside; the Man was hurting Mark. Buddy backed up and lunged for the door.

*   *   *

Kate heard the frantic chatter of paws on linoleum, then the softer drum of paws on carpet; Buddy was racing down the hall. *Come on Buddy*—come on!

Fechter's foot shot out and caught the den door, slamming it shut with a bang.

* * *

Buddy threw himself against the door, meeting it as it clapped into its frame. He reared up and scratched furiously at the knob. But it wouldn't open. He backed up, barked, whined. Listened. There was a scuffling sound from the den beyond. Mark was struggling with the Bad Man, and the Man's evil smelled very, very strong. A smell beyond bad—

Mark cried out. The Man was making grunting, laughing sounds. Mark's voice began to choke. He called Buddy's name. Buddy bolted back down the hallway, across the kitchen, through the dog door into the yard.

Then he began his run.

* * *

Past the fence, past the tree, past the shed, Buddy raced. Past the sand pile like a blur. Lungs burning, heart bursting, *Run, Buddy, Run.*

He flew. His paws scorched the ground.

He knew about glass. It was that strange stuff you could see through but couldn't walk through. He had hurt his nose crashing into a glass door when he was a puppy. He had stepped on glass. It was hard. It cut.

Faster Than Lightning!

He leapt—

75

Fechter bent obscenely over Mark, moving the whining silver instrument across his head in a slow circular caress. Mark bucked, spittle frothing past clenched teeth.

"Your son seems like an intelligent boy," Fechter said matter-of-factly, his voice jerking as he fought Mark's convulsive movements. "Perhaps we should alter that. How would you like a grade-one moron?" The instrument's tone dropped in pitch and intensified.

The curved disk crawled over Mark's forehead.

Kate raced through a mental maze. *Find the way to break free!* It was Fechter's voice and choice of words that had triggered the programming and given him total command over her. Even as he tortured her son, she calmed her mind, pictured Fechter speaking to her, and conjured his voice: *Kate, you are free to move—*

At that moment, the big den window overlooking the back yard exploded inward, a golden mass powering through the glinting shards like a cannon ball.

Buddy!

Fechter dropped Mark and stumbled, shielding his face with his forearms. Buddy rose from the floor, glass raining from his sides, hackles raised like a forest of golden needles. He growled a growl that was infinitely beyond a mere warning—it was a deep, mauling, fight-to-the-death rumble. Fechter crabbed backward.

Shocked away by the crashing glass, or perhaps responding to her own mental command, Fechter's restraining spell shattered inside Kate's mind and released her muscles to her command.

In one fluid motion, she snatched the Glock from the floor and leapt to her feet. She brought the pistol up and aimed. "You murdering—"

She squeezed the trigger. Fechter twisted as a fan of blood patterned the wall. Red blossomed across his right shoulder. He regained his balance and stared at Kate, eyes raging shock and hatred, purple lips drawn back in a ravening snarl.

Kate leveled the pistol again, steadying its aim against the tremor of her adrenaline-fueled muscles. Fechter's left fist shot down and seized Mark's hair.

In a growl and a blur Buddy charged and clamped his teeth onto Fechter's forearm, shaking it like a rag in a tug-of-war. Fechter screeched in pain, but maintained his grip on Mark. He ducked low, dragging boy and dog as he backed away.

Kate cupped the Glock in both hands and advanced, weaving the pistol sights between the flailing mass of bodies. Before she could get close enough for a clear shot, Fechter reached the door. He shoved Mark forward, and then swung Buddy thudding against the wall as he backed outside.

Kate rushed to Mark. He staggered to his feet. "I'm all right," he said, his voice shaking. "Don't let him get away."

If Fechter lived, he would return and kill them all—she *had* to stop him. She charged through the front door, her eyes darting up and down the street. An engine revved—*the van*! Not gray, but red, white, and blue, with the logo of some television repair business on the side. She aimed as it roared away from the curb. *Can't shoot—children in the yard across the street*. She ran to the sidewalk and screamed in frustration as the van sped away.

Tires chirped behind her: David's black Bronco.

"Get in!" he shouted.

She turned to the house. Mark was standing on the walk "Go on! Go on!"

She dove into the passenger seat and David punched the accelerator. Ahead, the van sped through a stop sign, bouncing as it hit twin dips. David raced across the intersection, flying off the blacktop.

Fechter fishtailed through a stoplight and screeched left.

"He's headed for the park," David said.

"If he gets inside, we'll lose him," Kate shouted. The area would be full of kids and families, and David would have to drive carefully. Fechter could shake them on the winding blacktop roads.

They sped downhill. Two blocks ahead, the park intersection crawled with traffic. David slowed. Fechter's van lurched from lane to lane as he flashed past cars. He was already getting away.

"Cell phone's in the glove compartment," David yelled.

Kate grabbed the phone and punched 911.

Horns blared. David swore. Kate looked up and saw taillights, swerving cars. Fechter raced through a stoplight at the bottom of the hill and arced across four lanes of fast traffic, attempting a left turn. A pickup truck's tires bellowed and smoked as it locked its brakes. It slammed into the rear of the speeding van, throwing Fechter out of control.

The van jumped the curb, hurtled backward across the sidewalk, and chopped through a wooden utility pole. The vehicle's rear wheels lifted off the ground as it slid onto the severed stump. The top portion of the pole tilted at a severe angle above the disabled van, and then rocked gently back and forth, suspended by the overhead wires.

David stopped and jerked the Bronco's door open. Kate bailed out after him and they jogged toward the wreck. She shouted the location into the cell phone, and then realized she still clutched the Glock in her right hand. *Good. If he isn't already dead, I'll kill him myself*. They threaded their way through the growing crowd.

People suddenly backed away as the van's door flew open and Fechter's left arm hooked outside, a pistol dangling from his hand. He placed a foot on the ground, and suddenly the window framed his enraged face. Glasses askew, blood slashed across his body, teeth bared—a mad ghoul scanning for its next victim.

A loud snapping sound came from the ruined utility pole. David grabbed Kate's shoulder. "Get away," he said. "The power line—"

Kate glanced up. Above the van, energy popped and hummed as the swaying high voltage lines touched, throwing a cascade of sparks from the disintegrating cables.

Fechter slid through the door like a maggot wriggling from the guts of a corpse. A high voltage wire separated with a loud *crack* and hit the ground. It coiled and whipped as yellow arcs of electricity jolted into the earth.

Fechter shuffled forward in a wide stance, arms out, lurching and waving the pistol. The second overhead wire snapped free and whistled through the air, sparked across the van's roof, and lodged against the open door.

In the shadows beneath the vehicle, a flurry of bright arcs crackled to the ground. Kate saw Fechter stiffen. His pistol discharged with startling *pop*, the bullet jetting up a puff of earth beside him. People screamed. The crowd turned as a single entity and ran.

Fechter's massive body began to shake. The glasses twisted from his face; the bloated eyes bulged, mouth gaping in a cavernous yawn, neck muscles stretching like steel cables. He let out a wavering, unearthly moan.

With a wet, cantaloupe-smacking-a-brick-wall *clop*, a pink mist replaced his cranium. Tethered by muscle and nerves, the eyeballs exploded out and dangled below his cheeks like a cheap novelty gag. He stood for a moment, limbs and torso quivering, as blood and smoke and steam spewed and gurgled through the great ragged opening above the crimson sockets. *Fechter, the human volcano.* The electrified body crashed to the ground, jerking, charring.

A soft *huff* and orange flames licked from beneath the van and curled up along its side, pouring out a dark plume of smoke. Sirens wailed in the distance.

David took the pistol from Kate's hand and tucked it into his jacket pocket. He pulled her to his side and they turned back toward the Bronco. Kate glanced at the burning van and the grisly remains twitching on the ground beside it. "Damn," she said. "And me without my camera."

They walked on in silence. As they approached the Bronco, Kate took both of David's hands, rose up, and gave him a deep kiss. "I love you, too," she said with a smile. "How's *that* for timing?"

76

Mark had lied. He was *not* "all right" when his mother and David Hightower had raced off to chase Fechter. Not at all. His ears rang, his vision in one eye had dimmed, and it was difficult to move his left arm. He suddenly became aware of Buddy's absence. Buddy would have chased Fechter to the van and all the way down the street. He stumbled into the house.

Buddy lay near the wall, a pool of red spreading from beneath his golden body, his breathing rapid and shallow. Mark dropped to his knees beside the dog. Suddenly the room swam; spots danced and hissed before his eyes. He lay down and heard himself sobbing over and over, "Buddy, don't die, don't die...."

* * *

A bright light stabbed his eyes. He winced, and then shrank as he saw a man in a white coat bending over him. *Fechter*! He yelled, threw his hands over his face in a protective motion. The man pulled away.

"Mark," came his mother's voice. "It's okay—it's okay." He turned toward her and the room came into focus. He was in a hospital. She held his hands. The man in white, a doctor, was smiling, jotting something down on a clipboard.

"He'll be fine," the doctor said. "We'll keep him overnight just to make sure there are no surprises." He looked at Mark, asked a few stupid questions: "What is your name? How many fingers am I holding up?" He smiled again, said they'd had hundreds of cases like Mark's since the attack on Colorado Springs. He left.

Mark blurted: "Buddy—? He isn't…"

His mother gave a thin smile. "The vet says he'll recover, but it'll take some time. He cut his leg when he went through the glass. Lost a lot of blood. Severed some tendons."

Mark sighed. "When can I get out of here? I want to see him."

"You heard the doctor. Tomorrow."

His voice hardened. "Did you get him, you know—*Fechter*?"

"He's dead," She replied, her voice dropping. "He crashed into a utility pole. Electrocuted." She made an exploding motion with her hands.

Mark folded his arms behind his head and relaxed into the pillows. "Wow," he said, raising his eyebrows as he pictured the event. "Excellent."

77

Mark spent all of his free time looking after Buddy. With the dog's right rear leg immobilized in a cast, taking him for walks was an ordeal. But Mark stayed with him constantly, and he seemed to improve daily.

On a Friday morning, ten days after Fechter's death, Kate and Mark drove to the law offices of Welsey and Benton, the partnership that had handled Thompson legal affairs since as far back as Kate remembered.

They met Kate's father and mother outside the nineteenth-century office building and went inside. The entire interior, down to the wallpaper, had been restored to its original 1890's style.

Leland Welsey, a short, balding man in his late fifties, greeted them and led them up a creaking staircase to his spacious office on the second floor. Kate sat beside her mother and father, with Mark occupying a chair behind them.

Welsey, being the senior partner, settled behind the massive oak desk, while Warren Benton stood beside him. Benton was tall, in his forties and, Kate thought, resembled an undertaker with his dark suit and somber demeanor. On the desk were the documents from the metal box O'Hanlon had found in the tunnel.

Welsey picked the yellowed papers up, adjusted his bifocals, and silently looked at his clients one by one. Kate thought she noticed a slight tremor in his hands as he lifted the papers off the desk.

"Jared, Kate, Jenny, Mark," he began. "We have contacted the Swiss corporations regarding the accounts listed in these documents. We have received faxed copies of the holdings. We researched the material and have confirmed, to the best of our ability, the following: you have access to cash accounts totaling over one million dollars."

Kate's heart leapt. She turned to the others and smiled. Her father gave her a look of surprise. She turned back to Welsey, who was looking at her over the top of his glasses. He glanced back at the papers and cleared his throat. "You have stocks and bonds in the Westinghouse Electric Company and General Electric Corporation that are currently worth—" he paused. A smile was beginning to crack through the normally inscrutable countenance, and Benton was already grinning.

Welsey continued. "—fifty-million dollars."

Mark whooped. Kate gasped. Her mother looked stunned, her mouth dropping open in a great "Oh." Her father's eyes sparkled, and he swept his hand slowly across his mustache, as if trying to stifle an outbreak of uncontrolled mirth.

But Welsey had not risen to shake hands and congratulate them. He remained seated, continuing to gaze seriously at his clients. He peeled off another page and held up a sheaf of papers secured with a paper clip.

"Now," he said with a tilt of his head. "These are faxed copies from several financial entities around the country and, of course, must be verified. But I have no reason to believe they are false or inaccurate."

Benton clasped his hands behind his back and began rocking on the balls of his feet. There was more to come. Kate noticed a further break in Welsey's composure. In fact, he seemed to be choking back some powerful emotion.

With a slow, almost reverential motion, he opened a leather folder resting on the center of his desk and removed a sheaf of papers. He again gave his guests a lengthy stare. "This is a contract, signed between Nikola Tesla and George Westinghouse in 1897. We believe it is still binding and fully enforceable." He clutched the contract in both hands. "The bottom line is that the Westinghouse Corporation is obligated to pay you twenty cents for every horsepower of electricity generated by the Tesla inventions at the time you should decide to collect it." He paused briefly. "Back then, they had no idea how much the electrical power industry would grow, or that the Tesla designs would have such great longevity.

"We did some research, interviewed some engineers and industrialists, and we came up with a rough figure of how much money this would be." He shifted in his seat. "Now, of course, there will be a fight. There will be litigation, and debate over specifics. *But*—" He paused, a wicked little grin crossing his face. "Today, this contract calls for the payment of over two *billion* dollars."

Kate thought she would faint.

"It appears," Welsey continued with a chuckle, "that one way or another, you, my friends, are about to become fabulously wealthy people."

Epilogue

Laughter and the scent of oatmeal cookies drifted in from the kitchen. Mark was seated on the big leather couch in the ranch house den, guitar on his knee, strumming the song he had just completed. Andrea was beside him, humming the melody. The song ended and Andrea turned to him and smiled, her auburn hair catching the honey-yellow glow from the log fire.

Mark looked past the glittering Christmas tree, through the front windows, beyond the area where the old barn once stood. Snow was falling in a soft hush, mantling the woods and meadows in perfect crystalline white. Fading rays of sunlight pierced the unraveling clouds and softly touched the foothills with shifting patterns of red and gold.

Maybe they'd be snowed in for a few days. That would be fine with him. They'd take the cross-country skis and head across the meadow, climb the hill, and schuss into the west woods. The dogs would follow, just like they had today, bouncing and charging through the white powder.

In a few hours, his mother and David Hightower would be on another talk show, touting her new book and video and warning about First Amendment restrictions, government black projects, and the need to be ever vigilant. David accompanied her wherever she went, an excellent arrangement, because he'd keep her safe. Mark knew they were an "item," and he'd considered the idea of having David for a stepfather. That would be okay. It didn't mean letting go of his father's memory. That could never happen.

Their house in Colorado Springs hadn't sold yet. Real estate was sluggish since the town had so much rebuilding to do. But it didn't matter. They had already tapped into some of their newfound wealth and purchased a big two-story house a few miles from the ranch.

He heard someone humming his new song from across the room—Charles Holt, one of two FBI agents still assigned to watch out for everyone, in case there were more Fechters creeping around.

His grandfather would be coming in the back door soon. He and Carlos were attending the horses in the new stone and brick stables built just north of the old barn. Jared planned to expand his operation and had replaced his lost champion quarter horses with some of the finest breeding stock in the country.

He thought about O'Hanlon, who was overseeing the construction of the new wing at the museum, also financed with some of the family's wealth. The professor had no family, and Mark thought Christmas must be a lonely time for him.

And Alex; he might as well consider Alex as a brother, because he was living with them while Alex's mom completed her rehab. He could hear the constant clacking of the computer keyboard in his grandfather's office—Alex gathering data for the new *Keep the Internet Free* web site. Not only was his family paying to ensure Alex's mother had the best available doctors, they would be paying for Alex's college education, assuming he ever got his grades up enough to graduate from high school.

O'Hanlon would be arriving for a New Year's Eve visit, so there was a lot of partying to look forward to.

The attorneys were still bickering about the Tesla-Westinghouse contract, but it was certain, like Welsey had said, that his family was going to be tremendously wealthy. For Mark, this simply meant no worries about his future. He could major in music, keep his band together, and continue writing songs.

He smiled at Andrea. They had been friends forever, and he knew without a doubt that the future would hold something more.

*   *   *

Buddy stretched out on the rug beside Mark and Andrea and huffed a contented sigh. He closed his eyes, feeling the warmth of the fire and smelling the enticing aromas from the kitchen.

His injured leg was still tight and stiff, and although the wound had healed, he couldn't jump anymore. He could no longer leap after the Frisbee, or even run as fast as before.

So now, when the afternoons were warm, Mark and he, accompanied by Higgins, would climb to the little lake above the new barn, and Mark would throw rubber balls far out into the water. Buddy would dive in and retrieve them, sometimes two at once.

Chasing Frisbees had been great fun, and he'd always remember Go, Buddy Go! *Faster than lightning*! He longed to jump and sail through the air once again, free as a bird. But, as he drifted off to sleep, listening to his master humming away, he dreamt of splashing into the lake's cool, clear water and paddling out to retrieve balls for Mark—because *that* was even better.

Photo by Terry Spearman

Lloyd Ritchey has authored screenplays, novels, non-fiction titles, and interactive media. He has produced special effects for stage and screen and performed grand-scale demonstrations of the dazzling apparatus described in Stormdragon. He lives in North Texas with his wife and two much-loved, hyperactive Border collies.

For information about the science and history woven into *Stormdragon, The Kellsbrg Vampire,* and about forthcoming books and events, please visit the author's website: www.LloydRitchey.com

Wildgrave
www.wildgravepublishing.com

Something is killing people in Sheriff Greg Colvin's small town, an entity that harvests flesh and spawns living abominations. As Colvin investigates, the real horror begins, and he must confront an evil beyond his darkest nightmares.

"...Excels in detective work, twists and turns and intrigue...A recommended pick for mystery and detective readers alike." *Midwest Review*

THE
KELLSBURG
VAMPIRE

LLOYD RICHEY

Available wherever books are sold

www.ingramcontent.com/pod-product-compliance
Lightning Source LLC
Chambersburg PA
CBHW030650120726
47905CB00001B/136